Eva Glyn fell in love with Croatia during her first holiday there in 2019; the incredible scenery, the delicious food, the country's dramatic twentieth century history all played their part, but most of all it was the friendliness of the people.

One of these was tour director Darko Barisic, who told an incredible story about growing up in underground shelters during the war in the 1990s, and she knew she had to write a book around his experiences. This became her first Croatian novel, *The Olive Grove*, and she and Darko have become good friends and he continues to advise her on all aspects of Croatia.

Eva delves into Croatian history and everyday life for her inspiration, and visits the country as often as she can, having uncovered so many stories by talking to local people. Travel in general is her passion, followed closely by food and wine, which also find their way between her pages.

Although Welsh by birth she now lives in Cornwall with the man she met and fell in love with almost thirty years ago. She also writes as Jane Cable.

www.janecable.com

X x.com/janecable

f facebook.com/EvaGlynAuthor

○ instagram.com/evaglynauthor

BB bookbub.com/authors/eva-glyn

Also by Eva Glyn

THE DUBROVNIK BOOK CLUB

EVA GLYN

One More Chapter
a division of HarperCollins*Publishers*
1 London Bridge Street
London SE1 9GF
www.harpercollins.co.uk
HarperCollins*Publishers*
Macken House, 39/40 Mayor Street Upper,
Dublin 1, D01 C9W8, Ireland

This paperback edition 2024
1
First published in Great Britain in ebook format
by HarperCollins*Publishers* 2024

A catalogue record of this book is available from the British Library

ISBN: 978-0-00-864811-4

This novel is entirely a work of fiction. The names, characters and incidents portrayed in it are the work of the author's imagination. Any resemblance to actual persons, living or dead, events or localities is entirely coincidental.

Printed and bound in the UK using 100% Renewable Electricity
by CPI Group (UK) Ltd

A Brief Glossary of Croatian Words

Knjižara Svih Nacija – the bookshop where all are welcome

Family relationships:

Nono – grandad
Baka – grandma
Tetak – uncle
Mama – mum
Tata – dad

Swearing:

Sranje – perfectly safe to use in mixed company
Bože – rather blasphemous for those who worry about it
Šupak – an anatomical insult, somewhere the sun doesn't shine
Jebem ti – only for extreme situations

Being polite:

Dobar dan – good day
Dobra večer – good evening
Mogu li vam pomoći? – can I help you?

Food & drink:

Krofne – small, fluffy doughnuts filled with jam, chocolate or custard
Dzezva – pair of long-handled jugs, one smaller than the other, used for making traditional coffee
Čupavci – small cakes dipped in chocolate and rolled in coconut
Bijela pita – oblongs of layered sponge and vanilla cream
Pašticada – slow cooked beef stew
Maneštra – orzo pasta bake with beef and tomatoes
Burek – filo pastry, normally filled with meat or cheese
Brudet – seafood stew
Spomilje – lemony Viennese whirls
Rakija – grape spirit firewater
Slani inćuna – salted anchovies
Crni rižot – cuttlefish and squid risotto, blackened with their ink
Ćupteti – open dough parcels stuffed with sausage meat
Sir i vrnhje – cottage cheese and sour cream
Bučnica – butternut squash and cheese strudel
Šporki makaruli – macaroni with spiced beef and tomato sauce
Orahnjača – sweet yeast dough with nut filling, rolled like a Swiss roll
Kiflice – crescent-shaped pastries

This book is dedicated to Jim, Stella, Chris, Jacquie, Gill, Sally, Jim, Angie, Matt, Cathy, Adi, Sally, Ian, Julie & Kev.

Thank you for sharing one of the best weeks of my life.

Prologue

He raises his head from the sink and looks in the mirror. Sunken eyes, stubble. The bruise a livid purple-red on his cheek. Beneath his palms the enamel feels cool and smooth. Solid. He pushes on it. Levers himself away, down the hall, into the bedroom.

The silence surrounds him. Unnatural. Bouncing from the glossy white wardrobe doors, refusing to be muffled by the duvet cast onto the floor. A lipstick has rolled against its folds and he stoops to rescue it, setting it on the dressing table amongst the mess of mascara, foundation, perfume, and the brown ring from a coffee cup.

Didi, this has to end. The words – his words – echo from the walls. He raises his fingers to his face, swollen just a little now. Whatever the rights and wrongs there is no going back.

He touches her phone and the screen lights, popping with notifications. 11.08. The numbers penetrate the fog in his brain. Too late. Too long. Too late. Too long.

The wind gusts against the patio door as he wrenches it open, a billow of curtain escaping across the terrace in his wake. Rain needles his skin. His legs unlike his own as one foot follows the other down, down, down the concrete steps towards the sea.

The tide rolls, an unbroken heaving mass of gunmetal grey, funnelling into the bay beneath glowering clouds. Peaks and troughs. Troughs and peaks. Nothing else moves in the water.

Faster, faster, stumbling as he scans the churning waves. Her robe, abandoned on the jetty, dripping in his hands. Heavy. Heavy with rain. Dragging him down, into the depths with her.

And he runs, back up the steps, two, three at a time, clawing at the slippery rail. Breathless, blood pounding from his neck to his temples, the door shuddering closed behind him.

His phone. Torn from his pocket. His voice. Not his own.

"Help me. Help me, please. My girlfriend went swimming two hours ago and she hasn't come back."

The Welcoming Bookshop,
Knjižara Svih Nacija

JANUARY 2022

Claire

"Right then, darling, off you go." Her grandmother handed Claire a Tupperware box full of freshly made pasta salad with a paper bag of homemade *krofne* resting on top. "These are to share," she added, "with your new colleagues."

"Thanks, Gran." Claire tucked them into her bag, alongside her purse and antibac. Giving her grandmother a hug, she inhaled her special scent of herbal shampoo and cake mixture, which for a brief moment brought the comfort of childhood. It was rubbish, of course; she was twenty-three years old and a good two inches taller than Gran these days. And she was in Dubrovnik, not London. And much as she longed to, staying in the kitchen all day, chatting and baking, was not an option.

Gran gently pushed Claire away, rearranging the cowl neck of her top as she did so. It felt strange to be wearing work clothes after all this time. Tailored trousers, pumps, the earrings shaped like little dolphins her parents had given her for Christmas. And as for makeup ... it had taken her three attempts to get her eyeliner even remotely where it should be.

Nono Jadran stood from his place at the table and fetched

Claire's coat from the hallstand before helping her into it. "Your grandmother's very proud of you," he told her. "We both are. It won't be an easy day, but we know you'll do your best."

"Thanks, Nono." She looked into his face, his tanned skin soft like crepe and far more wrinkled than when he had come into their lives twelve years before, but still the same tall, handsome man who had swept her gran off her feet. And in that time Claire and her sister Belle had learned to love him too.

"Right. I'd best be off." At least she sounded confident. That was a start.

Closing the front door behind her, Claire ran down the black and white tiled communal staircase, her heels tip-tapping on the marble. Glancing back at the apartment she noticed Gran standing in the living room window. Giving her a cheery wave she set off at a brisk pace towards the steps that made up this part of the narrow street.

It wasn't until she rounded the corner in front of the Museum of Ethnic Life that she slowed, fingering the mask in her coat pocket like a tiny comfort blanket. Her legs felt almost as unsteady as they had on the Long Covid bad days, but there was no other sign to indicate she was actually ill; no blinding pain shooting across her forehead, no random aches in her chest. And, thank god, energy rather than exhaustion. Nervous energy, making her tremble and feel slightly sick.

Who was she kidding? This wasn't nervous energy, this was fear, pure and simple. Fear of catching that terrible disease again. Fear of it stealing another fifteen months of her life. It had taken her so long to get well, so very long, there was no way she could risk catching it again. But what was the alternative? Hiding in her bedroom forever, dreaming about the countries she might have been visiting, the children she could have been teaching to read, if sodding Covid hadn't happened? Right at this moment, hiding in her bedroom sounded quite appealing.

Claire ground to a halt next to a stone archway and leaned against the parapet, gazing over the jumble of terracotta roofs below her towards the city walls, and the greens and greys of Mount Srd rising beyond. Gran didn't understand; she clearly thought these new variants were harmless. She'd even told her she wouldn't need to wear a mask at work, for god's sake, when she hadn't left the house without one for months.

Why, oh why had she ever agreed to work in a shop, of all places? And not just now when the city was quiet, but all through the busy summer months when it would be rammed with tourists? It was crazy. Crazy. Claire reached for the arch to steady herself, her fingers tracing the rough mortar between the blocks of stone. She couldn't do it. Couldn't go on. In fact, she could hardly breathe, just little gasps, as though her chest was closing down again. But it wasn't, it wasn't. She was not ill. *But you could be, especially after the flight*. The reminder was cruel, paralysing her.

If she couldn't go forward then she certainly couldn't go back. Could not let her grandmother down after she'd put her forward for the job. But if she'd never interfered Claire wouldn't be in this position. Gran should have kept her nose out, left her to find a call centre gig from home or something. Except she hadn't. She had been moping. Grieving for everything she'd taken for granted; her job at a top London bookshop, Foyles, her frenetic social life, her plans to volunteer her way across the world. Poor old Gran's only crime was trying to make sure she got at least some of that life back.

Above Mount Srd the sky was a clear, pale blue and the bright green leaves of the nearby fig tree were just beginning to unfurl. It struck Claire that the old grey stones she was leaning against had witnessed plague and pestilence many a time. Not to mention wars; even now the bullet marks from thirty years ago were still obvious on Dubrovnik's streets. People here had survived, people like Nono Jadran, who had lost so much yet still got on with their lives. Could she do the same?

Already her breathing had steadied, and slowly Claire set off again, down the slopes and steps towards the city centre and Ulica od Puča where the bookshop was. A woman leaning out of a window, hauling a line of washing across the narrow space, called *"Dobar dan"* and Claire returned her greeting. Normal. Everything was normal. She was just a young woman going to work on a January morning.

Somehow she managed to keep moving, counting the stairs, the flat areas of paving between them slippery beneath the soles of her pumps. Birdsong pierced the sparkling air, a washing machine or dishwasher rumbling beneath it, and as Claire walked on, the aroma of baking drifted from a window. Normal, normal, normal. In a few weeks' time, with any luck she'd be over the worst of the fear; the part that was making her feel physically sick at least. But for the moment, however she felt inside, she had to appear normal as well. *Fake it until you make it. Fake it until you make it.* The rhythm of the words fell into time with her steps.

Turning the final corner she could see the shop in front of her, Knjižara Svih Nacija written in a curve of gold paint across the top of the arched window. The name in itself was wonderful, meaning "the bookshop where all are welcome". Even damaged souls like her. It would be her ethos as manager too: to welcome everybody. She paused for a moment to straighten her shoulders, then pushed on the door and with the biggest smile she could muster said in Croatian, "Hello, I'm Claire Thomson and I'm so excited to be working here."

"Claire, welcome." She recognised Simeon Boskovic, the shop's owner, from her Zoom interview. Tall and thin, he was probably about her father's age, but his grey jumper and monk's tonsure haircut made him appear older.

"How is your wife?" Claire asked.

He shrugged. "The chemotherapy, it takes it out of poor Nadia. I will be glad to finish working after tomorrow."

Claire nodded. Two days. That's all he was giving her to learn how to run this place. It must have shown on her face because he smiled.

"Do not worry. It is a simple business, and Luna Raic, our shop assistant, knows almost everything. You can always message me if there is a problem."

"I'm hoping there won't be." He was relying on her so much, which made it doubly frightening. Did he not realise she hadn't worked for the best part of two years?

Behind her the shop bell rang, and Claire spun around, her bag almost knocking a pot of pens from the antique oak table that served as a counter.

"Ah," said Simeon, "here's Luna now."

The young woman who walked into the shop was no more than five foot tall, her short dark hair cut in a loose chop and shaved high up the back of her neck. Her oval face accentuated almond-shaped eyes that looked almost black, but what struck Claire most was the mobility of her features as she unzipped her bright orange puffer coat and sprang towards them, smiling one moment and grimacing the next.

"Hi, you must be Claire. Sorry I'm late. Not impressive, day one. But the bus was stop, start, stop, start. All the way."

"I've just got here myself," Claire told her. "And it's only a ten-minute walk for me."

"Neither of you is late," Simeon interjected. "Especially as we don't open until ten in the winter. Now, Luna, if you can make the coffee, I'll show Claire around."

Claire pulled the doughnuts out of her bag. "Gran made *krofne*."

Luna clapped her hands. "Oh, I hoped Fran would send you with some of her gorgeous cakes. Big plus point of having you here." She grinned at Claire and the warmth of her smile seemed to stay in the shop like the Cheshire Cat's as she disappeared through a red velvet curtain into the room behind.

The retail space was compact, to say the least, situated as it was on the ground floor of a double-fronted medieval merchant's house. Having visited Dubrovnik many times since Gran married Nono, Claire knew about these buildings' history and marvelled at how so many of the asymmetrical arched windows and window-cum-doors that characterised them still survived. They were the very essence of the city's shopping streets and despite her anxiety, a part of her – the part she needed to channel – was thrilled to be working inside one.

What was more, unusually the bookshop had retained what looked like some of its original stone corbels, and the white-painted bookshelves were built around them, filling every wall right to the beamed ceilings. Claire inhaled the same wonderful new-book smell that had permeated the stockrooms at Foyles. She had loved working there so much. Another reason to be positive about today.

The table with the till was end on to the arched display window, which Claire noticed was arranged in exactly the same way inside and out, so if someone in the street liked the look of a book they could come in and pick it up easily. When she remarked how clever it was, Simeon told her it had been Luna's idea.

"She's good at the arty stuff," he continued, "and she likes it. You know what I'm saying?"

"Of course I do. I certainly don't want to ruffle her feathers. It's probably as nervous a time for her as it is for me."

"There's no need to be nervous, Claire. I have every confidence in you."

Which didn't make her feel as good as it should have.

Simeon continued the tour, explaining that the English language books, which were the shop's bread and butter, were wrapped around the counter from the window to the arch, which led to the kitchen and office behind. Beyond them, facing the shop door, were a few tourist guides, some graphic novels of various nationalities and a *Game of Thrones* section, which needed to be regularly restocked in the summer as so many visitors came to see the filming locations around the city. To the right of the door the shelves were packed with books in other European languages, together with a small Japanese section.

"You're very geared up for the tourist trade," Claire said. "How do you manage in winter?"

"The Christmas market extends the season, but now it will be quiet for a few months. It's the language students at the university who keep us ticking over. We stock the books they need for their literature courses."

The aroma of coffee was beginning to drift into the shop and Simeon held open the curtain, allowing Claire to pass into the small kitchen behind. Three stoneware mugs stood in the centre of a scrubbed pine table and Luna was stirring an enamel *dzezva* on the small electric ring, which was balanced on a cupboard that had been painted pale blue some time in its distant past. Through the window above the sink was what appeared to be a small courtyard.

"Oh, lovely," Claire said. "Proper coffee."

"You like it?" Luna arched her eyebrows. "I thought in London everyone drank lattes."

"A lot of people do, but since Gran's been living here so much of the time I've come to prefer coffee the Croatian way."

"Fran is half Croatian, yes?" Luna asked.

"She would say the older half. Although she was born here she left for England as a baby and didn't come back until she retired. But she met Nono Jadran during her stay, and although she still has her house in Chichester they spend more and more time in Dubrovnik."

"Well, I am glad," said Simeon. "Not only is she a good customer, but she found you for us. It is perfect to have an English manager for our English bookshop, isn't it, Luna?"

"Oh, yes." Luna beamed. "Especially one who brings homemade cakes and drinks proper coffee."

It was a good couple of hours before Claire found herself in the shop, after Simeon had spent most of the morning going through the paperwork she would need to do. It had felt like a reprieve to sit in the tiny office beyond the kitchen, listening to Luna charming what customers there were. She was clearly a natural. Perhaps Claire could leave her to it most of the time and work in here?

In her heart of hearts she knew that wasn't possible; it would shoot any credibility she had to pieces if she hid herself away. And besides, the best thing about her job at Foyles had been helping readers to choose a title they would absolutely adore. It was what bookshops were about, surely? Browsing, picking books up and putting them down again, sharing recommendations. The pure joy of discovering something new that no algorithm, however clever, would have ever picked for you. She needed to be brave and get out there.

All the same she waited until the shop was empty before slipping through the curtain. The low sun would barely reach the narrow street at this time of year, but still the brightness of the day crept into the small room and the glow of the spotlights made it feel very cosy. Luna was humming to herself as she stuffed a receipt into the till.

"I love the way you've dressed the window," Claire told her.

"Thank you."

"I'm rubbish at stuff like that."

"Good." Luna glanced at her. "*Sranje*. What I mean is, I am pleased because I can keep that job. Not that I am pleased you are bad at something. I speak before I think sometimes." She flashed Claire a smile.

"I guess … having me here will be a big change for you."

Luna nodded. "I like working with Simeon. He's a kind man. He doesn't get angry if I make mistakes."

"Well, I'm happy about that, because I'm bound to make mistakes too."

"But you have worked in a big bookshop in London."

"A big bookshop is very different to a small one. Easier, I think. I have a lot to learn. And in a foreign language too."

"Your Croatian is quite good."

"I'm doing an online course and Gran has been teaching me, although I may still need to rely on your help."

"I would like that." Luna nodded, as if to herself. "And you can help me with my English. It will be fun."

As Claire agreed, the shop door opened and a long-haired man in a navy anorak walked in, hands in pockets. It was all she could do not to take a step back as he coughed into his hand.

Claire knew she should greet him, but her feet felt stuck to the floor. How could she approach him? How could she not? Her heart was thudding so loudly she was sure Luna would hear it.

She cleared her throat and asked, *"Mogu li vam pomoći?"*

"I don't need help. I'm just browsing," he replied, and Claire nodded, the lump in her throat full to bursting point.

Luna scribbled a note on the pad by the till and pushed it towards her. *Comes in most lunchtimes. Hardly ever buys.*

Time seemed to hang in the air between them as the man moved along the graphic novel section, coughing every now and then. Claire could almost see his germs. God, she couldn't do this; she couldn't. She would let everyone down. Simeon who needed to spend time with his wife; Gran who'd recommended her for the job in the first place.

Luna was looking at her, her face screwed into an expression Claire couldn't quite read. "Why don't you get a breath of fresh air while I hold the fort, then we can swap around? I like to see daylight at lunchtime, and it's much too cold to sit in the courtyard this time of year."

Without even thinking to grab her coat and bag, Claire thanked her and escaped, all but gulping the fresh, clear air outside. A cool breeze whipped up the street and she shivered, wrapping her arms around her. Sod it, she couldn't even antibac her hands. *Oh come on, Claire, talk some sense into that germ-obsessed head of yours. And walk. Walk to keep warm, if nothing else.* She couldn't help but wonder if Luna had sensed her fear, and if so, should she explain?

The heels of her pumps clicked on the shiny paving stones, echoing between the golden-grey walls of the buildings that huddled on either side of the street. There were very few people out and about and most of the shutters were closed. She looked at the signs on the nearby shops. A gelateria, a jewellers' and a gift shop; none of them likely to open much before Easter. The doors of the Orthodox church were ajar though, and the lights were on in the tiny supermarket further along the street. A woman with a pushchair strolled towards her and she could see an elderly couple in the distance, no doubt heading towards the Green Market in Gundulićeva Poljana.

The Orthodox church was set back a little from the street, allowing the pale sunlight to bathe its creamy frontage. Behind the elaborate railings that protected its terrace were half a dozen or so of the old town's stray cats. A huge ginger beast wrapped around the terracotta support of a potted palm, watched from a safe distance by an equally impressive white one with black and tan splodges. Several more stretched out on the paving, making the most of what little warmth there was in the rays of the sun.

Claire adored cats. They'd always had one at home when she

was growing up; ever since a stray tortoiseshell had turned up at the back door, just as they were settling into their house in Chiswick. A movement behind the palm caught her eye, and two kittens emerged, eyes wide and tiny tails upright, before starting to tumble together, a mass of ginger and white fur.

Their innocent play was infectiously joyful and Claire could not help but laugh. She had to recapture that joy in life for herself and the only way to do it was by losing her fear. She forced herself to remember how much fun it had been working at Foyles, how rewarding. All she had to do was make The Welcoming Bookshop the same. Right now it seemed an impossible ask, but somehow she had to find a way. A place to start, at any rate.

No one had passed her while she was watching the cats. There were so few people about, bookshop customers would be scarce. While it was bad for business, in the short term it would certainly help her to cope. Because cope she had to. Claire didn't just want this job to work out, she wanted her life back, full stop. And however terrified she was, she knew there was only one person who could make that happen.

It was too cold to stay outside for long so Claire retraced her steps, relieved to find Luna in an otherwise empty shop. But Claire was determined to serve the next customer, however wobbly the thought made her feel.

"I put the coffee on," Luna said. "To warm you up."

"Thanks, that's very thoughtful." Claire rearranged a book that didn't need rearranging before looking at her. "I'm sorry about that. I had Covid very badly and it makes me nervous around people, especially in small spaces. I mean, I've hardly been anywhere at all these last couple of years, but I know I need to get over it."

"Oh. OK."

"It should be fine, shouldn't it? I mean, it doesn't seem very busy at this time of year. It will let me get used to it gradually."

"I wasn't thinking about the shop, I was thinking about the book club."

"The book club?"

Luna nodded. "I thought … I thought it would be a way to get more customers here in the winter and the first meeting is next Tuesday evening. We already have eight people signed up, including your gran. I thought she might have said. We've made a big thing of having an English manager to lead it."

Eight people. In this tiny space. Had Gran told her, there would have been nothing more guaranteed to send Claire heading for the hills. As it was she had that awful feeling of her chest tightening and her feet being stuck to the floor again.

"*O bože!* You look awfully pale," said Luna. "I'll pour you that coffee."

Alone in the shop, Claire spun slowly around. Eight people. They'd be too crammed together, surely? But no, as she mentally pictured where chairs could be placed she realised that if they put the old oak table with the till against the bookcase they could fit up to a dozen. She reached for the nearest shelf to steady herself.

But before the pandemic Claire had absolutely adored a book club. She had belonged to three different ones at university, made some really good friends through them. Friends who had proved their worth when she'd been ill, when others had drifted away. They'd even had a Zoom version during the lockdowns, but then everyone else had got their lives back, whereas she…

Oh god, it was just too soon. Next month, maybe, she would have had time to build up to it, but next week … all those people in an enclosed space. The invisible belt around her chest tightened another notch and for one awful moment she really did wonder if she'd caught Covid on the plane or somewhere.

She was aware of Luna beside her, pressing a mug of coffee into her hand.

"You will be able to do it, won't you?" The pleading note in her voice surprised Claire. This clearly meant so much to her. There was no way she could let her down. Or Simeon. Or Gran. The list was growing. *Fake it until you make it.* The phrase started to beat its rhythm into her head. A rhythm she knew was vital to this new life.

She looked at Luna and nodded. "The book club is a great idea, and I'd be honoured to lead it."

Vedran

Vedran Novak hurried across the bridge that linked the new town to the old and through the grey bulk of the Pile Gate, already late for Sunday lunch. Of course he had called Tetak Jadran from the car, claiming unexpected roadworks, but the reality had been his own paralysis this morning, the all but impossible task of leaving his apartment.

He couldn't entirely blame the amount of whisky he'd put away last night; that was a symptom, not the cause. The cause was the latest addition to the list of things he was too frigging pathetic to face: seeing Claire for the first time since she'd arrived. Claire, who'd adored him since she was thirteen when, as a new graduate, he'd lived with her family in London during his internship with a City law firm. The precious little sister he'd never had, and since her grandmother's marriage to his uncle, Vedran's honorary cousin.

Worrying how Claire would react to what had happened with Didi had created a whole new shit-storm in his head, but it was one he had to face. He couldn't exactly hide from Tetak and Fran for the next year, so it was best to get it over with. But if Claire turned her back on him as well… He couldn't even bring himself to think how that might feel.

Head down he passed Onofrio's Fountain, where rather than flocks of tourists a solitary pigeon perched on one of the waterspouts, then he rounded the corner into Ulica od Puča. Past the boarded-up cafés and bars that would open only for the summer trade, the art galleries and jewellery shops abandoned for winter too. On a grey Sunday morning, the street had a neglected air that reflected his mood, and not so much as a cat slunk past as he began to climb the steps towards the place that more than any other he regarded as home.

He and his uncle had become so close over the years. Tetak, good and solid Tetak Jadran, had been his anchor and his rock, but now he had a potential dementia diagnosis hanging over his head. It was as well he didn't know the whole sordid story of the aftermath of Didi's disappearance, but not being able to confide in his uncle made everything so much harder. Ach, who was he kidding? There were things he could never tell a living soul. Secrets he would take to his grave.

Fran's request sliced clean through the mid-afternoon fug of too much roast pork, cooked the English way with apple sauce and crackling, as Vedran helped her to stack the dishwasher.

"You will come to Claire's new book club, won't you?"

He loved Fran to bits, but honestly, this was too much, too stupid… And what was more, her words were delivered with all the guile of a velvet-gloved assassin.

"I hardly think that would be wise."

"Why not?" Those big black eyes of hers, her fluffy grey halo of hair. A picture of septuagenarian innocence, if ever there was one.

"You know very well why not. My reputation would precede me."

"You need to stop thinking that way. People forget remarkably quickly."

"I don't." He glowered at her, before ramming a plate into the back of the washer with considerably more force than was necessary.

"Mind my best china," she said mildly. He grunted, and carried on slotting in the rest of the dishes, but with just a little more care.

"She could do with your support, Vedran. She's so nervous about it. I don't know whether she's more worried no one will turn up, or that too many people will and one of them will have Covid."

"Another reason I'd be one too many."

"Not to Claire."

He stood, leaning against the table and folding his arms. "How much does she know about Didi?"

"That she went swimming and didn't come back."

"And everything that happened afterwards?"

"Of course not."

Ha. That was why Claire had been pleased to see him. "Oh, so you haven't told her? You're ashamed of me too. Well, I can't say I blame you." He knew he was choosing his words to rile her, spoiling for a fight. These days a vague, undefined anger was never far from the surface. He closed his eyes and shook his head, then felt Fran's arms around him.

"You silly, silly boy. Of course I'm not. You have nothing to be ashamed of, nothing at all. But we agreed not to tell Jadran the whole story and it felt wrong to say anything to anyone else."

God, he needed this hug and he returned it ferociously, resting his chin on the top of her head. "I'm sorry," he muttered. "I'm all over the place, don't know what I'm saying half the time."

"That's not surprising. Yours isn't a simple grief, and under the circumstances, it can't be. Not only because you can't get closure, but because of everything that happened afterwards. It's going to take you some time to process it all before you can even begin to move on. But none of that makes you a bad person."

'You don't know the half...' He was that close to saying it, but how could he? Even to Fran, even with her arms around him. Even though he knew she'd had her doubts about him and Didi... Instead, he shrugged.

"Vedran, look at me." He lifted his face. "I know grief distorts, but you cannot let people who don't even know you grind you down. Don't do that to yourself. Remember that kind young man who befriended a lonely tourist all those years ago? You're still him inside, I know you are."

But he wasn't; how could all that had happened with Didi not have changed him? But it wasn't somewhere he wanted to go. Not now. Not ever. It was far easier to return to their original conversation.

"How about I tell Claire enough for her to decide whether or not she wants me at the book club. Will that satisfy you?"

Fran nodded. "I guess it will have to."

Vedran knew Claire would be curled up in the living room with Tetak, keeping him company watching television, but he needed to get her alone.

He stopped in the hall and messaged. *I'll be going soon. Fancy walking to the Pile Gate with me? Fran wants us to have a chat.* For good measure he added a rolling eyes emoji.

Her reply was instant. *Sure. Bet it's about the book club.*

Got it in one.

Who's giving who the pep talk? ;-)

His cousin repeated her question as they watched a couple of kids kick a football around one of the few level parts of Ulica Ispod Mira as it ran below the city walls. Vedran had played up and down these alleyways himself once, dribbling the ball with a reasonable amount of skill; young, free, not a care in the world... Now they'd had to take this rather circuitous route to minimise the risk of him running into anyone he knew. At least it gave him time to build up to the conversation he was dreading.

Maybe this was a place to start. "Fran thinks I should go to your book club, that you need my support."

"She thinks I should persuade you to come because you should start to get out more." Claire laughed. "On the other hand, she thinks I need to get out more too. I've only been here a week and already it's something of an obsession."

"That she knows it's hard, but she doesn't want you to waste your life..."

"That most of what you're frightened of is fear itself..."

"That people have short memories..." *Sranje!* How the hell had that particular phrase slipped out? He could have kicked himself. He wasn't ready ... hadn't screwed up the courage ... and now he'd have to explain.

"Nope. I haven't heard that one. One–nil to you!" She looked at him, her blue eyes, set in a round face so like Fran's, a picture of puzzlement. "But why would she say that? Surely you don't want people to forget Didi?"

Vedran began to walk on, following the alleyway as it snaked inside the towering walls, then around the corner into the square dominated by the solid bulk of the Jesuit church. Its frontage glowed golden-grey in the last of the daylight, the rich sound of its organ drifting through the open doors to welcome worshippers to Vespers.

He gripped his hands in his pockets, what was left of his fingernails digging into his palms. "It's what happened afterwards. Fran hasn't told you because we're keeping it from Tetak, but, well…" Oh god, he couldn't look at her. "There were people who believed I'd killed Didi."

"Vedran! No! How could anyone think that?" Anguish and concern filled her voice and he knew it was going to be OK. It really was. He felt as though he could breathe again. Surely he'd told her enough? There wasn't any need for her to know all the gory details, and he fervently hoped she never would.

"I guess … I guess … there not being a body led to rumours."

"But you couldn't hurt anyone. You're one of the kindest people I know."

"You're horribly biased, but even so my confidence could do with that kind of boost." They passed the church and Vedran paused at the top of the Jesuit Stairs, the streetlamps flickering on around them as they gazed at the narrow street far below. "So if your confidence would be boosted by me coming to your book club, well … I will try to do it. But you must realise it could be a distraction if anyone recognises me."

"Honestly, I think it's unlikely. There are only a few students signed up, and Gran and her friend Paulette. I know it's meant to bring more people into the shop, but obviously for reasons of my own I'd prefer it to start small." She bit her lip. "I don't want you to be uncomfortable, though, or for it to stress you out."

They started down the steps, perpetually crowded in summer with *Game of Thrones* fans taking selfies. Today it was deserted, thankfully, or it would probably end up being his own walk of shame. Would the book club be any better? When the time came, would he even be able to leave the safety of his apartment?

Claire stopped. "You know what this place always makes me think of?"

"The same as every other tourist?"

"No. Well, not only that, but it is to do with *Game of Thrones*.

Remember when you took us all to the River Café to thank Mum and Dad for putting you up for your internship?"

"Of course I do. That guy who played Jon Snow was there and you had a massive crush on him…"

"Except I was far too tongue-tied to do anything about it. But you … you just strolled across to his table and persuaded him to come to say hello. If you weren't my hero before then, you certainly sealed the deal that day."

"I'm no hero, Claire."

She hugged him. "You are to me. Which is just one of the reasons I'm so sad we're having a conversation about you being uncomfortable at the book club. You used to be comfortable anywhere before this happened. And you showed me how to be, too."

"And now we're both a couple of hermits." He tried to laugh.

"Yes, but we have to believe it's only temporary, that we will find our ways back, however unlikely it feels at the moment."

Was she right? Looking at her earnest expression, he so wanted to believe her. Wanted to make it right, if not for himself, for her, and for Fran and Tetak, because against all the odds, they still believed in him. So if he could help Claire, then he certainly would.

"I'll try to come to the book club, but I won't make you a promise I may not be able to keep when the time comes. Would that be OK?"

"Of course it is. Even without people being so horrid, you've lost someone very dear to you, and in awful circumstances as well. I totally get it you don't want to go out. Especially as I don't want to either."

"Then we have a deal, hermit to hermit."

She nodded, and he tucked his arm through hers. They strolled across the deserted marketplace, the honeyed stone of the former mansion houses glowing under the streetlamps as the cathedral bells began to ring. A scrawny black cat crouched in a doorway, and Claire bent to stroke it, but it dashed away with an affronted swish of its tail.

"Got to love their attitude." She laughed, and Vedran found himself joining in. God, this felt normal. Well, as close as he came these days, anyway. It gave him at least a tiny sliver of hope that Claire was right, and he could somehow find a way back to himself after all.

The Thursday Murder Club

Luna

Luna counted the chairs again. She'd set out ten, even though only eight people had signed up, and it was super-hard to squeeze between them. No wonder Claire had turned white and disappeared into the back room. And that was just the chairs, not the actual people. *Bože*, this was going to be some sort of disaster.

Come on, Luna, stay positive. Claire had said she'd do this. Promised. And she didn't seem the sort to break her word. But on the other hand, she was really petrified. A couple of times today she'd done that thing she did when the shop was busy, reaching for a bookcase and breathing in and out really fast, and Luna'd felt so guilty. As long as she could prise her out from the back room she'd help her to get through this. Really she would.

Last Monday morning Claire had been a slightly scary stranger, but even from that first day, her honesty about everything, including her own failings – well, especially her own failings – had won Luna over. Far from faultless herself, she was terrified by people who exuded perfection and she had been so, so relieved her new boss was not one of those. Thinking about it, it had probably been a mistake to read *The Devil Wears Prada* just before she arrived.

She moved the stool where Claire would be sitting as far as she could from the front row, then checked the window display for a final time. The book Claire had chosen had a disappointingly plain cover; white with red and black lettering, the only image the tiniest silhouette of a fox. Unusually, the author's name was larger than the title, but Claire had told her he was a famous television presenter, and the book had been the biggest seller in Britain last year. Luna was excited. She loved a good mystery.

As Luna pulled back the curtain to the kitchen, Claire emerged from the toilet, looking wan.

"Are you OK?" Luna asked. Claire nodded, more than a little unconvincingly, but before Luna could probe further she heard a gentle tap on the shop door, and seeing the panic return to Claire's eyes, ran to open it, sending a chair flying in the process. *Sranje* and *sranje* again.

A tall man – dark, and probably handsome, if you liked that sort of thing – stood in the shadows outside, the light from the old-style carriage lamp on the gelateria opposite making his strong features look gaunt, his eyes sunken. OK, not so good-looking then. But when Luna opened the door she realised they were soft eyes, kind eyes, despite the bruised circles beneath them.

"Welcome to the book club," she said. "You're a little early, but do sit down. Or browse. Yes, please browse. I'm afraid you've arrived before the wine."

He lifted a bag from his side. "I've brought the wine. I'm Vedran, Claire's cousin. My uncle's married to her grandmother."

Luna nodded, her mind racing. "She said you might be coming. She's in the kitchen. Through that curtain. And she's super-nervous."

"I'm on it."

He crossed the room in a couple of strides and before the

curtain closed behind him, Luna caught a glimpse of him embracing Claire warmly.

Now that was interesting. Not that he was hugging Claire – she'd said they were close – but the fact his name rang a bell. Luna had wondered back in the autumn if the Vedran Novak all the fuss was about was any relation of Fran's, but hadn't really known her well enough to ask. Glancing over her shoulder, she whipped out her phone and googled him. No way! It was the same guy. A murderer in their midst when they were going to be reading a murder book. What were the chances? But he had such kind eyes, and Claire obviously adored him, so…

The shop door opened again and Fran bustled in, carrying a small stack of plastic boxes. "My goodness, there's hardly room to swing a cat in here."

"I hope no one will be bringing a cat," Luna replied with a laugh. "Or keep the door open long enough for one to creep in. But never mind that; you've brought some treats."

"They're not all for you, young lady, but have a cheese straw to keep you going." Luna took two, winking at Fran, then headed for the table by the till to collect the list to tick off her name and add Vedran's.

So, who else were they expecting? Fran's friend Paulette, another regular in the shop, and her husband, who was apparently called George. Jozo, a waiter who normally bought graphic novels but wanted to improve his English; someone called Karmela, whom Claire must have signed up, and three girls studying languages at the university who always came into the shop together. Luna ran her fingers over their names. One of them, Aklina she thought it was, had a fabulous arse. She could barely take her eyes off it when she crouched to look at the lower shelves. OK, the chances of her being gay as well were minimal, but it didn't hurt to look, did it?

Luna had hoped, well, expected, really, that Dubrovnik would be rather more broad-minded than Šipan, the small island where she'd grown up, but so far that hadn't proved to be the case. She'd dreamed of tolerance, of gay clubs and bars even – that would be absolutely banging – like she'd read about in London and Amsterdam and other western European cities. She'd been pretty confident that here she would meet people who'd accept her for who she was, find her own tribe, but she was no nearer achieving this than she had been when she'd first arrived almost a year before. For a start she never went out anywhere. Bloody Ezra and his hermit-like tendencies.

But apart from his not wanting a social life, Ezra was not a bad flatmate. Not really. They'd been friends since their first day at school so she'd always known he was geeky, but not that he was a virtual monk as well. He'd thought it was enough to invite her to join in with his online games. As if. Luna wanted bright lights, laughter and excitement. The opportunity to make new friends with real people, not avatars.

The book club was her chance. Her only chance. Especially with Claire too scared to go out either. She sighed. If just one of those students, or this Karmela person, turned out to be all right, perhaps she could ask if they wanted to go for a drink. But would that sound like a date? Of course not, because she wasn't out. But later, when she'd plucked up the courage … how would it seem then? *Jebem ti!* This whole coming out thing was not only terrifying, it was also far more complicated than she had ever imagined.

The shop bell rang, making her jump. Paulette and a man who must be George. She hurried to greet them, ushering them into the front row seats closest to the window. Then Fran appeared with plates of nibbles, Vedran trailing behind her with a tray of glasses. She'd look up more about him later, but then Jozo arrived, closely followed by a woman Luna did not know.

"Hi, I'm Luna. Welcome to the book club."

The woman didn't smile, not even a little bit, as her dark eyes flicked around the room. It was only when she caught sight of something close to the ceiling that her whole face lit up briefly, making her long nose seem less hawkish and her chin a little softer. A favourite book maybe? Or better, one she wanted to buy.

Luna waved the list at her. "Can I take your name?"

"Professor Karmela Simic." No wonder she seemed so up herself. Luna knew trouble when she saw it. She looked just the type to complain about everything.

"Please, sit where you like and someone will bring you some wine." Lots of wine. That might soften her up a bit. But Luna found herself talking to the woman's back as she beetled off to the furthest corner.

Claire emerged from behind the curtain and gave Luna a weak smile before heading straight for her stool. Yes, she should be greeting their guests, but Luna knew her limitations. She had half expected Claire to make a bolt for the back door, then shimmy up a drainpipe in the courtyard to make good her escape.

With her back to the room, Claire shuffled her papers as the last few people arrived, and Fran and Vedran edged between the chairs handing out nibbles and wine. Fran had a kindly word for everybody, and Luna thought how alike she and Claire looked, once you got past the fact Claire was blonde with blue eyes and her grandmother's eyes were almost black, and her hair a soft grey. Both had the same generous curves and such lovely smiles. Assuming Claire could manage to raise another one. She'd better, Luna thought a little grimly, or people would think she was as unfriendly as that Karmela woman.

Claire did not let Luna down. Once everyone was settled she welcomed them warmly, her voice shaking only a tiny, tiny bit.

"Good evening. I am Claire Thomson and I'm the manager of The Welcoming Bookshop. It really is wonderful to see you all and I hope, through the books we read, we will become friends. In a moment I'm going to ask you all to introduce yourselves and tell us about what you like reading, but in the meantime I'm going to explain the club's rules."

Rules? They hadn't said anything about rules. What the hell was she on about? This was meant to be fun. Luna was about to fold her arms in front of her, but stopped just in time. Claire was smiling.

"There is just one rule; a simple one. As its name implies, this shop is for everyone and so is the book club, so all I ask is that you leave any prejudices you may have about people and their reading choices outside. Let's learn from each other."

There was a murmur of agreement. Luna wriggled more comfortably into her chair. It was going to be all right.

Karmela

The book club had not been a complete waste of time, Karmela supposed, stuffing the so-called cosy crime novel into her rucksack. Not her sort of book at all, but the shop itself had more than made up for the disappointment.

In fact its medieval detailing had been superb. One glimpse through that red velvet curtain at the unplastered walls of the back room beyond had entranced her. She had to go back, had to read that damn book if necessary, if only to see if she could get a closer look. The intricate corbels that held the beams in the shop itself had convinced her there might well be more treasures to see.

Normally Karmela would never have countenanced joining something so potentially intimate as a small book club, but when she had seen the notice in the city archives and realised it was to be held in that strange little bookshop with the elaborately scrolled keystone above its window, she had made a note in her diary. She'd known it would be a golden opportunity to study whatever architectural treats lay within, so one visit would not be a waste of her time. It was not as if she would have to talk to the other members, and experience had taught Karmela that in new situations it was best to observe people from a safe distance before attempting to interact.

She had used the tediously lengthy introductions to look around the room. This little shop really was a Ragusan gem, and Karmela's passion for the Ragusans burned bright. The wonderful civilisation that had ruled Dubrovnik in medieval times was her work; her world, if she was honest. Now, as she strolled between the boarded-up shops on either side she wondered if any of them had such fine stonework built into the tops of their shelving. The ones in the bookshop had been marvellous; the usual plain corbels alternating with patterned cornices that reminded her of diminutive versions of the capitals of Roman pillars. Unfortunately, the designs had been too worn to make out what they were from her seat, and she yearned to be able to take a closer look.

The night was cool and she walked quickly, soon finding herself in the square in front of the Sponza Palace, which housed the city archives where her precious research materials lay. This was her favourite corner of Dubrovnik and she stopped to gaze at its beautiful round arches with their oak leaf decorations, illuminated by the single lamp that hung in front of the great door. A huge rusted bolt was drawn across the small rectangular opening cut into the larger arched one, the metal studs that covered them both glinting under the light. The paint on the Ragusan coat of arms, still used by the city today, had been flaked away by the years, but Karmela loved it all the more because of it.

In the middle of the square outside the palace was the column where the famous statue of Orlando normally stood on its three-tiered granite plinth. Sadly the knight himself had been taken away for restoration, and she hoped he would be back in his place before she had to return to Zagreb ready for the new academic year in September. After all, he had graced this place in one form or another since the dawn of the fifteenth century and had played an important part in Ragusan life. If she closed her eyes she could almost see the bustle of the medieval market around him.

She was about to turn away when a familiar figure emerged from the narrow street next to the palace and lurched into the square. There was nowhere to run, nowhere to hide, the long, wide street of Stradun to her left completely empty.

"Karmela! How are you?" Her neighbour Rafael's voice boomed between the buildings, even louder than his considerable bulk might suggest.

"Fine, thank you." Good manners dictated she should return his enquiry, but she had no desire to prolong their encounter.

"And where are you off to on this cold night? Somewhere nice, I hope."

He was standing just inches away from her, and she could smell the *rakija* on his breath. "Yes. I have been to a book club. An English-speaking one."

His forehead wrinkled as he frowned. "But why? Are there not good books in our own language?"

"Of course there are. This is just a little more … challenging."

"And you are a clever lady." Nodding to himself he fished in his anorak pocket and thrust a small metal hip flask into her face. "Can I offer you something to keep out the cold?"

Instinctively she stepped away, almost stumbling backwards into one of the palace columns. "Thank you, that's very kind, but no. I must get home for supper." She dodged past him and trotted briskly up Zlatarska Ulica, the direction he had come from so he would have no reason to follow. Oh, no doubt Rafael meant well, but he had absolutely no idea about personal boundaries, and life had taught Karmela to value hers greatly.

All the same she did not relax until she was halfway up the hill, in front of the little church of Sveti Nikola. She stopped to catch her breath after the climb and to admire its narrow renaissance frontage, glorious in its simplicity. Just gazing at its plain rose window and neat oblong stones, some blackened with age, calmed her soul. How lucky she was to be able to live here, if only for a short while.

Karmela had fallen in love with Dubrovnik's medieval Ragusa Republic as a history undergraduate more than twenty years before, and the chance to research in the city was a dream come true. The archives in the Sponza Palace were full of hidden academic gold, and she was here to mine them for every last nugget she could find about the lives of Ragusan women. Such history, history that she could reach out and touch with her hand, made her heart sing in a way that nothing in Zagreb did.

And the women she was discovering, hidden as they were beneath years of patrician rule, were widows, mainly, who had taken their husbands' fortunes and made even larger ones for themselves. Intelligent women. Women like her. She would love to have lived in that peaceful, cultured age. She shrugged. It was not possible. She knew it was not. But bringing the Ragusans back to life through her studies was the next best thing.

Claire

Even in the middle of January, spring was definitely in the air as Claire made her way to work. The leaves of the fig tree near the museum were rapidly gaining their recognisable shape, and the tiny green bulbs that would form the fruit were just visible beneath them. The breeze from the sea felt softer somehow, although Nono was convinced it would rain later so her mac flapped around her legs as she walked.

How many days since the book club? Seven. And she still felt perfectly well. No sign of a headache, cough, or wheezing. Had she dodged a bullet this time, or was the city as safe as Gran would have her believe? Those first few days she'd been so very scared, secretly taking her temperature every morning. But somehow, having got through the evening unscathed, she did feel just a tiny bit more confident.

And she wouldn't have to run that particular gauntlet again for almost another month, anyway.

Monday mornings always seemed to be particularly quiet, so Claire and Luna lingered in the kitchen over their coffee and Fran's *čupavci*. Claire loved the shop's kitchen best of all, because here she felt safe from the customers and their germs. She knew she needed to overcome her fears and she was trying, really she was, but it was still so very hard, especially when someone sneezed or was continually wiping their nose. She promised herself that this week she would do better.

Wiping the stray crumbs of desiccated coconut from her lips, Claire asked Luna what she thought of the book club cosy crime novel.

She wrinkled her upturned nose. "I love mystery stories almost as much as romance, and although at the start I was not sure I would like this one, it became really good fun. It's so cool when ordinary people solve a mystery."

"Perhaps some of them were not *that* ordinary."

"Yes, but they were not the police. They were cleverer than the police. But all the same, I came to like those characters too."

"The police don't always get it right though, and I suppose that's a good premise for..." She stopped, noticing Luna was looking at her with a rather odd expression.

"I wonder," she said slowly, "are you thinking of the crimes from years ago in the book, or about your cousin, when you talk about the police not getting it right?"

Claire licked her fingers. What on earth did Luna mean? Vedran had told her some people had thought he'd killed Didi, but surely he hadn't meant anyone ... official?

"I don't know anything about Vedran and the police," she said.

Luna's dark eyes were like saucers as she gripped her mug. "*O bože*, I've put my big nose in it massively, haven't I? It was just that it was fresh in my mind while I was reading the book because after meeting him I looked up everything again. I never dreamed you didn't know," she gabbled.

Claire's mind began to race. Didn't know what? "I wasn't here, remember? Of course Gran told us poor Vedran's girlfriend had disappeared, was assumed to be drowned. That was bad enough. He's such a darling…"

"Oh yes, yes, he seemed really nice. Gentle. Nothing like the monster portrayed on social media. It was brutal."

Monster? Vedran a monster? "He did not kill Didi." Claire thumped the table and Luna jumped back in her chair, causing Claire to apologise profusely. It was so not like her to leap down anyone's throat.

"No, it's my fault," Luna replied. "I would never have mentioned it, but I assumed you knew."

But why didn't she know? Of course, Vedran had said the reason it wasn't talked about was Nono… How much could she trust Luna to hold her tongue? She hardly knew her, not really, but she needed to explain her lack of understanding of Vedran's situation. The last thing she wanted was for it to come over as some dark family skeleton.

"Can you keep a secret?" she asked.

Luna leaned forwards. "Of course."

"OK. We don't talk about it at home because we're keeping it from Nono. They're testing him for dementia and Gran doesn't want to add to the stress."

"Poor, poor Fran. I'm so sorry, Claire, and of course I won't say a word." Luna stood and began to rinse the coffee cups under the tap. Without turning to look at her, she carried on. "The question is, how much do you want to know about Vedran? I mean, we need never mention it again, but what if they've all got it wrong? What if we could clear his name? Solve the mystery like they do in the book?"

"Oh, Luna, it's so sweet of you, really it is, but the book is a book. You can't do things like that in real life."

"I don't see why not. Not if you want to."

Claire sat back in her chair and gazed at the chipped paint between the narrow beams that crossed the ceiling, trying to order her thoughts. If only it was possible … but she had so little to go on. It seemed even Luna knew more about what had happened than she did.

"On one level I'd do anything for Vedran. I've known him since I was thirteen and he's one of the kindest, gentlest guys I have ever met. Fun, too; really outgoing and sociable. Or at least he used to be. Now he's just … broken." A tear escaped and she brushed it away, no doubt leaving a trail of mascara across her cheek. Broken was exactly the word; he didn't even stand up tall anymore, he was permanently hunched, as if he was hiding from the world. Which he probably was. Claire bit her lip. "I mean, he's lost his girlfriend, hasn't he? Someone he loved. And not knowing exactly what happened to her must be eating away at him like anything."

"Isn't that another reason to find out the truth?"

"But the police must have—"

"All they did was arrest an innocent man when they should have been looking for her. Or, at the very least, her body. As things stand there's no proof she's even dead. Or alive. Just think about it, Claire, if we could solve this it would be so much easier for him to move on. I'd be more than willing to help you, you know." She turned, then swore under her breath. "I was about to say it would be fun, but not when it's making you sad. My big mouth. Words out before I think. Again."

The shop bell rang and, smoothing her short plaid skirt, Luna scurried through the arch. Claire pulled her mirror from her bag and began repairing her mascara. It was so kind of Luna to care about Vedran, but the reality was, what could the two of them do? Whatever Luna said, the police must have searched for Didi at the time, talked to people who might have seen her in the water… But why on earth had the police even considered Vedran some sort of suspect? Claire knew they always looked at people's partners as a matter of course, so maybe the rumours had sprung from nothing more than that.

So why the vitriol against Vedran on social media? Why portray him as some sort of monster? Didi had drowned, hadn't she? Simple. But if she hadn't, could something have been missed? There was no way Vedran would have had anything to do with it, and that being the case, it would be quite something if they could find out what had really happened. But no, that was the stuff of fiction, big time. *Get real, Claire. And get into that shop and do your job.*

She stood and rinsed her mug, gazing out over the courtyard, which was now filled with mizzle, making everything seem fuzzy. She felt fuzzy too; at sea, her loyalty to Vedran torn. If he'd wanted her to know more he surely would have told her, and yet she was desperate to know. Maybe it was all too painful for him to talk about. But he'd need to talk, wouldn't he? To heal. And if she knew what had happened then…

Oh god. She hated, hated, to see how much Vedran was struggling. He just wasn't himself anymore, and she could only imagine how much shit he was going through. If Luna was right then it wasn't just grief making him a prisoner, it was vile rumours stirred up by social media trolls. And that was so totally wrong. They shouldn't be allowed to ruin his life. Or anyone's, for that matter.

But what was she really dealing with here? She didn't know, and that was the problem. Just because it wasn't talked about at home… No, Claire decided she needed to know. She wasn't just being nosey; the first step towards helping Vedran must surely be to fully understand exactly what had happened with the police, what had been said at the time. Never mind solving any mystery; simply having a grasp of the facts would mean she could support Vedran so much better. Just like he'd supported her at the book club. She had to do it.

She followed Luna into the now empty shop. "Right. I've decided. I need to find out more about what happened with Vedran. Can you tell me?"

"Honestly, I'd just google it. You'll get a much better idea if you see all the shit yourself. You can always ask me if there are words you don't understand. The shop's super-quiet this morning, so why not hole up in the office for an hour or so and do it now."

"You don't mind?"

"Well, I did start this, didn't I?" Suddenly Luna grinned. "If we have a sudden rush I can always call you."

Click. Click. Click. And there it was. It hadn't been hard. A video on the local news channel, a reporter in a black raincoat standing on the shoreline close to Vedran's apartment. It was bleakly factual. Or at least Claire hoped it was; Didi Kelmendi had left the flat she shared with Vedran Novak at around nine o'clock to go swimming. The weather had been stormy, but she swam every morning, whatever the conditions. No one had actually seen her go into the water that day, although Vedran had later found her towelling robe in its usual place on the jetty. He had phoned the emergency services at about quarter past eleven, having been in a Zoom meeting that had lasted a couple of hours, after which he had realised Didi was not in the apartment. The police were searching the bay, but had so far found no trace of her.

There was a huge lump in Claire's throat as she watched the report. She tried to imagine how Vedran must have felt when he found Didi's robe; his panic, his devastation. And then as the hours ticked by, how terrified he must have been that they'd never find her, and later, how overcome by grief. She tried to put herself in his shoes, but she absolutely couldn't. That someone she loved had gone through all that was just so hard to grasp.

It had taken a few days for things to get nasty, after an interview with his upstairs neighbour appeared in an online newspaper. She'd said she'd often heard Vedran and Didi arguing, and when she'd seen him pick up her robe and gone to see if she could do anything to help, he'd had a livid bruise across his cheek he had failed to explain. And Didi had been such a strong swimmer too... After all, she had worked on tourist yachts before they met.

Claire felt physically sick. That awful, awful woman. As she clicked again and again, she realised what a furore the neighbour had unleashed, anger building inside her at every new comment or post. Luna appeared behind her and rested a hand on her shoulder. Claire looked up, her eyes swimming.

"It's frigging trial by media."

"And social media," Luna said quietly. "That was probably worse. There was some lowlife on Insta kept filming outside your cousin's flat. And a crackpot who claimed Didi had reached her from 'the other side', wherever that is."

"Oh god." Claire buried her face in her hands. "It just gets worse."

"Then stop looking."

"But I still don't get why he was arrested. Surely the police didn't believe those idiots?"

Luna shrugged. "Maybe they felt there was no smoke without fire."

The phrase lodged in Claire's head as she typed *Vedran Novak arrest* into Google. The first thing that popped up was some wobbly camera-phone footage of Vedran being led from his apartment to a waiting police car. As she watched the clip she began to shake, huge, hot tears running down her cheeks. She was so unbelievably angry. At the police, at the arsehole who'd posted the video, at Vedran's neighbour who'd stirred up the shit storm, and in part at herself, for thinking, just for a moment, that Luna's words could be right. Vedran could not be implicated. He could not. She'd never even heard him so much as raise his voice; she refused to believe he was capable of murdering someone.

Although she continued to search there was no reason given for his arrest, nor for his release the next day. There seemed to be no statements made by the police at all, only one from Vedran's employer, saying the inspector in charge of the case had apologised for his mistake in arresting him in what was, after all, a tragic missing person enquiry.

Social media had exploded; didn't everyone know that corrupt lawyers and police worked hand in hand? They were expected to protect their own, and poor Didi Kelmendi's murderer would never be brought to justice, even though everyone knew who it was. It seemed, to the world in general at least, that someone had to be blamed for her disappearance, and that person was poor Vedran.

Claire put her head in her hands, trying to make sense of it all. She had never, ever, envisaged it could be this bad. No wonder Vedran didn't want to go anywhere; she wouldn't either. If it was her, she'd want to hide away forever. But even so, he'd braved all this to come to the book club for her. It was the very least she could do to try to help him in return. She simply had to do it.

Leaving her phone in the office she walked slowly into the shop, inhaling the comforting new book smell. Luna turned from the box of paperbacks she was unpacking.

"*Sranje*, you look awful. I'm so sorry, Claire. I should never have started this. I feel terrible."

"No, no … it's not your fault and I needed to know. I didn't realise … even half … half… of what Vedran has gone through. Perhaps now I can support him better."

"But what about solving the mystery?" Luna asked. "Can we try to do that as well? At least that's something I can help with."

Claire crouched next to her, taking a book from the box. "I

wish we could, but I wouldn't even know where to start. Would you?"

"I do have one idea. My flatmate, Ezra, works in cybersecurity. I'm not sure exactly what help that could be, but I could always ask him."

"Do you trust him? I mean, absolutely trust him? I wouldn't want him to go on social media too."

"No, he'd never do that; it's just not his thing. And anyway, we've been best friends since we were seven and he may be a geek but he's one of life's good guys."

Claire knew it was a complete shot in the dark, and most likely nothing would come of it, but now her anger was fading, for some reason she still felt uneasy. Because they might unearth something she didn't want to know? Crap, crap, crap. That was so much crap. Vedran was innocent. Of course he was, so where was the harm? And if there was even the tiniest possibility of helping Vedran begin to heal, of finding out what really happened to Didi, of clearing his name, then it would be so, so worth it.

"OK then," she told Luna. "Let's do this."

Karmela

No. No. This was really too much. Again. All this noise again. How was she supposed to concentrate with Rafael yelling at poor old Paval downstairs? If her research had been going better, she might have been able to tolerate it, but so far she had wasted all morning going down blind alleyways riddled with superstition and folklore, in search of genuine evidence about a reluctant nun with arsonist tendencies. It was fair to say Karmela was not in the best of moods.

She pushed back her chair and strode onto the communal landing, ready to call down the stairwell, but to her surprise Rafael was standing in front of her.

"Ah, good morning, Karmela," he said, a grin splitting his greying beard.

"It is not a good morning. Not now you have come back, shouting and bawling."

Two furrows appeared between his eyes, his full lips pursing into something close to a pout, which looked frankly ridiculous on a bearded man.

"What do you mean?"

There was just a hint of menace in his voice, and Karmela regretted her hasty choice of words. It was better to be rational, civil. Especially as he appeared to be sober, which very often he was not. Appeal to his better nature, and she might have a chance of making him understand.

"I was working and your very loud conversation disturbed me."

"It was not loud. And anyway, Paval is deaf."

"Not that deaf. Could I ask you, please, to moderate your voice in the communal areas?"

"Moderate your voice in the communal areas?" he mimicked. "What does that mean? Don't you speak normal Croatian in Zagreb or wherever you come from?" Karmela was too shocked to reply, automatically taking a step away from him, but he followed, towering over her and prodding her arm to emphasise his point. "I will do what I want in my home. *My* home. And if you do not like it, well, go back to yours."

He stomped into his apartment, the cheap wooden frame reverberating as he slammed the door behind him. Karmela was shaking a little as she backed towards her own entrance. She had never expected him to get physical. But why not? Her father had in his darkest days. She could not let herself remember the fear, creeping around that awful flat in Berlin where they had been housed as refugees, with nowhere to escape to.

Karmela knew from bitter experience how frightening drink could make a man, yet Rafael had appeared stone cold sober, with not even a whiff of stale *rakija* on his breath. That in itself was unsettling. How dangerous could he be? She had always known he was a little unpredictable, but this… Should she call the police? And yet he had only prodded her arm. It was hardly an assault. They'd laugh at her, of course they would. She would just have to be careful about locking her door. And remember how kind Rafael could be sometimes. And that Paval had told her he was a good man, really. That "really" had just taken on a rather sinister meaning.

Rafael's television blared from across the landing, far louder than any reasonable person would need. Damn the man; she did not want to have to move; apartments just outside the old town were like gold dust, and with the tourist season only a couple of months away, even more so. Anywhere becoming vacant was quickly put on Airbnb or one of the other holiday rental sites. She would just have to hope he calmed down.

In the meantime, there was no point in staying here and trying to work. She had yet to start that stupid book club mystery, so perhaps she would treat herself to lunch out and take it to read. She had noticed yesterday that one of the restaurants just along Stradun from the Sponza Palace had put a few tables outside, and today it was warm enough to use them. From there she could gaze at her favourite building in the world.

The palace had survived, that was what drew her to it. Survived the earthquake of 1667, when most of the city had not. Indeed the event had been so cataclysmic it was often said to have brought about the end of the Ragusa Republic that Karmela held so dear. Of course, the truth was far more complex, but this last famous relic meant a great deal to her and just being near it would soothe her soul. Even if she had to read that damned book while she was there.

Although her lunch with its glass of wine had made her feel rather better, and she had become quite engrossed in the book club read, Karmela was still a little reluctant to return home. Of course she must go; she needed to work, but a walk around the old harbour first would certainly do no harm. It would be good to feel the fresh sea air on her face.

The harbour had been at medieval Ragusa's heart. She passed

the Sponza Palace, then continued under the arch beneath the clock tower. She knew the elegant grey stone finger pointing into the sky today was not the original – it was less than a hundred years old – but the bell was the same one the Ragusans would have heard, and it gave Karmela goosebumps every time it chimed.

Given the choice, Karmela would have gone back to that era in a heartbeat. Never mind the inconvenience of medieval living, never mind the lowly place of women in society. Her studies were proving that some had forged an independent life of sorts, some clever ones, like sixteenth-century Filipa Menčetić, a widow who had built a business empire following her husband's death. She was the main focus of Karmela's research, but she had not lived in isolation and although women were practically invisible in the records of the time, she was determined to root out whatever information she could about Filipa's female contemporaries.

There was no doubt the Ragusan Republic had been a strongly patrician society, but that had been the way of the world back then. What Karmela admired most about them was their expert diplomacy, never resorting to war with anyone, and becoming a most lucrative trade bridge between the Venetians to the west and the Ottomans to the east. A stable time. A peaceful time. That was the most important thing of all.

It had been one of the happiest moments of Karmela's life when she had won the funding for her research, together with a sabbatical to complete it. Although she loved sharing her passion for history with students, the false camaraderie of the staffroom at the university, hiding as it did a welter of backstabbing and jostling for position, irked her. Far better to keep her distance, although she knew behind her back her colleagues disliked her for it. Well, that was their tough luck.

For as long as she cared to remember, Karmela had struck out on her own. Certainly since leaving Sarajevo. Before that, of course, she, Emina and Nejla had been inseparable from the day they started school. Until the night after shots had been fired on a peace march, and Karmela's parents had packed their possessions into the car and done a moonlight flit. She had not even had the chance to say goodbye. A last goodbye, as it happened. Someone told her mother Emina had been killed, and Karmela had made no attempt to trace Nejla after the war. What would have been the point? In Berlin she had become a different person.

She closed her eyes, listening to the wash of the waves against the harbourside and willing herself into a more comfortable past. Instead of the fishing and pleasure boats in the shadow of Svetog Ivana fort, she imagined Venetian galleys filling the quays, and she could almost smell the spices being unloaded – cinnamon, cloves, nutmeg – and hear the rustle of merchants' fine silks as they passed, the creak of the wind as the sailing ships rocked against the quay. In Dubrovnik her escape into the Ragusan world could be complete.

Except in reality it was not. She could not stand here dreaming all afternoon, especially as she was only putting off going home in case Rafael was waiting to pounce. But no, she would not cower. Another lesson she had learned the hard way. She pulled her shoulders back, glorying in every single one of her five foot eight inches. She had ground to make up from this morning, and there was no way she was going to let anyone or anything come between her and her work.

On her doorstep Karmela found the most enormous bouquet of flowers wrapped in a cellophane bubble. Deep pink roses, orange tiger lilies and dark red gerbera tried, but failed, to clash. She took a moment to enjoy them, then bent to read the label to see where they needed to be redelivered.

My apologies. Rafael.

They really were for her. She was so stunned she failed to hear his apartment door open.

"Do you like them?" he asked, his voice coming from close behind her. She nodded. "I behaved like an animal earlier. I am ashamed."

She shifted on her haunches to look up at him. "They are beautiful. I can't remember the last time anyone bought me flowers."

"Then I must argue with you every week, so you can have some more."

"I would rather you did not." The words came instinctively, before she had time to consider them.

He nodded. "No, it is not good to be fighting with neighbours. Fighting full stop. That, at least, I should know."

He surprised her once again by settling on the top step, twisting around to look at her. Clearly he expected them to have a conversation. She pushed her desire to get on with her work to the back of her mind. For the sake of her peace and quiet at least, bridges needed to be built, so she sat beside him, tucking her knees into her arms.

"I do not want us to argue either. It is unnecessary and stressful."

"Stress, I think, is the problem. My problem at least." He shrugged. "Since the war I have not been the same man and that is the truth of it."

"But that was a long time ago."

"To me, it is like yesterday. I was only nineteen, you see, when it started." Rafael paused. "I thought the most exciting thing that would ever happen in my lifetime was when the computers arrived at work. I wanted to save my money, to travel, see the world. I was young, blind to the political situation. It was such a shock when the Serbs invaded."

"I think it shocked the world."

"But no, it didn't, not at first and not enough. So the government thought; sacrifice Dubrovnik and then the world would have to look. The city had already been a UNESCO site for more than ten years, so many foreigners had been here, surely everyone would rise up and help little Croatia. But the reality was in this city we had to help ourselves."

"You fought? But you were so young."

"Young and old. We fought together. What else could we do? Refugees streaming in from the countryside, telling such awful tales… They thought they were safe here. We had no arms, no power, no water. Nothing. But we could not let them down. Or our city. My gun … my gun…" He gulped, tears fresh in his eyes. "I took it from the body of my best friend's father. Or what was left of it. He was hit by a mortar."

Karmela could see the pain in his face, even after all these years. The poor man, living with such nightmares he felt he had to tell a virtual stranger about them. Not everyone, by any means, suffered this way; some were luckier, thank goodness. But having been whisked away from the country on the eve of war it was something she could not relate to, and experience told her that a kindly platitude was often the safest answer.

"It must have been very hard."

He shook his head. "No, it was worse than that. But it should not be an excuse for bad behaviour and again I apologise." He hauled himself up on the metal banister, then turned to give her a tired smile. "We won though. Against all the odds. And I was there, on Mount Srd on the sixth of December." He pointed to his chest. "I, Rafael Babic, was part of that miracle."

And miracle it had been. A handful of men had somehow turned the tide of enemy troops and saved the city. "You must be very proud," Karmela murmured, impressed despite herself.

"It is something, yes. Anyway, I cannot sit gossiping here, I have a business to run. Enjoy your flowers."

"Thank you."

But as she arranged her bouquet in an old chipped vase she had found under the sink, it occurred to Karmela that Rafael did not have a business to run; she had seen him in his uniform so often she knew he was a porter at the hospital. And if he lied so easily about that, were his war stories the product of a damaged mind too? She closed her eyes. War hurt everyone, in large or small ways. Even if your family had run away.

Luna

Luna replaced the display copy of *Girl, Woman, Other* the smartly dressed American lady had just bought with a new one fresh from the box, angling it this way and that until it caught the light perfectly. It had been Claire's idea to change the window for Sveti Vlaho Day, and it was filled with books with predominantly red, white and yellow covers. Just like the long flowing banners she'd seen the workmen erecting on poles along Stradun, the city's main street, on her way to work yesterday.

Sveti Vlaho was sodding everywhere. The saint's day was a stupidly big deal in Dubrovnik, and Simeon had even called to say they could close the shop at eleven o'clock so they could join in the fun. Fun? Since when had church been fun? Going to some religious love-fest was the last thing she wanted. Luna'd had more than enough of church, thank you very much. The teachings her parents subscribed to would stop them ever accepting their only child as she was and that freakin' well hurt.

Well, OK. Going to Sveti Vlaho wasn't quite the last thing Luna wanted to do. The last thing was to go home and spend the unexpected free time on her own. She'd rather be working, she honestly would. To top it all, when they'd been locking up last night, Claire had mentioned perhaps they could watch the procession together. That had come right out of the blue, really it had, and Luna hadn't known what to say. So she'd said yes. Except now she had distinctly cold feet. It would be so, so hypocritical. But the alternative was to be on her own. Again.

Claire turned the shop sign to closed. "Where should we watch the parade from, do you think?"

Luna pursed her lips. "Are you sure it's a good idea? It'll be massively crowded." Perhaps she could persuade her to do something else. Maybe head out of the old town, away from all the hymn singing and flag waving, and take a stroll around Gradac Park. Not that a stroll amongst the trees would be Luna's normal choice of entertainment either, but the bakery opposite the Imperial Hotel would be open so at least they could grab something delicious to eat.

Claire screwed her face into a crooked smile. "I know, but I really do want to see it, because it might be my only chance. At least it's outside, and I need to try to start worrying less about Covid if I can, if only because Gran's giving me a hard time about it."

"Are Fran and your *nono* coming too?"

"He has a touch of bronchitis so they're staying in. It isn't as though they're religious."

"They're not?" This surprised Luna; she had assumed it was the same here as on Šipan, where most elderly people were quite devout. And bigoted with it. But now she thought about it, it was hard to imagine Fran, one of the friendliest people she had ever met, being judgemental. Claire didn't know how lucky she was.

"Not in the slightest. None of our family are, but that isn't unusual in Britain."

"It is here."

"Really?"

Luna snorted. "Back home I'm the strange one because I don't go to church." They'd think her strange for other reasons too, if they knew. But they didn't. Wouldn't ever. Even if she ever, ever, managed to screw up the courage to come out in the city she could never tell anyone at home. And how she'd find the words to talk to Ezra… "Come on," she told Claire, "let's cash up, then we'll have time for a coffee and some cake while everyone else is still at the service."

At least the cake was an upside. Big upside. And it was what friends did for each other, wasn't it? She didn't begrudge Claire, not really. She was lucky to have a boss who could be her friend as well. Super-lucky. But would that change if Claire knew her secret? It could so easily slip out. Even today. What if it did? Luna felt her buttocks clench in fear. She could almost hear it, play it forward in her mind. Claire watching a man walk past the coffee shop, saying he looked nice, asking Luna if she fancied him… And then she'd have to make a choice; come clean or perpetuate the lie she was living with yet another person.

So many times as a teenager. So many times sitting on the beach after swimming, nudging each other and looking at tourist boys. How could she ever have told them she looked at the girls? Not her friends, not them, of course, but at the slim, tanned bodies of young women in the tiniest of bikinis; that's what had made her heart race and covered her with shame.

Oh, she'd found out pretty quickly from the internet it wasn't wrong to be a lesbian. In most modern places it was entirely normal; it was just that on Šipan it was absolutely unheard of. And certainly not allowed by the church. Well, only if she didn't do anything about it, and she wasn't going to live like that. She could only envy the openness of gay women and men in the big European cities. The homosexual community might have equal legal status in Croatia, but attitudes could fall far, far behind. Especially on small islands.

The thought of telling anyone back home she was gay made her feel really sick. It would be around the village in minutes and her mother would be so ashamed. Ashamed and disappointed; no wedding to look forward to, no grandchildren. And her father would go absolutely ballistic. He'd probably try to lock her in her room. And blame poor Mama like he always did. She couldn't let that happen. Absolutely no fucking way.

But would it be the end of the world if Claire knew? She was from London, after all, one of the gay capitals of the world. But you could never tell with people, not really. She'd only known Claire a month, after all. Plus she was her boss as well. It would be a massive, massive risk.

All the same she'd imagined it so many times. Casual, as if it didn't matter, so the words would not stick in her throat. City sophisticated. The other answer she could give, if Claire asked her if she fancied a man. The brave answer. "No, I don't have boyfriends, I'm gay." And Claire would nod and smile, maybe even say, "Cool. My best friend at home is too." And in an even wilder fantasy – and, let's face it, a world without Covid – she might even ask where the best gay bars were in Dubrovnik because they were always so much fun.

Except there weren't any. Even if Luna was out, there'd be nowhere to go. Of course she knew the jazz café actively welcomed the gay community along with everyone else, but with open displays of affection frowned upon how would she ... how could she ... let anyone she met there know who she really was and what she wanted? Let's face it, she even struggled to imagine how it might feel, being out. And if she couldn't imagine it, how could she be brave enough to...

No. Not today. Not that same old roller-coaster today. It was going to be hard enough to swallow all that religious shit and pretend she was happy about it. Cake. Think about the cake.

As they approached Stradun Luna spied a free table outside a café on the corner and grabbed Claire's arm.

"Come on! Let's sit here before anyone else spots it. They do fabulous *bijela pita* and we'll get a view of the parade."

The moment they sat down, Luna could tell Claire was far from comfortable, as she pulled her chair closer and closer to the table and away from other people, her breathing so shallow it was almost as if she was trying not to inhale at all. *O bože*, this was going to be awful. Whole new level awful. What could she do? Looking around for inspiration, she spied a vaguely familiar face.

"Isn't that Karmela from the book club?" she asked.

Claire glanced in the direction she was looking, and nodded. It was definitely Karmela. That sharp geometric cut that made her dark hair gleam like a helmet above her high forehead and arched eyebrows, her strong face completely devoid of makeup. She might not exactly be pretty, but she was certainly memorable. And she was looking for a seat.

Luna waved, making Karmela start, so she jumped up. "We work in the bookshop, remember? Would you like to join us?"

"I would not wish to intrude," said Karmela, backing away slightly.

"No, honestly, it's fine. It would be nice to get to know you better." Well maybe not, but it would be a distraction for Claire. Already she looked less like she was going to bolt at any moment, because now she couldn't. She was far too British and polite.

The older woman hesitated before saying, "In which case, thank you."

There was an awkward moment while Karmela sat down and wrapped the straps of her rucksack through the legs of her chair, but the waiter bustled over to take their order, and by the time he'd left Luna had thought of something to say.

"So you have the day off work too?"

"I have given myself the day off. I am on a sabbatical at the moment to do some research."

"That sounds interesting. Into what, exactly?" Claire asked. Good. She was going to join in the conversation. That was promising, at least.

"The position of women in Ragusan society. It is quite a broad topic, but I do not return to lecturing until September so there is plenty of time."

"You teach at the university?" Luna asked.

"Not here, in Zagreb."

"Does that mean you haven't seen the Sveti Vlaho procession before either?" Claire asked.

Karmela shook her head. "I am looking forward to it; there is such history attached to these traditions. And it is wonderful to see ordinary people in the streets dressed in traditional costume. I think, perhaps, it is something that has not changed in hundreds of years."

"So the Ragusans would have seen it too?" asked Claire.

"Sveti Vlaho was their patron saint because they believed he raised an army to save the city from the Venetians in 972, so they are calling this year the 1050th celebration. Of course that is not strictly accurate, firstly because the original date is disputed by historians, and secondly, when Napoleon's France ruled the city, public celebrations relating to the church were banned."

"Good for Napoleon," Luna muttered, but Karmela either didn't hear her or took no notice because she carried on with what was increasingly sounding like a lecture.

"Many aspects of the feast come from Ragusan times. Like these banners we see everywhere with the initials SB for Santa Blasius in Latin. The idea is at least six hundred years old. Images of Sveti Vlaho were used everywhere; on the city gates, on hallmarks for precious metals, the shipping fleet's flags."

"So he was more than just a religious figure?" asked Claire.

Sranje, she was good at keeping this woman talking, but it didn't seem to take much.

"Oh yes. But in those days it was hard to properly untangle the church from the state. While it can be said that many Ragusans had more interest in wealth than piety, religion was certainly used to keep the masses in their place."

"And women," added Claire.

Luna snorted. "That hasn't changed, has it?" Karmela and Claire both looked surprised at the force of her words. "I mean, where I come from what the priest says is the law. To the old folks especially, including my parents. Patriarchy is alive and well."

"I have male colleagues who certainly believe it should be," said Karmela.

Luna leaned forwards. "Then you get it. You know what my father said to me when I moved here? That he would *allow* me to because it would help me to find a big strong husband to work in the olive grove. I'm almost twenty-one!"

"Now that is bloody medieval," said Claire.

"But true."

"Where do you come from?" Karmela asked.

"The island of Šipan. And no, it's not in the back of beyond. It's all of twenty kilometres from here."

The waiter arrived with their order, unloading a small cup of local coffee for Karmela and two cappuccinos, as well as three neat oblongs of *bijela pita*, the layers of fluffy white sponge oozing vanilla buttercream.

As Luna lifted a large forkful to her mouth, Claire asked Karmela about the women she was researching.

"In the main they have been almost completely erased from the historical record, but in Dubrovnik the city archives are very good. Even so, most of them I can only find in marriage agreements. The young women from noble families were no more than pawns in building dynasties, but to a certain extent so were the young men. They were all under the control of their fathers as heads of the family. The only possible freedoms were given to widows and there is one in particular I'm looking into: Filipa Menčetić."

Claire nodded enthusiastically as Karmela continued to ramble on. And on. To Luna she sounded just like the teachers at school, and she was paying her about the same amount of attention. Why on earth would anyone think it important to find out what went on hundreds of years ago in such tedious, tedious detail? What relevance could it possibly have to women like her today?

But worse, much worse, was that the sound of brass bands and choirs singing hymns that had been circling through the air was becoming louder and more distinct. The procession was clearly approaching and Luna really, really, did not want to be anywhere near it. What could she do?

Karmela stood. "Come on. We need to get a bit closer so we can see it properly." Claire levered herself slowly from her seat, but Luna shook her head. Think. Think. Then inspiration came.

"It's fine. I'll stay here and keep our table. I've seen it before," she lied.

The edges of the street, marked by the rows of huge cream, red and gold banners, were crowded, and Luna watched as Claire hesitated. She jumped up after her and gave her shoulder a squeeze.

"You can do this," she whispered.

Claire turned her head, and although her eyes were troubled she tried to smile. "Thank you. I'll try. But I know where you are if I can't."

Despite people standing two or three deep in front of the café, as she swilled the last of her cappuccino around her cup, Luna was still aware of flashes of the priests' red robes as they passed. She could certainly hear the noise, the church bells adding to the cacophony, making her squirm. Above the watchers' heads the red canopy covering the elaborate silver casket that supposedly held the saint's relics swayed as it was carried along by a troop of men in red and gold jackets. Luna heard someone remark what a spectacle it was, a source of civic pride, something all Dubrovcani could come together for. Not her though, she was outside, as per usual. Different. Strange. Even Claire and Karmela, neither of whom lived here permanently, were more involved than she was and it sucked.

Following the procession were families wearing traditional dress: women and children in gold-braided waistcoats, men in collarless jackets and shirts, and round red felt hats everywhere. Rather than the wonderful historical spectacle Karmela had enthused over, all Luna saw were full-grown adults dressing up. Not families having fun, but walking symbols of all the things that needed to change. But was she wrong? Was she the intolerant one? Either way, she did not want to be here and was desperate to slink away. But to what? At least with Claire and Karmela she'd had cake, and maybe once this sham was over, she and Claire could go and do something nicer. Anything nicer. She didn't care.

Lifting her eyes from the parade towards the top floor windows of the building opposite, something entirely unexpected caught her eye. For real? Was it? Could it possibly be? A rainbow flag sticker? Super-freakin'-amazing! The shock gave way to a small smile, a moment of hope. Maybe she wasn't as alone as she felt after all, and she needed to cling to that thought. Bloody right she did. Things would get better. Not only did she have to believe it, but she needed to find a way to make it happen.

Coming Back to Me

Vedran

The second book club should be easier than the first, Vedran told himself as he locked his car and hurried up the ramp and through the low arch of the Buža Gate. Last time no one had recognised him, and despite his nerves he had almost enjoyed it. Well, as close as he came to enjoying anything these days. It had certainly been good to see Claire projecting a confidence he knew she didn't feel, and with so much polish and poise. His little cousin had grown up.

What was it she said? Fake it until you make it? The English phrase rolled around his head. He certainly needed to do that tonight, because the ball of anger that was his constant companion was scarily close to the surface. It rose like a poisonous bubble at just the smallest of things. This time it had been that stupid woman upstairs ignoring him when he'd bumped into her in the car park behind his apartment. Like she always did these days. So why he was letting it chew him up so badly, he did not know.

Sod her. He was damned if he was going to move. He wasn't going to end up some sort of miserable wanderer, trailing from place to place, trying to find somewhere he felt comfortable. The waterfront apartment on Zaton Bay was his home, whatever memories it held. As a child he'd hated the way his parents never settled anywhere, so he was damned if he was going to repeat their mistake.

Tetak had always lived in the same apartment and it had become his stability, teaching him to love the old town in all its moods. Tonight it suited his own; the dark and empty bars and restaurants, their closed shutters in need of their pre-season lick of paint. Some stayed open all year, of course they did; it was where he had met Fran, a winter tourist, some twelve years before, and introduced her to Tetak. Watching their romance blossom in their sixties ought to have taught him a lot about the importance of kindness and mutual respect when it came to love. But it hadn't, had it? That and more had been his for the taking, but he'd thrown it away with barely a thought.

He'd met Didi in the winter too; right on this street, he realised. He stopped halfway down the slope, well outside the yellow arcs of the street lamps. Had he come this way without thinking? Or to deliberately sabotage himself? He tried to tell himself it didn't matter. The nightclub wasn't here anymore. After Covid it had reopened as a *Game of Thrones* themed bar for the tourists, but leaning against the wall opposite its barred windows and locked door, and half closing his eyes, he could still sense the thud of the music, the tang of cigarette smoke that had filled the air. Too late, he tried to stop the memory from coming, but it was already consuming him; drawing him into a place he no longer wanted to go.

It had been his colleague Bruno's stag night. After dinner they'd stumbled, ridiculously wine-fuelled, into the club, and there she had been. Sitting on a high stool at the bar, wearing a silver lamé top and a tiny mini skirt, blonde hair cascading over her face as she bent to fiddle with her ankle chain.

He'd just about had time to clock her incredibly sexy legs

before she glanced up and looked at him. Her huge, cat-like eyes had worked their way languidly from knee level to his face, lingering here and there, and it had been the most erotic sensation he had ever experienced. It was almost as though he'd been naked before her and he hadn't minded one bit.

Buying the next round of drinks at the bar, he'd felt the warmth of her hand on his shoulder. "I know you from somewhere, don't I?"

It was a line. Of course it was a line, but he hadn't cared. "Perhaps," he'd replied. "Although I'm not sure I'd forget a face like yours."

"Well, I haven't forgotten you." She'd sounded so genuine he'd wondered for a moment if they had in fact met before. He certainly wanted to meet her again, but why, when he had a long-term girlfriend? Then, for the first and quite possibly the last time, he had felt properly ashamed, being so completely entranced by another woman when he should be thinking of Malina.

So he'd quickly ordered the drinks then strode away to join the others, all the time aware of her eyes on his back. Or maybe he had just wanted her to be watching him.

An hour or so later, as the party began to break up, he'd sensed her behind him.

As soon as he'd turned she had asked, "Just one dance before you leave?"

He might have said no. Might have. But probably wouldn't. His friends had urged him on. Part of the fun of the stag night. To their whoops and cheers he had led her onto the small dance floor, where she'd kicked off her ridiculously high-heeled but oh so sexy shoes, and when, after a few numbers the music slowed, tucked herself under his chin.

The pure physicality of his reaction had rocked him. Her hand on the small of his back burned right through his shirt, and when she spoke the warmth of her breath was feather-like in his ear.

"We fit so well," she'd murmured, her voice sensual, exotic, with its slightly imperfect Croatian. And she'd been right; it had felt as though they'd been built for each other, her hand sliding onto his buttock, guiding his groin into the softness of her belly. Right at that moment she'd been everything, everything he'd wanted.

Vedran raised his head, the roughness of the wall behind him tugging at his hair, trying to tip the tears back into his eyes. What the frigging hell was he crying for? He knew, he knew ... but this grief ... it wasn't normal ... wasn't ... couldn't be ... after what had happened... *Jebem ti!* He should never have come this way. One more bloody time, he'd let Didi break him. One more bloody time. When would he learn? And he wanted to howl; howl like a wounded animal. But real men didn't do that, did they?

Ach, he should go home right now, open a bottle of whisky. He was no frigging good to anyone. But he couldn't; he'd promised Claire. He shook himself like a wet dog. He needed to get his shit together, that was for sure, and he wouldn't be able to do it standing here.

He jogged down the steps towards the bright lights of Stradun before crossing the main street as quickly as he could, reclaiming the safety of the shadows. In the deserted alleyway opposite, he stopped. At least the tears had washed his anger away, but which was worse? He was shaking inside and out, too shaken to go on, but Claire needed him. *Frigging hell, pull yourself together, man, if that's what you are.*

Claire would be faking it again tonight, he knew, so he'd better do the same. Surely it wouldn't take much if he put his mind to it. All he had to do was force a smile as he handed around the wine, then sit in the corner until it was over, trying not to think of everything he had lost.

Karmela

Karmela locked the door of her apartment and tiptoed down the lino-covered stairs before slipping on her shoes and heading into the dusk. She hated having to creep around like this, but if Rafael heard her he would no doubt pounce and expect a rambling conversation. Tonight she had no wish to be late.

She passed the locked and silent cable car and rounded the corner next to the fire station. In front of her the walls of the old town rose, bathed in the too white glare of the floodlights. Impressive as they were, the Ragusans who built them all those years ago had never intended them to be seen this way, and she was not entirely sure she approved. Yet something about the sight made her smile inside. Difficult neighbours notwithstanding, she was absolutely loving her time here.

Walking briskly up the ramp between the parked cars she entered the old town through the diminutive Buža Gate. Most tourists never came this way, quite rightly in her view, because this entrance to the city had only been in use for a mere one hundred and fourteen years, but for her it was convenient. After all, the magic was inside, and the joy of it never seemed to pale.

Tonight, however, she found herself a little distracted from the beauty around her. She had received an email from her mother just before she came out, politely enquiring about her health, which had made Karmela realise how long it had been since they had spoken. And that they probably should, even though her mother had little interest in her research. It was probably best to replace their alternate Sunday morning visits to coffee shops with calls, but without the hustle and bustle of a café to spur them into conversation it would be hard to know what to talk about. Maybe the book club could fulfil that purpose.

To her surprise she had finished the mystery Claire had chosen and made extensive notes to share with the group, although she was unsure whether or not she would tell them she enjoyed it. It was not exactly serious, and she was a professor, after all. Not that most of them knew that, because she had not mentioned it at the first meeting for fear of intimidating them, but Claire and Luna did, and they would surely expect more from her because of it.

Karmela followed the man she thought of as the wine waiter into the shop, watching him embrace Fran before disappearing into the back room, presumably to open tonight's bottles. She needed to work out how she could get in there herself; she had hoped there would be an opportunity to ask Claire on Sveti Vlaho, which was the main reason she had accepted Luna's invitation to sit with them, but she had been unable to turn the conversation in an appropriate direction.

Claire stepped forwards to greet her, asking how she was.

"Very well, thank you. And you?"

"Fine, thanks. Although a little nervous about what everyone thought of the book. It's such a responsibility choosing one, isn't it?"

"I enjoyed thinking about what my choice will be."

"You have your selection with you?"

When Claire had emailed a reminder of the meeting she had

asked everyone to bring their choice along on a folded piece of paper, which she would put into a container to draw out randomly.

Karmela pulled it from the book in her hand, where it nestled with her typewritten notes.

"Thank you," said Claire, popping it into a cardboard box decorated with silver stars. "Don't worry, I'll mix them up – yours won't stay at the bottom. I have to say I'm sorry I didn't think of it before. It feels a bit wrong to have asked my cousin to pick the next one, but I needed to order the copies."

"It is a practical solution." Karmela shrugged her shoulders, then hurried away to her seat in the corner next to the international bookshelf. That was quite enough conversation; she wanted to enjoy her surroundings before the meeting started.

The thought that this room would have been some sort of shop for generations thrilled her, and once she had a glass of wine in her hand she allowed herself to drift into a happy fantasy where a Ragusan spice merchant was showing his wares to his wealthy customers, the candle-lamps flickering on their fur-trimmed robes. She had recently discovered that Filipa Menčetić's family had lived in this street; maybe it had even been one of them? Highly unlikely; but the idea was rather marvellous all the same.

Before Karmela knew it, Claire had climbed onto her stool next to the till and was welcoming them. As she did so the elderly lady called Fran, who had been busy with the crisps and olives, plumped herself down in the spare chair next to Karmela with a soft sigh, settling her rather ample bottom over the seat.

Glancing at her, Karmela could see a resemblance to Claire; her grandmother, perhaps? Neither was tall and both had rather round faces, and Karmela could tell the older woman would have been just as pretty, especially with her lively jet-black eyes that seemed to dance as she looked around the room.

Luna was the first to give her opinion of the murder mystery, saying she had enjoyed it and thought the crime well-constructed and the setting, in a retirement village, unusual. Most of the students had liked it too, and one made much of the fact that the straightforward use of the English language had made it a good first choice, something that Karmela had stressed in her notes as well. Neither of the men had read it; the wine waiter, as she thought of him, because he had been too busy with work, and the older one because his wife had taken too long to finish it.

"I didn't get on with it at all," she explained. "Not its fault; just not my cup of tea." The students started to giggle and for a moment she looked affronted, before Claire explained that "not my cup of tea" was a perfectly normal English expression and not, in fact, a joke.

No one's critique of the novel was quite as long as Karmela's so she rather skimmed through her notes, although she was delighted when one of the students challenged her on a point. She missed the cut and thrust of academic debate, and although this was rather low-key she relished the discussion that ensued. Perhaps next time she would be deliberately controversial to encourage more of the same. If there was a next time, of course.

Eventually Claire turned to Fran, who laughed.

"How on earth would I follow that? All I can add is that I really liked the fact the characters were oldies. Given how successful it's been, I hope more authors will be brave enough to follow suit."

Now the meeting moved on to the next book, which was apparently the wine waiter's choice, although Claire introduced it. So he was Claire's cousin, which would explain the warm embrace with which Fran had greeted him, and perhaps also why he had looked so uncomfortable at the last meeting. It must have been a family three-line whip or something. Claire referred to him as Vedran, and Karmela stored that away with the other names she would need to remember if she returned for a third visit.

That seemed rather less likely when she realised the next book was a sportsman's autobiography. It was hardly going to be literature, was it? First cosy crime, now this? What sort of book club was Claire running? She had a whole catalogue of wonderful English literature, from Shakespeare to Hilary Mantel, and she let her cousin choose this? Karmela was tempted to say as much, but the Englishman piped up that he had read it some time before and it was brilliant; more about the man's struggles with mental health than cricket, which had been ground-breaking for an athlete to reveal at the time.

"When I asked Claire to pick a sporting biography," said Vedran, "I suppose I had thought of a footballer, someone really famous like David Beckham or Lionel Messi. My apologies. I should have not been lazy and chosen it myself." He folded his arms, then hurried on. "It isn't Claire's fault, it really is mine. It was kind of her to do it for me. I have been so busy."

One of the students piped up that this one sounded more interesting, although if there was very much cricket involved it would be hard to get to grips with a sport she knew nothing about, but the man who had read the book assured her she could easily skip over those parts and still get a lot out of it. Karmela remained unconvinced; neither sport nor mental health were of any interest to her at all.

As soon as the meeting broke up Vedran made his apologies and left, so, realising it was a way to see what was behind the curtain, Karmela helped Claire to collect the empty wine glasses and carry them into the small kitchen at the back of the shop. It was a cosy space with a pine table in the middle, the rough walls decorated with a few old book posters, but best of all, over the archway was the echo of a scrolled keystone that matched the one above the front window. Battered and worn it might be, but it was still an unusually decorative item to have survived, and Karmela could barely drag her eyes away from it.

Hearing Claire run water into the sink, she reluctantly joined her on the other side of the room. "It is marvellous these old merchant houses are still used for the purpose for which they were built," Karmela said as she picked up a tea towel. "It must be wonderful to work in one."

"God yes. They mightn't be convenient but they make up for it with bags of character." Claire handed Karmela a glass to dry. "Thanks for doing this, by the way. Gran had to head off home and I guess Vedran did too."

"It is no problem."

"And the way you led the discussion on the book and got everyone talking about it was great too."

"Well, when I am lecturing, that is my job."

Claire nodded. "I can't wait to hear what you make of the cricket book. I think it's going to be challenging in all sorts of ways."

Although during the meeting Karmela had been on the verge of questioning Claire's judgement, to do so alone with her in the kitchen might seem rather rude. But she wanted to be honest as well. "I do not usually read contemporary autobiographies."

"Which will make your views even more interesting. A completely new genre for you to explore." Claire smiled at her. "That's the essence of a book club, isn't it? Trying different things. Give me that tea towel; you'll need to grab yourself a copy before Luna cashes up."

So that was that. She had been trapped into committing. To buying a book she did not want in the least. But now she had seen the kitchen, it did not absolutely mean she had to come back. Did it?

Luna

L una threw herself onto the seat of the bus just as it moved off. *Sranje*, she ought to be able to get up in the mornings. It wasn't as though she didn't absolutely adore her job, but she was reading this super-dreamy romance and she'd been awake so late… Of course, she had the hots for the sassy best friend and not the bloke, but books about people like her were few and far between.

She had a sneaking suspicion there might be at least a few in English, but she could hardly ask Claire, could she? Not unless she told her something else first. Luna squirmed in her seat. She should. She really would. Perhaps asking about gay romances would be a way in. It was an idea. Defo. She'd do it today. Really.

Except she knew that she wouldn't. She liked Claire, not in a fancying sort of way, thank *bože*, and working with her was so much more fun than when Simeon had been running the shop. Nothing wrong with Simeon, of course there wasn't, he was kind and patient. He was just a bit … well … old. Claire was kind and patient and young.

Yep. She'd tell Claire today. Luna nodded to herself. She would do it. Her stomach clenched. But what if Claire didn't like it? The problem was, Luna wouldn't know. Because Claire was kind. And ever so polite. She would just gradually withdraw from her, and Luna wasn't sure she could bear that. Claire was becoming her friend and she didn't have enough of those to lose.

Fran had sent Claire to work with enough salad for both their lunches, which was just as well because Luna had eaten her sandwiches by ten o'clock. She was always hungry and Claire told her for the umpteenth time how she envied her tiny frame.

"I'm forever fighting my weight," she complained, "especially with all Gran's baking."

"I don't know why," Luna said through a forkful of tomato and olives, "it must be nice to be curvy."

"You sound just like Gran. But when the evenings are lighter I'm going to start jogging after work as well as on Sundays, and once it gets too warm for that, I'll go swimming. Every night if I can."

"I'll come for the swimming bit. Not the running, though." Luna shuddered. "Ezra does it and he comes back disgustingly sweaty."

"That is rather the point."

Luna took another mouthful. "Which reminds me, he needs a picture of Vedran's Didi. He says the ones he can pull off the internet aren't working well enough. No idea what he's up to, although he did say something about the best way to clear the man's name was to find the woman."

"That's one way of looking at it, but it does rather rely on her being alive, and Nono said her body could have been carried anywhere by the currents."

"I don't suppose you could ask Vedran?"

Claire couldn't look at her. "Not really. I haven't told him what we're doing yet. I kind of want to get somewhere with it first. Not build up his hopes or cause him any more pain."

"You're sure that's a good idea?"

"What? Telling him or not telling him?" Claire's laugh didn't sound right.

"There might be more info we need from him at some point, and anyway, you don't look comfortable going behind his back."

"I'm not. It's his life we're interfering with, and apart from that I don't like there being secrets between us, but he's not the Vedran I remember in so many ways, not half so … I don't know … approachable. Hardly surprising, I suppose, given what he's been through. It breaks my heart, really it does."

Luna so wanted to hold her hand to comfort her, but how might that be read later? Sod it, sod it. Claire was right. You didn't want secrets when you were close to someone, so why couldn't she share hers? Common sense told her that Claire would understand, but it was just so damned scary… She hadn't told anyone. Ever. She wouldn't know where to start.

"I know," said Claire, "I'll have a look at Vedran's Facebook account. He hasn't used it for ages but I'm sure there were photos of Didi there – unless he's taken them down."

She opened her phone and began to scroll through, frowning slightly. "Here we go. The last picture of her is with Vedran last summer. Looks like he took her to Restaurant 360, lucky thing. It's of both of them together, but she's looking straight at the camera. Is that the sort of thing Ezra wants?"

Luna studied the picture, surprised how much younger Vedran had looked less than a year before. There was no sign of the tiny wisps of grey at his temples and no lines around his eyes, although they could have been hidden by his sunglasses. Nothing hid Didi's eyes, however, large and catlike, her blonde hair swept back from her perfectly made up face, her full lips somewhere between a pout and a smile. She was an absolute top tier sex goddess, but Luna slapped the thought down.

"Great. Save it," she told Claire, "but let's look to see if there's one of her on her own."

Claire peered at the screen again. "Going back there are quite a few."

Together they picked the best ones and Claire airdropped them to Luna, but as she was about to put away her phone she stopped and smiled.

"Look what's just popped into my feed," she told her, angling the screen so Luna could see it. "It's Belle, my sister. The LGBTQ+ Society at her uni organised a Valentine's burlesque night to raise funds for the local hospice. There she is, in the middle. Doesn't she look amazing?"

Luna could tell they were sisters straightaway, although Belle's face was less full. She was wearing a shiny black halter neck that reminded Luna of the film *Cabaret*, and she and her friends all sported bowler hats with the slogan "Pride Stands up to Cancer".

Luna's mouth was dry again. If only she'd known about Belle before it would have saved her so many sleepless nights. Now she could tell Claire with no fear of the consequences, but all she could manage was a feeble "That's so cool." *Jebem ti!* What was wrong with her?

"Brilliant, isn't it? I don't know how she does it; she must never sleep. She's getting fabulous grades, having one hell of a social life and doing all sorts of good stuff like this." Claire flicked to another photo where Belle and a redhead wearing a turquoise feather boa were posing for a kiss on the lips.

"In England … in England, that is OK in public?"

"Why wouldn't it be?"

"Then she is very lucky," whispered Luna, before, much to her own surprise, dissolving into tears.

Claire jumped up and was putting her arm around Luna when the shop bell rang. "Bugger," she said, "bugger, bugger, bugger."

Alone in the kitchen Luna sat up straight, willing the tears back into her eyes. Now they had started they didn't want to stop, falling in a silent cascade down her cheeks. Like an enormous dam had burst somewhere inside her. This Belle could not only kiss her partner, but in public too, and put it all over social media. In England it was normal. *Normal.* Oh, it just wasn't fair. And she … she … couldn't even find the words to tell Belle's sister she yearned for the same. Luna started to sob again.

Even by the time Claire returned, she barely had her tears under control.

"Do you want to tell me what's wrong?" Claire asked.

"Yes, yes I do." *Breathe, Luna. Get it said.* "You see, I'm gay too, but not out. The situation is different in Croatia so I can't be as open as your sister is. It makes me happy for her, but jealous too."

Claire sat down next to her. "I didn't realise it was like that here. Are people really still so very prejudiced?"

Luna nodded, catching her breath. "Certainly on the island where I come from. Religion is important; the church has such a hold. I could never tell my parents. They'd be horrified."

"You can't live a lie, Luna."

"I know, I know. It has been so hard. More than hard. Although now I have told you… Perhaps that might change." She sniffed. "But still there are many problems. Too many maybe."

"Like what?" Claire's voice was gentle.

"Like finding other people like me. There are no gay clubs or bars."

"Even in Dubrovnik?"

"Even here. And I came to the city because I thought it would be easier. The jazz café near the cathedral is for everyone, but as it's for everyone, how would I know who…"

"There must be a way, and if there is, we'll find it."

"Thank you … thank you for understanding."

They sat in silence for a moment. No earthquakes. No thunder and lightning. No terrible finger pointing from the sky. Just a normal Tuesday lunchtime. Luna frowned, trying to put the feeling into words. "It feels strange, someone else knowing." She wanted to say it was like she felt naked, but that would be so, so wrong. What the hell sort of impression would that give?

"So you're not even out to your flatmate? I thought you said you trusted him."

"Oh, I do. But you have to understand … Ezra … he's the ultimate geek. Don't get me wrong, he can be funny and kind, but he's so wrapped up in his cyber world it feels like sometimes he doesn't live in the real one at all. When he's not working he's always hooked up online playing games." She shook her head. "You know what worries me most? That I tell him and he barely registers what I've said."

"Oh, Luna. It must be so lonely for you. And I'm no good; I'm too scared to do more than sit outside a café, let alone go to a jazz club."

"No, no. Claire, you have been wonderful. So kind to me, so understanding." The lump reappeared in her throat. "But it's down to me, isn't it? I came to Dubrovnik to live the life I want and I need to find a way." Some help would be nice, but she couldn't ask. Already Claire had given so much and she didn't want to push her luck. Or push Claire outside her Covid-induced comfort zone, more to the point.

Claire hugged her again. "Well, you've made two steps today."

"Two?"

"You're out not only to me, but at work as well. How would you feel about changing the window display to a rainbow one?"

"No…" Luna whispered, "I mean, it's a lovely thought … but what about Simeon? It's his shop and he might not like it."

"You don't want me to tell him?"

"No, oh please, no." Did she sound ungrateful? "I need to get used to you knowing first."

Claire looked thoughtful. "And I need to understand not to rush you. It's just at home the culture is so different, thank god, although I am sure there are plenty of British gays who struggle to come out as well. With Belle it never had to be a secret and her experience is far more typical. One day I hope it will be the same here."

Luna nodded, feeling shaken and strong, all at the same time. "I hope it will too."

Vedran

Vedran looked at his phone. *Sranje.* He had messaged Claire to tell her he was too tired for their usual Friday night supper, but it hadn't put her off. Not one bit.

Gran has made a ton of food for you – as per usual. I'll bring it around but won't stay long. Shall I pick up a pizza too?

Damn her, why couldn't she take a hint? But if she did bring a takeout at least they could eat it quickly, then he could get rid of her. But why hadn't he told her the truth? That he didn't want company tonight. Not even hers. Because on top of everything – everything – he was pig sick with anger and disappointment that an important deal had fallen through at work, and all because he'd been stuck in the back room and not at the negotiating table.

Back in October they hadn't exactly told him it was the only way he could keep his job as a corporate lawyer. Just that they were sure he would understand if he couldn't be a public face of the firm until "all the fuss died down". At the time, he'd been grateful; he hadn't wanted to see a living soul, after all. Couldn't face the looks, the comments behind his back. After all, everyone on the call the morning Didi disappeared would have seen the bruise on his face, however low he'd turned the lights in his study. So he'd hunkered down at home and got on with it.

But sealing the deal was what he was best at. Lubricating the iron wheels of the law, listening to everyone's points of view, keeping the negotiations moving forwards. It was a rare skill and one that had earned him early promotion. Possibly the one that had generated sufficient goodwill to keep him in a job. Except he wasn't allowed to do it. And much as the thought of being back at the table terrified him, today his frustration at seeing yet another transaction fall at the final hurdle was boiling over.

Because he was on a permanently short fuse? It wasn't like him, not the him he remembered, anyway. He'd always been the reasonable one; the person everyone turned to, to pour oil on troubled waters. Except he was the troubled water now. More like a frigging storm. A storm that could roar out of him at any moment.

The devil on his shoulder told him that if it did, wasn't Claire partly to blame? Didn't she deserve his vitriol for choosing that bloody biography about a guy having a breakdown? What the hell did that say about him to all those people? He'd been welcomed so warmly at the second meeting he'd been feeling quite hopeful the book club was somewhere he could actually go. Well, not anymore.

Sranje. What was wrong with him? He mustn't, mustn't direct his anger at Claire. She might have been thoughtless, but that wasn't so great a crime. He was the one being unreasonable, not her. He was the frigging liability and he knew it. The disaster waiting to happen. No, the disaster that *had* happened. But that didn't mean he could add to his multiple sins this evening.

He had to call off her visit. Perhaps he could suddenly develop a migraine, or a stomach bug? Like that was going to work; being Claire, and every inch Fran's granddaughter, all she would probably do was offer to stop by the pharmacy on her way.

The alternative was to calm himself down. Have a quick whisky or two perhaps? That would help. It wasn't as though they had wine or anything on her Friday visits, so he wouldn't get drunk; Claire was far too nervous driving Tetak's car on the unfamiliar roads to Zaton Bay in the dark to risk even a single glass. He stood and headed for the kitchen, turning on the lights as he went.

By the time Claire arrived Vedran was three glasses down and feeling no better. Together they unloaded Fran's plastic containers of *pašticada*, *maneštra* and British cottage pie into his fridge, along with a flaky *burek* filled with spinach and cheese.

"We could have eaten that," he told her.

She shook her head. "It's you needs fattening up, not me."

"Like pizza's slimming."

"I've started jogging, I'll have you know. I'm allowed a treat or two."

If pizza was OK, then why not the *burek*? The contradiction lodged in his brain like a worm, although he tried to ignore it as they took the pizza from its box and shared it between the two plates he'd been warming in the oven. It looked stodgy and unappetising; the portion too huge. He really would have preferred the *burek*.

Normally they'd take something like pizza through to the lounge, but tonight they ate at the kitchen table. Vedran watched as Claire tucked in with alacrity, while he had to force the doughy, cheesy mass down. No, he mustn't be like that; she'd chosen his favourite, artichoke and mushroom. And the quicker he ate it, the faster she'd leave.

"You really are tired, aren't you?" she said, breaking their silence.

"There's a lot on at work."

"Are you able to go into the office?"

"By which you mean, do they let me?" He spat the words out.

"Sorry, Vedran, I was trying to be tactful."

More tactful than she'd been over the choice of book. "It's OK."

"You hate it though, don't you?"

"Yes." Perhaps he shouldn't be so short with her, but did he really need to explain? There was a wariness in her blue eyes, different eyes in a face otherwise so like Fran's. Fran whom he loved and trusted implicitly. As he did Claire. He had to try harder. "What I used to enjoy most about my job was the people; face to face, helping clients to solve their problems, making deals happen." He shrugged. "But all that's gone now. I'll just have to get used to it."

"I still don't really understand why. I mean, didn't the police admit they were wrong in arresting you?"

How the frigging hell did she know that? He'd never told her he'd spent a night in the cells, that was for sure. He picked up a piece of pizza then set it back on his plate. It was even harder to swallow now it was getting cold.

"So as it's causing you a problem, what if … what if … you could clear your name?"

What fucking planet was she on? He glared at her, not trusting himself to speak.

"If you could find out…" She paused. And the pause became longer.

"Well?"

"I don't know how to say this without hurting you."

As if he could hurt anymore. "Just say it. Or change the subject." That would be a good idea, but she didn't take the hint.

"If you could find out what happened to Didi." The words rushed out, the words he'd been half expecting, yet dreading. He couldn't, couldn't go through that mill again. The police … they'd taken him apart. And no one had bothered to put him back together again. Not even himself.

He folded his arms. "It's impossible."

"Just because the police—"

"Exactly. The police couldn't do it, so how the hell could I? She drowned, Claire, that's the long and short of it. She's gone. And I have to live with that. Every single sodding day."

"But Vedran, you need to get some closure. And I don't think the police did try very hard at all. When I looked up what happened—"

"Oh, so you couldn't resist either?" The betrayal was a hollow thud in his chest. "So now you know what a shit I am, perhaps you'd like to leave?"

Claire leaned forwards. "You might be in a shitty mood – which is quite understandable, by the way – but you're not a shit."

"Why thank you."

"Vedran, please…"

Come on man, this is Claire. Claire. Give her a break. "Sorry," he mumbled. But he wasn't listening to his better self. If she thought there was more to Didi's death than the simple fact she drowned, then by implication Claire believed he was involved. Her faithlessness gave a focus to the anger he was battling to contain, rising through him like a storm. *No. He had to keep control.*

"I'm sorry too, if you didn't want me to look," she continued. "I only wanted to help, and Luna told me—"

"Luna? What the frigging hell has Luna got to do with it?" He was yelling at her now, he knew he was, but he couldn't help it. The rawness, the redness, was surging through him. He gripped the edge of the table, watching the joints of his fingers turn white.

"We … we were talking…"

"So you didn't only dig, you gossiped too? How could you do that? So much for fucking trust."

She hung her head. "We thought we could help," she whispered.

If he moved he would tip the table over, pizza flying

everywhere, Coke cans spewing their contents in fountains over the white-tiled floor. Instead he gathered every last shred of restraint he could find.

"Claire. Please leave. Now."

"I'm so sorry, Vedran, I—"

"Go! Before I say or do something I really regret."

Her chair scraped back and she swept her coat and bag from the marble worktop, her low heels tapping across the floor. The back door closed quietly behind her and after a few minutes he heard the car engine start. Still he did not open his eyes. Did not move.

His fingers were stiff when he finally peeled them from the table top, his body so rigid he hobbled as he cleared the congealed remains of cold pizza into the kitchen bin. Hobbled like an old man. An exhausted old man. Turning off the light he groped his way along the hall to his bedroom, where he sunk onto the duvet, head in hands. He was poison. Poison. He could even taste it in his mouth.

Maybe poison was the answer? The way out? He pushed the thought aside. Thought instead of his parents, of Tetak and Fran. He owed them more. But the lows were getting lower and there weren't any highs. No, cling onto family. Don't cause any more hurt. Or maybe one big hurt, and get it over with? No. Think of Tetak; if he did have dementia the shock could push him over the edge. His uncle had already lost too many people. *Hold on, Vedran, crush that demon. Hold on.*

Slowly he straightened, reached for the light switch next to the bed and turned the dimmer up to full. Brightness engulfed him, bouncing off the shiny white wardrobe doors, hurting his eyes. Behind those doors were Didi's things. He should let them go, but he just couldn't do it. Not because he thought she might come back … just because he couldn't. He couldn't.

Anger dissipated, he was too tired to sleep, too exhausted to think. On the floor by the bedside table was the bookshop bag. He thought of Claire, driving home, hurt and upset. Then he tried not to. Tomorrow. He'd sort that one out tomorrow. When he had the strength to do it properly.

Bending over he picked up the book. The man on the cover's startling dark blue eyes gazed out at him in challenge. He read the title. Yes, he'd like to come back to himself too. Perhaps this guy, whoever he was, could help him to find a way.

Claire

S hould she tell Gran what had happened, or should she use Vedran's story of tiredness as an excuse for coming home so early? Even as Claire began to climb the steps towards the apartment, she was undecided. Undecided, guilty and more than a little scared; the feelings she'd tried so hard to push to one side while she was driving, simmering to a head.

What if Vedran's anger had taken a self-destructive turn after she left? Oh, god, she'd never, ever forgive herself. Should she even go back? But no, she couldn't do that. She couldn't have stayed ... not after the words he'd used when he told her to go. *To leave before he said or did something he might regret.* She didn't think she'd ever forget them.

It was not a cold night, but Claire began to shiver uncontrollably. What sort of *something*? His fury had been terrifying, and now there was a small unwelcome voice in her head asking what he might be capable of. What he might have done. She wrapped her arms around her chest, sure she could feel her heart beating beneath her coat. No. This was Vedran, not some monster invented by social media trolls. She had to believe in him.

Had to. Although this evening had shown her a side to his character she'd never have imagined in a million years. How well did she know him, really?

She trudged upwards, past the painted front doors, the pots of plants that were starting to show their colour, even under the yellowish street lamps. The black and white cat that lived opposite appeared and wound itself around her legs. As she crouched to stroke it she was glad of the comfort of its silky fur, the soft rumble of purring. She waited until it tired of her attentions and slunk away before slipping her key into the door and slowly making her way upstairs.

"You're home early." Those inevitable words. Even before Claire had taken off her coat.

"Vedran was tired." Her fingers fumbled the buttons.

"Grab yourself a glass. We've opened a bottle of Plavac."

A drink would be more than welcome. Plavac Mali was Gran and Nono Jadran's favourite wine, their shared love of it going right back to their courtship. When she went into the lounge they were sitting together on the squashy plum-coloured sofa, shoulders touching, with a photograph album across their knees.

"Oh goodness, I hope I'm not disturbing your date night. Perhaps I should go straight to bed."

"No need for that, darling, we're just having a little reminisce."

"While I can still remember what we're meant to be reminiscing about." Nono laughed. "That's why your gran had all these photos printed off, but it is lovely revisiting the wonderful places we've been. Look, this was in Yosemite National Park. I'm sure that brown blur to the left was a bear. Anyway, let me pour you some wine."

He filled her glass almost to the top. She had become used to the matter-of-fact way he was facing the threat of dementia, but at times like this, when she was feeling so fragile, it brought her close to tears.

Gran turned to her. "So what do you think was wrong with Vedran?"

"How do you mean, wrong?"

"You said he was tired."

"That's what he told me." Claire sipped her wine, giving herself time to consider her next words. "He'd had a rubbish day workwise too." She paused again. "So, Nono, was it a bear or not?"

He turned the page. "Of course it was. Look, we managed to get a bit closer."

Gran snorted. "You did, you silly old fool. I was all for climbing the nearest tree."

"As if the bear couldn't have followed you."

They continued their progress through the album, Claire squeezed onto the end of the sofa next to Nono with a lump in her throat. She hadn't cried when she'd left Vedran's apartment, she'd been too damned stunned for that, and now she wasn't sure whether her emotion was due to their argument or the poignancy of the conversation unfolding next to her. Or even the deeply unsettling feeling that perhaps she didn't know her cousin as well as she thought.

Gran's voice reached her through the fog. "So, Claire, are you going to tell us what's bothering you?"

She jumped, almost spilling her wine. "Sorry, I was miles away. What are you looking at now?"

"How is Vedran, really?" Nono asked. "If that isn't a stupid question, given what he's going through."

How much did he really know? Gran and Vedran may have tried to shield him from the aftermath of Didi's disappearance, but it occurred to Claire he was just as capable of looking at the internet as anyone else. She'd done it, after all, and that had been the cause of their argument ... or was it the fact she'd talked to Luna about him? It was all a little blurry now.

They were both looking at her, Nono with his head on one side, Gran's eyes sharp behind her reading glasses, although her face was full of concern. Oh god, it had always been practically impossible to lie to her.

"We had a disagreement," Claire said.

"What about?"

She looked into the red depths of her wine. "I did stick my neck out a bit, I suppose. I suggested he might get some closure if he knew what had happened to Didi. Without a body ... and I know, Nono, you said she could have been carried anywhere by the currents, but I guess ... I guess... Anyway, it caused a bit of a row."

"A bit of one?"

"Well, all right. A lot of one. He went from grumpy to absolutely furious within seconds. It was so not like him ... and really quite scary."

"And quite understandable." Nono spoke quietly. "Grief does that, Claire, or at least it can. It did to me, when I lost my first wife and daughter in the war. I was a ball of anger, and suppressing it all the time was so hard. But mine had a focus – the Serbs who killed them – and wrong as I later realised that was, the war gave me an opportunity to channel it. Vedran doesn't have that, and I'd guess it's been building inside him for quite some time."

"Until my stupidity..."

Nono took her hand. "Don't blame yourself. Maybe you were just in the wrong place at the wrong time, and anything might have lanced the boil."

She wanted to downplay this for him if she could. "Maybe you're right. Come to think of it, he was pretty arsy about why I'd bought pizza when Gran had made *burek*."

"Understandable, too." Nono laughed.

"But I am worried about him, what he might be going through there on his own..."

"Perhaps alone is the best thing for him right now. He might smash a few plates, yell at the ocean, sob for hours… He might need to, and he couldn't do that if you were there. He has a lot of pride, Vedran, and he's been putting on a very brave face for us all, but my god, he must be hurting." He put his head in his hands, then almost at once raised it again. "Best thing is for me to pop over there tomorrow. See how he is."

Claire was about to climb under her duvet when there was a knock on her bedroom door.

"So tell me properly about this argument." Gran perched next to her, resting against the wicker headboard and wrapping an arm around her shoulder. "I knew you were holding back in front of Jadran."

"I didn't lie to him…"

"But there were sins of omission."

Claire nodded. Having said so much already it would be good to unburden herself completely, so she told her how she and Luna had wanted to try to find out what had happened to Didi, and Vedran's close to violent reaction at the idea.

"He scared me more than a bit, if I'm honest. I've never seen him like that before, but what Nono said made at least some sense."

Fran nodded. "The first time your *nono* spoke to me about his war I found it hard to imagine the man I knew behaving as he had, but intense grief can be a kind of madness. Vedran's going to be hurting for a good while yet, and him feeling everyone is pointing the finger at him has made it a hundred times worse."

"Which is another reason why Luna and I wanted to find out what really happened, if only to shut them up."

"It's very noble of you both, but I can't see how you might do it. The police…"

"Luna said they didn't try very hard, just arrested Vedran."

Her grandmother sighed. "And she could well be right. Thousands of people go missing, after all, and once they were satisfied there was no foul play, maybe they just didn't have the resources. Especially when everything pointed towards her drowning. But all the same, it's Vedran's life and you must respect his decision about this. If he doesn't want you to look into it, then don't." She paused. "Perhaps focus on yourself instead – for once."

"What do you mean, for once?" Bugger. She hadn't meant to get arsy with Gran.

"You're too like me, Claire. Just about everything you do is to make other people happy. I know you only came here so you didn't let me down, and I have to admit I played on that a little, because I knew it was the best thing for you too. But right now you need to concentrate on solving your own problems."

"My own?"

"Getting your life back. Oh, I know you think I'm nagging and you've made good progress so far, but I honestly believe you're ready to take the next steps and start to go out and about a bit."

Claire fingered the tassels of the pale blue throw that was draped across her bed. "I don't think I am. Ready, I mean." Much as she had enjoyed watching the Sveti Vlaho parade, it had stretched her tolerance of crowds to its absolute limit, and it had taken her quite some time to stop shaking afterwards. She really wasn't sure she could go through that again, although she had to admit her confidence was growing. In the bookshop at least. Even with two or three customers at the same time. Surely that counted for something?

"You can't put it off forever," Gran continued. "In another six weeks or so the tourists will begin to arrive so things will get busier, and I can just see you using that as an excuse. Go out to a bar or for a meal, Claire. Just once. Go with Luna, I'm sure she'd like to."

Was Gran right? Was it time to push herself further? But this evening her heart was too heavy with thoughts of Vedran. She couldn't begin worrying about herself, but she needed to get her grandmother off her back somehow. "Luna has mentioned the jazz café."

"Really? She likes jazz?"

"I … I don't think so. Someone just told her it was a nice place to go."

"Then do it next week. It will take both your minds off trying to find Didi." Gran gave her a hug, but Claire was feeling far from ready to commit and her avoidance tactics seemed to be backfiring spectacularly.

"I'll think about it."

"Is that the best I'm going to get?"

Claire nodded, feeling more like a recalcitrant teenager every minute. Which Gran definitely didn't deserve. She gave her a squeeze.

"Sorry."

"It's all right, I do understand. Perhaps more than you know." She kissed her on the forehead and stood to leave. "Oh, and darling, don't worry about Vedran. You need to trust Jadran on this one. He knows him better than anyone."

Vedran

Vedran set down his razor and gazed at his reflection in the mirror, checking for any stubble he'd missed. The man looking back at him looked grey and haunted, and at least fifty years old. He honestly felt he didn't know him anymore, let alone feel capable of dealing with the mess hidden behind his neat and tidy exterior. And he was a mess; nothing was more certain.

Of course, the sleep deprivation didn't help. Sleep deprivation and a strange emptiness now last night's anger had left him. This morning everything seemed to be spooling out in ultra-slow motion, but if he didn't get a shift on he wouldn't be dressed by the time Tetak arrived, no doubt to tear him off a strip about the way he'd behaved towards Claire. Which he thoroughly deserved. And then some. Especially as he still hadn't even sent her so much as a text to apologise.

From the kitchen window he watched Tetak's car pull up outside, and his uncle walk briskly across the tarmac, his silver hair glinting in the sunlight. His movements were those of a far younger man; it was only his weather-beaten face that gave away his true age. He even managed to hide how much his memory was beginning to fracture … most of the time, at least.

Tetak embraced Vedran warmly when he let him in, almost reducing him to tears. Tears that had been close to the surface for most of the night; tears only kept at bay by the book that Claire had chosen for him to read. The book he'd been reading almost until sunrise, which had given him at least a paperback-sized life raft to cling to when he had needed it the most.

"How are you coping this morning?" Tetak asked.

Vedran turned away. "Coffee?"

"Later, I think. Talk to me first."

"Then let's go through to the lounge."

The room was in darkness until Vedran pulled back the curtains, light flooding the faux-marble floor and black leather sofas. Tetak eased himself onto one of them and indicated Vedran should sit next to him. Clearly there was to be no escape.

"I will apologise to Claire, you know."

"I know you will. You always do the right thing. But you gave her quite a fright, until I explained that anger is a normal part of grief. An important one at that. Cathartic."

"It's still no excuse to lash out like I did." Vedran ran his hand through his hair. "Especially at Claire, poor kid."

Tetak sat back. "It made me wonder just how long you've been suppressing that sort of rage. When I lost Leila and Kristina mine was almost instant – at the Serbs who launched the mortar that killed them, and at myself for failing to shoot it down."

"I bet you didn't take it out on—"

Tetak held up a finger to silence him. "I did. And worse. Much worse. There was a war on, remember. That in itself made me a killer, but I didn't have to be a cruel bastard with it."

Vedran shook his head. "I can't imagine you being like that."

His uncle leaned forwards. "And that's the point. Grief distorts, Vedran, it bends a person completely out of shape. Ach, we should have had this conversation before, but I didn't think you were ready."

Vedran rubbed the heels of his hands into his eyes. "I'm not. I'm ... it's all ... swirling around, like I can't get a handle on anything." Oh god, he so wanted to open his soul to Tetak, but how could he when his uncle knew so little about what had happened? How could he add to his burden when he was ill? He looked up at him. "I just need time, OK?"

"Too soon to begin to look for that closure Claire was talking about?"

How much did Tetak know about last night? What had Claire told him? Vedran could do without having to cope with all these unknowns, exhausted, struggling to keep it together as he was. He felt as though he was looking at his uncle through a curtain of rain, rain like there'd been on the day Didi disappeared. He turned his gaze to the windows and the light, pale sunshine sparkling from the tips of the waves, mocking him so very gently. His grief ... it wasn't even what Tetak thought it was. Nobody knew the real reason, and nobody ever would.

"Like I said, I'll apologise to Claire," he croaked. That's why Tetak had come, wasn't it? Now perhaps he'd go away. "I'll wait for her ... after work ... do it face to face. It's best, isn't it?"

"Yes. And you know, Vedran, when you are ready to take the next step, I am here for you. I won't be gaga for a long while yet." Tetak levered himself from the sofa. "But right now I'll leave you to it. You look as though you still need some space."

Wordlessly Vedran followed his uncle to the door. Tetak knew him so well. It broke his heart he could never tell him the truth.

The least he could do for his uncle was to keep his word, so dusk found Vedran skulking in a doorway just off Ulica od Puča in the fading light, waiting for Claire to walk past. He didn't have the balls to go to the shop, to face Luna as well, have her witness his apology. That would be a step too far at the moment.

Keen as he had been to get rid of Tetak this morning, his words had stayed with him, especially the part about anger being a natural part of what he was going through. From what he had said, his uncle had been there himself, although in most of the ways that mattered, his loss had been about as far from Vedran's as it was possible to be. But he supposed that in some ways grief was grief, whatever the circumstances. That's what Tetak had meant, he was sure, and that's what had stayed with Vedran and helped him to face the day.

As soon as he heard Claire call goodnight to Luna and start up the slope he stepped out of the shadows, so as not to frighten her. Her fair head was bent as she climbed, and he had to say her name to make her look up.

"Vedran!"

Was that relief in her voice?

"I want to apologise. Claire, I am just so sorry. I behaved abominably."

"Nono said—"

Vedran shook his head. "He didn't ask me to do this, I was going to anyway. I knew I had to the moment you left last night, but I wasn't…" Brave enough? Strong enough? Somehow the words choked in his throat, so he simply shrugged.

She stepped forwards and took his hand. "It's OK. As long as I've got my cousin back."

"Unfortunately you haven't. Not by a long chalk. I don't even know if that's possible, but…" *Sranje*. Was he destined to leave every sodding sentence uncompleted? "Fancy a walk?"

"Sure, but I need to message Gran."

"She knows. She's holding supper until we get back."

They returned to Ulica od Puča and passed the bookshop, its window covered in red and white "sale" signs. He listened as

Claire told him they were trying to shift old stock and the day had been particularly busy, with a special discount for students.

"You were OK with all the people?" he asked.

"I have to be. It's my job. And Gran's still on my back, so Luna and I are actually going out next week."

"So one hermit at least is coming out of their shell."

"Only a little way. And only because other people want me to. Luna is so excited, bless her."

The market traders that gathered daily in Gundulićeva Poljana at the end of the road were long gone, and a plastic bag blew forlornly around the poet's statue, so often surrounded by people and stalls, but now glorious in his isolation. Around the corner there was still a bustle on the terrace outside Gradska Kavana, customers wrapped in coats and colourful scarves under the heaters, laughing and talking, and Vedran wished he had the guts to take Claire there. But he hadn't. And that was that.

They walked under the clock tower and climbed the narrow street towards the Ploče Gate. He wasn't sure why he was coming this way, except he wasn't quite ready to stop walking yet, although once they had crossed the Revelin Bridge he knew he was running out of places. The piazza was deserted, too early in the year for there to be tourists admiring the view of the harbour and the solid bulk of Svetog Ivana fort beyond it. On the quay below, the street lights were beginning to flicker on and the rows of white boats, including Tetak's *Safranka II*, rocked gently in the swell.

Claire followed a few steps behind him.

"Sorry again. My long legs."

She smiled ruefully, massaging her heel. "And my silly work pumps."

"Thoughtless bastard, aren't I? Making you come so far."

"Distracted, that's all."

He turned his back on the old town and perched on the low

wall, Claire settling on a bench opposite him and looking up expectantly.

"That book you chose… I couldn't sleep last night, so out of desperation I picked it up. God, you never know with people, do you? Never see behind the mask. Until it slips so badly there's no hiding anymore."

Claire nodded, but said nothing.

"I mean, there he was, at the top of his game. Literally. Then bam. Illness. Depression. I never knew it could affect people so badly."

"Do you think you could be depressed?"

"Did you when you chose the book?"

"No. I just wanted a human story that people who weren't that into sport could relate to as well, and in the catalogue it said this one won awards when it came out. That it was ground-breaking at the time."

"Really?" She was being straight up with him, he could tell. "And I took it so personally, that you picked it because you thought I was screwed up."

"Well, you are, aren't you?" Although her voice wobbled slightly it was teasing, and he felt his shoulders settle to a more normal level. Why hadn't he been able to react so rationally last night? Why had he felt the need to hurt her? Claire, of all people.

"Screwed up as they come. But not ill, thank god. Not that." He shuddered. "But also in the book there was quite a lot about the media reaction." He leaned forwards. "Those tabloid shits even made up a story about his wife having an affair with one of his best mates, saying that had caused his breakdown. And in a strange way it made me feel less alone, less like the only person they'd ever got their claws into."

"It was worse for you though, because there's social media now, and that seems to be what caused most of the problem. Everyone had a sodding opinion, most of it provoked by your neighbour upstairs." Claire sounded really angry, and it brought it home to him how much she cared.

"Didi always said that woman wanted to be the centre of attention." He shrugged. "I guess she didn't like it because she did as well."

"She was beautiful enough to be."

How should he respond? With the truth? Or something close to it at least. Let Claire know that he still trusted her, even if that feeling was a little dented right now. "On the outside. I think Fran twigged she could be ... difficult. Has she said anything?"

"No."

"I know we joke about her, but your gran is one frigging amazing woman. It was a good day indeed when Tetak met her."

"Which you arranged, if I remember rightly."

"At the time it was nothing. But it became everything." He smiled at the memory, looking at Claire through the deepening dusk. In the nearby trees the chirping of the birds began to still, the waves washing gently below them at the foot of the wall.

He levered himself from his perch and joined Claire on the bench. "The truth is that Didi and I had run our course by the time she disappeared. So people saying they heard us argue was right. But somehow ... somehow ... I couldn't let go." He gazed at the uneven paving stones beneath his feet, feeling them more than seeing them in the fading light. "You see, I'd never met anyone remotely like her before. She dazzled me from the first moment, and even though she could wind me around her little finger I was more than willing to let her do it."

He looked at Claire. "And she could be kind, really she could be. We'd only been together a few days when you went into hospital and she was amazing. Refused to leave my side until we knew you were OK." He shook his head slowly. "I was in tears, you know, not very manly, but it didn't seem to put her off at all."

"And that changed?"

"Oh, don't get me wrong. We were happy … happy for a good long while." The birds above them were silent now, and Vedran shivered as the night stole the last of the heat from the stones. What more could he say? How could he find the words? "Perhaps there is more I should tell you but right now I can't; I just wouldn't know how. I don't know if I ever will be able to tell anyone the whole truth about how it was."

Claire's hand was warm on his arm. "What you choose to tell me or anyone else is your prerogative. Totally."

Across the harbour light shone from the arches of the Arsenal restaurant, its reflection shimmering across the water. Could he share what had happened the night before Didi died? But Claire had seen his anger, would it make her think the worst of him? Yesterday he'd believed she did and it was hard to shake that feeling entirely. He needed to know. If he'd destroyed her faith in him there was no way he could confide in her, and right now, this was as near as he'd come to being able to tell anyone anything near the truth.

"Claire, when I lost it with you last night, did it make you think I was capable of killing?"

She scuffed her shoe against the paving; heel toe, heel toe.

"You did, didn't you?"

"In the heat of the moment – and, to be honest, afterwards, when I was walking home from the car park – but the logical side of my brain dismissed it pretty damn quickly. I'm sorry if that isn't the answer you hoped for, but I don't think this is the time to lie."

"I thank you for that."

"Why did you ask me?"

"Because I'm trying to weigh up whether to tell you what happened the night before Didi died." He shrugged. "I don't even think I can. Not even Fran knows, and certainly not the police. It wasn't exactly my finest hour. But I swear to you, I did not kill Didi."

"I know that. Everyone gets angry from time to time, Vedran, but it doesn't mean they commit murder."

There was a long silence before Claire carried on. "Tell me when the time feels right, when you feel you can trust me again. And I do get that my talking to Luna about you might mean it takes a while, and I'm sorry for that too. I should never have tried to interfere. But don't forget I'm here for you whenever you're ready. Next week, next month…"

"…Next year… Oh god, Claire, I really do want to move on but I'm stuck where I am, and I have no idea whether talking would help or not. It's just all too damned difficult." He put his head in his hands.

She squeezed his shoulder. "I think it's great that you're even just thinking about it. That's definitely a start."

"It's all I can do at the moment."

"And that's fine, it really is. Accept it as progress, and stop beating yourself up." She squeezed him again, before she stood. "Anyway, I can feel you shivering and I'm getting cold too. Gran's cooking *brudet* – proper comfort food. That'll warm us up. Come on, a brisk walk back won't hurt us either."

She'd let him off the hook. Or maybe even thrown him off it. Perhaps she wasn't ready to know either, maybe the need to steady their trust in each other went both ways. That she was willing to try was more than he deserved. And he should try to trust her again too. Tetak had said something about anger being cathartic… Maybe, despite its destructiveness, it had set him on the course for change.

Luna

Luna nibbled her thumbnail, watching Claire lean into her bedroom mirror to put on her lip gloss. *Sranje!* She was even slower than Luna had been getting ready, but she got it, really she did. For a couple of *kuna* she'd have happily stayed in Fran and Jadran's apartment all evening too, but that could not happen. Tonight was going to be the night.

She swept her coat from the end of the bed. "Come on. You look perfect and I'm losing my nerve."

Claire grinned. "Can't have both of us doing that."

They ran down the stairs and into the street, bundling scarves around their necks. Thank *bože* the jazz café had outdoor heaters and throws. Luna had walked past often enough to know its layout intimately, and tonight, finally, she'd get there. Excitement thrummed through her, mixed with pure blind terror. What if nobody spoke to them? What if there was no one else there?

Claire stopped outside the Museum of Ethnic Life and gazed over the city towards Mount Srd. What was she waiting for now? She must have seen the view about a million times before. But what kind of friend was Luna, thinking that? How bloody selfish.

She was all over the place, and this was as tough for Claire as it was for her, so she tucked her arm into Claire's and waited.

The silence stretched. "You all right?" Luna finally asked.

"Yes … yes. Just thinking about the first time I went up there."

"Up where?"

"Mount Srd."

"Oh. In the cable car?"

"Yes, but Dad, Vedran and I walked down. It was what made me think of it. Luna, do you mind … if we put looking for Didi on hold for the moment? I … I don't think… Well, anyway, I've got cold feet about the idea."

"Sure, I'll tell Ezra." Oh, so that's what had been on her mind. Why hadn't she just said so before? Well, that was easily enough resolved. Luna tugged Claire's arm and they moved off, walking more slowly this time, and, unusually for them, in complete silence.

Silence that gave Luna time to think. Too much time. The knot of anxiety hardened in her stomach until it physically hurt. She almost stopped in her tracks. Claire wouldn't mind if she backed out now, would she? She probably didn't even need an excuse … but then it might look like she was in a strop because of what Claire had said about Didi. *Come on, Luna, come on. You have to do this.*

They both did. They'd come this far. Leave behind those negative thoughts buzzing around her head. Talk about ordinary things. Like they did in the shop.

"You must have visited Fran a lot since she's lived here."

"Every year, but never in the summer, because they normally spend the warmest months in England. It's going to get really busy, isn't it?"

Luna nodded. "Super-busy like you wouldn't believe. And hot. But the shop's cool. There's an aircon unit, and there's always the courtyard. Our side of it doesn't get much sun."

"It's the people bit I need to get my head around."

"Tonight's the start." Luna made the biggest effort she could to sound braver than she felt.

The jazz café was tucked into the corner of an odd-shaped square behind the cathedral. There were no inside tables at all, which was one of the reasons Claire'd been happy to come here, just a few high stools to one side of the door and two distinct areas of seating; one tucked into a corner beneath the cathedral walls, and the other under an awning which stretched along the street leading towards the Rector's Palace.

Luna chose a table in the square, her back to the cathedral she was trying hard to ignore. She was just trying to get cosy, nestling into a snowy white throw, when it made its presence felt with a sudden peal of bells, making her jump. Fuggin' hell. Couldn't she get away from religion, even here?

Claire ordered a carafe of wine to share and as she poured it, Luna studied the other customers. On the high stools directly outside the café door were two old boys, muffled in woollen scarves and smoking like chimneys, and a few tables away were a couple of women in their forties, heads bent close. Were they gay or just gossiping? *Sranje.* She didn't know. How could she?

"What if … what if… I mean, Claire, how are we going to talk to anyone? Never mind find out if they're … like me."

"You mustn't think of tonight like that. We're just here to watch and learn, build a bit of confidence, then we can work out a plan of action. You need to go inside at some point too, to the ladies. There might be some notices for events or groups."

"Oh, OK." Disappointment punched Luna in the stomach. It was stupid, she knew, but she'd screwed up so much courage to do this; pinned so many hopes on the outcome. And of course she was impatient; it was just so hard because she'd never knowingly met another gay person. Her fingers clenched around the stem of her wine glass.

"You know it makes sense." Claire's voice had a smile in it that grounded her.

Luna shrugged. "I wouldn't know what to say."

"Of course you would. You're never normally short of a word. You're far chattier than I am with customers in the shop."

"That's different."

"In what way?"

"Because … well … obviously … they're not gay."

"Firstly, how do you know? And second, why would you treat a gay person any differently to a straight one? I get it if it's a woman you fancy – that might make you a bit tongue-tied, like I would be with a gorgeous bloke, but otherwise I don't really get what you mean."

"I suppose … I suppose I did mean gay and I like them."

"It's not for me to say, but maybe get used to being out first? Having gay friends, being part of the scene? Look, I remember being desperate to lose my virginity too, but god, I wish I'd waited. He turned out to be a right selfish tosser who'd definitely watched too much porn."

"Yes, but I've waited longer. I've never even kissed." Another thought that terrified her. Would she even be able to do it right? What if she was useless?

Claire sat back in her seat. "Have you come out to Ezra yet?"

"*Bože*, no!"

"Why not, if you're so ready? You might need to take someone home."

Sranje and sranje again. Maybe she wasn't ready to come out at all. She hadn't thought about half of this. A quarter even. Or maybe she just needed to calm down. They were here. Finally. And what Claire was saying did make sense. "OK. Tonight. Scouting mission only."

"You need to tell Ezra. You keep saying how much you trust him."

Luna buried her chin in the throw, and picked up her glass.

They watched as a slim woman with almost purple hair and wearing combats and a thick jumper arrived with a much younger man, probably in his mid-twenties. She said "*dobra večer*" as she passed, then the couple set about pulling two of the tables under the awning opposite together. The waiter came out to help them, then brought carafes of water and wine, and dishes of olives.

"I'd guess they're regulars," Claire said.

"But they're a couple, they're straight."

"So am I. But I'm not jumping to conclusions. They look quite alike so they could be related."

Before Luna could reply, three young women appeared, two dressed in jeans and the third in a miniskirt not unlike the one she herself was wearing. She had amazing legs, and Luna gazed at them from beneath her eyelashes. Even that made her feel so very guilty. But it shouldn't. Looking didn't hurt anyone and she'd always done it. Why was this suddenly so confusing?

Once the noisy greetings subsided from the table opposite them, Claire leaned close to Luna.

"Didn't the blonde come into the shop last week?"

She'd been too busy gawping at miniskirt's legs to notice much about her companions, but she couldn't admit that to Claire. She was getting into a right proper tizz. *Breathe, Luna, breathe.* She shrugged. "I didn't see."

"Good."

What the… Claire turned around, looking over her shoulder. "I'm sorry to interrupt, but I'm sure I recognise you from the bookshop. Am I right?"

The blonde woman grinned at her, pushing her floppy hair out of her eyes. "You are. I knew I'd seen you guys somewhere, but I thought it must have been here." Her voice was soft and exuded warmth.

Claire shook her head. "First time we've come, although

Luna's wanted to for ages." Luna felt a gentle kick against her ankle. "Haven't you?"

She turned to face the other table, feeling a flush of colour rise up her cheeks. "Yes. I … I'd heard good things about it."

"How tolerant and welcoming it is," Claire added, and Luna's buttocks clenched with embarrassment. But why? Why? Wasn't this what she wanted?

The older woman who'd arrived with the man gestured in their direction. "Why don't you join us? Then we can make sure it lives up to its reputation."

Claire jumped to her feet. "That's so kind, we will. I'm Claire, by the way, and I'm English so forgive me if I don't understand everything. And this is Luna. We work in The Welcoming Bookshop."

"And is everyone welcome there?" The girl in the miniskirt asked pointedly.

"Of course. My sister's gay so I feel very strongly about inclusion," Claire replied.

She nodded. "I'm Senada," she said, then pointing to the others, introduced them in turn. "This is Dusana, and Vanesa, and Meri, and her son Zak."

Luna memorised the names: Senada with the fabulous legs, Dusana the blonde, who liked books, Vanesa wearing enormous statement tortoiseshell glasses, and Meri. Meri who looked so unlike anyone she had ever met before. And right now she was laughing.

"I know, I don't look old enough to have a son his age, but I was only sixteen when I had him so we've kind of grown up together."

"That's pretty neat," said Claire.

"And what about you, Luna?" Dusana asked. "You're very quiet."

What could she say? But Claire was squeezing her hand under

the table. "I come from a small island and I've only recently come out. Just to Claire, no one else." Tears swam into her eyes.

"Oh, honey," said Dusana, "that's just the toughest time. No wonder you look a bit overwhelmed."

"If you need guidance about anything, just ask," added Senada. "We're all gay or bi except Vanesa and we've all been through it. My brother still doesn't speak to me, but it's his loss."

"Thank you." Luna took a slug of her wine, and it did at least push the lump in her throat back down a little so her voice didn't sound so strange.

Claire grinned at her. "There, that wasn't so hard, was it?"

Meri shook her head. "We're the easy part, believe me. But hell, we're here to have a good time, not talk sexual politics. Let's have a whip round to see how much wine we can afford. Are you girls in?"

Luna waved to Meri as she got off the bus, leaving her to continue her journey to Mokošica. What a woman! She'd seen it all, done it all, and had an opinion about absolutely everything. It was amazing they lived in the same direction, Luna thought, and that Zak had gone home with his boyfriend, so she'd had the benefit of all that experience to herself on the journey.

Experience and life story. Luna had never, ever, met anyone like Meri. She was so totally confident in her skin. When she became pregnant within days of her sixteenth birthday, Zak's father had denied all involvement, but her parents had supported her, allowing her to continue her education once the baby was born. She'd never considered herself bisexual until she'd fallen for a colleague, but the affair hadn't lasted long, and she'd been in and out of relationships of one sort or another ever since.

"Best way," she'd told Luna. "I have all the love I need in my life from Zak and my folks. I don't really trust anyone else so if I do hook up it's just for fun."

Emboldened by wine, Luna had asked if she knew any lesbians who'd been together for a long time. She'd snorted. "Of course I do. Don't let what I like colour your view, although I do think it's a good way for you to start. Experiment a bit, build your confidence. Know what I'm saying?" Luna nodded, although she wasn't entirely sure she did. "But don't forget we all have a different journey, and yours won't be like anyone else's. Same goes for your straight friend. It's just your path could be a little bumpier than hers, so you need all the support you can get."

Luna snuggled her chin into the soft collar of her puffer coat as she walked down the hill, towards the port of Gruž and the tower blocks where she and Ezra lived. Support. Good point. She had Claire, she maybe even had these women, but what about Ezra? Was it too soon to tell him, or should she be brave while her Dutch courage lasted? It wasn't only the wine; the whole evening had left her buzzing. She knew other gay people. She was almost properly out.

Senada was super-cute too, with her slim face, rosy cheeks and ready, over-sized smile, but Luna had sensed from the chat around the table that the deal in the group was they remained friends and no more. And she got that, really she did. Something told her these women would become a place of safety she could launch herself out of and return to. She wouldn't mess that up for anything. Oh, no.

She let herself into the lobby of the apartment block, almost tripping over a bicycle before the automatic lights switched on. Rubbing her shin, she climbed the linoleum-covered steps to the third floor. She had to be quiet. Ezra was bound to be asleep by now. Just as well. She wouldn't know what to say.

Quiet or not, inside the flat she all but swore. At the end of the hall a light glowed from the open-plan living area. He'd left the freakin' thing on. Again. He never thought about her share of the bills. Not to mention saving the planet. But as she threw her bag towards the sofa she realised he was there, sitting at the kitchen table, his long fingers wrapped around the mug of coffee in front of him.

"I was about to come to find you," he said. "Except I had no idea where to look."

"But why? I said I was going out."

"For a couple of drinks. It's gone midnight."

How did he manage sweet *and* grumpy, all at the same time? "You could have messaged me."

"I did."

She fumbled in her pocket for her phone. He had, as well. She just hadn't seen it; she'd been too busy chatting to Meri. "*O bože*, I'm sorry. I didn't mean to worry you. We … we met some people in the bar and one of them got the same bus as me, so we were talking… I didn't even look."

"Well, as long as you're all right." He shrugged, pushing his hair back from his forehead. "It felt a bit odd here without you."

"I'm amazed you noticed. Is your computer broken or something?" She unbuttoned her coat and sat opposite him.

"*Sranje*. I'm bad, aren't I?"

"You're not much company, but I suppose I was kind of expecting that before I moved in. I just didn't think you'd spend all of every single evening online." She rolled her eyes.

"I asked you to play too."

"Not my scene."

"And tonight was? I'm pleased, Luna, really I am. I was just worried when you didn't come home."

Her head spun, mainly with the wine, but also… He obviously cared enough to stay up. Plus she had his full attention for once. *Spit it out, girl. This may not happen again.*

"Very much so. We went to the jazz café. It's the closest Dubrovnik's got to a gay bar."

"Oh." He looked up from his coffee and grinned. "So are you trying to tell me something I've suspected for a while?"

"Yes ... but how did you guess?" How had she given herself away? She'd been so very careful.

"Never had a boyfriend? A pretty, sociable girl like you?"

"I've never had a girlfriend either." She sat up straight, folding her arms.

"Don't be defensive. It's me you're talking to, remember, not some dinosaur olive farmer who's never going to leave Šipan. We're here because we both have dreams, Luna. And they don't involve existing in some half-life on a tiny island."

She looked around the kitchen, its ill-fitting cupboards and tatty old cooker lit by a single bulb. Of course she had dreams, but she'd never stopped to wonder what Ezra's might be. And that made her a bad, bad friend. Too wrapped up in her own shit to even wonder. And with him being so *nice*.

"What are your dreams, Ezra?"

"To run my own cyber-security firm. But for the moment I'm learning, learning all the time. And saving, now that you're here to help with the bills. I don't just play the games for fun, it's working out how to beat them, what's going on inside the code. And how to hack them too. The ultimate challenge. Other than robbing a bank, or stealing someone's data, that is. And that's not me."

"I never knew."

"Just goes to show, Luna. We've been best buddies for almost fifteen years, we share a flat, and yet we haven't shared some of our most important secrets."

"Claire said ... Claire said ... you shouldn't have secrets from friends, and when she did, I thought of you."

He shrugged and stood. "All out in the open now though, all good. And we both need to work in the morning."

She went to the sink to fill a glass with water, then turned. "Ezra, you won't tell anyone at home about me, will you?"

"You really should think about talking to your folks. Your *mama* at least."

She shook her head. "No… I can't… They won't understand. You … you won't say anything, will you? Please, Ezra."

"Of course not. What do you take me for?" He shook his head sadly. "Now go to bloody bed."

"Ezra," she called after him.

"Now what?"

"I'll cook you supper tomorrow if you'll come out of your room to eat it."

He nodded. "It's a deal."

Ordinary Thunderstorms

Karmela

When Fran left straight after book club somehow Karmela found herself helping Vedran to collect the empty wine glasses, while Claire and Luna stood at the till for the other members to pay for their books. She really was not sure what had drawn her back – except that books were solid and safe ground for her fortnightly phone calls with her mother. Not that she'd told her much about the sportsman's autobiography, it would have been too embarrassing. No one needed to know the ins and outs of mental breakdown in such excruciating detail. Why it had won an award, she could hardly imagine.

At a loss for something to say as she filled the sink with soapy water, Karmela asked Vedran if he had heard of the author Paulette had chosen.

He laughed, the first time she had heard him do so. "You're asking the wrong person."

"Why is that?"

"I'm not the greatest of readers. I don't have the time."

"And yet you come to a book club."

"I told Claire I would join, and I don't want to let her down."

"So did you read the book Claire chose for you? I noticed you did not say very much."

He shrugged and looked away, but Karmela understood. At times the discussion had been more than a little awkward, given the subject matter. In all honesty, she had not contributed much herself. She remembered Vedran saying he would have preferred a straightforward sporting biography, and tedious as that would have been, she was minded to agree with him.

Luna breezed into the kitchen, closely followed by Claire, who disappeared into the office with the cashbox. Vedran picked up an open bottle of wine from the table.

"There's enough here for a glass each," he said. "Not for me, obviously, I'm driving, but it would be a shame not to finish it."

"Shall I make you a coffee?" Luna asked him.

"I really should go."

"It won't take me a moment. Honestly."

"Then that would be kind. Thank you." Karmela thought she detected a note of resignation in his voice. It was time she found her coat and said goodnight too. She had no wish to intrude.

Claire emerged while Luna was busying herself with the *dzezva* and Vedran poured three generous glasses of wine. The third one must be for her. No one had asked Karmela whether she wanted to stay, and she was rather surprised to have been included. It would be embarrassing to leave now that the wine had been poured. All she had to go home to was the sound of Rafael's television through the walls. That and his occasional weeping, presumably when he was drunk, which was disturbing in an entirely different way. A good reason to stay if ever there was one.

She pulled out a chair and tucked her knees under the table. Claire sat opposite and there was a brief silence, while Vedran watched Luna make the coffee. After a few moments Claire asked

Karmela how her research was going. How nice she remembered and was interested.

"It is stop and start, truth be told," she replied. "I have enough information on two women for my case study, but I would like a third. And the two I have found are both widows of wealthy merchants so I need some sort of contrast."

"Someone poor, you mean, like a maid?" asked Luna, pouring Vedran's coffee into a mug and sitting down. He, however, remained leaning against the sink, as if ready for a quick getaway.

"That would be very unlikely as the working classes from the time are completely invisible. I was thinking of a nun from the St Klarisa monastery and there was one who started a fire in order to escape, but with that degree of notoriety it is hard to separate fact from folklore."

"Escape?" said Luna.

"Oh yes. These women were seldom nuns because they had a vocation. They were normally younger daughters of noble houses sent by their parents. The oldest sister had to marry, of course, but they would not have wanted to waste dowry money on the others. Much as I admire the Ragusans, it is good that society's expectations of women have changed."

"It hasn't on small islands," retorted Luna.

"You said that with some feeling," Karmela replied, remembering what Luna had told her about her father on Sveti Vlaho.

She watched as Claire glanced at Luna and gave her a half-nod, but with barely a shake of the head the younger girl looked down and away. Something else was going on here, but Karmela was unable to guess what it might be. Vedran had clearly noticed Luna's discomfort as well, and finally joined them at the table, probably as a distraction, then asked Claire if she had read Paulette's choice of novel.

"Not this book, but several others by the author. He's won

loads of literary prizes, even been short-listed for the Booker. I don't want to set expectations too high though, just in case."

Karmela smiled at her. "That sounds most impressive. I like an author with a pedigree and I shall look forward to reading it, although I have to say I was not over-enamoured by the cover." She paused. "I suppose that is rather the point of a book club. Reading titles you would not have chosen for yourself."

"You were very insightful about the structure and language in Vedran's book," Claire said, "but I didn't get any feeling of whether you might have enjoyed it."

It was a question asked honestly, and as such deserved an honest answer. "I would not say enjoyed, no, it was rather too … um … intimate for that. Not in a sexual way, of course," she carried on hurriedly, "but I was surprised to find anyone being so open about mental health."

Claire leaned forwards. "Don't tell me it's something else that isn't spoken about here? I love this country, but in so many ways it needs to move on. So much of what should be out in the open is brushed under the carpet. It's good to talk about these things."

Was it? Not to Karmela, definitely not, and she did not like the way this conversation was going. Before she knew it, Claire would be asking how she *felt* about the book, not what she *thought*, which would be completely irrelevant and without academic rigour.

She drained her glass and stood. "Thank you for the wine. It has been pleasant talking to you all, but now I must go."

Claire beamed at her. "You, too. And thank you for helping with the clearing up."

"It was my pleasure."

And it had been, up to a point. Which had proved an excellent moment to leave. So much for the British stiff upper lip she had heard so much about. But Claire was young, she supposed. They did tend to view things rather differently. Which, now she came to think of it, was one of the aspects of lecturing she enjoyed, and missed. She paused outside the Orthodox church. Had she been too hasty? Could she have turned the conversation around? Luna's comment about the position of women on small islands would have been a far more appropriate topic, and completely relatable to her research as well. It seemed like an opportunity lost.

While far from being academics, these were interesting people, Karmela thought, as she strolled through the darkness, admiring the way the lamps cast their shadows on the venerable old masonry, chipped and scarred, and in her view all the better for it. Claire was clearly well read, with a quiet intelligence and enquiring mind, and she admired Luna for her fiery opinions that showed a certain desire to break the mould. And Vedran ... he did not say very much, but he was honest and considerate. There were definitely worse people to spend an evening with.

It was years since she had sought the company of others, because she did not need it. It was not as though she was lonely; she had learned to appreciate the quiet and calmness that solitude brought her. But it had been pleasant to spend half an hour or so, sipping a glass of wine in that beautiful room, with at least the potential for intelligent conversation. As she passed Orlando's empty column she realised why; they had not made her feel like an outsider at all.

Luna

Luna raced up the steps to the apartment two at a time. She and Claire had been to the jazz café last night, and tomorrow she was going to an author talk at the university with two of the girls from the book club. She actually had a social life and the thought made her tingle with excitement. So tonight was all about – and only about – her laundry.

As she unlocked the door Ezra met her in the hallway. "I think I've found her."

"Found who?"

"Didi Kelmendi, of course."

Luna was stunned. Open-mouthed, almost. It had been weeks since they'd mentioned Didi, and she'd almost forgotten... But what else had she forgotten? The thought crept into her mind, making her stomach squirm. Surely she'd told Ezra Claire wanted everything put on hold? *O bože*, she must have done. Or – and the thought trickled in from almost nowhere – had she been too wrapped up in her own shit to remember?

Only one way to find out. "But I told you Claire was having second thoughts."

He folded his arms. "No, you didn't."

"But … but I must have done."

"Nope. I think I would have remembered something as important as that."

"Important? It's not that important … just a bit of f—" No, not fun. A rush of guilt flooded through her. What sort of friend was she?

"Of course it's important, clearing that poor guy's name. And anyway, it's a brilliant test for my app."

"Your app?" He'd said nothing about an app, that was for sure.

Ezra sighed. "Let's crack open a beer and I'll tell you about it. And show you what I've found."

Luna followed him into the living area, drawing the blinds to shut out the arc lights from the port below while Ezra made a beeline for the fridge. *Sranje!* If Ezra had found Didi, what was she going to do? Claire would be angry, and rightly so. She wasn't sure which was worse: saying she'd forgotten to tell Ezra, or lying and telling her that they'd ploughed on anyway, in total disregard of her feelings. Neither exactly looked good, but she couldn't go as far as to blame Ezra for it. That wouldn't be fair.

When she turned two bottles of beer were on the kitchen table. Slowly she crossed the room and took a glass from the cupboard.

"You can wash it up," said Ezra.

"I will. I always do."

"Why are you being so arsy about this? I thought you'd be pleased."

"Because it isn't what Claire wants."

"Why not?"

Luna shook her head. "I don't know. I … I don't suppose I really understood what she meant when she told me … maybe that's why it slipped my mind…"

"Or perhaps deep down you knew stopping was wrong. This Vedran has been falsely accused of something terrible, and if I'm right he can not only clear his name, but he'll know what happened to his girlfriend too. Win-win."

Well, put like that … but he had said *if* he was right. Perhaps he wasn't and she was worrying over nothing.

"OK. What have you got?"

"About a week ago, my app turned up a match. It's face recognition, you know."

Luna nodded, worried he was about to go off on one of his technical explanations that went way over her head. "So it recognised her face."

"A face. I'd had a couple of false positives but this time something just looked right. It was a holiday photo on Facebook, taken in Antigua. Some people were tagged and others just named, and I worked out the woman was calling herself Deirdre Kaye. Same initials. So I had a dig around the social media of the other people in the picture, and she turned up again. A better picture this time."

"Show me."

He put down his beer. "It's clearest on my desktop."

Luna followed him into his room. It wasn't somewhere she ventured; it was his private space as much as her bedroom was hers, and she was surprised how tidy it was in comparison. Tidy and sparse. His bed was made, there were no stray socks or, even worse, underpants on the floor, and his workspace was lit by a slim white LED light that flooded his keyboard and screen. Two hard drives whirred under his desk, masking the sound of the traffic below.

Ezra's fingers flew over the keyboard and his computer sprang to life. He clicked on an icon and the best of the photos of Didi that Claire had given her appeared on the left-hand side of the screen. Another click and a second picture popped up on the right. A bit on the grainy side, and the woman had different hair, but those cat-like eyes and those lips…

Luna put her hands on her hips. "Is that the best you've got?"

"No. This one's clearer."

Luna leaned over his shoulder as the new image appeared. Those eyes again, and something in her expression too as she posed for the camera. Brazen. That was the word. But you wouldn't be brazen if you had something to hide, would you? It must be some sort of coincidence. It couldn't be the same person.

She shook her head. "I'm still not convinced."

He looked up at her. "Best let Claire and her cousin decide then."

"Why bother them with this, when we're far from sure?" Her stomach was turning somersaults. Who was she trying to kid? Brazen or not, the woman looked a lot like Didi Kelmendi. But if Ezra was wrong it was pointless upsetting the apple cart. Not only for herself, but more importantly for Claire, and especially Vedran. Yes. Especially Vedran. It was him she ought to be thinking about.

"I'm as sure as I can be. I've tested this app on close to two hundred other faces and it's right ninety-four percent of the time. And given the woman is using the same initials and has no social media profile of her own..." He shrugged. "As I said. Best let Claire decide. I'll send you the pictures and you can show her tomorrow."

Luna stood back, hugging her arms around her. "I'll think about it."

"Think about it? It's a no-brainer."

"Is it? Is it really?" Close to tears, Luna walked out of his bedroom and back to the kitchen, where she picked up her beer.

Ezra followed. "Well, if you won't tell Claire then I will."

"You don't even know her!"

"Yes, but I know how important this is."

"She didn't want to find out, remember? She changed her mind." Luna clutched the glass to her chest. "I've let her down so badly."

"Luna, for once this is not about you. And now we've found out Didi Kelmendi's alive we have to tell her. Have to. It's our moral duty."

"Fuck you and your morals, Ezra Baca. She's my friend and I'll decide."

The slam of Ezra's bedroom door was so ferocious the lightbulb swayed from the ceiling. This was bad, so bad. And Luna had no idea how to stop it. She'd messed up. Big time. With Claire as well. Claire whom she cared about more than anyone. Never mind Ezra being mad at her; they'd fallen out dozens of times and always made it up. Her biggest problem now was putting this right with Claire.

Claire

O ver the weeks Gradac Park had become the regular destination for Claire's Sunday morning jogs. Exercising once a week was far from enough, but last night the clocks had gone forward so she'd be able to run or swim after work too, and hopefully the extra pounds would begin to fall away. She couldn't begin to imagine having to diet in Gran's house, with her generous kitchen and persuasive ways. It would be frankly impossible.

The sun split the clouds as she crossed the bridge outside the Pile Gate and almost immediately felt its warmth on her back. Mount Srd rose impressively to her right, Fort Imperial perched precariously on top, high above the dark green tidemark of trees. To her left the blue-grey sea churned around the rocks that supported the walls of the old town, the gentle breeze blowing the swell from the south.

She ran down the steps, past pots of brightly coloured geraniums, and along the Western Harbour, where lace-edged waves rippled over the pebbles in the sheltered bay. Past the shuttered Orhan restaurant, venue for so many family dinners over the years, and up the shallow-stepped backstreet that led to the promontory. All was peaceful, all was quiet. Just the faint hum of traffic and the bells of a nearby church calling the faithful to Mass.

She paused when she reached the road which led higher still to Gradac Park. She was sure she'd run faster this morning, she was ever so slightly out of breath, and that must be good. Once she was at the top she'd reward herself with a gentle jog along the seaward path, then loop back through the car park on the promontory.

As Claire trotted up the steps she noticed a man perched on the stone balustrade at the top, facing away from her. He turned at the sound of her footsteps and to her absolute astonishment, said her name. She stopped, stunned, looking at him.

He stood. "I'm sorry to startle you. I'm Ezra Baca, Luna's flatmate."

"Is she all right?"

"Yes, although my life will probably be in danger if she finds out I'm here, but I need to talk to you." Even the half-smile changed his face completely, and instead of seeming too narrow his chin looked stronger and in balance with his straight nose and almond-shaped eyes. Like her, he was wearing running gear, tracksuit bottoms and an over-sized T-shirt advertising the Dubrovnik 10k billowing around his slender frame and muscular arms in the breeze.

Slowly she climbed the last few steps until she was level with him. "How did you know where I'd be?"

He studied the scrappy grass beneath his feet. "Luna mentioned you ran on Sundays … and I saw your Strava route on her Facebook. I know Luna's login, but I'm not exactly proud of using it." He looked up, and nodded towards the ornamental pond and the wide gravel path beyond it. "Shall we walk?"

Could she trust him? She knew Luna did, but was he really who he said he was?

"I'm sorry to ask this, but do you have any ID? I need to know you really are Ezra."

"Fair enough." He pulled out his phone. "Face recognition to open it, OK? So it really is mine. Now, here's a banking app with my name on … and, oh yes, a photo of Luna I took on the ferry when we went home for Christmas." He shrugged. "It's not conclusive, but hopefully it's enough."

Claire nodded. "It is. And I guess what you have to say must be pretty important for you to take all this trouble tracking me down. I thought you lived miles away."

He shook his head. "Less than 3k. No distance at all."

"Luna said you like to run."

"It gets me away from my computer screen. About the only thing that does."

They walked side by side along the wide path that led from the pond with its trickling fountain, then beneath the Aleppo pines on the slope above them, bent at crazy angles by the prevailing wind. What on earth could he want to say that he'd gone to these lengths to meet her?

"So what do you want to talk about?"

"Your cousin. I think I've found Didi Kelmendi. Luna doesn't agree so she doesn't want to tell you, but I'm pretty sure it's her."

It took Claire a moment to take his words in. "But … but I asked you not to do anything, hold off for a while. Vedran isn't…" What could she say to this stranger? "What I mean is, I don't think Vedran is ready."

"Losing her must have been a huge blow to him. I do get that. Never mind all the vile stuff that followed. But having found something, I can't not tell you, can I? It wouldn't be right."

"No, I don't suppose it would. Just like if you're right I can't not tell Vedran." She shuddered, remembering how he'd been the night they'd argued about it. How could she go there again? "Oh god … why did you carry on with this when I told you to stop?"

He looked at his feet once more. "Luna and I had a difference of opinion about that. She swears she told me, but I know she didn't. You have every right to be angry, but I can't let your poor cousin keep thinking his girlfriend is dead when I'm pretty damned sure she isn't."

Claire nodded. She almost hoped Ezra was wrong. What the hell would she do if he wasn't? She was only just starting to regain Vedran's trust, never mind shattering it all over again. Whoever had said, or not said, what, at least Luna had somehow understood the predicament this would put her in and tried to protect her, but she couldn't blame Ezra for wanting to tell her the truth. This was turning out to be more than a mess. Why had she ever agreed to do this in the first place?

She steadied her voice. "Tell me about it. From the beginning." As much as anything, she needed time to think.

"I used the photos you gave Luna in a facial recognition app I've developed. I work in cyber-security, so I do know what I'm doing, and during testing the app worked in well over ninety per cent of cases. It takes a while though. It kind of crawls around the internet looking for matches. And then it hit something."

He carried on, explaining how he'd found first one image then another, and the name the woman was using. When he said the pictures had been on a yacht in the Caribbean, Claire's heart sank.

"Didi worked as a yacht hostess before she met Vedran."

Ezra stopped and she looked up at him. "There was a new picture yesterday. At a beach barbecue. The post said something about their hostess Deirdre knowing all the best places."

"Shit."

"Why don't we sit on that bench and I can show you?"

Claire felt her chest tighten in the same way it did when she panicked about Covid. Ezra's evidence was all adding up to the woman being Didi, but the picture would be the incontrovertible truth. The truth that she had at worst rigged, and at best suggested, her own death, in order to leave Vedran when their relationship had been more or less over anyway. But why would anyone do that? The only reason Claire could think of was if they didn't want the person they were leaving to follow them, if you were scared of what they might do… Shit, shit, shit. Surely, surely, Vedran could not be that person.

Claire dropped onto the bench with what felt like an audible thud. She had to pull herself together, in front of Ezra at least. Normal, normal. Fake it until you make it and all that crap. She took the deepest breath the invisible band around her chest would allow, and gazed over the ocean, so mocking with its sparkling kaleidoscope of blues, while Ezra took out his phone.

It took all the courage she had to look when Ezra showed her the photos, but she couldn't be sure who the woman was, not really. It was a thread of comfort to cling to. "It looks like Didi but I can't say for certain because I never met her. I just can't imagine why anyone would, you know, stage their own disappearance," she murmured.

"Perhaps it was nothing to do with your cousin. Maybe she had money problems, got involved with drugs … who knows? But the fact is, it looks like she's alive, so none of those social media trolls should be blaming him for her death."

A straw to cling to. Why the hell hadn't she thought of that? The simple explanation. And there she'd been, ready to blame Vedran all over again. Thank god for Ezra's quiet common sense. But all the same, she would still need to show Vedran the pictures and she really couldn't imagine how she might do that.

"You make it sound so simple," she said.

"I know it's not. I do understand that, Claire, and perhaps you would have preferred I hadn't told you but…"

She sighed. "You did the right thing. I just … I just need to work out the best way to handle this. What makes it worse is that Vedran always comes to Sunday lunch so I'll be seeing him in a couple of hours. So I've no time at all to think everything through."

"I'm sorry. My timing is absolutely lousy. Luna will tell you … I'm so bad at seeing things from other people's points of view sometimes."

"I don't know. I think you've handled this pretty sensitively."

"I'm just glad you're not mad at me. Luna is going to be absolutely furious."

Claire shook her head. "Don't tell her. Not today, anyway. I'll talk to her tomorrow, explain I'm OK with it. What's done is done, after all."

"Oh no. I've landed enough on your plate. And although I swear she didn't tell me to stop, I feel as though this one really is my bad."

Claire could understand why Luna trusted him. He was so straight up and honest, and there weren't many like him around. "Fine. But if I give you my number, message me once you've spoken to her if you feel I could help calm things down. I know you guys have been friends for years and I wouldn't want anything to jeopardise that."

"Me neither. She's a precious little bird, our Luna."

Claire nodded. "She is that."

Precious, but infuriating or just plain forgetful? Why, oh why, had Luna not nipped this in the bud when she'd asked her to? Claire thought as she retraced her steps past the Western Harbour once she and Ezra had said their goodbyes. She knew if she'd had the emotional bandwidth she might have been angry, but there was just too much shit about Vedran running around in her head. She should be happy that if it was Didi then Vedran would have the means to clear his name, but instead she was scared of his reaction, how this might damage the fragile trust that was growing between them again.

The one thing she could do was make sure Ezra and Luna didn't fall out over this. Claire checked the time on her phone. Even if he was a really fast runner he wouldn't be home yet so she messaged Luna:

Ezra found me and told me about Didi. He did right to tell me the truth, so don't get mad at him. And please don't think I'm mad at you either x.

Friendships were precious, after all. But not as much as family. As she increased her pace to jog up the steps towards the Amerling Fountain her head began to thump in time with her footfalls.

Her shower didn't shift it, neither did the pills she took. It was a good old-fashioned stress headache, the likes of which she hadn't had since she'd sat her finals. She couldn't face Vedran – she just couldn't. Even though Ezra had given her an alternative version of events she was desperate to believe, she still couldn't quite dislodge the thought that Didi might have been running from Vedran. After all, he'd told her himself he hadn't exactly covered himself with glory the night before she disappeared.

One thing was certain, there was no way she could face Vedran right now. First and foremost she needed to work out how best to tell him, never mind getting her own head straight. This was about him, after all, his feelings, his life. And, assuming it was Didi in the pictures, he would be hurt beyond belief by her actions. Or consumed by guilt. Or in denial. All Claire wanted to do was curl under her duvet and pretend this morning had never happened.

Gran was sympathetic about the headache, telling her she would save her some lunch, sending Claire's stomach into a nauseating downward spiral as her skull continued to thud. Even her bed offered no comfort as she tossed and turned, her mind twisting this way and that, refusing to let her rest.

She heard Vedran arrive, then the kitchen door was closed, presumably to keep things quiet for her. She wanted nothing more than to weep, and she almost did when she received a text from Luna saying she'd only been a little bit cross with Ezra, so Claire could be a little bit cross with her too. It was so very Luna, so… But Claire's eyes remained resolutely dry. Resolutely dry, and open.

She was still staring at the ceiling when there was a gentle tap on the door, and Vedran peeped around it.

"I've brought you a cup of tea and some of Gran's *spomilje* cookies. How are you feeling?"

It was far too late to pretend she was asleep. "Pretty rough. My head's still thumping fit to burst."

"Have you taken anything?"

"This morning. Didn't touch it. If I could only sleep I know it would go."

He reached into his shirt pocket. "Here. Try these. They'll knock you out if nothing else, but you shouldn't take them on an empty stomach so you'll have to force those biscuits down. Unless I can get you something lighter, like some yoghurt?"

God, he was just the kindest man. Like he always had been, ever since she'd been a young teenager with a massive crush on him. How could she have believed he was anything but her big-hearted cousin? That he was capable of… And yet, to her massive shame, she had.

Her head lurched alarmingly as she struggled upright and took the mug from him. "I'll stick with the cookies."

"They are pretty awesome. You're lucky there are any left."

She nibbled around the edge of a *spomilje*, the Viennese whirl-like pastry melting on her tongue. She eyed the pills he'd set down on her bedside table.

"You take them?"

"They're amongst my very best friends." He laughed.

"Oh, Vedran…" She would cry any moment, she knew she would.

"Now don't get all teary on me. Concentrate on that biscuit. I promise you once you've taken the tablets you'll sleep like a baby for hours."

Claire could only blink back her tears. "Thank you, Vedran. Thank you so much."

When Claire woke she could tell it was morning by the pale sunlight reflecting from the golden-grey stone of the apartments opposite. Those pills had certainly made her sleep. She hadn't even got up to close the curtains. In fact she could remember hardly anything after taking Vedran's tablets, but at least the headache seemed to have been reduced to a shadow of its former self.

She groped for her phone, finding it wasn't on the bedside table. Oh no, don't say she'd lost it. That was all she bloody needed. But Luna had messaged her yesterday … and the whole damn nightmare about Ezra most likely finding Didi came flooding back.

Swinging her legs over the side of the bed she waited for the thudding in her skull to begin again. It didn't. That was good. After checking everywhere she thought her phone might be she wandered through to the kitchen where Gran was reading, her book propped against a large blue and white striped milk jug.

"Oh, there you are. How are you feeling this morning?"

"Much better, but I can't find my phone."

"It's here. I crept into your room and took it away. It was easier than working out how to open it and turn off your alarm." Gran pushed her mobile across the table towards her.

Her alarm. Oh my god, she hadn't even thought about the time. She glanced at the kitchen clock.

"Bloody hell – I'm so late. Why didn't you wake me?"

"Because you needed to sleep. Nono popped in to tell Luna on his way to the harbour to fiddle around with the boat, so you can sit down, have some breakfast and tell me what you think was behind a stress headache that bad."

Claire knew she was cornered, but common sense told her Gran was the best person to help her decide what to do about the pictures. And what was more, she'd be able to speak openly without worrying about Nono overhearing. Her hand shaking only a little, she helped herself to coffee from the *dzezva* on the stove.

"I do know why. Luna's friend Ezra was waiting for me when I was jogging yesterday because he reckons Didi is alive. More than reckons actually." She wrapped her fingers around the mug. "He's found some pictures of a woman who looks very like her. She appears to be working in the Caribbean."

"Is he sure? That would be … remarkable." Gran was frowning. As well she might.

"He says the recognition software he uses works more than ninety percent of the time, and the pictures certainly look like her. But of course I never met Didi so…" Suddenly it struck her. "You have though."

Gran raised her eyebrows. "Oh yes. I think I'd know that little minx anywhere."

"Little minx?"

"I'm being polite."

It wasn't like Gran to mince her words. And it wasn't like her to dislike people either. Not without very good reason, so perhaps Didi had been capable of faking her own death without a thought of how that might hurt Vedran. Maybe she had been that sort of person. Vedran himself had said she could be … what was the word he'd used? Difficult? Challenging?

Claire opened her phone, then her photo file where Ezra had airdropped the pictures. She handed it to Fran.

"Scroll up. There are a few with her in."

She watched Gran's face as she studied the screen. Part of her was willing Ezra's software to be wrong, but eventually Gran nodded. "That's her. The way she holds her head, like she's constantly flirting. Definitely the same woman. Lord knows, there can't be two."

"Oh." Claire's forehead thudded and she rubbed it.

"Headache coming back?" Claire nodded. "Then spit out what's worrying you about this. It should be very good news for Vedran. He can take these to the police and clear everything up."

"I know … I know all that…" Oh, she could never tell Gran how badly she'd doubted Vedran, not now it seemed it was Didi who was the nasty piece of work. "The thing is, he told me not to do this, didn't he? I thought I'd made Luna understand that too, but obviously not, and last time he was so, so angry."

"But this is different. This is hard evidence. Remember, he's grieving for Didi. He thinks she's dead." Gran frowned. "But this will bring him a different sort of pain entirely."

"That's what I'm worried about. I know I have to tell him. I can't have a secret like this between us, I know I can't. But honestly Gran, I'm so scared of upsetting him or making him mad again."

"And upset him it will. You're absolutely right. There's no rhyme or reason why she would have done this, even given my doubts about her. This totally beggars belief."

"Ezra wondered if she was in debt."

"Unlike her not to dip into Vedran's wallet when she wanted something."

"You really didn't like her, did you?"

Gran sighed. "I always thought she was a bit, you know, sly. Maybe that's not the right word, but they never seemed as though they fitted. Not like he and Malina always did, and I never really understood why they'd split up. But Vedran was so head over heels, and at first Didi doted on him too. But later something changed; she started criticising Vedran a lot, and that's never a good sign in a relationship. Not that we saw much of them. I don't think she was keen on Jadran and me." Gran set Claire's phone on the table. "However none of that helps you to tell Vedran, does it? How would it be if we did it together?"

Claire got up and walked to the kitchen window, gazing into the courtyard below. Tiny stars of white blossom covered the orange tree, made all the more stunning by the dark glossy leaves that cradled them. She remembered a family barbecue under it; three, four years ago? With a different Vedran, relaxed and happy with Malina. Teasing and joking, comfortable in himself and with everyone else.

She could never, as long as she lived, admit to him or anyone her crazy doubts about him. She had to put that behind her. What she needed to do was work even harder at rebuilding the trust between them – and what she'd said to Gran was right, that was never going to happen if she didn't tell him the truth.

Claire had to find the courage to talk to Vedran, like she had with the book club, and with going to the jazz cafe with Luna. It must be inside her somewhere if she dug deep enough.

"Thanks, Gran, but I'll tell him on Friday. And I'd prefer to keep you out of it. If he hits the ceiling again, if he hates me for it, at least the door will still be open for him to talk to you."

Gran nodded. "That's very thoughtful, Claire, and I think it's the right decision. Lord knows, he's going to need all the support he can get."

Karmela

Karmela looked from her kitchen window towards the austere yet comforting bulk of the old town's walls. It was a beautiful evening, the soft rays of sunshine making the roofs glow between her and the perfectly circular form of the Minčeta Tower, rising majestically into a clear blue sky. It was certainly too nice to waste indoors, especially as she had been crouching over her computer all day. She stretched her complaining spine, reaching her fingers to the ceiling. She would stroll along the moat to the Western Harbour, and perhaps have a glass of wine there if the cafés weren't too crowded now the tourists had started to arrive.

She all but ran down the stairs and into the warm April air. The gentle breeze from the sea was wonderful this time of year, bringing a freshness to the evenings, and in the stepped alley that led to the main road the overhanging bougainvillea was just beginning to show its summer colour. Above her the wires carrying the cable cars to the top of Mount Srd hummed gently; another sign that the seasons were changing.

She was passing the cable car station itself when she spotted Rafael walking towards her. Immediately his face split into a grin.

"Ah, Karmela. It's too good a night to be inside alone."

She nodded. It had been a while since she had seen him, having avoided him even more after hearing his night-time tears, but he looked so happy it struck her as a good opportunity to fulfil her neighbourly obligations and pass the time of day.

"Yes, that is what I thought."

To her horror he grabbed her hand. "Then come, come with me."

"No, I…"

"But yes. The cable car has opened today and it is about to leave. Also I know the man taking tickets. More importantly, he knows me."

He must have sensed her hesitation. "Have you ever been on it?" he asked. Truthful to a fault, she shook her head. "Then what are we waiting for?" Still gripping her hand he more or less dragged her to the gates, where they were waved through like royalty, making Karmela cringe with embarrassment. It was only once they were in the cabin that Rafael released her. "Now, stand at this end to enjoy the view."

There was a click and hum as they began to move. Rafael stepped away, ushering a French family into the space, so they could make the best of the experience too, and Karmela smiled at his kindness. He might be impossibly impetuous, but his heart was in the right place.

Below her the walls of the old town seemed to sway as she became accustomed to the movement of the gondola, a blur of grey arms encircling the sharp angles of the roofs and their punctuating church towers, the boats in the old harbour. To her left the dark green bump of Lokrum island rose from silver-blue seas, the horizon tinged with orange as the sun began its descent. Directly below them the tips of the trees rippled as they passed, and looking outwards again the cabin was now so high the massive fortress of Lovrijenac seemed no bigger than a child's toy.

The terrain directly below was nothing but scrub smattered with loose shale. The higher they climbed, the steeper it became, the more studded with rocks. Looking back down now made her feel quite sick, the height was so dizzying, the tourist boats on the sea mere specks with wakes like matchsticks. She was relieved when a soft judder told her they had reached the station at the top.

"You liked it?" Rafael asked as they left the gondola.

"It is an impressive view. Thank you for suggesting it." She had expected him to join the short queue to go straight back down, but instead he said that now they were here, perhaps they should enjoy the panorama. Never having been to the top of Mount Srd, Karmela agreed.

Karmela had thought that by panorama he had meant the scene set out below them, but in fact Rafael had been referring to the restaurant and bar of the same name. As they were shown to a table on the terrace Karmela detected the faintest whiff of alcohol on his breath. This was not a good idea – from her point of view anyway – but there was nothing she could do about it now. Just one drink to be polite. Then she could make an excuse and head home.

The waiter brought Karmela a glass of golden-white wine and Rafael a beer with a *rakija* chaser.

He shrugged. "He knows, you see."

"Knows what?"

"Same as on the cable car. That I fought for this. That I was here on 6th December 1991."

This again. But if she asked him to tell the whole story it would not only pass the time, but she might even be able to ascertain if any of it was, in fact, true. Given his fantasy that he ran his own business, it seemed pretty unlikely.

A muscle twitched beneath his beard. "It is not an easy story to tell, but for you I will try. We were lost, you see, in this city, abandoned. Hung out to dry by the government. I still believe they wanted the enemy to take Dubrovnik, so the world would see how evil and greedy they were. So we, the citizens, had to stop them.

"Thirty-two men manned Fort Imperial. Just thirty-two. Exhausted men, hungry and thirsty, the occupying army surrounding them on almost every side. Well bedded-in, those Serbs were, had been for months. Over there behind me," he waved his hand, "is the village of Bosanka. They have rebuilt it now – just some ruins so no one forgets – but it was fought over so bitterly. The Serbs had proper tanks and weapons, you see. Not ones made in a converted broom factory like ours. And of course they had ammunition. We had next to nothing in Dubrovnik; no water, no food, no power…" He raised his glass to her. "And only a little *rakija*. For courage, you know?

"Well, ammunition was the problem but proved to be the solution. The men in Fort Imperial up here at the top had nothing left at all, not a bullet or grenade between them, so under cover of darkness they started to creep down the mountainside. This we did not know, because starting out in the woods at the bottom, a group of us began carrying crates of ammo up. The days were short and the nights long. If we were lucky we wouldn't be seen. But of course when you cannot see yourself the climb is all the more treacherous. I volunteered because I was young and fit, and when I was a boy my father used to take me hunting in the hills."

He paused for a moment, to gesture to the waiter for another *rakija*. As he leaned towards her the alcohol enveloped her like a cloud.

"Of course, we met the shattered defenders coming down, but we would not give up, no! So we persuaded them not to either and they turned around and helped us to carry the crates back up. But what were we? Thirty-eight men against an army. But we fought like tigers…" Rafael hiccupped. "Fucking tigers, if the lady will pardon my language."

The waiter brought his *rakija* and he downed it, wiping spittle from his beard with the back of his hand. As she tried not to edge away from him, it struck Karmela that his story sounded very practised, despite the fact he was clearly drunk. Was it a spiel he gave to tourists for tips? Supplementing his income by accosting them at the cable car station and offering his personal account of the war? Would he want to show her around the museum in the fort next? Then ask her for money?

"We thought we would not get out alive," Rafael continued. "That we would fail, and they would take the fort. Because once they had it they would have won. But eventually we had to retreat inside. No ammo again. Not even enough to cover our retreat. Not that we would have retreated. We would have rather died." Rafael's eyes were watery now, as he gazed out over the city, the terracotta roofs far below bathed in the glow of the setting sun.

He cleared his throat. My, this was an accomplished act, but he must have told it so many times. "So what did we do? We sang. We sang so fiercely and bravely that we must have sounded like a thousand men. They said later that the Serbs thought reinforcements had arrived. No such luck, but we had our voices. And we held the fort. We held it."

As he finished his tale, Rafael shook his head slowly, as if even now in disbelief at what they had achieved. It had been told with a great deal of passion, but was it really true? Karmela knew the bones of the story were right, but had he been one of those men? What struck her most was the lack of personal detail. He could have learned it all from newspaper stories or gossip at the time.

"It is an incredible story," she said, knowing he would be unlikely to question her careful choice of words. "I read somewhere the acoustics in the fort are very good so they magnified your voices."

He sat back and folded his arms. "Oh, so you know all about it anyway."

"A little. As you say, it was an important day in Croatia's history."

He turned and looked over his shoulder at the monument on the lookout point behind him. "That flag … we fought for that flag, our generation. It is ours."

Was he saying it was not hers too? Something about his insinuation rankled, even though she would never have described herself as much of a nationalist. "Not every Croatian's?"

"Not in the same way. We suffered for it, bled for it."

She folded her arms. "People suffered in the war who did not fight." She thought of her father, of Emina. "Children died. Innocent non-combatants. Slaughtered for their ethnicity…"

He held up his hands. "I'm talking about Croatia, not Bosnia."

"It happened here too. And everywhere, everywhere, people made sacrifices. That flag belongs to us all."

"To the people who ran away the moment the fighting started? To the ones whose grandparents went to America and Australia, who've never even been here yet claim it as their own?"

"Of course. It is their heritage as well." His words had wrong-footed her, putting her on the defensive. Her parents had run away, as he put it. Her father had not stayed to fight, yet the war had broken him all the same. Perhaps for that very reason. Why had she not thought of it before? Now she had, it felt as though a piece of a jigsaw had slotted into place. He had paid with his life, albeit on the streets with an empty bottle in his hand. "And it is my heritage too," she said, quietly but firmly.

"Where did you spend your war, Karmela?" Rafael sneered. "Zagreb was a comfortable distance from the front line."

She took a deep breath. "We were not in Zagreb, we were in Germany. We had to leave everything behind in Sarajevo. Everything. And that was not easy…" She had been going to say

150

that of course it had not been as tough as it had been here, but he did not let her.

Instead he stood, a mountain of a man towering over her, flecks of spittle spattering her face. "Scum! Weak, feeble, scum! How dare you tell me that flag is yours; you've done nothing to deserve it."

Silence settled over the tables around her as he stormed from the terrace. But there was none of the cringing embarrassment she might have expected; instead Karmela felt completely numb. The calm before a storm. Or after one. Slowly she picked up her wine and took a cautious sip. She was aware of someone moving behind her and a woman crouched down.

"Are you OK?" Her English was spoken with an American accent, her eyes concerned behind gilt-rimmed glasses.

"Thank you. Yes." Karmela zipped up the emotions that had been threatening. Hard.

"Of course I don't speak your language, but that sounded more than heated at the end. Your husband…"

"Oh, no, no, no. He is not my husband. He is my neighbour, and he is a little drunk." She tried to smile. "Do not worry, it will be fine."

"You just be careful, honey, you hear?" After patting her shoulder the woman returned to her table.

Karmela supposed it had been kind of her to come over, but all the same it was a little embarrassing to be singled out in that way. She hurriedly finished her wine, but rather than heading straight for the cable car she found herself drawn to the flag that fluttered alongside the stark grey stone cross of the memorial. The viewpoint around it was crowded with tourists, trying to capture the purple-orange glow of the sunset on their cameras and phones, so she hung back, gazing up at the rippling fabric, red, white and blue against the vivid sky.

It was only a flag, wasn't it? She could hardly believe it had caused such an argument, but perhaps Rafael would argue about anything when he was drunk. The thought that he might be waiting to start round two when she got home was at the back of her mind, but she had become used to creeping up the stairs to avoid him. It just all felt rather … unsettling. Yes, that was the word.

So why had she not simply agreed with him, just to keep the peace? Was it all bound up with Sarajevo, with her father, with losing Emina and Nejla, with the bitter loneliness of being a refugee? All the things she had tried to forget. And yet, tonight, they were creeping back into the darkest corners of her mind.

She looked at the flag again. It was just a piece of fabric. Was there some sort of deeper identity woven into its threads, woven into her life? She had always felt like an outsider, so maybe Rafael was right and it was not hers after all. But no, she was Croatian. It was the nationality on her passport, if nothing else. But did that mean she belonged?

And what was belonging? It seemed a pretty meaningless word to her. She had always been perfectly happy on her own. Well, maybe not always, but she had become used to it. When she and Mama had arrived in Zagreb at the end of the war, she had found she had no experiences in common with her fellow students who had lived through the bombings and deprivation. Leastways it had marked her out as different, and she had already learned in Berlin that different was never good.

For a Bosnian, born a Yugoslavian, now living in Croatia and knowing all too well about the divisions caused by the recent past, it had been far safer to burrow into history, to a time and place that no longer had the power to hurt. Somewhere she could lose herself. So she had found her precious Ragusans. Her solace and her joy. The place she had carved out for herself in the world. But tonight the comfort seemed strangely hollow. There was a lump in Karmela's throat, and it was not a feeling she was used to.

Claire

Claire watched Vedran stow the last of Fran's goodies in his fridge.

"She really must stop doing this," he told her. "I'm coping better these days so I'm sure I can manage to cook. And of course tonight I have." He gestured towards a simmering pot on the hob, rich with the aroma of olives, tomatoes and beef. "Smells good, huh?"

Claire nodded, although for once she was far from hungry. Vedran might very well be eating alone – or not at all – after what she had to tell him. Oh god, could she even do it? She'd been working herself up about it all day, and trying not to let it show, but failing miserably. In fact she'd almost snapped at Luna when she'd asked what was wrong, then muttered something about PMT. Thankfully she had taken her excuse at face value.

But now she was here there was no point in delaying. She needed to get it over and done with.

"Vedran, we have to talk."

"On the terrace with a drink? It's a lovely evening. First time this year it's warm enough to sit out."

Oh no, he was in such a good mood as well. As relaxed as she'd seen him since she'd been here. "Inside would be better. I don't want us to be overheard."

He looked over his shoulder as he stirred the ragù. "That sounds a bit ominous."

"Yes and no. Will you just hear me out without exploding?"

"Explode? What do you think I am, a gas canister someone left too close to the barbecue?"

She couldn't look at him. It didn't help that he was joking around. Well, trying to.

He turned to face her. "It's about Didi, isn't it? That's the only time I've exploded at you." Claire nodded, and he folded his arms across his chest. "Don't even think about asking me to open that whole can of worms again, because the answer is still no."

Shit. Shit, shit, shit. What could she say? She couldn't invent another story. That wouldn't be right. And he needed to know. He needed to know. He may not want to, but even Gran had agreed… She took a deep breath.

"I promise you, I did tell Luna not to do anything. I told her I had cold feet, but somehow … somehow … it got lost in translation and her flatmate went ahead anyway."

"Her flatmate?" Vedran's eyebrows were close to his hairline, but at least his voice was fairly even. So far.

"He works in cybersecurity and he has this app … for facial recognition. Anyway, the long and short of it is, he thinks he's found Didi."

"He thinks he's *found* her?" His Adam's apple bobbed violently as he frowned.

"The woman's in the Caribbean, but she's using a name with the same initials, and working as a yacht hostess so…" Her mouth was too dry to say any more.

Vedran's hands slid behind him, his fingers gripping the edge of the marble worktop as if he was trying to steady himself. She could barely imagine what he was going through. What she was putting him through. What was he thinking? His face gave nothing away.

"Do you want to look at the pictures?" Her voice trembled as she said it.

He shook his head. "I can't take it in. Not one little bit."

Oh god, he looked so white, almost as though he was going to faint. And she'd done this to him. But there was a little voice inside her, telling her it was better he knew the truth, that once he was over the shock…

Right now he needed her to support him. Physically, by the look of it. Crossing the kitchen she took him by the arm, guiding him towards a chair.

"How about that drink? You look as though you need it."

He shook himself, like a dog that had just got out of the water, loosening his arm from hers in the process. "Maybe that's not such a bad idea. I'll open the wine if you sort out the nibbles. There are some olives in the fridge, and a lump of Grobnički cheese, too, if you fancy it." He glanced out of the window, then cleared his throat. "And let's not waste the last of the sunshine either. It'll still be warm enough on the terrace."

Was that it? Was that all of it? But Vedran had closed up on her completely. He had slipped behind a veneer of normality, of a pretence that nothing had been said, and nothing more could be, with his insistence they had their drinks outside. She had no idea what she'd expected, but it certainly wasn't this. But she got it, or at least, she thought she did. Didi's disappearance had blown his world in two; what she had told him had probably just done the same, all over again. He'd need time to process the information, for sure. Maybe the fact he'd taken it so calmly was a positive sign, but it left her in a strange sort of limbo, not knowing how to behave.

As she started to cube the cheese Claire could almost hear

Gran's voice in her ear telling her you couldn't make an omelette without breaking the eggs. She glanced at Vedran, still struggling to remove the cork from the wine bottle. Oh yes, he was scrambled all right, but hopefully, hopefully, this evening would set him on the path to healing. And at least she was here, beside him, and she'd just have to follow his lead and pretend that nothing had changed, that everything was normal. Perhaps he was right and it was for the best.

Vedran

For the first time since October, Vedran walked down the concrete steps to the jetty. Darkness settled around him, a cool breeze swooping from the hills and rippling the calm waters of the bay. It hadn't been like this on the day Didi had disappeared; the waves had been rolling in from the sea, perilous peaks and troughs through a curtain of rain. But what if ... what if ... she had never gone into the water at all?

The pictures in his inbox would tell him the truth, one way or another. Or rather they might, if this woman was indeed Didi. He'd asked Claire, just before she left, to email them to him. She hadn't stayed much beyond supper and he couldn't blame her, given how stilted their conversation had been. But at least while she was here he'd been able to pretend that nothing had changed.

At first when she'd told him, it had felt as though an earthquake was rumbling beneath his feet. The room really had seemed to pitch and toss as his mind fought to make sense of her words. Rearrange them in a different order, so he could understand them properly. His only defence had been to grip the worktop until he felt less like he'd collapse to the floor, then try to pretend they had never been said.

But you couldn't unsay something like that, could you? At least Claire hadn't told him his life would be all roses if Didi was found, and she didn't know the half of it. It was not that simple. It never had been, not really. Well, maybe at the beginning, but that was more than a lifetime ago. And if Claire was right, the way she had chosen to leave him…

That was the hardest thing; not that Didi was alive, but that she had *chosen* to do this. Not met with an accident at all. He needed to get used to the idea before he did anything else, because if it was true, so much of what he'd gone through these last months… It didn't make sense. Every single thing he thought he knew about what had happened had been turned upside down in moments. No wonder he felt slightly sick at it all.

But what if the photos weren't her? He ran his finger over the top of his phone in his trouser pocket. No. He wasn't ready, no way. There was too much he needed to work out first. Because if it was Didi in the pictures he would have to go to the police, and he simply could not. Going through all that again … being locked in a cell like a criminal … he just wasn't strong enough.

He sat on the bottom step, the chill of the concrete seeping into him as he gazed at the spot where he'd found her robe. He could still feel it in his arms, heavy with rain and spray as he'd run back to the apartment, still hear his heart thudding in his chest. The terror ripping through him had been real. Real. Which made Didi's behaviour way, way beyond cruel. But she had proved herself more than capable of it. Many times.

He could never pinpoint exactly when it had started. He supposed he had slid into it so gradually, a fraction of himself at a time, that he had come to accept it as the way things were. The way he was. Not quite enough. One small step away from not being loved. From not being lovable. Desperate to please. Grateful for crumbs. A victim. But he should never have been a victim; he was a man, for god's sake. An intelligent one at that, or so he'd thought. But she must have spotted some weakness to be able to reel him in like that.

Maybe it had even started as early as his lockdown beard. But no, they'd been blissfully happy then, cocooned in the little world they had created here. He'd had no responsibilities; his parents had been living on Korčula, and Tetak and Fran in England. Work had been reduced to a smattering of Zoom calls as the country held its breath. So he and Didi had been able to lose themselves in each other completely.

Lockdown beards had been all the rage, so she'd suggested he grew one. He'd never tried before, so had shrugged his shoulders and agreed. And he'd persisted, even though she'd complained bitterly at the harsh, stubbly stage, and it had itched like hell, but after that she'd found it very sexy. Until she didn't, and said he should shave it off. It was a bit scrappy, not as manly as she'd hoped. All said with a giggle and a stroke of his thigh, of course.

Ach, he'd been such a fool. Worse than that. If he could see it so clearly now, why hadn't he then? They say love is blind, and in his case it had been true. And he had loved her; to absolute distraction. To the exclusion of everything, even himself.

Of course the beard had only been a bit of fun … so when had it really begun to sour? The wheels of the world had started to turn very slowly again in the May, when a few more shops were allowed to open and public transport of a kind resumed. But there'd be no tourist season as such that summer and Didi had been distraught. How would she survive? How could she pay her way? And he'd reassured her there was no need to worry; he would look after her.

Even when offices reopened his firm allowed everyone to work where they felt most comfortable. Left to his own devices he might well have gone back, but Didi had been so scared of infection she'd persuaded him not to. If he was honest, it hadn't taken much. So they'd continued in their little bubble of love for quite a few months more.

Then Tetak and Fran had been able to return to Dubrovnik, provided they isolated once they arrived. So of course he had needed to shop for them and run errands, and although they had hardly been demanding, Didi hadn't liked it one bit. It was a risk going into the old town. Didn't they have neighbours? Were they always so needy? It was the first time they'd argued and she'd slapped him across the face, immediately collapsing into floods of tears of remorse.

The stresses and strains of Covid were making everyone crabby, so he'd known it wasn't her fault, not really. He'd been extra-attentive afterwards and she'd loved it. Loved him all the more, it seemed. Was that when the increasingly poisonous game of withholding and bestowing her affection had started? That his reaction had caused it to happen? Why was he even wondering? Didi had left him in no doubt that any problem in their relationship was either in his imagination or entirely his fault.

Vedran wrapped his arms around his knees, hugging them ferociously. The lights from the village of Zaton across the bay reached him as a faint glow beyond the black bank of trees that covered the far shore. After a moment he stood, rubbing the stiffness and cold from his legs. Should he look at those photos or not? To do so would set off a whole chain of events he didn't even know how to face.

If he went to the police the whole sorry business would be opened up once more, the inevitable glare of publicity... And he'd still be cast as the monster. How could he not be, when a woman had gone to such lengths to fake her own death to leave him? He couldn't, couldn't go through all that again. And he could never tell them the truth. It was too damn humiliating.

If it hadn't been for something Claire had said he'd have

opened those photos straightaway, if only to find out one thing. But if Didi had been heavily pregnant there was no way she could be working as a yacht hostess. She'd carried out her threat all right, even without the money she'd demanded from him to pay for her abortion. If he closed his eyes he could still see his hands, moving towards the base of her throat…

But he didn't close them. He opened them, snapped his head back. His child was dead. Aborted, not drowned. But still, as he gazed at the water, the pain threatened to overwhelm him, and he gripped his shaking hands into fists to make it stop. His hidden grief. His real grief. How it had happened should be immaterial. But it did matter, oh god it did, and a cold flame of anger ignited inside him.

Telling him she was pregnant and wanted a termination had been her last and greatest crime as far as he was concerned. The crimes of Didi Kelmendi. The phrase ran through his head as he climbed the steps to the apartment. The whisky bottle sat on the coffee table and he eyed it for a moment, but his lawyer's brain was kicking in. Perhaps it was self-protection, he didn't know, but he was going to use it. And tonight the whisky would play no part.

While his computer churned into life in the narrow room that served as his office he made a *dzezva* of coffee and after pouring himself a mugful, left the rest to keep warm on the hob. He crossed the hall, then swung slowly in the black leather chair, this way and that, thinking, thinking, before finally settling in front of his keyboard.

He listed the evidence with as much detachment as he could muster. Didi's nipping and niggling away about Tetak and Fran, so they hardly ever saw them. Her complaints against his friends for looking at her tits and their wives and girlfriends for hating her for it. Begging him not to go out in case he brought infection back. Until last summer when she had been able to work again, and she was hardly ever here. Leaving him in the isolation she had carefully woven around him.

Furiously typing he recorded individual incidents too. Some he even managed to date, like the time she'd burned him with her hair straighteners. He remembered it specifically because they'd been getting ready to go out to dinner for Tetak's birthday – a rare enough occurrence as it was – and one that had made him so happy he'd kissed her neck as she was doing her hair. She'd flown at him in an absolute rage. Then fallen to her knees sobbing and begging forgiveness.

They'd been late of course, and Didi had been red-eyed. Naturally Fran had noticed but she'd held her counsel. It was only some weeks later when she dropped around for coffee, knowing Didi would be at work, that she asked if everything was all right. He remembered clutching his arm as he answered. She wouldn't have known why, thank god, the scar was above the line of his sleeve. And he'd said yes, of course it was. She'd nodded but told him to remember they were there for him if he needed them.

So many times he'd almost spoken to her or Tetak. So many times. But he was ashamed of the pathetic excuse for a man he'd become. Didi had told him so often enough and he'd come to believe her. Still did now, truth be told, so she must have been right. These lists of her wrongs were somehow not helping. Yes, of course to his lawyer's brain, they did, but the fact that something deep inside refused to listen was most frightening of all. Didi's version of himself had become the real thing. Whether she was alive or dead would do nothing to change that.

Vedran sipped his coffee, long gone cold, so he stretched and returned to the kitchen to refill his mug. The blinds were still up and dawn was streaking the sky over the mountains, reminding him of that last morning with Didi. It wasn't true when he'd told the police they hadn't spoken after their row the previous night, oh no. He'd begged her to consider keeping their baby, to start again. Begged her. And she'd laughed in his face. With a terrible clarity he had seen it for what it was: a deliberately provocative action.

So he'd told her it was over and she'd laughed again. Said he'd never survive without her, and when she left it would be on her own terms. But all the fight had gone out of him so he'd retreated to his office and closed the door.

On her own terms. At the time he thought she had meant money to pay for a termination, but looking back at her actions now – assuming it was her in the pictures – her words made perfect sense.

So was he ready to look at those photos? Perhaps he didn't need to. Perhaps he already knew the answer. But as he'd realised on the steps, positive confirmation Didi was alive would mean he had to do something about it and for that he needed more time. Tomorrow. He'd make his decision tomorrow.

Downing his coffee he returned to his study and powered off his computer. The birds were singing outside the small window. It was already tomorrow, a fresh new day. And he was going to bed.

Sense and Sensibility

Luna

Finally, finally, the day of the LGBTQ+ women's cruise was here and Luna was hyped. A whole Sunday with something to do. Easter Sunday at that, when her parents normally expected her to waste the day in church with them. She'd always dreaded Easter before, and while Mama's disappointment that she wasn't going home had made her feel just a little bit guilty, there was no way on earth she was going to miss this.

Next to her Vanesa pushed her tortoiseshell glasses up her nose, then eased the lid from a cardboard cup of coffee. The engine murmured and chugged beneath them, the smell of diesel mixing with the sweetness of frying doughnuts drifting from the stand on the old harbour. Luna was really struggling not to bounce up and down, but the last thing she wanted was to spill Vanesa's coffee on her new sundress. That would be such a bad start to the day.

Dusana and Senada appeared on the top deck and sat down opposite. They were all coming, the regulars from the jazz café, all except Meri, who'd said that a tourist cruise was the last thing she wanted to do, however high it was waving the rainbow flag. So where the hell was Claire? Luna craned over the side, looking back towards the city walls, and spotted her, caught up in a group of young women, chatting and laughing.

Luna grinned at Senada. "See, you didn't have to worry there wouldn't be enough people. Sod all those places that refused to put up your posters – this boat is jumping!"

Senada laughed. "Luna, the only one jumping is you. But all the same I can hardly believe how many women signed up."

The cruiser was buzzing with female voices in at least four different languages as locals and tourists alike crowded on for their trip along the coast to Cavtat. Luna leaned over the side and waved frantically to Claire, who thankfully noticed and waved back.

Three women followed her up the steps. "I met the English contingent," Claire told them. "This is Brianna, Louise and Jo."

It was Louise who stole Luna's attention. All her attention. She had incredible cheekbones, the sort only super-models were blessed with, but they were teamed with endearing dimples when she smiled, which she did a lot, and hazel eyes that darted around, taking everything in. *O bože*, this woman was gorgeous, and Luna's stomach did a backflip. But was one of the others her girlfriend? Or was she a gay ally like Claire? What was the deal with her?

Without Luna noticing, the boat had slipped its mooring and was leaving the shelter of the harbour. The morning sunlight bathed Svetog Ivana fort on one side, and on the other the protective mole sheltered the yachts and launches owned by locals. She tore her eyes from Louise, and started to chat to Vanesa.

Although the sun was beginning to make its presence felt, the breeze ruffling Luna's hair was fresh and she was glad of her hoodie, which she pulled over her head. Claire had told her she planned to swim today – she was completely mad, as far as Luna could see, but Vanesa's towel was peeping out of her rattan bag, so clearly she wasn't the only one.

At first the boat hugged the coast between the string of hotels clinging above the sea and the lush green vegetation of Lokrum island opposite. The sun sparkled on its wake and gulls wheeled above them, Luna digging in her bag for her shades as Claire pointed out the local landmarks to Louise and her friends. Hoodie and shades? Was that a cool look, or was it ridiculous? And why did she care? But Luna knew why, and as she flicked a glance in Louise's direction she noticed she was looking at her too.

In no time at all the boat rounded a peninsula fringed with Aleppo pines dipping their branches almost into the sea. Ahead of them was a long, squarish tongue of water, then buildings began to appear: green-shuttered houses with the terracotta roofs so typical of the area, a church with a round tower perched on top of a square one, a restaurant terrace shaded by palm trees.

It was near here the boat moored, and Luna felt strangely self-conscious as she followed the others onto the quay. Why? Why? *Sranje*, she knew why. But she mustn't, mustn't let Louise's desirability spoil her day, so when Claire asked if she wanted to go swimming she answered with so much mock shivering it made everyone laugh, and said she was going for coffee.

Dusana agreed, and Brianna asked if they could tag along too. Luna wondered if she dared single Louise out and walk with her, but the moment was lost when Brianna fell into step beside her and asked if she'd been to Cavtat before.

"Sit with me on the way back?" Louise asked as they returned to the boat a few hours later. No reason, no excuse, needed. Luna looked over her shoulder, smiled, and nodded.

They had been in each other's orbit all day, without really having a conversation as such. Drinking coffee, browsing the shops, taking selfies around the picturesque harbour; all part of the larger group. At lunch they'd been sitting diagonally opposite, and Luna had barely been able to take her eyes off Louise's incredible cheekbones, except to allow them to slide towards the tanned cleavage peeping from her top. It had reminded her of the way she'd looked at the tourist girls back home, except it was no longer pointless lusting. One thing she had managed to ascertain from Brianna was that Louise was lesbian and single too.

Luna's palms began to sweat. Louise was here on holiday. There was no question of a relationship, of course there wasn't. But what had Meri said about starting with hook-ups? Well, a hook-up this soon was beyond her wildest dreams, but a little flirtation wouldn't hurt, maybe even a kiss... *Sranje*, she was absolutely longing for that kiss. More than ever as she watched Louise freshen her lip balm before they boarded the boat.

Could her feelings be reciprocated? Maybe, just maybe. And when Louise chose a short bench on the lower deck, with room for just the two of them, Luna prayed she was right.

But how to start this? How to flirt? She was too used to hiding her feelings, her sexuality. Why hadn't she realised before how hard this would be? Asked one of the others for some advice on how to begin?

"So do you like Croatia?" she asked, as the boat began to move beneath them. Boring question, or what? Louise would think she was so, so dumb.

"It's beautiful." Louise's hazel eyes sparkled. "And everyone is so damned friendly. Although I was surprised there's no real gay life in a city like Dubrovnik."

"We're really behind," Luna told her. "But there are rumours of a new club opening this summer. It's all a big secret though. Maybe they want to be sure of their licences first, or something."

"But it is legal to be gay here?"

Luna shrugged. "Sure. But the law isn't everything. There's a big church-going population and they have opinions and clout." She told her how the boat owner had washed his hands of the booking when he learned what it was for, leaving his daughter and son-in-law to crew for the day.

"For real?" Louise's mouth actually dropped open.

"For real. My parents would be the same. I can't even tell them I'm gay."

"No way!"

"Every way." She laughed, but it sounded terribly self-conscious. "I'm almost twenty-one and I've only been out a couple of months. Claire's sister back in England's lesbian, and things seem so different for you."

"Perhaps," Louise mused, "we don't know how lucky we are. But you're lucky too, Luna, in a different way. You live in such a beautiful place, for a start, maybe that's the payoff. And anyway, sometimes if you have to work hard for something you appreciate it all the more. But not everything." She laughed, and slid her hand along the bench until it was holding Luna's.

Another person's palm against her palm. The last time that had happened had probably been her mother's when she'd been a child. Oh wow, wow. Feeling Louise's warmth she realised there was something super-intimate about your hand being held. More so than a hug, or an arm around the shoulder. This was not just comfort or friendship. It was the first step of a dance. An unfamiliar and exciting one.

She wriggled her fingers further between Louise's, enjoying the sensation of skin on skin. The Englishwoman was smiling down at her, but her eyes were serious.

"I'm going home tomorrow and I don't want you hurt. I don't want you to start your journey with a bad experience."

So this was what she was offering. Something deep in the pit of Luna's stomach flipped. She nodded, uncertain how to reply.

"But you're so gorgeous, Luna, I can't resist at least asking.

There's an energy about you; I was watching you browsing the shops with your friends. You're like a warm, fuzzy little bee making everyone laugh."

"And you…" Luna stuttered. "You… I couldn't take my eyes off you at lunch. Your face…" Instinctively she reached out and ran a finger along her cheekbone.

"You just gave me goosebumps."

Luna's courage was building by the moment. "Good." She wanted to kiss Louise right now, but why rush? It was far too soon. And rather too public. Still holding her hand, she settled back in her seat. "So tell me about your life in England."

There was no awkwardness between them as they talked, and their fingers remained entwined as they left the boat. On the quayside the group began to drift apart, including Claire, claiming a family Zoom call, but a good number headed for the jazz café, where Brianna ordered Prosecco for them all to share.

"If we're going home tomorrow then we might as well party."

"You want to?" Louise asked Luna.

"You bet."

They didn't stay long. Luna toyed with her glass, taking only the occasional sip. She didn't want her senses blunted for what she hoped was to come. Her first kiss. Maybe even more, if that was what Louise wanted too, but she hardly dared to look that far ahead. *Stay in the moment, Luna, stay in the moment and enjoy.*

As dusk fell and the piano-player started his set they left. Luna led Louise along Ulica od Puča so she could show her the bookshop, and her hand was gripped tighter as Louise said,

"That's lovely. I can picture you here now."

"And where can I picture you?"

Louise took out her phone and googled something before angling the picture of an enormous ugly grey tower block towards her. "There you go." She laughed. "My ward's on the fourth floor." They clutched each other, giggling, as though it was the funniest thing in the world.

As they walked on, Louise tried to tuck Luna under her arm but she wriggled away. It would be too, too obvious. If anyone she knew came it was easy to loose hands, but this...

"I'm sorry..."

"Me too," replied Louise, "but I get it after what you've told me. You live and work here."

Past Onofrio's Fountain and through the Pile Gate. They stopped in Brsalje, the piazza overlooking the Western Harbour and leaned against the rail, shoulders and hips touching.

"This is so beautiful." Louise sighed.

The setting sun had left the faintest purple-orange glow on the horizon beyond Lovrijenac Fortress, turning the sea into a pot of molten bronze. They watched until the last of the light faded, the sound of traditional Croatian music and clattering cutlery from the nearby restaurant terrace and the aroma of grilling meat filling the air.

What now? Luna thought. The bus home left from the street behind them, and Ezra knew, so she could ask Louise ... but what if that was more than she wanted? But asking ... what did she have to lose? The touch of their hips through her sundress and Louise's shorts was running shivers up and down her legs and deep into her belly.

It was Louise who spoke. "We're staying in an apartment about ten minutes' walk from here. It's nothing special, but I'd love it if you came back. No pressure though, if that's not what you want."

"It is what I want. For sure."

Before leaving they took a selfie with the harbour behind them, which Louise promised not to share. "Thank you for trusting me. Not just with the photo. For wanting me to be your first. I'm honoured."

"I'm honoured it's you."

They separated to walk along the crowded harbour front, where tables from the restaurants and bars spilled onto the quayside, but as soon as they reached the quieter streets beyond, Luna felt for Louise's long fingers and wound hers through them. Fingers that would soon be touching more than just her hand. She felt hot at the thought, then cold, then wobbly inside. But more than anything, she felt it was right.

Louise led her up a flight of narrow stone steps, fringed with bougainvillea that brushed Luna's shoulder as they passed. At the top was a terrace, a table covered with a red and white checked oilcloth. Luna perched on the corner while Louise fumbled for her key in the light of the old-fashioned carriage lamp that hung above the door. Beyond it, through it, lay her first step into her future. And although she felt strangely breathless it wasn't even a tiny bit scary. Not anymore.

Inside, a single room served as kitchen, diner and lounge, the centrepiece of which was a red corner sofa, scattered with colourful cushions. Without letting go of Luna's hand, Louise turned on a lamp in the corner, and they sat as one, bathed in its glow.

Then her palm was on Luna's cheek, tilting and turning her face into hers, as she leaned towards her and their lips touched. Softly at first, no more than a butterfly making her tingle, but soon becoming a press that opened both their mouths, tasting each other in a way that would have made Luna cry out, had she been able. But as the kiss drew to an end it was she who lay on the sofa, she who pulled Louise on top of her, reaching under her T-shirt. It might be just for tonight, but Luna's moment had come.

Claire

After yesterday's hectic day, Claire was enjoying the peace and quiet of being in the bookshop on her own. Monday mornings were never busy, and there was no cruise ship due in today, so when Luna had texted to ask if she could take a half day's holiday to have brunch with Louise before her flight home, she'd been delighted to agree.

It was just the best news that Luna's date had gone so well and Claire hoped it would be a watershed, a taste of better things to come. Luna still would not countenance coming out to her family and that seemed such a shame. Claire knew her own parents would support her and Belle however they lived their lives, but perhaps not everyone was so lucky.

She had reached a watershed yesterday too, and she hugged the thought to her. Since they had been going to the jazz café regularly she had become quite accustomed to gathering around a table with people whose daily lives she knew little about, and the fact she had remained healthy had buoyed her confidence to take another step towards banishing the fear of Covid from her life.

Initially she had been terrified of the idea of a boat full of people from all over the world, most of whom would have travelled through crowded airports then been packed onto planes in the few days before. But she had convinced herself she could stay on deck in the fresh sea air, and there'd been such a general expectation she would go, it hadn't been in her to let everyone down.

Despite a few wobbles, on the whole she had found she'd enjoyed the day and she knew in her heart of hearts it had been a significant step towards rejoining the world. Not one she could take comfortably – far from it – but definitely a box she now felt able to tick. She'd been quite elated by her progress, and the warm glow of achievement stayed with her even now.

Claire looked around the shop. Everything was ready for opening, but that was still almost an hour away. She walked over to the table by the till and picked up a copy of Karmela's book club choice from last week. It wasn't a novel she'd need to read; she'd studied it to death for her A-level, so the similarities between Karmela and Elinor Dashwood were far from lost on her.

She wondered what Karmela herself would make of the book; she'd admitted she hadn't read it, just chosen a Jane Austen at random. Would she even notice how like Elinor she was? Fond as Claire was becoming of her, Karmela didn't always strike her as the most self-aware of people, but you never could tell. Not really.

Claire was certainly having trouble understanding Vedran at the moment. He still hadn't looked at those pictures. Nor had he come to book club, just texted an apology. When Claire had called him afterwards he hadn't seemed willing to talk, leaving her tossing and turning most of the night. But in the morning there'd been a message on her phone, asking if there was anything special she'd like for supper on Friday, and Friday had been … well … normal. Claire sighed. She just needed to be patient with him. She knew it herself, and Gran had agreed.

She turned in a slow circle, inhaling that special new book

smell she never tired of. She'd come in early, looking forward to a good catch up with Luna about yesterday, so now what could she do? Then she remembered. Luna had spoken about cleaning the table and chairs in the courtyard, as now the weather was better they could sit outside to drink their coffee and eat their lunch.

The lock on the kitchen door was stiff after a winter of disuse, but eventually Claire managed to turn the large brass key, making a mental note to ask Nono for something from his toolbox to lubricate it. Rubbing her fingers, she stepped outside. The air was fresh and cool, but sunlight flooded the corner to her left, where she could see a pale pink metal table pushed against the wall, with two matching chairs folded beside it.

She crossed the flagstones, stepping over the weeds growing in the cracks. The buildings surrounded the space completely and all she could see above the fringe of terracotta roof tiles topping the walls was a glimpse of Mount Srd and an expanse of sky. Swallows flitted to and fro, disappearing under the eaves to their nests, and from the kitchen window of the restaurant in the far corner came the muted sound of a radio.

As Claire was opening the chairs and shaking off the worst of the winter dust, she heard the faintest of squeaks. She frowned to herself. No, it wasn't quite a squeak; it was more of a high-pitched half excuse for a mew, and she began to look around for its source.

Partly obscured by the bottom of a drainpipe she discovered a small ginger and white cat. Its head was beautifully marked, with dark orange stripes running between its ears to form a furrowed brow, but its body was painfully thin. When it tried to raise itself to look at her, its head wobbled violently from side to side, ears batting backwards and forwards like a pair of wings.

Claire sat on her heels. She'd come across a cat who did this before, when her friend's mother had adopted what she'd called a "wobbly kitten". It had been born with some disease with a long Latin name but it had been a darling little thing, although it walked a bit like it was drunk, and certainly couldn't jump and play the way other cats could.

She reached out towards the cat and it squeaked again, shuffling further into its corner, although it was far too weak to move very far. She spoke softly to it and ran her fingers along its back, feeling each and every rib along the way. Of course she couldn't be sure until she'd seen it walk, but a wobbly cat would hardly be able to hunt, would it? How on earth had it managed to survive almost to adulthood?

Very gently she slid her hands under its body and picked it up. It scrabbled weakly in her arms, its head shaking and ears flapping again. But after a few moments its whole body flopped and she was able to carry it towards the back door.

A movement in the kitchen caught her eye. Simeon. She wasn't expecting him today. Was something wrong? She'd hardly had time to think it when he appeared at the back door.

"Luna not in yet?" His voice sounded uncharacteristically sharp.

"N … no. She has the morning off."

"*Sranje*. I wanted to tell you both together. Now I will have to leave it to you."

"Tell us what?"

He sighed. "Sorry I snapped. This isn't going to be easy. Put that cat down and come inside."

Claire sensed this was not the moment to argue. The cat was in no fit state to go very far, so she set it gently under the table and followed him into the kitchen.

"Shall I make coffee?" she asked.

He shook his head. "Maybe after. Sit down for a moment."

She lowered herself onto the chair opposite him, full of trepidation.

"Claire, I am so sorry, but the shop will have to close."

"Close?"

"Yes. At the end of September." He spread his hands. "We tried. We really did try, and it could have worked. In fact with the tourists coming back it is working. But the landlord's increasing the rent. It will be almost double and we can't afford that. Even if I come back to run it myself."

"Oh, Simeon, I'm so sorry. You've worked for years to make The Welcoming Bookshop everything it is." There was a huge lump in her throat as she said it. First his wife's illness, now his life's work…

He shrugged. "Nadia is my focus now. And for you, well, it just means you will have to leave a few months early, but for Luna…"

The words hung between them. A bee buzzed outside the small square window, bumping against the glass. A bright little bee like Luna, so full of energy and joy. And just as her personal life was beginning to come together.

"I will ask for her in the other bookshops, of course," Simeon said. "But they keep so few staff all year I am not hopeful."

Claire found she was biting back tears. "Is there anything I can do to help?"

"Only tell her gently, please. I am so sorry you have to do this, but Nadia has an appointment with the nurse this afternoon, and her chemo tomorrow, and I can't miss those."

"Of course you can't. Don't worry, I can handle it." Could she? Well, she would have to find a way.

"Thank you, Claire. I know you'll be kind." His smile was a shadow of its usual self. "Now, how about that coffee? Then you can open up while I look through the paperwork. I might as well do that, seeing as I'm here."

Claire was relieved when Simeon left quite soon, and not just because she could rush back into the courtyard and set a dish of milk as close as she could to the cat's head. The shop bell rang just as she was doing it. Bugger. She'd have to come back later to see how it was getting on.

As the morning ticked by she became herself increasingly preoccupied with how she was going to break the news to Luna. Between every customer she found herself phrasing it a different way, but nothing she could think of would even remotely soften the blow.

Now it was sinking in she felt bad enough about it herself, sort of weepy and numb at the same time. She couldn't understand why she felt so bad. She'd never planned to be here beyond December. That had been the deal – a year. No more. But somehow the city had started to feel like home, and working in the bookshop felt so, well, safe. That was it; safe. It was probably an illusion, but at least in Dubrovnik there were a few places where she didn't feel as though Covid was lurking around every corner, and that meant a great deal.

A steady stream of customers kept Claire busy, so when Luna bounced through the door she was no nearer finding the right words. Except she'd decided it would have to be after work. It was Easter after all and the street outside was packed with people, most of whom seemed to be looking for reading matter or at the very least a city guide in English or Japanese.

It was almost an hour before they had time to draw breath, and Luna was positively glowing.

"I keep pinching myself," she said. "I can't believe it's finally happened. And Louise is so lovely." She twirled around. "Don't worry – no broken hearts – I mean, how can you fall in love when you only have twenty-four hours together? But Claire, Claire … being kissed … being…"

Claire tried her best to smile. "I'm so pleased it was everything you dreamed it would be."

"And more." She giggled. "Even Ezra ragging me about doing the walk of shame on the early morning bus. I don't care! I didn't stay at home long anyway – I had brunch with Louise and her friends overlooking the Western Harbour. They've invited me to London and everything."

"I've invited you to London," Claire pointed out.

"Yes, but this would be different." She gave her a hug. "You do understand, don't you?"

"Of course I do." Only too well. This was everything Luna had yearned for. So how on earth could Claire possibly shatter her bubble when it was still so fresh and shiny and new? But something about her manner must have given her away, because Luna stopped twirling and asked if anything was wrong.

Think, Claire, think. "I … I found a stray cat in the courtyard this morning."

"So?" Luna was right. Stray cats were all over Dubrovnik.

"There's something wrong with it. I think it's what we call a wobbly cat, but I can't be sure until I see it walk."

"It's not walking?"

"No, it's too weak, poor little—" But Luna was gone, leaving the curtain swaying in her wake, just as another two customers walked in.

Five minutes later she was flying back through the shop. "Oh, what a little darling! I'm just nipping to the minimarket for some cat food. I won't be long."

Another thing that was making Luna happy, Claire thought glumly as she filled the space on the shelf with another couple of guide books. Oh well, she'd give her tonight to enjoy the glow at least. Tomorrow. She'd tell her tomorrow. It would give her a bit more time to get over the news herself. And to work out what to say.

Karmela

Karmela set out early for the old town. She had already
been working for a couple of hours, pulling together her
research notes from the day before. She had quite a file on Filipa
Menčetić, and had begun to hunt down her sole notable
contemporary, Nikoleta Sarkocevic. While it was satisfying to
have got so much done, it had been deeply unsettling to have
been woken by Rafael's weeping. Again.

She had successfully managed to avoid him for a couple of
weeks after their argument, although she had heard him
stumbling up the stairs drunk on more than one occasion. Then
yesterday she had bumped into him as he was coming off a night
shift and they had nodded to each other, but his eyes had been
downcast and failed to meet hers.

Claire had texted her on Saturday to tell her a book she had
ordered had arrived, so she wanted to collect it before her research
slot in the archives later this morning. There was a gentle buzz
and hum around the narrow streets as locals and visitors alike sat
outside the cafés with coffee and pastries, bland Europop drifting
around them, mingling with the smell of bacon. How people

could eat such salty cooked meat first thing in the morning, Karmela did not know.

It was taking her a while to adjust to the city in the tourist season. At first it had seemed its history had disappeared beneath awnings and behind tables and chairs, but it was still there if you looked hard enough, and Karmela delighted in the thrill of discovery. A tiny statue of Sveti Vlaho high above the door of a former noble house in Prijeko Ulica, and close to the Minčeta tower, a perfect round stained-glass window that had somehow survived the mortars of the 1991 siege.

As she turned into Gundulićeva Poljana the Green Market was in full swing, the red and white umbrellas protecting tables full of aubergines and tomatoes and buckets of fresh flowers from the warmth of the morning sun. Now the season was underway the fruit and vegetable stallholders were joined by women with gnarled walnut-brown faces selling traditional goods for the tourists: homemade lavender bags, painstakingly embroidered in purple and blue, small bottles of *rakija* and olive oil, and slabs of traditional fig cake wrapped in cellophane dressed with ribbons.

Karmela loved the continuity of it all. People from the country had been coming to the city to sell their wares for generations. The women she was writing about would have seen them as well, although at that time they would have gathered around Orlando's column. Of course these wealthy ladies would not have shopped themselves, but perhaps they would have peeped between the curtains of their palanquins, where women of high birth were hidden from the world whenever they left their homes.

When Karmela arrived at The Welcoming Bookshop she was surprised the bell rang out into an empty shop. She waited for a few moments, then called Claire's name. There was no answer, then she thought she heard a muffled sob from behind the velvet curtain.

Without a second thought as to whether she should interfere,

Karmela peeped around. Both Luna and Claire were sitting at the table, Claire red-eyed, her arm across Luna's shoulder as she wept into her hands. The English girl looked up when she saw her.

"Whatever is the matter?" Karmela asked. Someone must have died, someone they both knew by the look of it. She hung back next to the curtain. Was she intruding or was there something she could do to help? And what could you do, in such a situation? Make coffee perhaps? But now she had asked she had to brazen it out before, she hoped, making a dignified retreat.

"It's the shop," Claire said. "It's going to have to close. I mean, it's sad for me, but for Luna it's totally heart-breaking."

Now that was shocking news. No wonder they were both so upset. "But that is awful. What will happen to this place?"

"I don't know. The landlord wants to double the rent and the owner can't afford it. We import almost all of our books so the margins just aren't there. It's not like we're a fast food joint or a tourist shop that can make a fortune in the summer and close all winter."

"Double the rent? That sounds like extortion." Karmela did not know much about business, but this she could barely believe.

"He must think someone will pay it."

"Someone who will no doubt ruin this beautiful old building." Karmela gazed at the alternating plain and decorated corbels supporting the pitted wooden beam that ran the length of the wall. It would be a travesty if that was allowed to happen.

Finally Luna looked up, her eye makeup smudging her cheeks like bruises. "And we'll lose our jobs. I can't go back to being a chambermaid. I just can't."

Karmela pulled out a chair and sat on the other side of her. "And neither should you have to, a bright girl like you. What about the big bookshop on Stradun?"

"Simeon said he'd ask," Claire told her, "but they lay off so many of their staff in the winter and Luna needs a year-round job to stay in Dubrovnik."

"And I can't go back to Šipan, I can't! Not when I've come so far … not when I've finally got a life."

Her words struck Karmela as a little hysterical. She was young, she would find something else, even if she had to go home to her island to regroup for a while.

"You see it's different for Luna," Claire said, squeezing her friend's hand. "She's gay, but no one on Šipan knows. Her parents are very religious…"

"The whole bloody community is," Luna mumbled. "I'd have to start living a lie all over again."

"I cannot stand that sort of prejudice," said Karmela. "Years ago I had a student who took his own life because of it, and it is something I have never forgotten."

Luna looked at her, blinking back her tears. "You understand?"

"Of course I do."

The girl looked so vulnerable. For a fleeting moment she reminded Karmela of someone, something, a long time ago, but the thought was gone before she could place it, leaving her with a desperate urge to rock Luna in her arms to protect her. She was way further in here than she was comfortable with, and needed to steer the conversation back onto solid ground.

She gave Luna's hand a quick pat. "There must be a way of saving the shop."

Claire shook her head. "I've been awake all night trying to find one. Although I have an escape route back to London, I don't feel ready to take it. I had Long Covid really badly and I feel so much safer here. Perhaps that isn't completely logical, but it is what it is."

"You and Luna are both too emotional to think straight at the moment. There must be something. How about we ask your cousin Vedran? I seem to remember him saying he was a lawyer, so he should have a different perspective." Most likely a dispassionate one too, but she did not say it.

"I guess … I guess he would," said Claire.

"Is there anyone else in the book club who might be able to help?" Karmela asked, warming to her task.

"Vedran is our best bet."

"Then it is settled. Ask him over here one evening after the shop closes and I will come too and bring pizza. Then we can put our heads together and see if we can find a solution."

Luna shuffled her bottom on the seat like an uncomfortable child. "I don't know if I should be there. Vedran … well … I've upset him, that's for sure. He didn't even come to the last book club."

Karmela noticed Claire shoot Luna a puzzled glance, but nothing was said, so she carried on. "Whatever your differences, surely you can put them behind you for the sake of the shop?"

Claire bit her lip. "It's … it's … complicated. And I'm not being funny, not telling you. It isn't mine to tell. Or Luna's either."

Luna sat up straight. "You're right, Karmela, the shop is more important. I'll stop being a coward and apologise. I should have done it way before now. Then it's up to him whether he accepts it or not."

Karmela stood, keen to be away before any more of these uncomfortable secrets reignited the atmosphere. "Good girl. Now, I came in to collect that Hilary Mantel you ordered for me, Claire. I am sorry it turned out to be at a bad time."

"I'd say your timing was pretty damned perfect. A dose of your common sense was just what we needed. We might have wallowed all day otherwise, and I don't know about Luna, but I certainly feel a bit more positive now. Even if it comes to nothing, at least we'll have tried."

"I am very pleased I was able to help." But all the same, the emotions swirling around her were making Karmela feel a little shaky. Best just pay for the book and be on her way to the archives where she could lose herself in the world of the Ragusans. Her happy place. Her safe place.

But the bookshop was Claire's safe place as well as Luna's best chance of an independent future. And safe places were very important, hard to find, and to be protected at all costs. This was not only about making sure the interior of this beautiful old building was preserved. There were other reasons to do everything she could to help them save it. But for now she had her own work to do.

Luna

For once Luna was far from hungry. Even the aroma of fresh tomatoes and garlic drifting from the bowl of *slani inćuna* salad Fran had bought made no difference. And she hadn't eaten all her sandwiches at lunchtime either.

She was dreading this evening. Claire seemed hopeful something would come out of it, but just what, Luna could not see. The job she loved was finished, over. And on top of that she would have to face Vedran. It was no wonder she couldn't eat. She so did not want to see him.

She had phoned him to apologise, like she had told Karmela she would, but it had not gone well. Oh, he hadn't been rude or nasty; in fact he'd been very polite. Chillingly polite. Totally awkward. After that she'd almost bottled this evening, but Claire had persuaded her Vedran was the one person who might be able to help save the bookshop.

Luna picked up a cloth from beside the sink, wringing it out viciously, then headed for the courtyard. She'd cried herself to sleep for the last three nights. Without this job she would lose everything – everything – she'd managed to gain so far. She couldn't go back to Šipan. Couldn't and wouldn't. But no way would she live on Ezra's charity. She shuddered. Anything but charity. Even in Dubrovnik there were so few year-round jobs, and her rather basic qualifications were nothing to write home about. Besides, the job she wanted more than anything was this one. This one! Tears pooled in the backs of her eyes again. *Jebem ti!*

Mis, the little wobbly cat who seemed to have adopted them, was stretched out in a patch of sunlight on the far side of the paving, but stirred when she saw Luna and staggered over with her strange waddle, bumping herself around Luna's legs while she dusted the chairs. She and Claire were feeding the poor creature every day, but what would happen to her when the shop had to close? This just got worse and worse.

"Oh, Mis, it's just so unfair. To both of us." *Bože*, she sounded like some petulant child from primary school, but she felt damned well petulant. She had every right to be petulant. Super-freakin' petulant. And some.

With a dramatic sigh Luna returned to the kitchen to rinse out the cloth. Claire was in the office, studying some figures Simeon had given her along with the lease. It was all right for her. She was clever. She could go home to England and get another job. Beyond September, Luna's life was empty. She hiccupped. *Fuggin' hell, Luna, get a grip*.

A few minutes later there was a rap on the glass of the door. Karmela or Vedran? Claire's head was still bent over the papers so Luna had no choice but to go. *Sranje*. It was Vedran.

At least she managed a sort of smile as she let him in. He was carrying two bottles of wine and set them on the nearest shelf before turning to her.

"Thank you for your apology and I'm sorry if I seemed ungracious. This whole thing is doing my head in. In some ways finding Didi is as hard as losing her."

He was hurting too. She should have known that, of course she should. But she'd let her own feelings take over, so she forgot everyone else's. Again. When did she get so selfish? She looked up at him. "I understand that. Well, I do now, anyway. I feel massively bad that my thoughtlessness has caused you so much upset."

He gazed around as though he had never seen the bookshop before, unable to meet her eyes. "It's just so … complicated. That's all. I can't explain."

"So the photos are Didi?"

"I haven't looked at them yet." He shrugged. "Every morning I tell myself today will be the day, and every evening I say it will be tomorrow."

Luna could relate to that all right. Telling him why was a risk, but she owed him big time, and anyway, her secret was hardly a secret anymore. Not in Dubrovnik at least.

"I so get that. I'm gay, you see, but for the longest time I wasn't out. I wanted to tell Claire for ages and it was exactly the same; every day on the bus to work I would promise myself I'd do it today; every night on the way home, it would be tomorrow."

"Do you mind me asking, what made you tell her in the end?"

"It was when she showed me a photo of Belle. It opened the door, you see."

"Hmm…"

"Vedran?"

"Yes?"

"Someone will open the door for you too, you know."

He half smiled. "You and your friend already have."

She shook her head violently. "All we have done is shown you a door exists."

"You are a wise little thing, aren't you?" he replied. "But come on, we have a bookshop to save and here's Karmela with the pizza."

Luna gathered the available cutlery and crockery, while Vedran opened the wine. She really wanted to make some cheerful conversation but the words would not come, and she was relieved that as soon as they went outside and gathered around the table Karmela got straight down to business by asking Vedran if increasing the rent so much was legal.

"It may not be moral, but it's probably legal. Unless there's something in the lease to prevent it. If Simeon was well advised at the time there might be, so I can only hope."

"It's a huge document," Claire said. "I was expecting a few pages."

"I'll have to take it away to look at so you won't have an answer tonight. I'll do it tomorrow, I promise, before I head off to see my parents in Pula. Although to be honest I am not hopeful about what I might find. This sort of thing is happening all over the old town. Already it is bad enough, but soon there will be only shops for the tourists."

"And no one living here either," Claire said. "Nono often talks about how much it's changed, how lucky they are to own their apartment. Nobody from around here can afford the rents and flats lie empty all winter because of it."

"I loved it here during the off season," Karmela said. "But I do not think I quite realised the impact on local people."

"Some weeks we didn't take enough to cover our wages," Claire told her, "but Simeon said not to worry because he had money in the bank from last summer. I'm just so sad for him," she carried on, the anguish in her voice making Luna well up. "It's his life work, and with Nadia being so ill too…"

There was a silence, which Karmela's calm voice broke. "Then perhaps we should not simply rely on the lease. We need to think of other ways to save the bookshop."

"Maybe we can speak to the landlord, explain. Tell him Simeon's wife has cancer and…"

Vedran shook his head. "Luna, I don't think that will work.

They will just see this shop as an asset to make the maximum money from. There's a whole raft of people in Dubrovnik who don't even work anymore. They own a property like this, or if they are really lucky, more than one, so they don't have to. Just buy swanky cars and clothes and sit around in the cafés all day."

"I didn't realise…" *O bože*. This was impossible. She'd been right all along. How had she let that little seed of hope creep in? She covered her mouth with her hand to prevent a sob.

"Come on, Luna, no tears. We have not lost yet," said Karmela. "We need to stay calm and think this through logically."

What the hell was there to think about? And yet it was hard not to trust Karmela, she was so assured, so clever. The exact opposite of what Luna felt right at this moment: too young, too inexperienced, and out of her depth. She reached down and fed Mis a piece of ham from her pizza. What could she possibly contribute? There wasn't so much as a single idea in her head. Even Claire was looking as though the cogs in her brain were whirring, while Luna's were in free fall.

"Right," said Karmela, "we should break the problem down. That always helps. In its most basic terms, the only thing the shop is losing is its place to operate from. Everything else is fine. So in essence we need to find a way to stay here – which Vedran will hopefully do with the lease – or work out where else we could trade from instead."

"So it really could be as simple as finding new premises?" Claire mused. "I have no idea why I didn't think of that."

"But where, apart from the old town?" Vedran asked. "You need to be near the tourists."

"There are other places," said Karmela. "I live near the cable car station and it is always busy around there."

"And the harbour at Gruž, where they come off the ferries," added Luna. "Or the airport." She thought again. "But no. That is too far for our local customers and the students."

"Maybe somewhere near the university," suggested Karmela.

"But then the tourists would not find us." Claire picked up her glass of wine, then put it down again.

"You cannot be in more than one place, though," said Karmela, "that would be even more expensive."

"Maybe ... maybe..." Claire started, "and I haven't thought this through ... there is a way to be everywhere and nowhere. We go online. A virtual bookshop. But how we'd do it and get the right profile... I mean, the competition in that market must be huge."

This was a question Luna could answer. "Ezra would know how to go about it." Of course he would. He'd found Didi after all. He was an internet genius. Suddenly hungry, Luna grabbed another slice of pizza. "And I know he'd help. Claire – you're really onto something."

"So," said Karmela, "we have a few things to work on. Vedran, you have the lease and staying here is still our best option. Claire, you explore whether it is possible to move online and how that might work." She frowned. "That leaves me looking around for other properties, but even though I do not know Dubrovnik that well I can make a start."

So she'd been left out. Luna slumped in her seat. Put down her pizza. They really did think she was too dumb to add anything to the process. Or at the very least, too emotional. They were right, but sod them all the same.

But no, no. She could not let that happen. It was her job, her life, more than anyone's. And she would not be a bystander.

"What about me?" she asked.

Claire reached around the table and gave her a hug. "You have the most important job of all. Someone has to run the bookshop while I'm in the back room crunching numbers and making plans. We can't let things slide. It's even more important we make as much money as possible this summer. We'll need every last *kuna* to make this happen."

Luna returned her hug. Claire believed in her, at least. "I won't let you down, I promise. Nobody will leave without buying at least two books. Three, maybe." This wasn't the moment to doubt if she could do it. What was it Claire told her she used to say when she was pretending not to be scared of Covid? Fake it until you make it? That was exactly what Luna was going to do.

Vedran

Vedran's heart sank when he saw the name of Simeon's lawyer as he pulled the lease out of its manila envelope. This would not be good. Oh, they weren't real fly-by-night boys; they just had a reputation for charging the minimum and doing the minimum too. Without even reading the document he already knew the landlord would be able to treat Simeon exactly how he wanted.

He flung the package onto his desk and escaped into the sunshine on the terrace. Already barbecue smells were drifting from the rental villa next door, and through the hedge came the sound of children laughing. In another life he would have been preparing to be a father by now. But he couldn't allow himself to think that way, it would drag him down, and today he needed to focus. Be sure he wouldn't miss any loophole that shoddy lease might present.

At least he could look at the bay without pain, and that must mean he believed it was Didi in those pictures. Claire's email was sinking further and further down his inbox as the days turned into weeks, and now it had fallen so far he no longer saw it every time he logged on. But he knew it was there; of course he did. Taunting him. Like Didi herself had done so many times.

The concrete felt smooth beneath his bare feet as he walked down the steps and sat on the jetty, cool ripples of water spreading around his feet. The frills of waves caressing the rocks sparkled in the fresh, clear light and in the distance a trip boat headed out to sea, no doubt taking tourists to see the famous Blue Cave on Koločep. Just a normal Saturday morning.

What had Saturdays been like before Didi? It seemed so long ago. Waking with his long-term girlfriend Malina, breakfasting on his terrace or the balcony of her apartment in Lapad. Looking forward to lunch with friends. Mutual friends he had completely lost touch with. Not surprising. He must have hurt Malina so badly, yet at the time he'd been too obsessed with Didi to do anything other than tell her he'd met someone else, then watch her walk away.

Obsession. That's what it had been. Looking back he had no doubt. Oh, he'd believed he loved Didi, and that she loved him. He'd wanted, hoped, dreamed of them being together forever. Right until the end, really. Right to the point she'd told him she was having an abortion, whether he liked it or not. She'd never even said she was pregnant. If he hadn't found the positive test when he was emptying the bathroom bin he might never have known.

But that would have been calculated too. Didi would never have made such a careless mistake. He punched his fist into his palm as anger flowed through him. If he could see it all so clearly now, why had he not been able to then? He was such a bloody fool.

He had confronted her as soon as she came home; her words, her laughter even, the realisation she had no intention of keeping their child, forcing through him like shards of ice. Ice turning to white cold fury. Fury like never before. His hands gripping her shoulders, moving towards her neck. The only time he had ever touched her, except in love. And in that moment he had known what she'd done to him, what she'd made him become. And he'd hated himself all the more.

Ach, this was getting him nowhere. Pointless introspection. Waste of time. Better to get angry about the lease that meant poor old Simeon could get royally screwed by his landlord, and Luna and Claire would lose their jobs. He had to find a way to help them. They'd helped him, after all, even though at the time he'd far from welcomed it. But in his heart of hearts he knew what they'd found was the key to getting his life back. A life, anyway. If only he had the balls to do something about it.

If he couldn't find the courage to help himself, then perhaps he could find it to help them? That was why he'd become a lawyer, after all. To fight injustice. God, that sounded impossibly up himself, but it was how he felt. Little guys in business should have rights too. And if it took him away from the safety of his study, to somewhere far beyond his comfort zone? Well, he'd cross that bridge when he came to it. But for Claire, and for Luna, he would do it.

But several hours later he knew for certain that Simeon had signed most of his rights away. There was no restriction on rent increases, no right of appeal. Nothing that could help. The best he could do would be to talk to the landlord, but inevitably his reputation would precede him. Would he even be taken seriously? Maybe he'd ask a colleague to do it instead. *Oh, you frigging coward, Vedran. Man up and look at those photos.*

He opened his mailbox and stared at the screen. From here it would take a scroll, then just a few clicks. Find the email, open it, open a photo. But his fingers froze on his keyboard as what would happen next flicked through his mind. The police station, the cell, the questions... Questions he could not answer then, and could not now. God, he'd been hiding so much it was little wonder they'd suspected him. But one thing was for sure, he couldn't bear the whole wretched cycle beginning again.

Vedran stood slowly, recognising the start of the road that led to the whisky bottle. He couldn't let that happen; couldn't lose yet another Saturday in a miasma of booze and tears. But what could he do? He spun slowly around, seeking inspiration. And then it struck him; there were Didi's clothes to clear out, for starters. Another job that was way overdue, but perhaps today was the day. If he did it before his trip to Pula, if he could obliterate the memories that lurked behind closed cupboard doors, when he came home he could start afresh.

His determination growing with every step, he marched to the kitchen and grabbed a rubbish bag from under the sink. Then on to the bedroom, yanking open the mirrored door of her wardrobe. Her perfume assailed him; stale now, but instantly recognisable as the Dior Private Collection smoked wood and damascus rose she'd begged him to buy for her, mingled with the salty sweetness that was Didi's alone. The vivid reds and purples she'd favoured pressed against his eyes; dresses, skirts, tops with plunging necklines ... an assault on his senses that was the very essence of her.

He reached out his hand, surprised to see it was shaking. It met with the silver top she'd been wearing the first time he saw her, but instead of dragging it from its hanger and stuffing it into the bag, once it was in his hands he found himself stroking the shimmering fabric, his fingertips tingling with memories and regret. He must have done something to make her behave as she had. Must have. She'd said it was all his fault. So many times.

He dropped onto the bed, staring at the river of silver in his hands. Slippery, slithering, so hard to hold onto. Just like Didi. She had never been his, not really. He saw that now. But he had been hers, all right, just where she wanted him. Whenever she wanted him. However she wanted him. And that was a shame he would take to the grave.

He didn't love her now, that was for sure. She had gone, months ago, so why was her hold on him still so strong? It wasn't the first time he'd asked himself that question, *sranje* no, but it was still too frightening to answer. He looked at the open wardrobe door; at the rows of shoes, the cerise leopard-print dress, the Bottega Veneta jeans he'd loved to see her wear, and had most likely paid for. He felt sick inside. He could not bear to touch them, let alone clear them away.

But neither could he let her win this particular battle. His fight back had to start somewhere. He stood, closed the wardrobe door, then took her silver top into the kitchen, where he grabbed the scissors, opened the bin, and cut it into a hundred pieces.

Claire

Claire had been more than surprised to see a WhatsApp from Ezra when she woke, asking if she was running this morning, and now she was waiting for him near the balustrade where he had waited for her not much more than a month before. And what a tumultuous month it had proved to be.

She didn't want to think about that now; she needed to escape for at least a little while, so she focused on the view in front of her. It was spectacular, making the jog up the steep incline worth every aching muscle and ragged breath. Straight ahead, colours muted by the morning sun behind it, stood Lovrijenac Fortress high on its promontory, surrounded by a sea that was almost silver blue beneath cloudless skies. Beyond it was the old town, a blur of terracotta roofs enclosed in a ribbon of iron-grey walls. Just looking at how strong they were, how long they had lasted, made her problems feel insignificant and small.

She heard running footsteps behind her and as she turned Ezra drew to a halt, pushing his overlong fringe out of his eyes.

"Thank you. Thank you for agreeing to meet me. Luna told me

you have an idea of taking the shop online, and she is so sad at the moment…" He shrugged. "I just want to make it better for her."

"So do I. She's come so far in recent months, but last night she didn't even want to meet the others in the jazz café."

They began to walk around the ornamental pond, their trainers crunching on the shingly gravel. "And what about you, Claire? You're losing your job too," Ezra asked.

"I was only ever meant to be here for a year."

"So you don't mind very much?" He looked at her with his soft brown eyes.

"Actually, I do. Half of me hoped that Simeon might keep me on longer."

"Half of you?"

"Yes, because it was a really selfish thought. It would mean his wife was still ill and all of us want her to get better more than anything."

"I get that, but it's good you are happy in Dubrovnik. You don't miss London?"

"I miss my parents but my sister's away at uni. And it's not as though I'm on my own here."

"Yes, Luna said you live with your gran and her husband."

"They're good people. I … I don't really want to leave them either…" Yesterday had been a bad day; Nono had forgotten he was meant to be stirring the risotto and it had burnt to the pan. And the more patient Gran had been with him, the more angry he had become at himself.

Claire suddenly found herself fighting back tears.

"Hey, hey," said Ezra softly, "you're hurting more than you're letting on, aren't you?"

"No, I'm fine." Claire sniffed.

"I bet you're the sort of person who says that whenever they feel someone's worse off than them."

"You sound just like my gran. And you're not wrong, either."

"It's good to be strong, Claire, but not all the time. If you want to give yourself a break, I'm listening."

She saw why Luna liked him. He was so much more than the geek she'd complained about, wrapped up in his cyber world. There was a sensitivity to other people's feelings in him too, a real empathy.

"This is just between us, OK? Although I have told Luna." He nodded. "My *nono*'s in the early stages of dementia. I mean, most of the time you wouldn't know, but yesterday was a bad day, and on top of everything else…" She stopped to gather herself. "I suppose it was a bit much. Even though they could do with my support, I know without a job Gran will send me packing. I lost so much time to Covid, you see, she wants me to get on with my life."

They reached a bench with a view out over the bay. A lone cypress guarded the long finger of rock that stretched across one corner, the rugged grey stones washed by the wake of a passing boat. The chug of its engine reached them, a deep counterpoint to the birdsong filling the trees.

"You had Covid badly?"

"Long Covid. For months and months … and every time I thought I was better I relapsed. Again and again. It took almost a year and a half for me to be completely right. Until I started at the bookshop I hadn't worked since March 2020."

"That sounds really tough. I can't imagine not working. I don't know how I'd fill my days."

"When you're ill you fill it with sleeping and watching trash TV. And feeling guilty because you're a burden on your family, and wondering if you'll ever be well again."

"But you are well now?"

"Yes." She lifted her fingers and crossed them. "So far, so good."

Ezra sat next to her, stretching his long legs towards the tile-topped wall. "So if we hadn't had a pandemic, what would you have done? What time did you lose that your gran is so anxious you make up now?"

"Good question. Workwise this job has given me the chance to get back on track. I'd never have got management experience so early at the bookshop where I worked in London. But what I really lost was the chance to travel, and I think Gran's so passionate about me doing it because she feels she left it almost too late in life to do so herself. I'd planned to take a year out, to volunteer on literacy programmes around the world. That isn't going to happen now."

"Why not?"

"For a start, the friend I was going with is busy planning her wedding. And I'm still too nervous of being in crowded places in case I catch Covid again. I mean, I have got better since I've been here, but I still struggle to go inside a bar or restaurant. Thank goodness the jazz café's tables are on the square."

When she glanced at Ezra he was looking at her intently, something about his expression making Claire want to blush. Had she over-shared? She hardly knew the guy after all. God, how embarrassing. Enough to make her toes curl in her trainers.

"That's quite enough of my woes," she said, as briskly as she could. "Tell me about yourself."

"It's not that interesting a story."

"I'd still like to hear it."

"Honestly?" That half-smile again; the one that seemed to change the shape of his face and light it from inside out. She nodded.

"OK … well…" He cleared his throat, then looked away from her, out towards the sea. "As you know I grew up on Šipan with Luna. I liked school, although we did not have many opportunities on a small island, but I was lucky and I got a job in

IT. I've been writing software since I was about twelve, taught myself online, so it was easy to pass their tests and get in."

"Is that why you came to Dubrovnik?"

"It was the excuse, not the reason. I work mainly from home so I could have stayed on Šipan but I found it overpowering living with my family. I wanted my own space and to be independent. I have a sister and brother still at home, and a married sister three doors away. There was never any peace. The reality is I could work anywhere and I was toying with the idea of becoming a digital nomad when Luna needed somewhere to live in the city."

"A digital nomad?" The term sounded vaguely familiar, but Claire wasn't entirely sure what it meant.

"Yes, there are quite a lot of them in Croatia, but you find them the world over. People who can work anywhere as long as there's a good internet connection. It struck me as a great way to see the world."

"Well, if you ever do it you'll have to write a blog so I can follow you vicariously." It was the closest she was going to get. The closest she wanted to, to be honest. Sure, it sounded exciting enough, but the reality of travel with Covid lurking around every corner was rather too much for her to contemplate.

"I won't be going anywhere for a while," Ezra told her, "I don't want to let Luna down. The worst thing about all this is she was getting her life so sorted." He paused, screwing up his mouth in a really cute way. "I still think she should come out to her parents, though."

"She says they'd never accept it."

"That's probably true."

"What are they like?" If she knew that, Claire might well understand Luna's reticence, and help her to overcome it.

"I think the real problem is her father. He's very traditional. And if I'm honest – although you mustn't say I've said this – not a very nice man. My mum went out with him for a while when they were younger and she once told me she'd had a lucky escape."

Claire frowned. "In what way?"

"I didn't press the question. But I'd guess it's because he's never wrong and he blames Luna's mother for everything. It doesn't make for a very nice atmosphere."

"It's amazing Luna's as bubbly as she is."

"She's a fighter, all right, and I suppose being relentlessly positive about everything is her way of coping. And while it's brilliant on one level, it can be really irritating before I've had my first coffee of the morning." He laughed. "I feel a bit bad talking about her behind her back, but the fact is you're really easy to talk to."

He was too, Claire thought. It was even comfortable when they lapsed into silence, watching the wisps of cloud skate across the sky as the pines rustled silvery-green against the blue of the sea.

Eventually Ezra spoke. "Still, what we're actually here to discuss is taking the bookshop online."

"It feels like something we should explore, but I know it won't be easy. Do you have any ideas?"

"A few. But they're not for now. I wouldn't want to exclude Luna from this, would you? How about we all get together to brainstorm one night this week?"

"Great idea. I'll talk to Luna tomorrow and we'll work something out."

It was only when Claire was jogging back down the slope towards the Western Harbour that she began to wonder why, if that was all he had to say on the matter, Ezra had asked to meet her. They could have very easily agreed it with a few messages. But whatever his reasons, she was glad. He was such a genuine guy, and Luna was lucky to have him as a friend. It had been a lovely respite from her growing list of worries to get to know him a little better.

Luna

"It's not like where you live," Luna gabbled. "I mean, super-not like. No marble floors and fancy ironwork. We're just kids from a small island. Don't expect too much."

Why she was so nervous about Claire coming to supper she didn't know. It was crazy, but everything seemed so stressful at the moment. *Calm down, Luna.* Claire was her best friend. She'd never judged anything about her and she wasn't going to start now.

As if to emphasise the point, Claire wrapped her arm around her shoulder. "All I expect is to have a nice evening with you both and hopefully end up with some ideas about how we can take the business online. I do know how lucky I am to live where I do, but the apartment has been in Jadran's family since the 1940s at least. And I know all about grotty flats from when I was a student."

Even so, seeing the entrance hall through Claire's eyes made Luna shudder. A lick of paint was too much to hope for, but a good dust to remove the dead flies shouldn't be beyond whoever owned this place, and some air freshener wouldn't go amiss either. At least that sodding bike wasn't here to trip over. And Luna didn't dare tell Claire she never used the lift because she'd found a syringe in it once, so instead she claimed climbing the stairs helped her to stay fit.

At least the apartment itself would be presentable because she'd spent yesterday evening cleaning it, and for all his faults, Ezra was hardly likely to have trashed it during the day. She'd kill him if he had. *Bože*, she was so bloody negative at the moment. So stressed. But she knew that, really she did. She'd given herself a stern talking to on the bus this morning. She would not give in. She was going to fight.

Claire was always good at seeing the positives, but Luna had to concede she wasn't going over the top when she exclaimed about the view. Below the living room picture windows the tongue of silver-blue water forming the port glistened, ferries and the small cruise boats that carried the tourists between the Dalmatian islands clinging to the quayside below them, their destinations distant hazy humps on the horizon.

"Ezra! We're home," Luna called, and he appeared, hair still damp from the shower and grinning from ear to ear.

"I only just beat you to it – I've been for a run."

"In this heat?" Claire sounded incredulous.

"It clears my head after work. And anyway, it's going to get an awful lot hotter before the summer's out."

"I hope you haven't left your sweaty gear in the bathroom," Luna told him, folding her arms. That would be bloody typical after she'd even gone so far as to shine the taps.

"As if. And before you ask, yes, I did remember to go to the supermarket."

"And you got everything on my list?"

"Look in the fridge. Everything, plus olives and a smashed avocado dip."

When Luna started to assemble ingredients for supper on the worktop, Claire offered to help.

"No, no," she replied. "I'm making *crni rižot* so it's easy. I'll stand here and stir while Ezra gives us his thoughts. A glass of wine would help though."

She made Claire sit at the table while Ezra poured the drinks and set out the olives and dip, then split a large bag of crisps flat in front of them. Luna rolled her eyes, but he shrugged.

"Why pretend we do otherwise?"

"Why pretend we normally have olives and dip?"

"I'm not." He looked genuinely puzzled. "We only have three bowls and you'll need them for our dinner. Although if I had thought about it, maybe I should have bought some more." Yes, maybe he should. It was ridiculous to have nothing to eat from. Especially when you had a guest.

Ezra sat next to Claire and opened a can of beer. "She's going to tell me off for not getting a glass," he said. "But I don't see the point in extra washing up."

"Me neither," Claire told him, grinning. There was an ease between them that Luna found surprising, given they'd hardly met before. Ezra wasn't normally this comfortable with people he didn't know, but at least that was one less thing for her to worry about. A super-small thing, but they all counted. *Positive, Luna, positive.*

"So," Ezra said, "this website. The technical side is simple enough. I can get some cheap shopping-cart software and build around it. I could have you up and running in a couple of weeks, but there would be no point if you didn't have distribution in place, and no one could find the website. I think that's the first thing: how is it going to work in practice? And who will your customers be? Because one kind of informs the other and I take it you're not setting up in competition with Amazon."

Claire looked thoughtful. "I guess our customers will be the same people: tourists visiting Dubrovnik, university students reading languages, and a handful of local people."

"The university students are easy. You could just deliver the books to their department for them to collect. Local people as well; the problem is the tourists."

"And they are the largest part of our income. I'd guess most of them don't even know they're looking for a book – they're just wandering around town and they find us. Even if they did plan their reading in advance, we can't send books off worldwide."

"No," said Luna. She stopped stirring the cuttlefish and onions for a moment, frowning. "But we could deliver them when they arrive; to the cruise ships when they dock, the big hotels. Perhaps even have a very small place where people could come to collect them." She sighed. "The best bit of my job is talking to customers and whatever we do, there won't be many opportunities for that."

"You can't be sure, Luna," Claire replied. "You never know, the landlord might respond to Vedran's email. And Karmela could come up with alternative premises we can afford."

Luna nodded. "You're right." She turned away from them to focus on the pan, hoping the gentle steam rising from it would disguise the tears she was desperately holding back. No. They were doing their best. She had to believe. Fake it until you make it, and all that. Except right at this moment it was like believing in unicorns, and one of those wasn't going to waltz through the door any time soon.

She added the rice and continued to stir, listening to Ezra and Claire discussing discoverability and visibility of the website, SEO and keywords, all manner of other things she struggled to understand. Why, oh why, was she so totally dumb? Her father had told her enough times... But hell, no, why should she believe him? Bossy, bigoted man, whose only use for his daughter was to catch a nice strong son-in-law to work in the olive groves. He could go sling one. She'd show him. Well, she would if she could.

"Luna? Luna?" Ezra's voice penetrated her fog.

"Yes?"

"How do you think we should arrange the webshop? In terms of categories, I mean."

"Oh, I don't know."

"Yes, you do," Claire encouraged her. "You really watch people when they come into the shop, and as you said, you talk to them. How do they choose their books?"

"By browsing. Which is most of the fun of it. But you can't do that on a website."

Ezra frowned for a minute, then grinned. "Just you wait and see. You'll have to help me though … or maybe I could come into the shop on Saturday to see how people behave?"

He was grinning at Claire as he said it, and she nodded. Woah, hold on. Something was happening here, Luna was sure of it. The start of something perhaps even they didn't know about? Top tier or what! This was such a joyful prospect in the midst of all the crap, Luna could barely stop herself from jumping up and down. They'd be so, so good for each other.

But knowing Ezra, he wouldn't have a clue there was any chemistry going on. No idea at all. After Claire went home she would have to point it out. And tell him what he needed to do about it. As far as she knew, he'd never even been on a date. The man was completely hopeless, but never mind, he had her in his corner.

"Yes, come to the shop," she said. Perfect. Absolutely perfect. And then another idea struck. A genius one. "We could all go to the jazz café afterwards. And don't look at me like that, Ezra – it's high time you met my new friends."

"I'm up for that," added Claire.

For the first time since Claire had given her the news about the shop, Luna found herself grinning from ear to ear. Getting these two together was a damn sight easier than saving the bookshop, and right up her street.

"Then that's what we'll do," she replied. If Ezra didn't have the nous to ask Claire on a date she'd just done it for him. "And in the meantime, pour me another glass of wine. Stirring this pot is thirsty work."

Vedran

Safranka II swayed as a nearby trip boat left its mooring, its thrusting engines sending silver-topped waves across the smooth waters of the old harbour. Tetak Jadran swore quietly.

"I'd just got that bloody wire back in too."

Vedran shrugged. "It's not like we're in a hurry. Want me to have a go?"

"Just pass me a smaller screwdriver. The yellow one."

He scanned the contents of Tetak's neatly arranged toolbox and leaned into the cabin to hand it to him, before returning to his position on the wooden deck, just outside the door, and raising his face to the sky.

"You look better after your trip to Pula," Tetak said. "Caught some sun."

"I didn't realise how much I needed the break, and it was great to see Mama and Tata so happy. If I didn't know better I'd tell you they'd settle there."

"Unlikely. You and I both know they never settle anywhere."

Vedran's visit to his parents had made more of a difference than he was prepared to share even with Tetak. The change had started at home though, before he'd left; a small and barely perceptible one, as though the single act of destroying just one item of Didi's clothing had begun to unravel the ties that still bound him to her. Added to that, he'd found such freedom in Pula. Just being able to sit outside cafés without fear of being recognised had made everything feel completely normal, and much of the tension he barely knew he'd been holding had disappeared. After a couple of days his mother had become quite emotional as she told him how great it was he was more himself.

He'd even wondered if moving there was the answer. Well, away from Dubrovnik at least. Somewhere he could be himself again, without having to live his life looking over his shoulder all the time. The only place outside his and Tetak's homes he could do that here was the book club, and even though he still hardly read anything, it had become a place of sanctuary and friendship. He was just glad they weren't relying on his efforts with the landlord to save it, because there was definitely nothing doing there. No reply to his email at all.

Which begged the question whether he could ever work effectively in Dubrovnik again. In a new city he wouldn't be stuck in the backroom, he'd be able to do what he was best at: explaining the intricacies of the law to clients face to face, helping them use any loopholes to their best advantage, leading negotiations, closing deals. He could bury the scars, re-invent himself. His current employer would probably be only too pleased to be rid of him.

Tempting as it was, could he really let Didi take the city he loved from him as well? Everything else had been systematically stripped away: his friends, the parts of his job he loved the most, his self-respect, his child… No, he couldn't think of the baby right now. And yet, somehow, he could. Not without pain, granted, but certainly without the twist of agony he'd come to dread more than anything. Maybe, just maybe, he was beginning to move on.

He gazed lazily around the harbour, at a little girl chasing one of the stray cats that begged at both restaurants and fishing boats, at a couple in denim cut-offs and white T-shirts taking a selfie, at the old men sitting in the sun on the benches beneath the fort. He'd lived most of his life under the protection of Mount Srd, today rising into a hazy blue sky, the cable cars like so many little red caterpillars gliding up and down its slopes. And from closer by came the chink of glasses and clatter of cutlery from the three broad arches of the renowned Arsenal restaurant.

It hadn't been good enough for Didi though. She had preferred the Michelin-starred glory of Restaurant 360. Of course she had; it was so much more Instagrammable. If he leaned a little further forwards he could see waiters moving along the curve of its terrace, so cleverly built into a fort on the old town's outer wall. Some places he would never go back to. Some places held far too much of Didi.

But not everywhere. There were places he should be able to go, places untouched by her memory. In not doing so, was he proving her right? Becoming that pathetic excuse for a man she'd told him he was; that he had come to believe himself to be. But maybe, just maybe, he was not that person after all. Well, not entirely, anyway.

He watched Tetak screw the panel back onto the boat's dashboard. Even if he moved away from Dubrovnik he couldn't run away from himself, but day by day his strength was building. Enough to mend his life here? Tetak fixed everything – sometimes to Fran's annoyance, when she'd rather have new – and he yearned to talk to him now, tell him the whole truth, ask his advice. But they were still waiting on his diagnosis, so that would hardly be fair.

But there were changes Vedran could make, big ones, and now was as good a time as any, before he lost his nerve.

"Fancy a beer?" he asked his uncle.

Tetak grinned. "Thirsty work, prepping the boat for the

summer. Why not?" He looked at his overalls and Vedran's grubby T-shirt. "Perhaps not at Gradska Kavana, eh? Somewhere a bit more down to earth."

Once Tetak had stowed his toolbox away they walked through the alleyways to one of the bars that the tourists would struggle to find. No more, really, than a courtyard with a dark room beyond. Tetak chose a round metal table under the shade of the single orange tree and they sat down facing each other.

"Thanks for your help today."

"I don't feel I did very much."

"You did a great job of cleaning the deck. You never were much of a mechanic, but you work hard." He winked. "And it's the company, you know. Safranka worries I can't cope with the boat on my own."

"Which you can."

"Unless or until I lose my confidence I'll be all right. Confidence is important to a man, isn't it, Vedran?"

That didn't sound like a casual comment. This was going somewhere. Vedran took a sip of his beer, then nodded.

"So how is your confidence?" Tetak asked.

He shrugged. "It must be improving. I'm here. Until Pula I hadn't been to a bar since before it happened."

"You're coping better?"

"Some days."

"It's a start. When I lost Leila and Kristina..."

"Tetak, it's not the same. Didi wasn't the love of my life... To be honest, things weren't great between us towards the end. It was blowing itself out anyway." He could never tell his uncle he'd lost a child too. But then it occurred to him: why not? Having been a father himself, he would surely understand. "However..." He started and then stopped. Tetak was looking at him intently. "This is for your ears only. Not even Fran's. Is that OK?"

"Hmm. What if I forget I'm not meant to tell her? My memory isn't the best."

"Well, if it happens, it happens. I need to get this off my chest. Didi was pregnant."

"Oh, Vedran." Tetak's hand on his was liver-spotted and weathered, and looking at it Vedran struggled to hold himself together. "So you lost two of them as well."

"Not like you did." Not in any sense. Tetak's daughter had been thirteen years old when the war had so cruelly ripped her and her mother away.

"It's not a competition about who had the biggest loss, you know." Tetak sounded sharp. "It's about how we move forwards. I took far too long and…"

"Well, well, Vedran Novak." A hand clamped onto his shoulder. "You must tell me, how come you get away with murder when I get locked up for shoplifting a few watches. Because you're a lawyer, is it?"

Vedran looked up, the sun and his unshed tears half blinding him. Shit. Not now. Not this animal of a man who had made his teenage years a misery.

"Srecko." It was all he could say. A lifetime ago the guy had recruited him into his little gang of mayhem at school – until Tetak had rescued him.

"Kitty got your tongue? Or have I struck a nerve?"

No words came. There was nothing at all that Vedran could think of to say. He just kept gazing into those glass-grey eyes and feeling a fraction of the man he ought to have been.

"Of course you've touched a nerve, you … you … *šupak*," Tetak spluttered. "Vedran's suffered a significant bereavement in a tragic accident. Show some respect."

"Accident, is it now? Everyone knows he killed her."

What could he say? If only he'd had the balls to look at those photos…

"Then everyone is wrong." Tetak drained his glass and stood. "There's a bad smell around here so I don't fancy another. I'll call in tomorrow to settle our tab."

Vedran left his beer half drunk on the table, praying Srecko wouldn't rise to Tetak's words. He'd left it to his elderly uncle, who clearly wasn't thinking before he spoke, to defend him. Didi had been right. He was a pathetic excuse for a man after all.

They were half a dozen paces down the street when Tetak stopped. "Don't look so shocked. Did you think I didn't know what people were saying about you?"

Vedran stood back against the wall to let a woman with a shopping basket pass. "I did think that, yes. Fran said—"

"Look, I appreciate you were both trying to shield me, but Vedran, I knew there was more to it and it took about two minutes on the internet to find out what had happened. I'm not gaga yet, you know."

Vedran nodded. "I'm sorry. I shouldn't have kept it from you."

Tetak looked thoughtful for a moment. "And I shouldn't be keeping it from you that I definitely do have dementia. Safranka thought it best not to say because you have enough to cope with, and I agreed. But it was wrong of me."

"How long have you known?"

"Now how do you expect me to remember something like that? Anyway, even before the official diagnosis it's been clear to me for a while. But it's early stages and there are drugs." He smiled, although his eyes were deeply tired. "And I'll take them for as long as I remember to. Then Safranka will remind me. Let's just see how it goes."

"I'm here for you too." Although he hadn't exactly been much help in the bar.

"Vedran, I know that. You have never, ever let me down."

"Not even back there?"

"You weren't the one being an arsehole."

Vedran smiled shakily, screwing up as much courage as he could. "Seeing as we didn't get to finish our drinks, shall we go somewhere else? And this time I'm buying."

Tetak slapped him on the back, grinning. Oh yes, Didi had taken so much, but in this particular round of the battle, once more she'd lost. Even after what had happened, he would go into a café again, another bar. As unpleasant as it had been, the world hadn't ended, so he must be getting stronger. Maybe, finally, strong enough to face up to those photos, to go to the police and to clear up Didi's disappearance once and for all.

Black Butterflies

Claire

"This looks just so beautiful," Luna breathed, stroking the cover of today's book club choice as she set it centre stage in the window, the flame-like shapes and colours on the shiny paper catching the sunlight. Unusually it was a hardback, only recently released, but when one of the students had suggested it Claire had been bold and asked the wholesaler for an extra discount. By some miracle they had agreed.

Knowing there was probably limited time for the club to run, Claire had been rather less random in choosing the remaining books than perhaps she should have been. This one, set in Sarajevo during the war in the 1990s, and loosely based on the author's mother's experiences, had leapt to the top of the pile. It was about the Balkans – relevant, given what was happening in Ukraine – and a peep inside had shown her the prose was exquisite.

She had also wanted to tell the members about the shop's potential closure, but Luna had been dead against it, without ever really giving a solid reason why. Although when she thought about it, Claire did kind of get it; saying it out loud to so many people would make it feel like an incontrovertible truth, and she wasn't sure she was ready for that either.

Neither did Claire want to dent what she feared might be a rather fragile resurgence of Luna's positive attitude. They'd had a really brilliant laughter-filled night at the jazz café on Saturday and Luna had spent quite some time flirting with a Scandinavian visitor, as tall as she herself was short, and had headed off with her back to her smart hotel. Claire knew these holiday flings would not be for her, but everyone was different, and she understood that Luna was finding her way, experimenting, having fun. And fun was a really good thing right now. A distraction from some pretty tough realities.

But was Ezra flirting with her? In his own way, of course. Claire couldn't work it out. He wasn't a natural flirter, any more than she was, but there were certainly moments when he held her gaze for longer than perhaps was necessary, or his smile seemed to be for her and her alone.

She liked him, of course she did. But what was the point if she'd be heading home in just a few months? They'd both only get hurt. But looking at him, with his long hands and slim, toned body, made her remember just how much she'd missed physical intimacy during the endless months since the pandemic had begun. Not just sex, but kissing, that feeling of comfort from being tucked under someone's arm. She remembered how Luna had longed to be kissed and now she was beginning to understand. More than two whole years out of the dating game. Was she ready to go back? In different circumstances, Ezra might have been the guy to persuade her.

Luna stretched, and reached for another book. "I'll put some local history titles in the window too," she said. "But these are so beautiful I want there to be more than one in the display. How about I pop to the stationer's for some coloured paper so I can make some flames as a backdrop?"

"Good call. You're so clever with this arty stuff, Luna."

"It's another thing I'll miss. Doing the windows."

"Well, if that happens you'll be busy tarting up the website instead."

"True enough. Once he got over his hangover, Ezra spent all day Sunday working on it. He's very keen, for some reason." Luna shot Claire a knowing glance.

"I expect it's because it's something different to his normal work."

Luna opened her mouth to speak, but the customer who had been browsing in the corner came over with two books in her hand. Claire took them with a smile, and put them through the till.

After that the afternoon became busier and once the shop was closed, Claire was glad to take a coffee into the courtyard. These tiny spaces tucked behind so many buildings had been a revelation, and although in the evenings the still air was often filled with the aroma of cooking from the restaurant or the rental apartments above, in summer they were cool as the sun only reached them for an hour or so at most.

She moved the metal chair away from the wall to avoid the drips from the air conditioning unit and gazed at the patch of sky. City sounds surrounded her; voices and footsteps from the streets, the pump of music from the bar in the alley, Luna hoovering the shop; yet for the moment she was completely alone – not even Mis had put in an appearance.

Gran would be here soon, with her home-baked nibbles and a carton of olives from the Green Market. Her grandmother loved book club nights, the lively discussions, the mix of people, and Claire knew she would miss it when it stopped. No, if it stopped. That was a point. She wriggled upwards on her seat. Maybe even without the shop the book club could live on. If all else failed it would be a way of keeping the name and the ethos alive. Everyone welcome. Nobody turned away.

The book club was certainly growing and it was entirely possible that soon there would be too many people to squeeze into the shop anyway. Claire could barely remember how terrified she'd been at the first meeting. She knew she was making progress; she no longer carried her mask everywhere and had even become quite used to popping quickly into a crowded shop for something. She wouldn't say she was comfortable, but at least she could do it. But it was summer, wasn't it, when germs went away. Winter on the London Underground would be a different proposition entirely and the thought filled her with dread. It was terrifying to think that her hard-won victories over Covid might count for nothing if she had to go home.

Once Vedran had handed around the wine, Claire asked Karmela to lead the discussion on the Jane Austen she had chosen. Everyone laughed when George said he had watched the film instead.

"I told him it was cheating," Paulette said.

"But I didn't get on with the language," George protested. "I know it was of its time, but it was getting between me and the story."

"I wish I'd known there was a film," added Vedran.

Karmela folded her arms, but she was laughing as she said, "I do not suppose you actually read it?"

Vedran shrugged. "It's still in the bag." Making everyone laugh again.

"But the language is an important point," Karmela continued. "You could find it off-putting, or it could carry you right back to the time it was written. What did everyone else think?"

Quite a discussion ensued, before they moved on to talking about the story itself, in particular how the two sisters who were central to this classic novel had developed and grown, how the emotional one had learned the value of common sense the hard way, and how the sensible one had learned to trust her heart, just a little.

Claire wondered whether Karmela herself was changing or whether she was simply getting to know her better. Perhaps her initial frostiness had been shyness after all, and now her reserve was breaking down, her true colours were shining through. She had certainly grasped the nettle when it came to saving the shop, adding some steel to their resolve with her forthright manner and common sense. Maybe Karmela was Elinor Dashwood, and if that was the case, Luna was definitely Marianne. Looking at it like that, Claire liked the novel just a tiny bit more.

So who was she? And who was Vedran? Edward Ferrers perhaps? He was definitely honourable enough, and hopefully, one day, he too would find his happy ending.

The discussion drawing to a close, Claire announced their next read. Aklina, the student who had chosen it, explained it had been recommended to her by a cousin living in England but whose parents were from Sarajevo, so she hoped, although a novel, the historical facts of the siege were correctly portrayed.

From her position facing the room, Claire could have sworn that Karmela's expression froze, but she was quick enough to start helping Gran to collect the glasses, as Vedran folded the chairs and took them through to the kitchen. The inner circle, as Claire thought of them, were staying behind, and Gran had brought a generous box of her mouth-watering *ćupteti* and some pasta salad for their supper.

In the kitchen, Claire was surprised to find her grandmother giving Karmela a hug. Gran was an enthusiastic hugger all right, but she'd never had Karmela down as much of a touchy-feely person, so what was going on?

Gran turned and beamed at her. "Karmela's coming to lunch on Sunday. Isn't that nice?"

"Fantastic. We alternate British and Croatian dishes so it'll be interesting to hear what you think of a traditional roast."

"I am looking forward to it," Karmela said, but all the same she sounded unsure.

"And you'll have my *ćupteti* for supper tonight," Gran added.

"Oh no, I cannot stay." Karmela extracted herself from Gran's arm and turned to Claire. "There is little progress on alternative premises, but I have a meeting with the university facilities manager next week so I will update you then." With that she grabbed her rucksack and left.

Gran watched her go. "You need to know," she said, "the choice of book upset her a bit."

"But why?"

"It seems she was brought up in Sarajevo until her family left as refugees when the war started."

"Oh no!" This was truly, truly awful. "I … I never thought. All this talk we have of trigger warnings and I never even… I have to apologise." She moved to follow Karmela, but Gran put a restraining hand on her arm.

"Leave her, darling. She said she needs time to think."

Claire wriggled free. "But this is my fault. I have to—"

"Claire, no." Gran's tone of voice made her stop in her tracks. "This is not your fault," she whispered, obviously aware of Luna in the shop, "it is just an unfortunate coincidence, and anyway, you are not responsible for Karmela's feelings. How could you have known? You have to stop thinking you need to fix everyone, darling, you have enough on your plate as it is."

Vedran appeared through the back door. "I took two extra seats outside. It's much cooler there than in this kitchen."

"We'll only need one," Claire told him. "Karmela couldn't stay."

"That's a shame. Oh well, all the more *ćupteti* for us."

"And I'd better be going," said Gran. "Jadran is meant to be cooking supper, but whether it is still in the fridge remains to be seen."

There was the tiniest of breezes outside and they settled around the table, Claire lifting Mis onto Karmela's chair, hoping that way it wouldn't seem so empty. Poor, poor, Karmela, walking home alone with god knows what memories. But at least the little cat seemed pleased by the arrangement, nudging Claire's arm whenever she picked up a fragrant sausage-meat pastry, a look of longing in her eyes.

As Claire fed Mis scraps, Luna asked Vedran if he'd heard from the landlord.

"Nothing. Not even an acknowledgement. It's as I thought, my reputation…"

Luna folded her arms. "His rudeness, more likely."

"Just like that ignorant shit in the bar," Claire added, then immediately bit her tongue as Luna asked what had happened.

Vedran shrugged. "Some guy I knew at school. He's been in prison for theft so asked me how I got away with murder."

"But Vedran, you didn't murder anyone. I hope you told him Didi's alive," Luna stormed.

"Of course I didn't. Why would he have believed me? And anyway, we don't know that for sure." He stuffed a *ćupteti* in his mouth and glanced sideways at her. "And don't look at me like that. I'm still working up to it. You, of all people, know how it is."

Luna nodded. "I do. And I also know how liberated you feel once you've screwed up the courage."

Vedran's face closed in on itself, his eyelids half shut and his lips pursed. This was not good. So many tensions, everyone so stressed… Claire supposed it was inevitable, but all she could think of was to move the conversation onto safer ground. "Karmela has a meeting with the university next week, to find out if there is any space for us there," she said, "and we're making great progress with the webshop."

"Both sound promising." He picked up another pastry, his gaze fixed firmly on the table.

"I'm sorry, Vedran," said Luna.

He shook his head. "Ignore me. It's the best thing."

Claire still didn't understand why Vedran hadn't so much as peeped at the photos. Perhaps he had, and just wasn't saying. She deeply regretted her honesty in admitting her trust in him had wavered all those months before, but at the time being truthful had seemed like the right thing to do. He'd been about to tell her something important then too, something about his life with Didi. Was it her fault he now seemed so stuck in the past with no one to help him to navigate his way out? Shit, everything felt like her fault tonight. Perhaps it was.

Gran had said Karmela needed space, so maybe Vedran did as well? But Gran had also told her – quite forcibly, in fact – that she should stop trying to fix everybody. Is that really what she did? She tried to help people, like she had Luna, but was she really trying to *fix* them? She was only twenty-three, with so little life experience. Especially compared to Vedran and, it seemed, Karmela, who had gone through so much.

The irony was that wanting to help, to put others first, had come from Claire's desire to emulate Gran. For as long as she could remember her grandmother had been the person everyone turned to, from caring for both her parents when they'd fallen ill, right up to finding Claire this job. But Gran had the wisdom of years behind her. The experience to know when to intervene, and when to leave well alone. Perhaps Claire needed to get real about what she could and could not do.

It was an intriguing thought, and not a little liberating, and she began to play with it, while Luna showed Vedran some sketches for the web pages she'd been working on.

Claire knew in her head, even if her heart remained unconvinced, that it just wasn't possible for her to put the world to rights. She couldn't make Nono well, invent some miracle drug that would cure dementia. And if Vedran and Karmela wanted space and time, all she could do was give it to them. And be there, if and when they needed her. And Gran was so right: what she had to do now was focus on what she could realistically change; throw her energies into that. Which basically meant doing all she could to save the bookshop. For Luna, for Simeon, for poor little Mis, who would surely go hungry without them. Perhaps even for her own future as well.

Claire felt just the tiniest weight shift from her shoulders. She tipped her head back, stroking the cat, both of them watching the swallows circle the heights of the courtyard as dusk settled over them, a creeping softness signalling the end of the day. Over the roof she could just make out the lights from the cable car gondolas crawling up and down Mount Srd like so many fireflies. This had to be the most beautiful city on earth, and it was wrapping its strength and warmth around her.

Claire wriggled up in her seat. She needed to stop navel-gazing right now, and roll up her sleeves to put together a knockout business plan. That was what was important. As Vedran topped up her glass, she took a gulp of wine then rejoined the conversation. And what was even better was that she didn't have to do this alone; she had people around her. Good people. Beautiful, flawed, wonderful people with baggage she might help them carry for a while, but that ultimately was down to them to unpack and sort out.

She beamed at Luna and Vedran. They had a bookshop to save. And along with Karmela they could do it.

Karmela

K armela pressed the entry buzzer then stepped inside the coolness of the hall. To her right and left were the solid wooden doors of the ground floor apartments, and in front of her a staircase with black and white chequered tiles that looked for all the world like marble. Given the elaborate leaves and scrolls in the wrought-iron balustrade it seemed entirely possible it was.

She heard footsteps above her and Claire leaned over, her blonde hair forming an unruly mop around her face.

"Come on up. Vedran brought some sparkling wine and he's opening it right now."

So Vedran was here too, but of course he was Claire's cousin so it was hardly surprising. And his calm presence at the table would be most welcome. He was so sensible about everything, and a dose of common sense was what she needed right now. She had to stop fretting about that silly book and put it behind her. It was just one book and she did not have to read it.

But all the same it had unsettled her. Memories of Sarajevo had been creeping, unbidden, into her quieter moments. Strange, small things; like her parents listening to jazz on the radio on summer evenings; going out for coffee on Sunday mornings, to that funny little café with its name in tiles above the window and old movie posters curling from the walls. Things that perhaps on the surface seemed harmless, but still cut her deep. And not understanding why was keeping her awake at night.

She was quite exhausted by it all and had almost phoned Fran this morning to cancel, but that would have been terribly rude when she had been so kind as to invite her. Besides, it would be a welcome distraction to have other people around her.

Reaching the top of the stairs, Karmela followed Claire into the apartment and across a modern fitted kitchen with a large wooden table, four chairs tucked neatly under it. Fran was standing at a square ceramic sink in front of the window peeling potatoes, and a delicious aroma of roasting meat filled the room while a dark sauce rich with onions and herbs bubbled on the hob.

Fran wiped her hands on a tea towel, then kissed Karmela on both cheeks.

"Oh, but you've brought wine, and flowers. That is so very kind. Vedran is already in the courtyard so you go on down. Jadran's been working on the boat this morning. He's just having a shower and then we'll join you."

A flight of steps punctuated with overflowing pots of herbs led down the outside of the building and Karmela could see Vedran sitting next to a table covered with a dark blue cloth. An orange tree dominated the space between the walls, offering welcome shade, and the trellis over the table was colonised by a deep pink bougainvillea, its sweet scent filling the May air.

Once he'd greeted her they sat down, sipping wine and chatting. Washing flapped from a line strung between windows far above, and a woman's voice singing drifted from roughly the same direction. Drinking it all in, Karmela felt something inside her settle.

"It is so very peaceful here," she said.

Vedran nodded. "This place, more than any, has always felt like home to me. My folks moved around so much and when I was growing up I came to hate it. A new bedroom, a new neighbourhood, sometimes a new school, but Tetak's apartment was always a constant. I even lived here for a while when I was a teenager. I went off the rails a bit, I suppose, fell in with a bad crowd ... at that point changing schools was a good idea."

"You must be close to your uncle," Karmela said.

"Very. My life would have been completely different without him, I think. I mean, I wouldn't like to give the impression I don't get on with my parents, it's just with Tetak it was like having an extra one."

His uncle's timing was perfect, Karmela thought, as a tall silver-haired man walked briskly down the steps, a bowl of olives in each hand. No doubt he would have been very good-looking in his youth, and as soon as he put the food on the table he shook her hand.

"Welcome to our home, Karmela. Safranka tells me you're a history lecturer and you're researching the Ragusans. May I sit next to you, so you can tell me all about it?"

Talking to Jadran, Karmela felt herself relax even further, the tension drifting slowly from her shoulders. This clever and charming man nodded at all the right moments and asked questions that made her think. Vedran, having fallen silent, smiled and topped up her wine, while they nibbled on olives, and cheese in oil which Fran had brought when she followed her husband into the courtyard. There seemed to be no immediate hurry to eat, although eventually Fran slipped away to the kitchen to finish preparing their meal, Claire following a few minutes later.

There was such warmth in this family, Karmela thought some hours later, after a delicious lunch of melting lamb, dressed in sharp mint and lemon, potatoes that had been roasted in the oven, fresh summer peas and beans, and the sauce, which they all called gravy. Contentment seemed to flow from the empty plates and topped-up wine glasses, and when Vedran went inside to make coffee she was sorry the afternoon was almost over.

Jadran sat back and sighed. "I am a lucky man."

"You have an incredible family, a beautiful home."

"And I appreciate it all the more because it has not always been this way. I had another wonderful family when I was young, but I lost them in the war and for many years I believed that was the end of everything."

A war story was the last thing Karmela wanted, so she made what she hoped was a sympathetic noise, which Jadran seemed to misread as an invitation to carry on.

"I was a Dubrovnik Defender, you see. Me, and Vedran's father, and so many others. One day during the siege, while I was manning a gun battery that was meant to protect the city, a mortar fell on the building where I lived and destroyed it and everyone inside."

Now she had to speak, but finding the words was all but impossible, faced with such a terrible loss. "That's awful. A ... a tragedy." An unfamiliar wave of emotion washed through Karmela, making Jadran's voice echo around her, the scent of the bougainvillea cloy in her nose.

"Yes. One tragedy amongst many others. After the war I moved in here with my mother-in-law and for years I did not live, I just went through the motions. I wasted so much of my life, trying to protect myself from hurt. Vedran and I were close, of course, and we still are, but I never thought I would love again." He reached out his hand and patted Fran's arm. "Until I met this marvellous lady."

Fran put her free hand on top of his. "We are both very lucky."

"All the same," Jadran continued, "the war left many scars.

Some healed quickly, some slowly, and some only in part. Maybe some not at all."

Even as he held Fran's hand, his eyes were focused on Karmela's and she had to deflect him. "My neighbour ... he told me he has not been the same since, and he was just a boy when it started. Only nineteen, but he still fought..."

"Young, old, the middle ones like me. We all did. Many sent their families away. I tried to send mine, but Leila would not go and it was my biggest regret I did not make her. But I think to be a refugee is a terrible thing as well."

Had Fran told him? But why would she not? Karmela had never said it was a secret, because it wasn't, not really. Just somewhere she did not want to go. Could not go. She cleared her throat.

"My neighbour claims he was one of the men who held Fort Imperial on the sixth of December. It is a fascinating story." It surprised her how little her voice shook.

Jadran laughed. "There were fewer than forty men up there, but you use the word 'claim' wisely, because there are hundreds who say they were. Tell me, what is his name? I might know him."

"Rafael. Rafael Babic."

"Then his story is true. He was one of the youngest – if not the very youngest. And they were all so brave. I did not know him before, so I cannot tell how he changed, but his is not an easy life. He can be a difficult man when drink and his emotions get the better of him, but he has a good heart. We do not meet often, but every year we gather under the flag on Mount Srd so we can all remember together. The camaraderie ... it is still there."

"Thank you. I will remember that when he's stumbling up the stairs shouting in the early hours of the morning." She tried to make a joke of it, but all she could see was the look of pride in Rafael's eyes as he had gazed at the flag, his huge hand shaking as it wrapped around his beer glass. Was she imagining those things?

She could not remember noticing them at the time, but now they seared into her.

"You all … lost so much. Gave so much," she murmured. Jadran nodded, the lines on his face telling far more stories than she knew he would ever share. Except, perhaps, with his Safranka, as he called Fran. But Rafael had shared his – or at least some of his – with her. Even so he had only scratched the surface; she understood that now. The lack of personal detail had been because it was locked too deeply inside. Too raw. Raw. That was the word. It was how she felt, exactly that, but why? She had experienced none of this.

"Everyone who lived through that war lost," said Jadran. "Even innocent children. Maybe especially the children."

He knew. He must do. It seemed as though he could see into her soul. She had to stop this and stop this now, or she would crumble. She could not bear the thought of weeping at this table, of the pitying looks, of Fran's arm around her shoulder, even though a part of her craved the comfort of it. She had been an island for so long, but now she felt her very self would dissolve in a sea of emotion if she let it.

She had to escape. The people, the heat, the wine … everything. But when she glanced towards the steps she saw Vedran carrying a tray of coffee and *kroštule*. There was nothing she could do – she was trapped. Trapped by their kindness and caring, their generosity to a virtual stranger. The best she could manage was a request to use the bathroom, where she ran cool water over her wrists for as long as she felt she could without being impolite, counting her breaths until they became more ordered, all the time avoiding her reflection in the mirror.

The old town was rammed with tourists as Karmela made her way home, but she hurried through the crowds, her head barely in the present at all. But this time the past was not her beloved Ragusan one; it was a mere thirty years ago, drawing her eyes towards every last bullet hole that marked the paving and walls.

If only, if only, Aklina had chosen a different book, then she would be feeling none of this. But would she be feeling at all? She brushed the thought away; what a ridiculous notion. Of course she felt. Everyone did, and she was no exception. The sunshine on her skin, the delight of discovery in her work, pleasure in the beautiful view from her kitchen window.

It was the shock that had put her out of kilter. The past forced into her present like the sort of battering ram Dubrovnik's walls were designed to keep out. But now her own barriers were breached it was gaining momentum. The past – the war – was everywhere she looked, in everyone she spoke to. Crushing her like the oppressive heat before a storm. And she did not want it. Not at all. And yet she was powerless to stop it.

What nonsense was this! She had to engage her brain, push these damned emotions away. But right at this moment the logical side of her brain did not seem to be working and that in itself was more than frightening. All her adult life her feelings had been kept tightly under control. It had been her only defence as the perpetual outsider. *You are not like them; they do not want you. You cannot show weakness. Do not get involved.*

There were so many people queuing for the cable car she had to step into the road to avoid them, but it did not matter because the traffic was pretty much stationary anyway. The fumes from the idling engines made her want to gag, the shimmering heat on the tarmac, the press of bodies, voices in every tongue. She needed to be alone. To clear her head. To think.

She slipped into the alleyway that led to her apartment and stopped under the bougainvillea, her chest heaving as she caught her breath. The hum of the bees, the delicate fragrance, transported her back to the calm of Fran's garden. They had tried to persuade her to stay – was that why she had run away? To give herself time to think? Or because she was frightened. Frightened of showing what was inside her, in case they cast her out too?

Oh, but this was ridiculous. She was close to tears and she could not remember the last time she had cried. Not in her adult life, certainly. What was it Jadran had said? That he had wasted so many years trying to protect himself from hurt? The thought occurred to her that perhaps she had been doing the same, but she pushed it aside. It could not be true. It could not.

Reaching the apartments she ran up the stairs and unlocked her door, heading straight for the kitchen, where she poured herself a glass of water from the tap. It was lukewarm but she gulped it, feeling a little calmer now she was back in her own space. She must be tipsy; that was what was making her think in this unfamiliar way – she needed to sober up. Yes, that must be it. No wonder Rafael was always so emotional, the way he drank. She needed to be kinder to him.

And kinder to herself? Oh, this rubbish again. She refilled her glass from the tap, put it to her lips, but somehow it was impossible to force the liquid down. Something was rising from deep inside her to meet it. Something she no longer had the energy to fight.

She set the undrunk water on the draining board and gazed out of the window. But instead of the city walls rising above the terracotta roofs she saw the needle-like tower and copper dome of the Emperor's Mosque in Sarajevo. Instead of the hum of the cable cars above her she heard the traders in the Ottoman Bazaar vie for custom, smelt the rich, strong coffee they brewed in *dzezva* on tiny stoves.

She had never been back there. Not when her father had lived there, nor when he had died. Not even to try to find Nejla. She had always told herself it was because Nejla might have been killed in the fighting too, but that was a lie. She knew that now.

The real reason was, if she found her, she would be sure to turn her back on Karmela who had run away from the war, and consider her an outsider as well. Because that's what she was, wasn't she? Outside of every place, of every thing. Her parents had made a decision that...

But no. Clarity seared through her. A clarity born of remembrance, of giving her strangled emotions life and breath. It was not her parents' fault for leaving. It was hers for not daring to live since coming back.

Karmela's grief was like a tidal wave, drenching every atom of her being and all but bringing her to her knees. Somehow she managed to make it to the sofa where she grabbed hold of the nearest cushion as if it was a life raft, clung to it and wept.

She had no idea how much later it was when she heard frantic knocking on the door. Knocking so rapid and persistent it could not be ignored. She struggled upright and wiped her face on the already sodden cushion before pushing it down the side of the settee and running along the hall.

"Karmela? Are you all right?" Rafael. Rafael, his eyes full of sympathy and perhaps his own tears. She gazed up at him, not knowing what to say.

"You are not all right. That I can see," he said with a brisk shake of his head. "You're trembling as though you're in shock. Wait there. Just one moment and do not move."

She was not sure she could have if she had tried. Her fingers found the door post. Why had she answered the knock? Why had he knocked in the first place? Had she really been weeping so loudly? Oh, the absolute shame of it. But he was right; she was shaking so badly her body could not even obey her brain's instruction to run back inside and lock the door.

Rafael reappeared carrying a bottle of *rakija* and two glasses. "For medicinal purposes," he explained, then gently put his hand beneath her elbow and led her into the kitchen, where he pulled out a chair and guided her onto it.

He sat next to her and poured two small shots of the clear liquid, pressing a glass into her hand. "It has herbs in. To calm you. Then you can tell me what has happened."

Karmela's teeth chattered against the glass as she sipped, while Rafael knocked his back in one gulp. To her intense relief he did not pour himself another, just sat and silently watched her.

But what could she say? That a couple of mentions of the war had pushed her over the edge? That all the tears she had buried inside her for the last thirty years had come out as a torrent she could not control. But of everyone she knew, oddly Rafael was the person who would probably understand about both. Except to him the fact her family had run away from the war meant she had no right to feel this way at all.

Best to tell him what it was not. She focused on her breathing, trying to calm herself. "It is all right. No one has hurt me and I am not ill. I have had no bad news…" She trailed to a halt. What other reasons did people have to weep as she had done?

"So what is it that has melted the ice maiden into a waterfall of tears?"

Despite her initial horror at the way he described her, she had to concede it was accurate enough, and there was a note of affection in his voice, so perhaps he would not be angry at what she found she so badly needed to say.

"Memories. Memories of the war. Now listen, Rafael, I know you think I have no right to feel this way because I left as a refugee, but…"

He slapped his hand on his forehead. "So that's what I said to upset you!"

"You mean you do not remember?"

He shook his head. "The drink is a terrible thing. One moment we were having a lovely time in the bar on Mount Srd, then we were yelling at each other, and when I woke the next morning … well, I knew it was something bad because you scuttled away if you even saw me in the distance. I had not the courage to ask. After all these years, I am a coward."

"No, you had the courage to knock on the door when you heard me crying." She wrapped her hands around her empty glass. "I have heard you crying too, and I have not been so brave."

"These walls are too thin. Much too thin. This war in Ukraine, it affects me. Brings certain things back I would rather forget, and that's what makes me cry. So I understand the pain in memories, Karmela, I understand it very much. But I think in a way it is good to let them come. When I do, despite the tears, I find I can face another day. It's when I fight the past that the bottle becomes my friend."

"It … it has not happened to me before."

"Really? Not at all?"

She shook her head.

"Then why now? Why today? An anniversary perhaps? Or a trigger?"

"A trigger. I think that is the best way to describe it, but not just one big one, a series of smaller things, one after the other."

"Tell me."

She clutched her fingers more tightly around her glass. "The first was on Tuesday night. I go to a book club and the next novel we are meant to read is set in Sarajevo during the siege. Sarajevo was my home, but I have never been back there, not even when my father died. I could not bear to pick up the book, but all the same, the memories began to creep back."

"Good ones or bad ones?"

She shook her head again, trying to clear it. "Good ones, I suppose. We left before anything really bad happened."

"So things you have lost?"

God, yes, what had she lost? At that moment it felt like

everything and tears threatened again. She grabbed the nearby tea towel and wiped them away.

"Let them come, Karmela."

"No, no, I want to finish telling you, or I might never start again. You see … you see … the biggest things I lost were my family and my friends. My dearest friends … one died, the other I don't know…" She scrubbed her eyes again.

"Perhaps I should start at the beginning. Or the beginning as I remember it. The barricades were our first indication something was wrong."

So she told him, how they had appeared all across the city, supposedly to mark ethnic boundaries, where none had been before. That every night they were thrown up; walls of old sofas, tables and barbed wire built by men with black stockings over their faces, men who did not want to be known. And every morning the people who lived nearby simply removed them.

"At first it almost seemed like a game to us kids. I was eleven, going on twelve, and I'd been best friends with Emina and Nejla since we had started school." Karmela could see them now, arms linked, walking along the pavement. Talking, talking, always talking. About everything and nothing. She wiped her eyes, then continued. "We were forever speculating if anyone we knew might be involved. Our scary maths teacher, maybe? The pale and skinny new neighbour who spoke to no one? Looking back, perhaps it was just as well we had no idea of what was to come."

What was to come had been ditches in the streets. Harder to move than the barricades. And then the looting and robberies had begun. Rumours the prisons had been opened and the criminals let loose. Crowds surrounding the police station on the corner. Her wonderful, peaceful home, consumed by hatred and fear. She put her face in her hands.

"Tell me about your friends," Rafael urged, "something good."

Good? Those friends had meant everything to her. She heaved

a shuddering breath. "Emina and I were only children, and Nejla's sister was five years younger, so we were almost like sisters ourselves. We shared everything: records, clothes, ideas. There were no secrets between us. Nejla was a fine, fine artist, Emina loved to write, and even then I adored research... Poor Emina. She never even had the chance to find out what she could become. And I ... I ... I never had the chance to say goodbye."

"So what happened?"

"The authorities fired on a peace march, and that night my parents packed everything they could into the car and we left. I suppose ... I suppose they thought they were doing the right thing, and given what happened to the city..."

He put his hand briefly over hers, but she did not flinch. In fact, she appreciated the comfort. "Poor Karmela, you were only a child. You had no choice, so you must not have regrets."

"My father... I think perhaps he regretted it, although it took me a very long time to even think it." In fact it had been on Mount Srd, after their argument, but that was the last thing she wanted to mention now. "The war changed us all, but it changed Tata the most. I wonder now if he started drinking because he really wanted to stay and fight, felt guilty that he had not. We were in a tiny flat in Berlin and my mother worked all hours to help other refugees. When I was not at school I was there with him alone and he became ... unpredictable." She looked at Rafael. "It is why I am nervous around you when you are drunk."

He looked at the *rakija* bottle and there was a note of regret in his voice when he said, "Then I will not pour us another glass. In any case I should not, because I am on shift tonight. Tell me what happened today."

"I went to lunch with a family I know through the book club. A warm, loving family, who welcomed me in, and although it was wonderful it made me feel sad as well, because ever since leaving Sarajevo I have not had that. Then the man ... he started to talk about the war here, what had happened to his first family. And how people had been scarred, whether they had stayed to fight or been refugees torn from their homes. I suppose I sort of half-realised that his words applied to me too." She shrugged. "I left early because I could not handle it. And when I got home, it overtook me. It is a little pathetic, I know."

"No, it's not. Not at all. But it will be hard, because that big strong shell you have built around you is starting to crack."

"Shell? What shell?" But she knew, really she did. She just had not realised it was obvious to anyone else.

"I am thinking perhaps you keep everyone at arm's length. Before I thought it was just me – with good reason, I may add, given what you have told me about your father – but now you have explained I am recognising something I have seen before. Veterans holding themselves in their own space, bristling with it, so you can almost see the ring of ice and fire around them."

"That sounds like what Jadran was saying about his past. He said for years he—"

"Jadran? Jadran Novak?"

"Yes. You know him?"

"A little. We all know each other to some degree, the Dubrovnik Defenders who are left. And he stayed inside himself for almost twenty years."

"Then what happened?"

"He met his Safranka, of course. But my guess is he was ready to change anyway and perhaps had been for a while. He just needed a little nudge. I think a nudge was what you needed too."

"None of it makes any sense." She was tempted to put her head in her hands and weep again, but instead she tried her best to hold his gaze.

"And perhaps it does not have to make sense in your head when it is about how you feel in your heart." He sighed. "I am sorry, but I must go now, Karmela. I know my timing is awful but

I need to get ready for work. And you need to sleep, and perhaps cry some more. But please, please, don't let that shell grow back. Learn from Jadran's mistake and don't waste any more of your life. You're as beautiful a woman inside as you are out, so what would be the harm in letting more people see you as you really are?"

He stood and nodded in the direction of the *rakija*. "Shall I leave you the bottle?" There was a playful twinkle in his eye, which made Karmela laugh.

"No, but perhaps bring it back when you are not working, and I will make supper to thank you."

"There is no need to do that, but I would like it very much." He placed his hand on the top of her head as if in benediction then let himself out.

Karmela stood, wrapping her arms around her chest. The shaking was starting again and tears were running down her cheeks. The damage, the damage that war had done to her family. They might have run from their country but the hurt had followed them; followed her father to his grave, made her and her mother virtual strangers, when before they had been so close.

But her mother was not dead, except perhaps inside, in the way Karmela herself had been. How strange, when she could barely see the kitchen through her tears, that thoughts, ideas, feelings, were more than crystal clear. Strong feelings, deep feelings. Those strangers she had so firmly pushed away. Could she find it in herself to welcome them back?

Claire

C laire parked Nono's car on the street in front of Simeon's house and took a deep breath before stepping out onto Mokošica's quayside. There was a peaceful quality to the late afternoon, the only sounds the puttering of a small boat making its way over the glassy blue inlet tucked between the steep hills, and the distant hum of traffic crossing the Franjo Tuđman bridge.

Simeon's was a modest stone property on a corner plot, the garage under a terrace shaded by a rattan awning, the white shutters in need of a lick of paint. Claire bit her lip. She was bringing bad news, but also hope, and she fully intended to focus on the latter, rather than add to the poor man's woes.

It took him a few moments to open the door, apologising profusely for not being able to come to the shop to talk to her.

"This round of chemo has really knocked Nadia sideways," he explained. "She is upstairs sleeping now, but if we talk on the terrace we will not disturb her."

He led Claire through an open-plan living area, the exposed stone walls and tiled floor making it feel both cosy and cool. Outside, even in the shade, it would be roasting, and Claire was relieved when Simeon fetched a jug of iced water, then turned on the fan in the corner.

"So Vedran has finally heard from the landlord?"

"Yes. He did apologise. Apparently he'd been away. But the long and short of it is that he won't negotiate. You see, he's had a better offer for the building. He claimed he didn't seek it out, and all he was doing by increasing the rent was asking you to match it, but Vedran isn't entirely sure he believes him."

"So what is the place to become?"

"A fried chicken takeaway. As if there aren't enough fast-food outlets in the city as it is."

Simeon shrugged. "It's where the money is, I suppose. Please thank your cousin for trying, Claire, it's very kind of him. If Nadia is a little better next week I will talk to my accountant about closing the business."

"That may not be necessary." Claire pulled from her bag the document she, Ezra and Luna had worked on late into the last two nights. "Take a look at this first. It's a proposal for how you might run things without an actual shop, a way it could work to take things online." She set it on the table. "Of course, it would mean many changes but we've done a great deal of research, have maybe even found potential premises at the university business hub, and costed everything out. Luna's excited and it really could work." She pushed the folder across the table towards him.

He picked it up and flicked through it, then set it back on the table.

"Claire, I am so sorry, but I don't have the mental energy for this. Nadia being so ill, it's exhausting. Most days it takes everything I've got just to hold it together." He ran his hand over his face. "I can't make a decision about this as well. And anyway, I've come to terms with letting the bookshop go. If we are lucky, and Nadia gets through this, there is so much else we want to do."

"Oh." What else could she say? She had never once considered that perhaps the rent increase was a blessing in disguise for Simeon. But looking at the greyish tinge to his skin, the dullness in his eyes, she understood. Sort of. Because her understanding was tinged with bitterness that he wasn't even thinking of Luna. But why would he? She'd only worked for him for just over a year, another in a string of employees who came and went. Looking at it like that, of course he had to put himself and his wife first.

Oh, god. Why hadn't she seen this before? Why had she built up Luna's hopes? She'd been on edge enough as it was, even kicking one of the courtyard chairs after a customer had been rude to her, something she'd normally take in her stride. Had Claire been cruel to lead her to believe there might be a way she could keep her job? And now she'd have to tell her that she couldn't.

Claire didn't ask how Simeon would make his living. It wasn't her business, and frankly right now she didn't care. Her eyes smarting with red-hot tears, she collected the plan from the table and put it back in her bag, then stood.

"Thank you for taking the time to see me," she said.

He looked at her. "I've disappointed you, haven't I?"

She nodded. "Yes. But I get it. You have to do what's right for you."

Back in Nono's car she sat for a while, gazing down the inlet towards the Tuđman bridge. The steel cables glistened white in the late afternoon sun as the traffic streamed over it, away from the city. There was no point in going back to the shop today, but she needed to get over herself and tell Luna what had happened.

Pulling out her phone, she typed a quick message to Gran, saying the meeting hadn't gone well so she would drop by Luna's flat on the way home. She didn't want to examine how much Ezra being there, Ezra with his quiet strength, played a part in her decision. She would have sought Luna out wherever she'd been, of course she would. And after all, she needed to apologise to Ezra for wasting his time too.

It was hard to find anywhere to park near the apartment so she left the car in the pay-and-display on Gruž's quay, before climbing the hill towards the blocks of flats. The temperature was almost unbearable, the pavement radiating so fierce a heat it almost seemed to burn through her sandals. Her eyes began to smart again, but she told herself it was the petrol fumes. This was no time for self-pity. This was about Luna.

Outside the dust-streaked glass doors of the apartment block she checked her watch; Luna would most likely be a little while yet, which meant she'd be able to tell Ezra and apologise to him first. Then they could both be ready to comfort Luna when Claire broke the news.

All the same, she hesitated when it came to ringing the doorbell. Ezra was bound to be working; would he want to be disturbed? Would it be better to sit on the steps and wait for Luna? But no, she knew him well enough now to tell him she'd sit in the kitchen with a glass of water, and not get in his way.

When Ezra opened the door his welcoming smile made his brown eyes sparkle and something deep inside Claire's stomach seemed to twist. He looked so open and friendly when he grinned like that, and it gave her the courage to say what needed to be said.

"I'm sorry to disturb you…" she began.

"That's OK. Any time. Literally, any time." He held the door open wider for her to pass, following her down the hall and into the living area. "How did your meeting with Simeon go?"

"Not good. Worse than that really. He doesn't want to know. Can't even think about it with Nadia so ill. I've wasted so much of your time and I'm really, really sorry."

"Oh, Claire, there's no way it was a waste of time and don't you dare think it." He wrapped his arm around her and she leaned into him, resting her head on his shoulder. It was only half a hug, but it was what she needed right now, and they stood, motionless, watching a ferry slip away from the quay below them, its churning wake sparkling in the sunlight.

"Thank you for being so understanding," she whispered. "I barely know how to tell Luna. I got her hopes up with my stupid plans and it was all for nothing."

"So what will Simeon do?"

"Close the business."

"Then perhaps it is not for nothing, after all."

She looked up at him. "I don't understand."

"Perhaps he would let Luna use the name, and she could do this herself."

"But it's going to cost money – for the website, the rent at the university, all sorts of things. And she has to live."

"I have some savings." He shook his head. "Although it might not be enough."

Claire turned to face him, but his hand remained on her shoulder, drawing them together. "My dad might lend me something to invest."

"Especially if you were to stay too. It would be so much better for Luna, particularly at the beginning, to have your help. Better for me too."

"I suppose you wouldn't have to worry about her so much."

"Having you here being better for me is nothing to do with Luna." He gazed at her for a long moment then dropped his lips onto hers, but before she had time to respond he pulled away, looking at the floor. "Claire, have I just made a massive fool of myself?"

"No. Honestly, no." She'd been about to kiss him back, had really wanted to… Why hadn't she seen this rush of feeling between them coming? Maybe because she'd been denying it, and after all that was the sensible thing to do. And she had to be sensible, and right now she had to think of Luna. She squeezed his hand. "Whatever happens I won't be living in Dubrovnik forever and … and … you're a lovely, lovely man, Ezra, but I don't want either of us to get hurt."

"But if you weren't leaving?"

She couldn't lie to him. She just couldn't, even though a little voice in her head was telling her that she should. "That would be completely different." Shit. She'd made it sound as though she welcomed the kiss, but then she had, hadn't she? It was just that…

This time Ezra was more confident, his lips firm on hers, but gentle at the same time. She should pull away, really she should, but she wanted this too much. As his tongue found its way between her teeth her whole mouth began to tingle and before she knew it her arms were around his waist as he pulled her to him. There was nothing she could do but sink into the firmness of his chest, the scent of his sweat and a faint hint of lemon shower gel, but above all the feeling of comfort and excitement, all rolled into one.

"Oh, so what have we here?" Luna's giggle filled the room as she slung her bag onto the sofa. Claire went to jump away, but Ezra's fingers wrapped more tightly around her shoulder.

"It's what straight people do when they're into each other." He grinned.

"Don't worry, gay people do the same. Honestly, guys," Luna continued, "it's about bloody time."

But it wasn't. The timing was anything but great. The storm of feelings the kiss had created inside Claire was making it hard to think. And think she must, and focus on Luna. God, they would seem so selfish and callous when she'd said what she had to say. But say it she must, and quickly.

She ducked from Ezra's hold and turned to Luna. "Ezra was trying to comfort me. That's how it started. You see … Simeon doesn't want to know about our plan."

Luna slumped down next to her bag. "What? Not at all?"

"He says … he doesn't have the mental bandwidth to deal with it right now."

"Oh, so he'll look at it next week or something?"

Claire shook her head. "I mean … he's not interested at all. Ever."

"But that's all right," Ezra chimed in, "because as he's closing the business it means you can get on and do this yourself. With help from Claire and me, of course. We'll need money and with you living here I've been able to save, so…"

"You may have been able to save, but I have not." Luna folded her arms across her chest.

"Well, I know that. What I'm saying is that I could invest in the business, and I don't need to charge you rent while you're building things up."

"I won't take your money. You're saving because you need it for your own idea."

"But I'm not ready—"

"And what about when you are? No, Ezra, this will not work." She stood and made for the kitchen area. "Let's just forget it. I need to find a new job, and that is that."

Her voice was breaking and Claire wriggled free of Ezra and followed her, touching her shoulder. Luna jumped away.

"Leave me be, OK?"

"I'm so sorry, Luna, I shouldn't have built up your hopes. It was wrong of me and I feel so bad about it."

Luna reached into the fridge for a can of beer, keeping her back to Claire. This was awful, awful. Claire's eyes were brimming with tears. She tried again. "Please, Luna, I am sorry, really I am…"

Luna sighed, turning to face her, her hands on her hips. "Like you will be when you run out on Ezra when the shop closes? You being sorry doesn't stop it hurting, you know."

Only the hum of the fridge filled the silence. Claire's eyes were fixed on the floor. Finally Ezra spoke. "This isn't Claire's fault. I'm a grown man, Luna, responsible for my own decisions."

"Then you've just made a bad one. Almost as bad as offering me your charity. Now if Claire will just get out of my way, I'll leave you two to your lovefest."

As Claire stood back to let Luna pass, she couldn't remember ever hearing her sound so bitter. Even remotely bitter, come to that.

Slowly she turned to Ezra. "What have I done?"

He stuffed his hands into his shorts pockets. "You haven't done anything, it's me. I pushed the charity button. That, on top of all the stress... God, I should have known better."

"The charity button?"

Ezra nodded, looking glum. "When we were kids, one year Luna's dad's olive harvest failed and they had to rely on handouts from the church. Luna had grown quite a lot and her clothes were getting too small for her, so when my mum bought new jeans for my sisters, she bought an extra pair for Luna too. Luna was delighted; she was so made up about the present, but when her father found out, the bastard dragged her down to our house and made her return them. She's hated any whiff of charity since."

"As you would. Oh, Ezra, this is all just so awful."

He took her hand. "Please, Claire, don't worry. She'll come out of her room in an hour or so, and then we can try again."

"You can, but there isn't a 'we', Ezra. Luna was right about that, at least."

"No, she didn't mean it..."

However shredded her emotions, she had to stand firm. "Ezra, we should not have kissed. What would we have? A couple of months? It just isn't worth it."

"But Claire..."

He reached towards her but Luna's words had brought her to her senses. She put a restraining hand on his arm. "Thank you for how your kiss made me feel, but it can't happen again. Let's just stay friends, OK?"

Somehow Claire walked out of the flat without looking back, down the stairs and into the street. The aroma of spices and roasting meat from the kebab stand filled the warm air and made her stomach churn as she traipsed back down the hill towards the car. Backpackers spilled out of bars, and a woman in a tiny skirt and high heels staggered past her, weighed down by bags from a nearby boutique. Everything seemed blurred at the edges, perhaps by the heat, perhaps by the tears in her eyes. God, she hated this city right now, with its fast food joints and drunken tourists. Its heat and the diesel fumes choking the back of her throat.

In the car she turned on the engine to activate the aircon then sat back in the seat and allowed herself to cry. Everything she'd achieved since she'd come here was in tatters around her; she had failed to save the bookshop, then let down the dearest, sweetest friend she had ever known to such a degree things felt like they might never be the same between them again. And to cap it all, she'd walked out on the first man in a long time she'd really liked.

But this was their world, not hers, which was why she hadn't stayed to try to comfort Luna. They would be here long after she went back to London, living their lives without her, and it would have been wrong of her to interfere. Or rather, to keep interfering. They were better off without her. All she had done was fetch up here for a year, with her desperate desire to fix everything for everyone, making Luna believe it would be OK, then shattering her dreams in a single stroke. All she would leave when she went back home was hurt. She clenched her fingers around the steering wheel. She would never, ever, try to fix anyone ever again.

And she certainly had to minimise the damage to Ezra. That wasn't fixing, that was just being kind. She knew, she supposed she had known for a while, that the long looks he gave her were echoed by her own, that if circumstances had been different... But they weren't, were they? And right now, more than anything she longed for the leafy avenues of Chiswick, for light summer rain, and a bloody big hug from her parents.

Stifling yet another sob, Claire watched as a cruise boat was untied from the quay, its sleek lines like the white and black layers of a modernistic wedding cake. Its motors kicked in, frothing the dark waters of the port behind it, while passengers leaned from the top deck, drinks in hand. They were leaving on an adventure, swigging champagne, while all Claire had was ashes and dust. She wasn't a tourist but she didn't belong here either. Perhaps it was time to make plans to go home.

Karmela

Karmela sat down next to the wonky pink courtyard table and turned over the novel in her hand, gazing at the firebird shapes and colours on the cover. Would it burn her fingers if she opened it? Or worse, burn her soul? Behind her the back door to the shop kitchen was open, and above the hum of the air conditioning she could hear Luna helping a customer to choose a book set in Corfu, the next port of call on their cruise.

Karmela had arrived early for their meeting to give herself time to buy the book, but the shop would be open for another twenty minutes so she had time to start reading it as well. But instead she gazed at the patch of blue sky above the golden-grey walls of the building opposite, Mount Srd peeping over the fringe of roof tiles above them in a haze of heat.

It was strange that Rafael had been the one who had persuaded her to read the Sarajevo story, yet over the last week or so the openness between them had been a revelation. The night he had come to supper she had been determined to stay behind her protective shell but he had not let her, and through more tears from both of them she had had to accept it was broken beyond repair. Could it be that Rafael was so unashamed of his emotions that something inside her was able to let go as well?

They had talked, they had cried, and they had laughed. He had made her feel safe to share these things, because he was sharing them too, as if they had found a common bond, even though their experiences had been so very different. Stories of war, of loss, of friendship, of courage, of fear passed readily between them and it had felt so freeing, so good. But how would it feel to be so open with other people?

What she and Rafael had not done was drink – or at least not too much. It transpired that what he was really ashamed of was the man he became with too much *rakija* inside him.

"If I drink like that, Karmela, you must take the bottle away and tell me to go home. I may be angry with you at the time, but I will thank you in the morning."

"Then it would be better if we did not drink at all."

He had shaken his head. "One glass. For medicinal purposes."

"Medicinal?"

"To loosen your tongue. Now I am finding the real Karmela, I do not want her to disappear up her own backside again." And rather than bristle with resentment she had found herself joining his laughter.

Mis slipped through the gap under the door of the storeroom belonging to the restaurant, and sniffed the air. Spying Karmela she shambled over with her strange rolling gait and allowed herself to be stroked, even to purr, before settling a couple of feet from the table, obviously hoping for food. Karmela smiled; the little creature was getting to know their habits well.

She heard Vedran's voice in the shop and checked her watch. Five minutes past closing time. Claire would be cashing up, so she went into the kitchen and took the olives, crostini and *sir i vrhnje* dip from her coolbag. Vedran appeared, a bottle of wine in his hand as usual, and kissed her on both cheeks before starting to open it.

"The news is not good," he whispered, "but we must wait for Claire to explain."

They carried the drinks and snacks through to the courtyard and set them on the table. Luna followed shortly afterwards, bringing a jug of water, but there was none of her usual spark about her, and they sat in silence while they waited for Claire.

She appeared a few minutes later, gripping a cardboard folder between her hands like a shield, and Karmela noticed dark circles beneath her eyes. Vedran poured his cousin some wine but she did not pick up the glass, just sighed.

"OK. First, for Karmela's benefit, the landlord will not budge on the rent. He's had an offer from some sort of takeaway chicken franchise so there's no reason he should. They will make so much money in the season they can afford to pay almost anything, I guess."

"Then it was lucky the university was so positive," said Karmela.

"Thank you so much for going there and speaking to them," Claire replied. "It was a lovely thing to do. But in the end … in the end … I'm afraid it was for nothing. Simeon wants to close anyway. He didn't even look at our plans." Her voice was breaking as she said it, and Luna put her arm around her shoulder.

"We have cried enough tears over this," she said. "There is nothing more to be done. We have to accept it."

Claire gripped her hand and nodded. "I know."

"It seems such a shame, after all your hard work," said Vedran.

Karmela could hardly believe what she was hearing. Were they really all giving up so easily? Even if Simeon could not be persuaded, surely there was another way to save the shop. A takeaway franchise with its greasy kitchen would be disastrous for this lovely old building. But now Karmela knew there was far more than history at stake.

She picked up Claire's folder and flicked through it. It was all there; mock-ups of the website, financial projections, appendices with market information. Vedran was right – Claire, Luna and her friend Ezra must have spent hours on this, and it made her angry it might all go to waste. There had to be a way. Had to be.

Clearly Vedran was thinking along the same lines. "So take me through this again," he said. "There is no way at all the business can continue if it isn't in this shop?"

"We looked at taking on the webshop idea ourselves," Claire told them, "Luna especially, because at first it will only make enough money to support one person."

"But money is the problem," added Luna. "I don't have any."

"I could invest," said Vedran, with a shrug. "It's not as though I'm spending my salary on anything else."

"No." Luna's rejection of his offer was firm. "Claire and I have been over this already; Ezra was all for us using his savings too, but no. I can't do it that way, even if everyone's kindness makes it seem less like charity. The truth is, it would be too much responsibility and it would make me worry so much I'd hate it. And anyway, it's working in the shop I really love. I don't have experience of anything else, certainly not running a business. We needed Simeon or Claire for that."

"I thought about working for nothing," Claire said, "but Luna wasn't comfortable with that. So there's nothing else to be done."

No. There had to be something. Something they had all missed. If they put their heads together, surely they could come up with avenues as yet unexplored. Quite what, she did not know, but the resignation in Claire's voice, the unshed tears that Luna was trying so bravely to hold back, galvanised Karmela. She knew how much they had wanted – no, needed – to save the bookshop.

She just had to remind them, make them see, there had to be more they could do.

"Luna," she asked, "how much do you want to stay working at The Welcoming Bookshop?"

"There's no point wanting what I can't have."

"You do not know you cannot have it."

"Oh, please, Karmela, there's no way and I can't bear to have my hopes raised and dashed again. I've been up, down, and sideways over this – I even had a go at Ezra and Claire, the two people I care about the most, because I've been so all over the place. This has to stop."

"Not until we have exhausted every avenue, and I do not believe we have. I understand why you do not want to be beholden to anyone by taking their money to set up a virtual business and I admire you for it. I also understand what you like the most is working in the shop. You said it yourself – you've been up, down, and sideways. Now we need to look at the whole problem upside down and sideways as well."

Vedran tapped his fingers on the table, the sound making Mis's ears twitch, and echoing up the walls, sending a couple of pigeons which had been resting on an upstairs windowsill flapping into the air. "I get what you mean, Karmela. I think I get what you mean. We have an important new piece of information we haven't even considered yet."

"What's that?" asked Claire.

"The next tenant. It's a really, really long shot, but what if there was something about them that might stop them from being able to take over the shop, like they were financially dodgy or something?"

"Exactly that sort of thing," said Karmela, more than relieved that Vedran, at least, had a concrete idea they could work on. "Luna, please, get back on that rollercoaster for just another couple of weeks. I know you can do it."

"And why do you care?" she shot back, then muttered her apologies.

Yes, why did she care so much? It was not just about the building, not anymore. It was about Claire having somewhere she was comfortable to live and work, about Luna having a future. And they mattered to Karmela because they had become her friends. Her first real friends since Nejla and Emina, and just at the time she was remembering what friendship really meant. But how could she explain? Make them understand? With honesty, that was how. Honesty and taking a risk with her feelings, however alien it seemed.

She turned to Luna. "It is a good question. A very good one. Especially because, well, I have been guilty, I think, of holding myself apart from you. From everyone, really. But despite that I very much hope that you are my friends, and I have come to learn that friends are precious. Friends are worth fighting for. I had two friends like you when I was very much younger and I did not fight..." Suddenly she was choked with tears, but much to her amazement, instead of feeling humiliated, she did not even try to brush them away as she told them about Emina and Nejla, about their childhoods and how close they had been.

"Nejla had a much younger sister and just before the war she was having a bad time at school because of her ethnicity. It was something that had never happened before, and it shocked us to the core. The last time the three of us were together we vowed that we would take on the bullies, but of course that night my parents decided to leave and I had to break my promise." She looked at Luna. "To be honest, Luna, you remind me a little of Sumeja, although I did not realise it until now. And perhaps, that is part of the reason—"

Karmela ground to a halt, the words sticking in her throat. Had she shared too much? Would they think her too emotional? Discount the value of what she was saying? But Claire's hand snaked across the table and took one of hers, and moments later Luna did the same. The sight of them, bound together in this way, the warmth and comfort of their touch, made her weep all the more, and she struggled through the story of Emina dying and of being too frightened to search for Nejla after the war, hiccupping and sobbing, strengthened by their support.

"You see," she finished. "What I never had the chance to do for them, I want to do for you. The book club and your friendship have made me feel part of something worthwhile for the first time since leaving Sarajevo. As a refugee in Berlin I was an outsider and I have carried that with me ever since." She squeezed their hands. "Until now."

"Then thank you for trusting us," Claire murmured.

Karmela turned to Luna, squeezing her hand tighter. "I have spent thirty years being frightened of my feelings. Please don't be frightened of yours, Luna. Don't be frightened of pain, because without it you will never know joy."

"I do know that," Luna said softly. "I struggled so much to come out. And I suppose once I did I thought my battles were over, but I was so naïve, so foolish." She paused, her brow creasing into a frown.

"You have so much courage – can you be brave again?" Karmela looked into Luna's brown eyes, now as tearful as her own. Was she wavering? How could she make her see? "Please try. This is not just for you, is it? It is for Claire, for all the book club members, everyone who comes into the shop. And you are not alone. We are here to help and support you. But we need you to be on board to have even a tiny chance."

Finally Luna nodded, something more than tears glistening in her eyes. "OK, Karmela," she said. "As long as you will all help me. I think … I feel … together we can be strong."

Karmela had almost forgotten Vedran was there until he spoke.

"Your courage is an inspiration. Both of you. Thirty years, Karmela, that is so long…"

"And it happened without me even realising it. That is the shocking part. But thanks to you all, and to Fran and your uncle, and my neighbour Rafael… Look, I won't go on. Let's just finish the wine and work out what to do next."

Luna

"I could do with another drink." Luna sighed as they locked the shop half an hour later. "Jazz café?" Dumb question. Where else would they go? But she definitely, definitely, needed to talk to Claire on her own on the way. Karmela's words had filled her with courage, but right at this moment she couldn't be sure how long it would last.

Claire put the key in her handbag. "All right. Just a quick one."

Quick was not what Luna needed. She needed slow. She needed more than the five-minute walk down the crowded street, dodging tourists at every turn. But how? She had to say her piece, put things right.

She knew her behaviour on Friday night had been pretty awful, and she had been massively relieved Claire had given her just the biggest hug when she'd apologised the next morning. They'd both got quite teary, in fact, then laughed at each other for being ridiculous. Almost everything had been put right without words, but the almost was what was bothering her, and words were what she so badly needed to sort out the rest. Words and a bit of time.

The queue outside the bakery gave her an idea. "I need something solid inside me before we drink any more," she said. "Fancy some *bučnica*?"

Claire wrinkled her nose. "I'm not really hungry, and Gran will have put some supper aside for me."

"So you want to be stumbling up all those steps and getting home with grazed knees?" Luna put her hands on her hips in her fiercest attempt to be bossy. She had to – had to – be able to say her piece.

"All right."

She was relieved Claire had given in so easily, but Luna'd had a bet with herself she'd be unable to resist the crispy pastry stuffed full of pumpkin and cheese. They were Claire's absolute favourite and they smelt amazing.

As they joined the queue Luna took her arm. "Ezra's so sad and I know it's my fault."

"You haven't fallen out over him trying to help you financially, have you?"

"Of course not. He knows when no means no."

"Then what is it?" Although she sounded innocent enough, Claire couldn't look her in the eye. Ha! She knew after all.

"I put you off him, didn't I? What I said."

"Of course not. It was only what I'd been thinking. There's no point if I'm going away."

"And if you weren't?"

Claire withdrew her arm and started digging in her bag for her purse. "Well, I am. Either at the end of September, or, if we manage to work a miracle in the meantime, December."

"But if you weren't? Please, Claire, tell me the truth. Do you like him?"

"Do you promise not to do any matchmaking?"

Luna could have kicked herself when she replied, "You didn't look like you needed it." That kind of response wouldn't help anyone, least of all Ezra, and she desperately wanted to get him and Claire together. She couldn't even remember him meeting a girl he'd really liked before.

"I suppose I mean … no interfering."

Luna crossed her fingers behind her back. "Then I promise."

"OK then. I do like him. He's kind, and clever, and funny. Not to mention pretty cute in his own geeky way. And I suppose it is because I like him, and I know he likes me, I don't want us to get involved because it can only end one way. Now, are you satisfied?"

Luna nodded. They had reached the front of the queue so she bought them a *bučnica* each with a generous dollop of sour cream on top. As Luna picked hers up from the counter she said. "There is just one thing … no, don't roll your eyes at me, listen and listen hard. Think about what Karmela said, all the years she wasted being frightened of her feelings."

"What's that got to do with me? She was making the point for you."

"Just think about it, OK? Later. Right now we're going to stuff these into our faces then go and get really drunk."

Perhaps that wasn't the best idea she'd ever had but right now Luna needed something to blunt her churning emotions, if nothing else, so she could sleep. Apart from coming out, what Karmela had asked her was the toughest thing she'd ever had to do. It would be so much easier not to hope; not to be disappointed. But how could she live with herself if she gave up before everyone else? No freakin' way.

She needed support. Not from the book club; they had enough on their plates without having to bother about her. And Ezra was no bloody use at the moment, moping around about Claire. He needed her too. She felt herself stretching, stretching, almost too far. But in heading for the jazz café she knew just who would prop her up. Those super-amazing strong women. They'd be there for her, she knew they would.

The moment they sat opposite Meri and Vanesa, it all spilled out. Total update on the bookshop, while Luna made inroads into the extra carafe of wine the owner had brought them. If they were going to help, they needed to know everything. Every sodding thing. It was only as she finally ground to a halt, Luna realised Claire had said nothing at all.

In fact she was looking at her phone, her drink almost untouched. Had she messaged Ezra? Oh, please, let her have messaged Ezra. But no, that wasn't it at all, and Luna only just stopped herself from thumping the table with frustration.

"I've heard from Vedran. That fast food franchise … the landlord did tell him their name so he googled it. They caused quite an uproar in Split when they opened a place near Diocletian's Palace. They ripped out a really old stone archway they were meant to preserve."

"Let's hope they don't do the same to your shop," said Vanesa. "If they get it, that is."

"Vedran wonders if what they did in Split could be a reason they don't."

Meri shook her head. "Money talks. And not just with landlords. It might mean the authorities keep a closer eye on their fit-out, but that's about all. Who are they, anyway?"

Claire looked at her phone again. "Priro Piletina. I know *piletina* is a chicken…"

"Huh." Meri sniffed. "It's short for Prirodni Piletina, which I think translates for you as country chicken. I read a blog about them a while back, written by a former employee. They have this all-natural image but he reckoned most of the meat came from battery farms in Poland and the moment he spoke out he was sacked. Maybe you could resurrect that story, splurge it all over social media."

"It might not be true though," Claire said.

"Since when has that mattered for stuff going viral? If it's out there, use it."

"It matters to me."

Well, of course it did, after Vedran, Luna thought, but Meri didn't know about that so she ploughed on. "This is no time for moral scruples, not if your only chance is stopping them getting that shop."

"Claire has her reasons," Luna said.

"Yes, I have. My cousin's life has been ruined by the lies people told about him online and I won't do that to anyone else."

"But this is a big company, not a person."

"A big company is made up of people. The people who own it, who may or may not be in the wrong, the people who work there and need to make a living. I won't stir up a hornets' nest based on a lie." She downed her wine and stood. "I'm sorry. It's been just the shittiest week ever and I want to go to bed."

Meri stood too, giving her a hug. "I am sorry, darling, I didn't mean to upset you, but to me it is common sense."

Luna watched as Claire threaded her way through the crowded tables. Was she just upset over the shop, or over Ezra too? *O bože*, she didn't want Claire to be hurting, but she didn't want Ezra to be either. And did a promise really count if you had your fingers crossed when you made it? How on earth could she get Claire to see sense?

Vanesa brought her back to the table with a bump. "So, what do you need us to do, Luna?"

"I guess... I guess..." She sighed, and reached for her glass. Again. "When we have a plan we'll let you know."

Vedran

Now that Vedran had finally decided to do this, he was going to do it properly, methodically, get rid of everything. It felt wrong to put Didi's expensive clothes, shoes and handbags into the bin, but if he bagged them all neatly then stacked them in the car port, he could work out what to do with them later. Perhaps Claire would have a few ideas when she came over for supper. The main thing now was to remove every trace of Didi from his home.

Vedran had been creeping closer to the decision since the four of them had met to discuss the bookshop last week. Something Karmela had said had stuck in his brain like a worm, about being frightened of pain for too long. All right, he was nowhere near the thirty-year mark, but what had really shocked him was her comment about the time passing before she'd really noticed it. Already it was eight months since Didi had disappeared, and two since Claire had emailed him the pictures.

He'd thought about looking at them this morning. Like he did every day, then somehow never got around to it. But this time he'd made a bargain with himself; dealing with Didi's possessions would be easier than facing the absolute truth of what she had done, so he would tackle that instead.

He started with the nearest wardrobe, the one with the full-length mirror she'd asked him to put on the door. He yanked it open, unable to look at himself, and after surveying the riot of colour in front of him pulled half a dozen black plastic bags from the roll and wrote out a label for each of them: shoes, jackets, dresses, skirts, trousers, tops. Now he was ready to begin.

Half an hour later he tied the top of the bag with the skirts in and sat back on his heels. It seemed light years since he had attempted to do this and failed, so what had changed? Had it been the trip to Pula, which had given him a chance to step away from the grimness of his everyday existence and gain some perspective? Or the encounter with Srecko, unpleasant as it had been, which had given him just a little more courage to know he could handle these things? Probably both, and Karmela's comments had been the final spur he'd needed.

So was he finally coming back to himself? Ach, that was impossible. The Vedran he'd been before Didi had been irreparably damaged. She'd opened his eyes to a whole world of manipulation and pain he had never imagined existed. And what was worse, he'd let her do it. What a frigging sucker he'd been. Never seen it coming. But how could he, when his only possible yardstick had been Malina.

Everything had been so easy when he'd fallen for her, and had stayed that way through pretty much their whole relationship. If he'd never met Didi they'd probably have been married by now. He dug his palms into his eyes. What-ifs were no sodding good. He couldn't turn back the clock. And anyway, he'd be no use to a woman like Malina anymore. Didi had damaged him beyond repair.

No. He mustn't let himself go there. Couldn't waste the positivity he'd felt not an hour before. So he pushed the destructive train of thought firmly to one side and concentrated on folding dresses and stuffing shoes into bags, which he carried through to the car port. God knows what the neighbours would think was in them, and frankly he didn't care. That ship had sailed a very long time ago.

He looked at his watch. Time was flying by and he needed to make the sauce for Claire's favourite *šporki makaruli* pasta, which needed a lot of cooking for the flavours to combine properly, and quite a lot of stirring. His little cousin had so much to deal with at the moment, she deserved a Friday night treat, and sod her perpetual diet. He could finish the bedroom clear-out later, but now he had started he was loath to stop, so once the pot was bubbling on the hob he pulled out a drawer and tipped its contents onto the kitchen table.

Big mistake. This was where Fran had stuffed Didi's makeup after her disappearance, so eye-liners, mascara, and all manner of other little tubes rolled onto the floor, scattering to every corner. Vedran swore. Bastard things. They weren't going to be bagged neatly like the clothes, they were going straight into the bin.

After a good few minutes scrabbling around gathering them up, Vedran returned to what was left on the table. A narrow leather belt had snaked undone and he picked it up, running his finger along its length. There'd been a scar the exact same width on his leg for weeks, just too low on his thigh for him to be able to wear shorts. God, he'd been such a fool. Not to nip it in the bud. To let it continue. He could see it so much more clearly now. But that didn't make it any easier to live with.

He swirled the mass of designer silk scarves under his hand before scooping them up, along with the belt. There should be another black bag really, labelled "accessories", but something dark was simmering inside him. Why not just tip the whole sodding lot into the bin?

He was about to do so when he spotted the embossed Gucci passport folder he'd bought for Didi at the end of the lockdown. Oh god, what a memory to turn up, just when he was beginning to feel a bit flaky anyway. He'd meant it to be a symbol of all the places they would go together when the world came back to itself, and she had loved it. They'd been so happy then, he could hardly bear to remember it.

Maybe he had reached the end of his endurance, done enough for today, and he ought to stop. He lifted the wallet to his nose, drinking in the slightly salty earthiness of the calfskin, picturing the look of delight on Didi's beautiful face as she'd tucked her passport inside it, telling him it was both a gift and a promise.

Almost without thinking, he eased the metal stud open. The shiny brown leather interior was empty, save for the photo of him she had asked for just after he'd given it to her. He stood, motionless, gazing at it. Where was her passport?

He scrabbled in the drawer, throwing the remaining scarves on the floor. Then ran to the bedroom, tugged the other drawers out, convinced it had dropped behind. Nothing. Nothing. But when would she have had cause to take it out of the folder, to use it even? They'd never gone anywhere. It had been easier to abuse him at home.

Vedran closed his eyes. He could see her now, taking her passport from the folder and putting it in the pocket of her swimming robe. Had she been wearing more than her bikini when she'd left the house? That robe could have covered a multitude of sins. God, he had some imagination, but somehow the image wouldn't leave him. If it was her in the pictures, working in the Caribbean, she would have needed her passport with her so something like that must have happened.

His brain began to tick. How had she done it? As far as he knew, no one had seen her go into the water, but no one had seen her come out, either. She'd have needed an accomplice. A man, probably. Either his replacement, poor sucker, or one of her Albanian relatives who'd motored up the coast by boat then taken her back there. Given how enclosed the landward side of the jetty was by buildings, most likely she'd swum to meet him. But how had she kept her passport dry? How would he have done so in her shoes?

Sranje! Vedran leapt up and yanked open his wardrobe door. Tugging his wetsuit from its cover, he threw it on the bed. No pouch. No neoprene pouch. It would have been big enough. Just.

She must have planned this. Must have. But when? How? She wasn't to know they'd have the most almighty argument, that he would tell her to go. Unless, of course, she had come to know him better than he'd known himself. Had played him along and reeled him in, right to the very end. He'd had a hunch it wasn't completely by chance he'd found the pregnancy testing kit in the bin. Had she somehow faked that as well? Had she been carrying his child at all?

He gripped the open wardrobe door to stop himself swaying, his wetsuit strangely out of focus, its plasticine smell catching the back of his throat. All those tears, all that anger … had they been for nothing? Had it all been an elaborate lie? But why? Why would she even do this? All he had ever wanted was to love her – and be loved in return. Had anything about their relationship been real?

He sank onto the bed. He would never know the truth. Even if it was her in those pictures, he knew he would never ask her. What would be the point? All he would get were more lies. Lies upon lies. He fingered the scar on his arm. That had happened all right. That was real. The manipulation, the violence … but maybe nothing else.

He tensed, waiting for the pain to thud into his solar plexus;

waiting to want nothing more than to curl onto the duvet and weep. But it didn't happen. His legs shook a little when he stood, but upmost in his mind was that supper needed stirring, so he shut the bedroom door firmly behind him and followed the rich aromas of garlic, tomatoes and beef to the kitchen. As he picked up the spoon they enveloped him in a familiar protective fug. *Get real, Vedran. This is now. This is what matters.*

He was thankful when he heard Nono's car pull into the parking lot. He would show Claire what he had found, see if she could make any sense of it. Maybe even tell her what had happened the night before Didi left. But just how much would he be able to share? Yet somehow he needed to. He knew it was time. And he knew Claire was the right person.

Claire called his name at the door, then let herself in as she always did, setting Fran's coolbag on the unit above the fridge before giving him a hug.

"Having a clear-out?" she asked, eyeing the almost empty drawer on the table.

"Didi's things."

"Oh, Vedran, I'm so pleased. It must mean you're making progress."

"I found something." He was surprised his voice sounded normal, given how every word felt stuck in his throat.

"What?"

"Her passport's not here." He picked up the Gucci folder. "See."

"And it was definitely in it?"

He nodded. "Something else is missing too. The waterproof pouch from my wetsuit. If she went into the water she'd have needed a way to keep it dry."

Claire thudded onto a kitchen chair. "So what do you think happened?"

"She swam to meet someone. Maybe they were waiting in the next cove, most likely on a boat."

"So she really did have it all worked out, all planned."

"She must have."

"But why?"

He shook his head, more because he did not want to answer than because he couldn't guess at a logical explanation. Logical to Didi, that was.

"I did wonder…" Claire continued, "or rather Ezra did, when he found the pictures, if she'd got herself involved with drugs or something, or was in debt. If she was frightened for her safety."

"Do you not think, with her gone, whoever it was would have come after me for anything she owed?"

"Not with you being accused of murder. They probably thought she was dead too. I mean … everyone did, until Ezra turned up those photos."

She'd thrown him a straw, an alternative reason for this, one that wasn't his fault. One that would mean he could walk away with his head held high, that no one need know the truth about how weak and pathetic he was, how easily manipulated. How just plain stupid. But finding her passport was missing … working out what she'd done … that wasn't his fault either. It was just plain evil. No one, no one deserved to have their life ripped apart like that. Not even him.

The thought gave him the courage he needed. Just enough. He turned off the heat from under the pot and rested the spoon on top of it. *One, two, three. Now.*

"Didi and I were in an abusive relationship. And I wasn't the abuser." The air felt thick around his head, and he didn't dare turn to look at Claire, didn't want to see the revulsion that would be written all over her face.

"Is that what you couldn't tell me before, that evening we walked to the Ploče Gate?"

"Uh-huh."

There was a long silence. Finally Claire said, "I don't know what to say. Everything I come up with sounds trite. I'm just … I'm just… Vedran, I can't believe the hell you must have gone through. And I suspect in Croatia, like gay rights and mental health, this sort of thing isn't talked about at all."

Finally he faced her. "Because men don't get abused. Only a weak bastard like me would let it happen to them."

"Men do get abused, all the time. If you were in London there'd be help available. The police would even have told you about it."

"The police don't know. Come on, Claire, how could I have told them? It would have given me a motive for killing her. And besides … I'm just so fucking ashamed I let it happen. I haven't told anyone until now."

Claire sat back in her seat. "And I suppose it started slowly, so it didn't really feel like abuse, and she tried to isolate you from your friends, and from Nono and Gran…"

"How do you know about this stuff?"

"Because in England it's talked about. Not like here. God, Vedran, I love Croatia but sometimes… Oh, I guess changing attitudes is hard with a generation who've had to fight for their freedom, but I'd never have believed how strong those traditional macho views were before I lived here. Look at Luna struggling to come out, then the way some people were really uncomfortable discussing mental health at the book club."

"It feels like … I'm the only man ever pathetic enough to allow it to happen. I let myself be well and truly manipulated, Claire. I allowed her to physically hurt me. That's nothing to be proud of."

"It's nothing to be *ashamed* of."

"Stop being so bloody nice!"

"Why? Because you think you don't deserve it? Classic symptom of abuse. But let me tell you, Vedran, you're not weak or pathetic. You're the kindest man I've ever met and that bitch took advantage of you. But you're stronger than you know and you will move beyond it."

Suddenly Vedran felt exhausted by it all, every shred of emotional energy drained. He shook his head. "Can you cook the pasta? I need a moment. I'll just take this drawer back to the bedroom."

"Sure."

He'd started something but he didn't know how to finish it. He sat on the edge of the bed and gazed out of the patio doors onto the gentle rise and swell of the bay. A day boat chugged past, taking trippers back to Zaton, greedy gulls swooping in its wake. Had a boat like that spirited Didi away?

He could hear Claire clattering cutlery in the kitchen. Normal life went on. His too. It was time to embrace it, if he could. Time to move on.

He knew what he had to do. He had to look at those photos, then, if they were Didi, go to the police. He could not be seen to be withholding information. Whatever came afterwards, well, he'd just have to deal with that too. He thought about Luna's courage in coming out. He thought of Karmela, weeping as she told the story about her friends. Proud Karmela, who had always held herself slightly apart from them before. Those tears must have cost her so much.

He took out his phone and messaged her. *Your courage inspired me to try to sort out my own life, but I'm stuck half way. Did that happen to you?*

It took her only a moment to reply. *Yes, but my friend Rafael forced me to keep ploughing forwards. Do you need me to force you?*

To his surprise, Vedran found he was smiling. *Claire's with me. She's more than capable ;-)*

Then you need to let her. Good luck.

He closed the doors on Didi's empty wardrobe, then slotted

the drawers back into the unit before returning to the kitchen. He angled his phone so Claire could read the exchange of messages.

"It's what you want?" she asked, looking a little nervous.

"No, but it's what I need. I have to tell the police about Didi's missing passport, but I need to look at those pictures first."

"The pasta's almost cooked."

"After all that, I'm not sure I can eat."

"But you're going to, just a little, and drink a glass of wine, then I will show you the photos."

"You sound so like Fran." He almost smiled. "But no wine. I need a clear head and at the moment it's far from it."

"That's hardly surprising."

"No, I don't suppose it is."

Good to her word, Claire dished up two small bowls of pasta and they ate in silence. Once they had finished he put them in the dishwasher and began to make coffee, but Claire stopped him.

"The deal is, we look at the photos next." She scrolled through her phone, then handed it to him. "There you go."

The tilt of the woman's chin, her outstretched arm. He knew instinctively she would be jangling those bracelets. Different bracelets. Different hair. Same old Didi. What was he meant to feel? He didn't know anymore. Grief, anger, bitterness. They had bundled themselves together and become completely indistinguishable, an amorphous ball of pain. The feeling he associated with losing Didi. A hole punched in his world. A hole he needed to clamber out of and into the light.

"I take it it's her?" Claire asked.

"Oh, yes. But I knew, Claire, I guess I already knew in my heart of hearts. I just couldn't face up to it, because it meant I would have to go back to the police." He spread his hands. "Pathetic. As usual."

"The damage that woman did. I don't think I've ever hated anyone before, but if she walked in here right now…"

"I would tell her to get out before you said anything you might regret. I did that, you know, the night before she left. I thought I was taking back control of my life, but now I can see she was just reeling me in for the kill one final time."

"What do you mean?"

"We had an almighty row. I'd found a positive pregnancy test in the bathroom bin—"

"Oh my god!" Claire's hands leapt to her face.

"She told me she wanted an abortion and I was devastated. But now I don't know if even the pregnancy was a lie, or if she was expecting and being opportunistic. It could well be that those final hours were stage-managed to get money out of me, then cause maximum damage when I wouldn't play ball. There's no reality I can hold onto. It's all shifting sands. Part of me knows what she's capable of, and the other part still believes that no one could be that poisonous."

"So what happened next?"

What had? The nightmare of it had been etched in his mind for so long, yet now the reality behind it was fragmenting. He needed to stick to the facts; the facts that he recognised anyway. That he had begged Didi to keep the baby and to stay. How she'd said there was no chance, and she needed money to pay for the abortion. And he'd refused, and begged again for her not to kill their child.

"She laughed at me, Claire. Laughed at me. And something inside me just flipped." He cleared his throat. "I put my hands around her neck. I just wanted her to stop laughing. To listen to me. It was the first time I touched her in anger, I swear. I didn't even squeeze, although I wanted to. The next thing I knew I was on the carpet with ringing in my ears and blood gushing from a cut on my cheekbone. She must have pushed me away and I hit my head on the coffee table as I went down. I could hear her in the bedroom, so I fetched a towel to stem the flow as best I could, then lay on the sofa. I didn't see her again until the morning."

"So what do you think she did?"

What, indeed? It was still almost impossible to comprehend, even from Didi, that she could have deliberately caused so much harm.

"I suppose … I suppose … she made her final arrangements to leave."

"So she scarpered the moment you began to fight back?"

He picked at his nail. "I suppose so."

"She knew then she couldn't continue to control you. That the game was up. OK, perhaps she was planning to go anyway once she got the money, but you not playing ball would have made her angry so she decided to punish you for it as well."

"Do you really think that's how it was?"

Claire nodded. "I do. And I'm not just saying it to help you to believe this isn't your fault, because your feelings won't change overnight. She's stripped away your confidence, embedded negative self-worth far too deeply into your psyche. God, Vedran, I don't know when I've ever felt so angry."

"The strange thing is, I don't. Not anymore. The more I think about it, the more I think she wasn't pregnant at all – she was just trying to get money out of me. And, of course, she'd have enjoyed the drama. She always enjoyed a bit of drama." He shook his head. "I've been grieving because I thought I'd lost a child and chances are I haven't. It never even occurred to me before, but I was so damn slow to face up to everything – to clearing her things, to looking at the photos – perhaps that isn't surprising. But what I do find strange is that I don't feel angry, I just kind of feel … numb. Like there's a big empty space inside where all those negative emotions used to be."

"So how are you going to fill it?"

Vedran sat back in his chair. "Good question. First and

foremost, with determination to clear up this mess once and for all. Tomorrow I'm definitely going to the police."

"Want me to come with you?"

"You'll be working."

"I'm sure Karmela will help Luna in the shop for a few hours. I don't want you to go through this alone."

He laughed. "Or you don't believe I'll actually go unless you're with me."

She bit her lip. "Well, there is that too."

He couldn't blame her for thinking it. She might even be right. So many times he'd almost had the courage and so many times … but it felt different now, although he couldn't be sure that wouldn't change in the morning.

He ran his hand over his face. "You're not wrong." Claire nodded and tried to smile, but she looked every inch as drained as he felt. Continuing this conversation would do neither of them any good. "Actually, Claire, I'm absolutely wiped out and could do with an early night. Though god knows if I'll sleep."

"You could always take some of those wonder tablets of yours."

"Another habit I need to break."

She held his hand across the table. "One step at a time, Vedran, and today's has been a bloody big one. You need to relearn how to be good to yourself as well."

But that was definitely for another day.

Claire

Never before had Claire felt so very out of her depth. Out of her depth, inadequate, and young. That Vedran had chosen to bare his soul to her in that way … it made her feel proud of their closeness, but completely useless when it had come to helping him. Certainly nothing beyond spouting all she could remember about abuse from every self-help article she had ever read… He'd still looked so broken when she left, and she felt broken too.

Broken, drained, exhausted. She couldn't face going home to Gran and Nono's inevitable questions. She'd only weep, and then she'd have to tell them … but she couldn't. She couldn't break Vedran's confidence, and knowing she was holding back would hurt them as well.

Damn it! She was hurting too. She pulled into the lay-by above Tri Brata beach, taking one deep breath after another as the headlamps from the cars on the main road above her came and went, casting brief arcs of light through the deepening dusk.

She dropped her head onto her chest, wrung out by emotion. But then the thought came to her that at least she'd supported

Vedran, after a fashion. Listening and shoring him up had been enough. Fixing him ... fixing this ... would always have been beyond her; beyond anyone who wasn't a skilled professional. It was too big, too ugly, too deeply rooted... Oh, her poor, poor cousin.

Claire stifled a sob. She was in desperate need of comfort herself and there was only one pair of arms she wanted to feel around her. A pair of arms she couldn't ... no, the right word here was shouldn't ... have.

For the last couple of weeks she had tried her best to put the issue of Ezra out of her mind. Even with Luna's attempt at a stern talking to last Thursday night, she had shunted him off to one side; too busy with the bookshop, dealing with the summer flocks of tourists, confronting a shoplifter in the street, and ploughing through internet searches about the chicken company that would be taking over the building.

At least Karmela had helped with the latter. She popped into the shop most days now, and when Claire had told her what had happened to the property in Split she had promised to look into that aspect at least, leaving Claire to ponder the morals of trying to use the disaffected employee's story to discredit them. All the time coming back to the fact that her morals would have to be practically non-existent to do so, given what had happened to Vedran. But if they had nothing else to fight with, what choice would she have?

She had been intending to talk the issue through with him, but of course that had proved impossible, and probably would be for a while to come. She needed to fall back on her own resources ... her own dwindling resources. She wriggled up in the seat. *Come on Claire, channel Gran.* Gran who always supported everyone. Gran who was so very strong.

But Gran was strong for herself too. It could not have been easy for her to leave her family in England to begin a new life with

Nono Jadran in her sixties. After all, up until that point she'd done everything for everybody; she must have known the void she would leave. But love had won through and the choice she had made had been for herself, and for Jadran. She'd taken a chance, and it had been the right one through and through.

The same sort of chance was being presented to Claire now, and she wondered why she had taken so long to see the parallel. Family history was repeating itself in the cruellest of ways. But was it cruel? For Gran meeting Nono had brought them both so much happiness. Could meeting a Croatian man she adored, and who adored her, do the same for her?

Oh god, what did she want? That's what it boiled down to. What she really wanted, if you took away the doubts and fears. If she could be anywhere now, with anyone, where and who would it be? She was pretty sure she knew the answer, but it was just so bloody frightening. But she'd done frightening before, hadn't she?

Music drifted from the beach below, and she could just make out a group of people sitting around the glow of a campfire or barbecue. Two small children, little more than silhouettes, played on the edge of the waves, a dog bounding between them, as the last of the purple and orange streaks of the sunset faded into the distant horizon.

If ever there was a moment to be brave it was now. She'd arrived here only five months before, a hermit glued to its shell, terrified of Covid and any situation in which she might even just possibly have been able to catch it. Scared of the future too, hiding the ache of dreams she was far too frightened to follow, clinging to the comfort of the small, almost pretending the big no longer existed.

Except it did. Out there beyond the sunset to her right and behind the hills to her left was a whole world, opening up every day, there for the taking. Slowly but surely she had crept further and further into it: the bookshop, the book club, the city streets, the jazz café, even a party in Senada's tiny flat. How much further could she go if she let herself? The thought made her feel slightly sick, but there was a tingle of excitement all the same. Could she? Could she?

Karmela had faced her demons head on. Vedran was doing the same, and the courage Luna displayed just about every day took her breath away. As the last glow from the horizon faded to velvet blue Claire decided. Borrow a little of their courage, add it to her own, and go for it. She had faced up to Covid, so surely facing her own feelings for a certain someone should be a piece of cake? No, of course it wouldn't be, but it was even more worth the risk.

The face of her phone lit the inside of the car when she unlocked it and began to type. A very few words, but words which could change the course of … no, not her life, that was exaggerating, but the next few months at least. Luna's reply came almost immediately and Claire started the engine, remembering at the last moment to message Gran to tell her not to wait up.

A puzzled frown crossed Ezra's face when he opened the door. "Have you come to see Luna? She didn't say." He turned towards her bedroom door, but Claire put her hand on his arm.

"I'm here to see you."

"Me?" He raised his eyebrows, but Claire could tell he was trying hard not to smile. "Are you sure?"

"Oh yes. I've given this a great deal of thought." Screwing up every last fragment of courage she possessed, Claire stood on tiptoes and kissed him, her lips gently brushing his in both question and answer. There was a moment when she knew she was holding her breath, then he pulled her into the hug she'd been longing for, and began to return her kiss.

He raised his head and she looked up at him. "I'm going to ask you again," he said, "are you sure?"

"Definitely. You're an even better kisser than I remembered."

"Then you'd better come in." He led her by the hand to the sofa, asking if she'd like a glass of wine or a beer.

"No thanks. I have Nono's car."

"You mean you're not staying the night?" He pulled a disappointed face, and she burst out laughing.

"I'm not *that* forward."

"A man can dream. But seriously, Claire, I'm just so pleased, so freakin' pleased, as Luna would say, that you've changed your mind. But I'm also wondering why."

"Let's just say I've had a challenging evening, and there was only one pair of arms I wanted around me. But I don't want you to think it was only that. I really have thought long and hard about starting something, and although it's a hell of a risk, and we could well be on a hiding to nothing, good guys like you don't come around every day of the week so I want to take that chance."

"How do you know I'm good?" His eyes were lit with laughter, but he was gripping her fingers so tightly it almost hurt.

"Because you come with the Luna seal of approval. She's known you forever, and that's good enough for me."

"That matters so much?"

"When you see people you care about hurt when they've trusted their judgement, sometimes it's hard to trust your own. But every instinct tells me you could be the real deal."

"I know you're the real deal, Claire. OK, so I don't exactly get out much, but I've never met anyone like you in my life. As I've got to know you I've watched you being so kind and selfless, putting everyone's needs before your own, and I've realised all I want is to put you first for a change."

"Oh." Claire put her hand over her mouth as she tried not to sob, the emotion of the evening catching in her throat. Ezra got her. He really did. And she got him. For the moment that was surely enough.

Swimming in the Dark

Claire

Claire cleared her throat. "Thank you for leading the discussion, Karmela, and everyone for your opinions on what I think we all agree was a very fine book."

"Even I might read it now," added Vedran. "Karmela telling us about her experiences in Sarajevo as a child brought it very close to home." Although he had deep circles under his eyes, this evening Vedran was as relaxed as Claire had seen him, with his arm stretched out across the back of Gran's chair. He'd told Claire he'd slept for almost twenty-four hours after their visit to the police station, and she hoped he was finally beginning to heal.

At first the police had been defensive about the missing passport, saying they would have checked it, but when Vedran told them Didi was an Albanian national they seemed to think that explained why it wasn't on their systems. Claire still didn't quite understand why that was the case, but she had been grateful because instantly the interview had become less confrontational. They'd actually been nice to Vedran after that, taken copies of the photographs, and promised to follow them up so the case could be closed.

Twelve faces were looking at Claire expectantly. It was time to grasp the nettle. She glanced at Luna, who was gripping the edges of her chair. She had something to say to the meeting as well, but they had agreed that Claire's announcement would come first. There was nothing for it but to plough straight in.

"Before we move on to this month's book I have some bad news. Unfortunately The Welcoming Bookshop will be closing at the end of September. The landlord's had a better offer from Priro Piletina and we can't match the rent they can afford to pay."

"Like Dubrovnik needs another fast food joint," said one of the students. "It's places like this we need; shops that serve the local community as well as the tourists."

"And certainly not lying bastards who claim they're ethical but aren't."

Claire turned to the girl who'd said it. "I did see that story online, but I didn't realise it was common knowledge."

"God, yes. I'm from Zadar and there was a big protest about it outside their store there. Not sure it achieved much though. There were huge queues there again the next day."

Well, that effectively closed down that line of attack, and Claire, for one, was relieved.

"Another thing we're looking into is the damage they caused to their premises in Split during the fit-out," said Karmela. "This is a lovely old building, and perhaps if enough people raise the issue, the city authorities might listen."

There were nods of agreement around the room, then smaller conversations broke out. Ezra, who had been sitting in the far corner with Karmela, stood.

"Social media is important too, but we need to use it positively with a 'save our bookshop' campaign starting right now. Luna's designed some leaflets for customers – including the tourists – explaining how important this is, and suggesting some hashtags.

It won't be easy but we need to all work as hard as we can to make an impact."

"Do you really think we can stop this?" asked Paulette.

Claire shook her head. "I don't know. But if you all feel as strongly about it as Luna and I do, then it's worth a try."

Ideas for spreading the message came thick and fast: offers to put up posters in the cafés and bars where the students worked, names of local influencers to target on TikTok and Instagram. The wave of enthusiasm was such that for the first time since her meeting with Simeon, Claire really began to believe that perhaps they might be able to save the shop.

Reluctantly she brought the discussion to a close. "It's getting late and we still need to announce next month's book. So over to you, Luna."

Luna stood next to Claire and faced the room, holding up the paperback with its striking image of a young man in profile, his hair a damp helmet and his freckled body glistening with drops of water. "I've chosen this book because novels about gay people are under-represented. I'm lesbian myself, you see, so it's something I feel strongly about."

There was a moment of silence in the room, when Claire held her breath, then Gran said, "That sounds fascinating, Luna. The reason I joined this book club was to read different things, and it's wonderful that it's something personal to you. Thank you for choosing it."

A murmur of agreement went around the room, and as she started to ring the copies of the book through the till Claire noticed Karmela give Luna a hug. How much had changed for them all since that very first book club meeting? How many friendships forged? How many brave decisions taken? She looked at Ezra in the corner, chatting to Vedran, and her heart warmed a little more.

This simply could not end. It was far too important to all of them. But tonight it really did feel as though together they were giving the future of the shop and the book club their very best shot. Whether it would be enough, only time would tell.

Karmela

It was strange walking through the deserted streets of the old town so early on a Sunday morning. A delivery truck crawled along Stradun, much to the frustration of the handful of tourists who had most likely skipped their hotels' buffet breakfasts to take some photographs before the crowds descended.

Karmela crossed the square in front of the Sponza Palace, her long strides scattering feeding pigeons. Poor old Orlando had not yet been reunited with his column, but today another aspect of the city's Ragusan history interested her more. The gems that might be hidden behind the bookshelves of The Welcoming Bookshop.

Earlier in the week she had suggested to Claire that it was difficult to make a convincing argument about preserving historical features when you did not know exactly what those features were. Apart from the tantalising glimpses she had observed on her first few visits and admired ever since, so much of the fabric of the building was hidden by the bookcases. Would it be possible to look behind them?

Initially Claire had been reticent, but had agreed to discuss the idea with the shop's owner, Simeon. Almost to

Karmela's surprise, he had agreed. He and his wife had apparently talked long and hard about the bookshop's future, and had come to the decision if, by some miracle, the shop could stay where it was, they were prepared to carry on as well. Karmela knew how poorly his wife was, and she wondered how much of their thinking was down to her wanting Simeon to still have a focus if the worst happened to her.

So today they were going to empty every bookcase, remove them from the walls, and record what they found behind. And that meant a very early start.

When Karmela arrived, Claire, Luna and Ezra, who now seemed to be Claire's boyfriend, were already surrounded by neat stacks of books. Karmela briefly wondered if there might, at some point, be room for a little romance in her life, but she knew she was far from ready to make a commitment to anyone. She was only just relearning about friendship, so love was very much a step too far.

The girls stood to greet her, giving her a hug that she returned with some ferocity. They were relying on her today and she needed to repay their belief. Yet deep inside she knew that whatever the outcome, their friendship was strong enough to survive it. There would be no sideways glances, no raising of eyebrows, no blame. They were in this together.

The rich aroma of coffee was drifting from the kitchen, and Luna invited Karmela to help herself. In the centre of the table was a plastic box of *orahnjača*, a traditional Sunday pastry stuffed with walnuts, no doubt homemade by Fran. Karmela picked one up and it melted across her tongue.

The only way to do this in the limited space was to tackle one bookcase at a time, and they had almost finished emptying the first when Vedran arrived, carrying an impressively large, battered metal toolbox.

"It's not mine," he explained, "it's Tetak's. I have a feeling he'll be along later to make sure I'm using everything correctly."

Karmela steadied the ladder while Vedran climbed to the top, then began to undo the screws holding the shelving in place, stopping every now and then to spray them with some sort of liquid from a can so he could loosen them enough to tease them from where they had been embedded for more than twenty years.

It was taking forever and Karmela began to wonder how on earth they would finish in a day. Whatever happened the shop had to be ready to open at nine o'clock tomorrow morning, before the first of the cruise passengers arrived for their city tours. And what if they did finish, and find nothing? The idea made her feel a little queasy; she had so much invested in this line of attack, because quite frankly they were running out of other options.

She needed to have faith. She had convinced Luna to do this, almost forced the girl to carry on, so they could leave no single stone – or in this case book – unturned. It would be far worse to look back and wonder if there had been a hidden treasure waiting to be discovered, then damaged beyond recognition and lost for all time because of her failure to act.

Eventually Vedran climbed down, and he and Ezra edged the huge bookcase away from the wall. It wobbled alarmingly when they tried to let go, so Vedran told Karmela to squeeze behind it to find out what was there.

Every crevice of the rough stone wall was filled with dust, and as it rose from her touch, Karmela sneezed. Some of the mortar came away under her exploring fingers too, raining onto the unpolished wooden planks like so many flakes of dandruff. A spider disappeared into a gap near the ceiling, but Karmela did not care. History was in her very hands.

She paused for a moment. What had these stones witnessed? Who had they seen? It was virtually impossible to place any but the most influential Ragusan families in a specific building, so many records had been lost, but the Menčetić family's residence had been in this street and for a moment she dared to dream.

"Can you see anything?" Vedran called, bringing her back to the twenty-first century with a bump.

"The stonework is fabulous, completely untouched. It looks as though it has never even been painted. And I can see the whole of one of the more elaborate corbels now too. It has a little curved decoration at the bottom, just like the keystone above the window outside. I will take a few photos with my phone, then you can put the shelving back and we can move on."

It was the same story behind the smaller bookcase that stood next to the arch to the kitchen. Wonderful untouched stones, but nothing that could not also be seen in other shops and bars that had kept at least some of their original features. Was that really all there was going to be? Karmela sighed to herself. It was entirely possible.

As she edged back into the room she apologised to the others, but no one seemed to mind, especially when Fran and Jadran arrived carrying a picnic lunch. Salads and rich, flaky pastries filled the kitchen table and Vedran reprised his role as wine waiter as all seven of them trooped into the courtyard, clustering around the small table, which Claire had moved to a shady spot.

"So what have you found so far, Karmela?" Jadran asked, tucking into a slice of his wife's *burek*, while fending off Mis's greedy intentions with a gentle nudge of his foot.

"Less than I hoped, but if I am totally honest, about what I expected."

"There are still two more shelves to go," Vedran reminded her.

"Let me put this another way," Jadran continued. "What do you hope to find?"

"In my wildest dreams? Something that would link the building back to a known individual, but that is practically impossible. I think the best we can hope for would be some carved stone, a lintel or part of a fireplace, preferably something early. Anything sufficiently rare to make the authorities think again about allowing the shop to be converted into a takeaway. Especially by a company with a dodgy reputation."

"Are there many known individuals in the city archives?" Vedran asked.

"Quite a few men, but hardly any women," Karmela replied, "which is why it is so important to me to research them."

"Did you settle on a third one in the end?" Claire asked.

"Almost. Having ruled out the nun who tried to set fire to St Klarisa's, my best option seems to be Cvijeta Zuzorić. She was very unusual in that she was highly educated, and although she was born here was brought up in Italy as her father had business interests there. She married a Florentine merchant and they returned to Dubrovnik to live, where she was renowned for her beauty and poetry. Until her husband's business went bust and they had to leave in disgrace."

"She sounds amazing," Luna said. "You shouldn't just be writing a research paper, you should write a book. A wonderful romance about her life. Except you'd have to give her a happier ending."

"If I did write a book, I would rather it was one about female friendship. My three women came from different times but I have often wondered what might have happened if they had met."

"They'd probably have tried to rescue that poor little nun," said Claire.

"You have to write it!" cried Luna, clapping her hands together in delight. "It would bring their stories alive and they're so relatable. And inspirational, the way they all do their own thing, despite living in a world controlled by men."

"It is years since I have written anything other than academic papers," Karmela replied. "If ever." But she had, she knew she had. She and Emina had always scribbled stories based on their history lessons, and Nejla had illustrated them with her wonderful coloured pencil drawings. It had been such fun in the long summer holidays, filling discarded exercise books with the contents of their imaginations. Oh god, she was going to well up again, and they really didn't have the time.

"Karmela?" Claire touched her hand.

"I am sorry. I was just remembering… I used to write stories with my friend Emina who died in the war, and Nejla used to draw the pictures, she was such a talented artist. How stupid to get all teary over such a happy memory."

"Then write it for them," Luna urged.

"Write what?"

"Your story. The three Ragusan women. You're clever enough."

Karmela could not help but smile at her enthusiasm. "I will think about it." She stood, and brushed the crumbs from her combat trousers. "But for the moment, we had better get on."

Jadran and Fran cleared away the picnic then left them to it. As Vedran climbed the ladder once again, Luna and Claire wiped the empty shelves of the second bookcase, ready to return their contents. The air conditioning hummed, keeping the worst of the heat at bay, and voices drifted from the busy street outside.

Next was the longest bookcase, which ran behind the till, and even with Ezra helping, it was a struggle for the two tall men to ease it forwards.

"It feels as though it's catching on something," Vedran muttered, "it could be another of those decorated corbels. Hopefully we won't cause any damage when we pull it away."

Ezra rubbed the sleeve of his top across his forehead to wipe the sweat. "Karmela, stand back a bit. I wouldn't want this to fall on you."

Karmela retreated to the corner next to the door. Only one more to do after this, and then she would know. One more shelf to save the shop. Was she being overdramatic? Making her role too significant? But this was so very important. To Luna, to Claire ... and they were important to her. Crossing her fingers firmly behind her back, she prayed to one Ragusan saint after the other that something – anything – would turn up.

"Don't look so worried," Claire told her. "A rare find is a nice-to-have, not a must-have. In any case, the social media's starting to take off. Ezra checked on a couple of the hashtags after lunch and they're trending already."

With a final tug the bookcase came away from the wall with a sickening crack of wood, enabling the men to haul it a couple of feet across the floor, making a horrible scraping sound on the boards.

"In you go," said Vedran. "It's just as well you're slim."

Karmela grinned. "It's the only reason I refused a second slice of *burek*," she joked. The real reason was she'd begun to feel a little queasy. She honestly had not expected it to get to her like this, but it mattered so very much. History was the only thing she knew; the one weapon she had to fight this. It simply had to succeed.

There was very little light behind the bookcase and to Karmela's disappointment, unlike the others, at some stage this wall had been plastered. But wait, there was something that looked like bare stone and it was protruding a little, so presumably was what the shelves had been catching on.

She edged in further, pulling her phone from her pocket to use the torch. The space had a ghostly quality as motes of white dust from the plaster floated in the still air, shimmering in the beam. Ahead of her, at chest height, jagged edges of stone emerged from the plaster, broken and battered; perhaps even deliberately damaged at some point, in an attempt to smooth the wall.

It was an attempt that had failed. The plaster was just not thick enough, and she traced the lumps and bumps behind it with her fingers. Could it be a mantelpiece? Or what was left of one. She tried to crouch, exploring downwards with her open palm. Yes!

There was an upright too, and a flurry of white flakes dropped to the floor, revealing the cool grey of stone; plain and tapered slightly inwards.

"Anything there?" Vedran's voice sounded a long way away.

"Yes," she breathed, "yes, I think there is. It looks like a fireplace. Wait a minute, some of the plaster is quite loose."

Her exploring fingers moved upwards, beyond the broken remnants of the shelf, brushing gently. There was something here too: a shape emerging from the mist of plaster dust; the outline of a small oblong panel with a carving inside. She struggled to raise her phone in the enclosed space, banging her elbow in the process, but she had to be able to see this more clearly. Her heart thudded. Please, please, let it be something important.

Plaster crumbling beneath her fingers, the pattern slowly emerged. No. No. She was hallucinating, surely; wanting this so much she was imagining it was there. But under her fingers, in front of her eyes, she began to make out a small tower, almost like a child's drawing, with a central arched door, two windows, and topped by three crenellations.

"Oh ... oh..." she gasped.

"What?" Luna was behind her, two sweaty bodies crammed into the tiny space.

Karmela twisted to look at her, her fingers still glued to the stone. "If I am not going completely mad, which I quite possibly am, this looks very like the Menčetić coat of arms."

Claire

Claire arrived at work first so she set the *dzezva* on the stove to make coffee. She'd already breakfasted with Gran and Nono Jadran, on a healthy bowl of muesli and fruit, but still she unpacked the *krofne*, hoping she could resist when Luna began stuffing them into her face. While Ezra claimed to like her curves, they still made her feel just a little self-conscious.

From the window she noticed Mis crossing the courtyard so she poured some dried food into her bowl. The little cat had come to depend on them feeding her; these days her coat was sleek and she seemed able to get around the courtyard pretty well, despite her ungainly gait. But Claire knew she was far too clumsy to hunt, so what would happen to her if they failed to save the shop, she dreaded to think. Mis was certainly too wobbly to jostle with the other cats for a place at the communal food bowls outside the Orthodox church. And Gran couldn't have her, because she would never get down the steps to their courtyard.

Come on, Claire, she told herself. Be positive; they would find a way to win. They had to. Maybe Karmela's discovery would somehow be the key. She knew she was trying to get in touch with a local antiquities expert, and Claire had her fingers firmly crossed.

The morning air was still cool in the courtyard, although the sun had already crept a good way down the wall. Claire tilted her face upwards for a moment, enjoying the glow of the terracotta roofs in the early light, then settled herself at the table with Mis crunching contentedly at her feet.

Opening her phone, she found a message Luna had left about twenty minutes before. *Sorry. Going to be late. Can't help it. Will explain.* Perhaps it was another of her assignations, although Claire didn't think she'd been going out last night. But Luna had such a lively social life these days she could never be sure.

Oh, well, it would be coffee on her own. After fetching a mugful, Claire returned outside. It was only twenty to nine, and everything was ready for opening, so she had time to check the shop's social media first.

After Ezra had posted a short video of Professor Karmela Simic discovering the hidden coat of arms on Sunday, the campaign had really begun to take hold. Views went into the thousands on Instagram alone, while the shares on Facebook were in the hundreds. They were tapping not only into book lovers but history buffs as well. And thanks to Meri the feminist angle relating to Filipa Menčetić's story was beginning to take off too. But while it gave Claire a very warm feeling, she was still pretty doubtful it could affect the outcome.

It felt as though she had been swaying back and forth like this for weeks, between blind optimism and black desperation. Now she was seeing Ezra, staying a little longer in Dubrovnik felt all the more important. Which was the last thing she'd wanted to happen. So far they'd been taking things really slowly, but on Sunday night as they'd sat on the rocks just outside the arc of light from the bar on the beach below Gradac Park, she had longed for more than just his amazing kisses. But would that be the right thing to do?

She didn't have long to decide. Tomorrow he was taking her out to dinner – a proper date, and she sensed it would be some kind of watershed. Maybe it would be best to tell Gran that she might not be coming home afterwards, tuck some condoms into her handbag, and go with the flow. How very un-Claire. How very Luna.

Laughing at herself, she left Mis snoozing on one of the metal chairs and returned inside to rinse her mug, then unbolt the shop door. Yesterday had been manically busy, so she hoped Luna wouldn't be much longer. If this morning was the same it would be hard to cope alone.

Her phone buzzed. Luna again. *So sorry. Had to buy Covid tests. Ezra's positive, but I'm not. Should I come in?*

Claire rocked back against the till table, almost knocking over the stool. She grabbed at the leather seat to steady it, but was far from steady herself. Thirty-six hours before, she'd been kissing Ezra. They might have been outside, but that would have given her no protection. And they'd been in here together for most of the day too. With Luna, and Karmela, and Vedran ... not to mention Gran and Nono at lunchtime. And they were old, and vulnerable.

She felt hot, and cold, and hot again. Oh god, she didn't have a fever, did she? No, no, she'd been fine a few minutes ago. It was the shock, that was all. But the chances were she was going to catch Covid and there was absolutely nothing she could do about it. She was holding onto the stool so hard it began to wobble again.

No. No. There were things she had to do. She needed to get a grip. First off, tell Luna to stay at home. She would have to manage without her somehow. If the shop got busy, then the customers would just have to be patient. But what if she was spreading dangerous germs as well? She couldn't just close though, they needed every last *kuna* they could make. *Think, Claire, think.*

OK, she needed to test. If she was negative the shop would stay open, if she was positive it would have to close. Simple as that. She replied to Luna to tell her to stay away, then messaged Vedran and Karmela. She was just about to call her gran when the first customers of the day strolled in, a couple in their twenties who were after a guide book. Keeping as far away from them as she could, she helped them to complete their purchase in record time. As they left she wedged the door open against the bookcase before hurrying to fling wide the kitchen window to encourage the air to flow through.

Karmela had replied, saying she needed to buy a test kit so could she drop one off for Claire too? Terrifying as the idea was, Claire was grateful for her thoughtfulness. Just as she was typing her reply a few more customers arrived, so rather than call Gran she dropped her a message too.

Oh god, this was like wading through treacle. Almost an out of body experience, making her fumble the buttons on the till. Her worst nightmare coming true. She didn't even carry a mask in her pocket anymore.

Somehow she struggled through the next hour. Where was Karmela? The not knowing was almost worse than … but nothing was worse than Covid. Except Long Covid. Another huge slice of her life was about to be taken away, just when she'd got it back on track. Tears burned at the back of her eyes, but with customers in the shop she couldn't let them fall.

It was almost eleven when Karmela arrived, clutching a bag from one of the chemists on Stradun.

"It's murder out there and I had to queue twice because they didn't have any at the first shop. Shall I go first or do you want to?"

"You."

"OK. How is Ezra?"

His message had been a vaguely bright spot in Claire's morning. "Just a bit wiped out. But he couldn't taste his coffee. That's what made him wonder," she told her.

Claire watched as Karmela disappeared through the curtain into the kitchen. In about twenty minutes she would know. Well, she'd know if she was positive. And if she wasn't, the waiting game would begin. She really wasn't sure how she could go through all that … and not just for her, but for Nono and Gran as well. By the time she had messaged they were already on their way to Trsteno Gardens for an early walk, and Gran had simply told her not to worry, they'd test when they got home. Like it was nothing. Just as Gran's attitude to Covid had always been.

"Your turn," said Karmela, materialising beside her. "I'll mind the shop."

It was strange, Claire thought, as she rubbed antibac onto her hands, how easily she had forgotten the testing routine she had once carried out almost daily. Since she'd been here in Dubrovnik, slowly, over the months, her terror of this awful disease had faded almost completely. Today just went to show how wrong she had been. Covid was there, inside her, an unwanted gift that had wormed its way into her system alongside a wonderful kiss. Oh, the irony. She had never even considered it. She fumbled the wrapper on the swab, swearing to herself. The whole damn cycle was starting again.

She stopped, biting her lip. Would she have done anything differently? She was honest enough to realise that would depend on the result of the test. And that in itself told her all she needed to know about the progress she had made. Maybe, maybe, this time it might be all right. It was just like saving the bookshop. She had to believe.

Twenty minutes later she and Karmela were high-fiving each other as the dreaded red lines failed to appear on their tests, but there was little time for celebration as they heard more customers come into the shop.

"Right," said Karmela, "you had better show me how to use this till."

Claire shook her head. "Don't you have your own work to do?"

"Nothing that cannot wait. How on earth would you manage alone? It is June, for goodness' sake." And as if to prove the point three backpackers walked in and began to browse.

Claire gave Karmela a quick hug, but it was only at the end of a very long day, when they were both sprawled in the courtyard, with Mis dozing on Claire's lap, that she was able to thank her properly.

"I'd never have coped without you."

"You seemed to be managing when I arrived."

"I meant … emotionally as well as in practical terms. I may have been functioning, but inside I was panicking like mad about getting Long Covid again, and about passing germs onto people. The whole frigging nightmare coming back."

"So how do you feel now?"

Claire screwed up her face. "Apprehensive. I think that's the best word. I need a few more negative tests behind us all to feel really comfortable. But I'm certainly not panicking about it anymore and I won't let it beat me. Having you here has helped no end."

"That is just as well," Karmela laughed, "because you are going to see a lot of me over the coming week. And no arguments. Now, more than ever, we need to keep the shop going. Remember, Claire, you do not have to do this alone. We are friends."

Luna

Luna sat cross-legged on the sofa, the blinds closed against the glare of the intense afternoon sun. The longest day of the year and it sure as hell felt like it.

She checked the latest message on her phone. "That's everyone," she called to Ezra. "Just you and Vedran positive, and he feels fine. In fact, he says he's pleased to get it over with while he's still mainly working from home."

Ezra appeared at his bedroom door. "I'm not sure Claire will ever forgive me though. She hasn't messaged since this morning."

"Ezra, that shop will be super-rammed. I know Karmela's helping, but she doesn't know the stock, or how to work the till, or anything very much. Claire won't have a moment to think, let alone message you. Stop being so needy."

"I'm never needy."

Luna rolled her eyes, then said, "To be fair, you're not bad for a man. If it was my father he'd be lying on the sofa groaning, expecting Mama to run rings around him all day. Which she would."

"I can't get near the sofa because you're sprawled all over it. Budge up."

Luna shifted towards the window, leaving just enough room for him to slump down.

"Your feet stink," he told her.

"All of you stinks. You haven't even had a shower today."

"It's not like I'm going anywhere, or anyone's coming here."

"What are we going to do, then?"

"Do?"

"After you've had a shower."

He settled himself further onto the sofa, stretching his legs in front of him and closing his eyes. "I'm going to chill for ten minutes, then get back to work. As you so rightly pointed out, I'm not that ill."

"I'm not ill at all. And I'm beyond bored."

"Don't you have a book to read?"

Of course Luna had a book to read. There were several new ones stacked on her bedside table, but rather than being her only companions, these days their main purpose was to fill a few hours on the nights she didn't go out. Her social life was about a million times better these days, and she knew who she had to thank for that.

"I hope Claire doesn't get it too. She was so scared of Covid when she first arrived. She must have had a hell of a morning, poor love."

"That's what I mean. She isn't going to forgive me."

"It's not your fault. I can't even work out where you've been that you might have caught it. It's not like you go out that much. Even with Claire."

"We were going for dinner tomorrow night, but up until now we've been far too busy saving the bookshop. Which is a lot more important than being romantic."

"You're sure?" Luna teased.

He looked at her, and she saw something close to fear cloud his eyes. "So tell me honestly, Luna, am I stuffing this up?"

Oh, bless. "Honestly? I don't think so. Apart from getting Covid … no, really, I am joking about that. I don't know what you're worried about."

He shifted sideways to face her. "Because it's Claire, that's why. You know as well as I do she was really hesitant about starting anything and I'm just so worried she'll see this as a reason to change her mind. She took a risk with me, didn't she? And she doesn't like risks. And this one might have seriously backfired so she'll head straight for the hills again."

"You can't let it happen. And I won't let it happen either. You guys are so good together, it would be a travesty. I bet she calls you as soon as she's finished work."

"Let's hope so." He stood and stretched. "And talking of work…"

"Ezra, there is one thing."

"What's that?"

"I've been thinking. While we're stuck here with nothing to do, how about we try to track down Karmela's childhood friend Nejla? She's done so much for the bookshop it would be an amazing thank you."

"You really want to go there again? After all the angst we caused Vedran."

"It came right in the end though, didn't it?"

"Yes, but what if this Nejla's dead? What do we tell Karmela then?"

"Nothing." She could sense he was weakening. He loved this sort of challenge. "Will you just think about it, Ezra? Please."

"Of all the hundreds of Nejlas who lived in Sarajevo in 1991?" he muttered. "Ask me something difficult, why don't you? We don't even have a picture this time."

"Well, we know she has a younger sister called Sumeja…"

He shook his head as he wandered away, but Luna was smiling to herself. He'd give it his best shot, she knew he would. In the meantime she returned to her phone to see if she could find any more BookTok influencers who might be persuaded to help them try to save the shop.

Free at last on Sunday morning, Luna flopped next to Senada, her bare legs relishing the chill from the seat of the metal chair. *Bože*, it was so, so good to be back at the jazz café.

"My quarantine lasted forever," she said. "Talk about stir crazy … but Ezra tested negative yesterday too so we're all good."

Senada laughed. "I can't imagine you stuck inside for all that time. I can literally see you bouncing off the walls."

"I came close, but we've had this little project to keep us occupied. We're trying to track down another missing person. Well, not so much missing as lost."

"Lost?"

"You know Karmela from the book club?"

"The one who found the fireplace?"

"Yes, that's her. She had to leave Sarajevo as a refugee in the war and completely lost touch with her best friend, so we're trying to find her."

"That's so sweet, Luna. Typical of you."

Luna grinned at Senada, delighted by the compliment. "It's so hard though, without a picture or anything. But Ezra's written a bit of code to trawl sites like LinkedIn for Nejlas with the right dates for school and stuff, then he gives the results to me to see if I can sleuth some more. We know she liked drawing when they were little so I've started with graphic designers and the like."

"No wonder it's difficult."

"As long as she still has connections with Sarajevo then we might be all right. But if she left too…" Luna shrugged.

"Practically impossible. My neck, it aches so much from looking at my phone. But we will keep going until we've tracked down every Nejla we can. But not today. I need a day off."

Luna sat back contentedly, surveying the scene. The tables in front of them were slowly filling with tourists, many seeking the shade of the enormous square umbrellas to drink their morning coffee. The cafés in the square beyond were buzzing too, but she could still hear the muffled notes of the organ from the cathedral. Back in Šipan her parents would be at Mass, and Luna was glad when the café's speakers burst into life, a tinkling jazz piano drowning out all memories of home.

"Got any plans for your first day of freedom?" Senada asked.

"Sit here for as long as I can make my coffee last, then maybe see if I can squeeze onto the rocks at Komarda for a swim. It's so damn hot."

"You'd be lucky. Maybe we should head over to Meri's at Mokošica. The sea will be far less crowded there."

Their cappuccinos arrived and Luna took a sip, sitting back with a sigh. "Decent coffee too. I got fed up of all that faffing around with *dzezva* by about Thursday."

"That's nobody's fault but your own." Senada picked up her own drink. "The social media for the shop's going well, isn't it? I saw several well-known British authors posting about it. All kudos to you guys."

"It's fab, isn't it?"

"There was a new one this morning. A German writer shared a post by one of the girls working at Bura Bar opposite. Said she was a book club member. I picked it up because it was hashtagged Gay Dubrovnik."

"I know who you mean. She's a student, but I didn't know she was gay."

"She's not. She was posting about you. How you're living

proof that The Welcoming Bookshop really is for everyone and is properly inclusive."

Despite the heat, an icy chill punched Luna in the stomach. "What, me? As in me by name?"

"Well, yes. She tagged you, but I guess there's so much in your feed at the moment you mightn't have seen it."

"*O bože*," Luna whispered. "*O bože*." Something seemed to shift beneath her feet as she grappled with the thought. This was some kind of disaster. The fact she was gay couldn't be more public if it tried and she was so not ready. So not. Her secret had seemed safe within Dubrovnik's city walls, but now everyone … everyone would know.

Senada frowned. "I don't get the problem."

"My parents … I haven't told them…"

"If they're anything like mine they won't have Instagram accounts, so why worry?"

"They don't have them, but other people on Šipan do. It isn't *that* backward. People I went to school with, people running tourist businesses, like the hotel where I used to work…" Her mouth was almost too dry to continue. "Suđurađ is a tiny, tiny village… This won't stay secret for long."

"Then you're going to have to tell your folks."

"I can't … I can't…" Tears burned the back of her eyes. How totally awful was this? Why hadn't she kept her mouth shut at book club? Why had she let Claire persuade her to choose a gay romance? None of this would have happened if she'd kept quiet. She brought her hands to her face, but it was no good trying to hide behind them. There was no hiding now.

Senada wrapped a comforting arm around her shoulder. "Look, honey, I know how hard it is, but it mightn't be as terrible as you think. People surprise you, in good ways and bad. One of my brothers hasn't spoken to me since I came out, but my *baka* is totally cool. So cool at first I wondered if she was too deaf to have understood what was going on. She was the one who talked my father around. Men normally listen to their mothers when push comes to shove."

Luna rubbed the back of her hand over her stinging eyes. "It's my father who's the biggest problem. He is just so traditional, really stuck in his ways. He'll try to order me back home. I know he will." She could picture him now; his face that horrible purple red it got when he was angry, his podgy hands grabbing at her arm... No. It was not going to happen. She sat up straight. "But he can whistle. I won't be going. Not now. Not ever." Her life here was too damn precious, and with Senada's arm around her shoulder, already she was feeling stronger.

"Why not ask your mother to pick a good moment to tell him?"

"Because there won't be one. And anyway ... oh, Senada, he'd just blame her. I know he would. He'd make her life hell and I can't put her through that. She can't escape like I have."

Luna felt Senada's grip on her shoulder tighten and she let herself sink into her warmth. "Is it really that bad?" her friend asked. Luna nodded. "You're not responsible for your parents' relationship, you know."

"I feel I am. I feel if I'd been the daughter Tata wanted..."

"Pah! He's a stupid, stupid man. He should want the wonderful daughter he's got."

They sat for a while in silence, as Luna watched the tourists laughing together, drinking their coffees, ordering beers. An elderly couple walked past in their Sunday best. Presumably the service in the cathedral had finished and they were heading home. Fuggin' church, Luna thought, teaching her parents to be so intolerant. It just wasn't fair.

But was it fair that Simeon's wife had cancer? That Claire's lovely *nono* was going to lose his marbles? That Vedran had been taken apart for something he didn't do? That Claire herself had been ill for so long? No, of course it wasn't. In fact most stuff wasn't fair, and she'd better get used to it. Take proper responsibility for the life she wanted. The one she had now.

"You could always get the post removed before many people see it," Senada suggested.

Luna sat up straight and looked at her. Just how brave could she be? But she had to be really; to do anything else would seem like a slap in the face to Senada and the others. And that was what mattered most to her now.

"No way. It's out there now and so am I. Sod what anyone thinks."

Senada cupped Luna's cheeks in her hands and kissed her gently on the forehead, in a way that sent shivers deep into Luna's belly. In a way that made her wonder if it meant anything. Then hope that it might.

"That's my girl," Senada said as she released Luna's face. She gazed into her eyes for the longest moment, then suddenly stood and swept up her bag. "Come on, finish your coffee. Didn't we say we were going swimming?"

Karmela

The knock on Karmela's door made her jump, and she glanced at the clock. How was it that time already? She leapt up and hurried along the short hall to let Rafael in.

She was not sure how their habit of meeting for morning coffee had begun, but they seemed to have fallen into it, on the days Rafael was on a late shift at the hospital at least. Like when he was on earlies she sometimes cooked them both supper. Having been in the bookshop helping Claire for the last week, and catching up with her own work in the evenings, she had not seen him, but now he kissed her on both cheeks, then followed her to the kitchen where he set an elaborately wrapped box of pastries on the table.

"I am sorry," she told him as she filled the *dzezva*. "I completely lost track of time."

"If you're too busy…"

"No, no. I need a break. I feel as though I am going around in circles."

"Then you are right. You need to stop. Clear your head of

those magnificent ladies you're studying if they are troubling you."

"Oh, it is not them. Well, one of them, and only indirectly. It is about the bookshop."

"I talk to all my patients about it, you know. How important it is to save a local business. One of them said they had seen it on their phone. How exciting is that? I told him my friend, Professor Simic, was one of the people behind the campaign." He beamed at her, his full lips emerging from the depths of his beard.

"It is exciting so many people are aware of it, but I cannot decide how useful it is. Half the city seems to know and support us, but it has changed nothing. Probably because the decision-makers do not spend their time on social media."

Rafael sat down, and started to untie the ribbon on the cake box, while Karmela spooned coffee into the smaller *dzezva*. "It could be because they're old, like me," he said.

"Exactly. I mean, not that you are old…" Karmela blushed, but Rafael tipped back his head and guffawed.

"Silly girl, of course I am. But I am not the subject of conversation here. Talk to me about these circles of yours that are going nowhere."

So she told him about the previous Sunday and how they had moved bookcase after bookcase, eventually finding the engraving that looked like the Menčetić coat of arms. She was still pinching herself about it, to be honest. It was almost impossible to believe.

"Karmela, you are positively glowing. These circles must be good for you after all."

"Yes, and no. I have done some more research since, and consulted with an expert from the Friends of Dubrovnik Antiquities, and we think there is enough evidence to positively link the family to the property. That in itself is of genuine historical importance, but I have no idea how to make anyone from the city council listen." And if they did not listen, well, it would be even worse, because something very precious indeed would most likely be destroyed. The thought of a fast food joint in Filipa Menčetić's home was perfectly unbearable. A bookshop was so much more … dignified, she supposed.

"So if they listen, what do you want them to say?"

"In an ideal world, that the building is too important to be converted into a takeaway by people who have a bad track record with heritage, so the bookshop can stay. I know they will look after what is there, and maybe they can even get a grant towards conservation. After that, the shop's owner will just need to persuade the landlord not to put the rent up too much."

"You don't ask for a lot, do you?"

"I know, I know. It feels impossible, but it is so important. You know how good Claire and Luna have been to me. They may be young, but they are some of the best friends I have had. And being part of the book club…"

He put his hand briefly over hers. "I know. You explained." They looked at each other for a moment, then he carried on. "So tell me, who is the landlord?" Karmela gave him the company's name and he sat back, frowning. "It is the family name of the brothers who own it. One runs the business, and the other is important in the city council."

Karmela's shoulders slumped as she picked up her coffee. "So that is that. There is no point in wasting any more time."

Rafael sucked his teeth. "I wouldn't say that. The older brother was a Dubrovnik Defender like me. In fact, he was in my unit and I do not think he's an unreasonable man."

"So do you have his email address? Or a phone number?"

"No, but I know the restaurant where he takes his lunch. And I also know his brother is interested in becoming mayor. So I had better not eat my cake." He downed his coffee and stood. "All the more for you, Karmela. I'll let you know how I get on."

She watched his retreating back in amazement. Well, you never knew. Stranger things not only could happen, they actually had, and she had no better plan. To think, she had unwittingly entrusted the future of the bookshop to the hands of an unreliable drunk... But no, she had entrusted it willingly to the hands of a very good friend.

Vedran

Vedran dodged the tour groups clustered around Onofrio's Fountain and the plain stone entrance to the Franciscan monastery church, then strolled down the wide expanse of Stradun. He was doing his best to appear so casual, and every inch the successful young solicitor, in his sharp-pressed navy trousers and crisp open-necked shirt, but his insides were churning. This meeting with the landlord of the bookshop, at Gradska Kavana, Dubrovnik's most iconic coffee shop, was pushing him way out of his comfort zone.

Yes, he was working back in the office now, and his boss had asked his contacts in the police force to issue a statement saying that Didi had been found. How much that would satisfy the trolls, Vedran did not know, but as far as his business life was concerned it would close the matter once and for all. He just wished the news was already out there. Today was far too important for some random person to stroll by and accuse him of being a murderer.

He had been more than surprised to receive an email from the owner of the building, requesting a meeting to discuss its future, but perhaps he shouldn't have been. The degree of social media support for The Welcoming Bookshop had reached the point that it might just be embarrassing, so either the landlord was thinking about changing his mind – or he was going to try to force them to give in gracefully, pay Simeon off perhaps. Which would be great for him, but wouldn't help Luna and Claire at all.

Stradun was bursting with visitors milling around and taking photographs, perusing menus outside cafés, or just standing and gawping in the middle of the street. He could not blame them; they were, after all, in the most beautiful city in the world. And right at this moment he was more than pleased to be lost in a crowd of strangers.

The mid-morning sun was burning hot, and he could do without the sweat pooling in his armpits. God, he was so unused to this, and only a year ago it had been his bread and butter. To start again with something so damn important, something that meant the world to him and people he loved... But no. He needed to calm down. Treat this as just another appointment.

He paused at the bottom of Gradska Kavana's steps. The arched windows behind the solid stone terrace loomed over him, the flags above the door limp and listless in the airless day. Every table was taken and a waiter approached, his white shirt gleaming, but after flashing him what he hoped was a confident smile, and clutching his leather document folder more tightly under his arm, Vedran headed straight inside.

There was a cool calmness to the interior of the café, which was rarely used by tourists. Below the smooth arches of the double-height ceiling stood tables draped in crisp white cloths, and chairs and sofas upholstered in rich yellows and blues, an unlikely yet perfect contrast to the muted terracotta and cream tiles on the floor.

Where was the man? Here or on the mezzanine? What would he be like? *Sranje*, he'd come so far, he couldn't let himself panic now. Taking a deep, slow breath, Vedran slid behind his business persona and gave a hovering waitress the landlord's name.

A portly man with streaks of grey in his hair and wearing an expensive pale blue shirt rose from a table beneath the striking panel of modern art that ran the length of the wall.

"Vedran Novak?" he asked. His words rang out loud and clear, and Vedran expected heads to turn, but there was no change at all in the beat of the conversations around him as he stepped forwards to shake his hand.

"Jacob Vukovic?"

"Indeed. I'm very pleased to meet you, Vedran. Although I have to say I was a little nervous until my cousin, a senior police inspector, told me your name is about to be cleared."

That was not exactly the phrase Vedran might have used. Was it a ploy to wrong-foot him? Best to ignore it, if it was. He shrugged. "Mistakes were made, and social media blew them out of all proportion. I can't say it hasn't been inconvenient. But life rarely is convenient, is it?"

"Indeed it is not. Coffee?"

Vedran sat down. "Thank you."

Vukovic leaned back, wrapping his fingers around his stomach. "Ah yes, the power of social media. Is that why you chose to harness it for the bookshop?"

"It was not my choice at all. My involvement is simply to give a little friendly advice to your tenant on his legal position."

"Nevertheless the campaign has been impressive."

"It has."

"And noisy."

"Yes."

Vukovic cleared his throat. "But more important is the discovery of the Menčetić coat of arms at the property. My brother in particular is keen to ensure its preservation. As a city councillor he has a great interest in Dubrovnik's history and culture in all its forms."

It hadn't taken him long to get to the point. The real point. Vedran kept his face neutral. "Then I suppose he is also concerned about the reputation of Priro Piletina, given what happened when they were fitting out their restaurant in Split."

"We were not aware of that when they approached us. And perhaps our advisers were not as diligent as they should have been. After all, money is not the be-all and end-all when it comes to protecting our city."

Oh, the man was such a good liar, but if this was the ball he had chosen to run with, then Vedran was happy to pick it up.

"A city we all love. And one of the most beautiful, most historic, in the world."

"It is. Which is why we have worked hard to come up with a solution. We have a property just outside the Pile Gate which is becoming vacant quite soon, and it is more suited to Priro Piletina's requirements."

Vedran briefly wondered which business was being screwed over now, but that was not his problem. "And the bookshop?" he asked, careful to keep his tone perfectly even. They both knew what an important three words those were, but it wouldn't do to show it.

"It can stay."

"At what rent?" Motes of dust danced in the air between them. Vedran knew Vukovic's silence was deliberate.

"That is open for discussion. There may be a certain amount of … leeway, shall we say? But first my brother would be interested to meet Professor Simic to see what she has found. He is anxious to be involved in the preservation of something so important."

"And presumably to be seen to be involved."

Finally Vukovic smiled. "I think we understand each other very well, and that is always a good beginning to a negotiation. I am sure we can reach a conclusion that will leave all parties content."

"I am sure we can."

It was after noon when they shook hands and left the café. Vedran stood for a moment in the doorway, elation mingling with disbelief seeping through him. Had they really done it? Had they won? Against every single obstacle that had been raised against them? And it had all happened so quietly, so calmly… But as he gazed up at the dome of Sveti Vlaho, the sun glinting off the cross at the very top, he knew it was true.

What had been achieved this morning was as remarkable as it was unexpected, and now he didn't know quite what to do. It was a cause for celebration, certainly, but it was so long since he'd had anything to celebrate, he didn't really know how it should feel, either. Should he be jumping up and down like Luna surely would? Punching the air? Not here, certainly, but what he could do was return inside and book a table at the adjoining Arsenal restaurant so they could mark the occasion properly. Did he have the balls to do it? Why the hell would he not? Without another moment's thought he walked back across the café and through the connecting arch.

A woman wearing a fitted navy skirt and striped open-necked shirt was approaching from the harbour entrance, chestnut hair swinging like a shining helmet on either side of her heart-shaped face. He stopped. There was no possibility of retreat, no escape at all. But then he realised Malina was smiling.

"Vedran! How are you?" She stopped short of shaking his hand, or kissing his cheek. Of course she did. This was one woman who really did have every reason to hate him; the woman he'd left for Didi.

"OK," he faltered. "Yes, OK. How about you?" he added, remembering his manners.

"Good, thank you. Happy to be back in Dubrovnik."

"You've been away?"

"I went straight after lockdown. The bank had a position in Frankfurt and I needed a change of scene."

"I'm sorry." He hung his head.

"It was a good thing. Career-wise at least. I've just been made head of ethical investments."

"Congratulations. That's wonderful news. I'd offer to buy you a drink to celebrate, but I guess you're already meeting someone." Where had he found the courage to say that? It was already a miracle she hadn't slapped him across the face, so he shouldn't be pushing his luck.

She nodded. "I am. But I hear on the grapevine things haven't been quite so good for you." Oh, so she knew. Of course she did. Everyone did. "I was out with some friends last week and one of them let slip what had happened to Didi. I'm ever so sorry, Vedran. It must have been awful."

"Yes." How else could he reply? Except... "It's really kind of you to say so."

"If I'd known at the time I'd have dropped you a message or something, but everyone kept it from me. Saving my feelings, I guess."

She was being so nice about it all, but it was making him feel guilty as hell. Perhaps that was her intention? But no, this was Malina, remember. Not Didi. With a supreme effort he looked her in the eye. "I want to say sorry again for the hurt I must have caused you, and tell you how much I mean it, but I don't suppose it will count for much."

She nodded. "It counts for something. And just for the record, I don't believe you did anything bad. The Vedran I knew simply couldn't have."

"Thank you. Thank you so much for your faith. It means more than you can ever know. But also for the record, Didi is alive. A friend of mine tracked her down to the Caribbean. The police say they'll make a statement, but they're taking their time."

Over her shoulder Vedran saw two men in suits approaching and Malina turned. "Here are my guests," she told him, "but Vedran, if you really do want to buy me a drink to celebrate my promotion, my number's still the same."

He tapped his pocket. "And it's still on my phone."

Vedran watched as she shook hands with the men and the maître d' led them to a table close to the harbour front. What had just happened was frankly unbelievable, but he thanked his lucky stars it had. He could never expect her to love him again, but perhaps they could be friends.

It was only on the café steps he realised he'd completely forgotten about booking the table, but he could always phone them later. Steering around a tour group gawping at the Rector's Palace, he headed for the Green Market, and then on to Ulica od Puča. Despite his sudden urge to run to the bookshop to tell Claire and Luna, he would stop at the bakery for some cakes. They had to mark the good news somehow. But wait. What about Karmela? He'd give her a quick call. Get her over here pronto. They needed to be together for this.

Vedran was grinning from ear to ear. Today was turning into a really exceptional day.

Everything Is Beautiful

Claire

The champagne cork arced across the courtyard, causing Mis, who had been dozing on the sill of a blanked-out door opposite, to startle and skitter away, almost falling over as she tried to look resentfully over her shoulder. Claire giggled. She wouldn't look so grumpy if she knew what they were celebrating, that was for sure.

It had been such a surreal day. Karmela had rushed in at about eleven o'clock because Euronews had called her to ask if they could film the Menčetić coat of arms that afternoon. All hell had broken loose as they moved everything around, trading from the tiniest space ever, while a hastily put together working party of Karmela, Ezra, Nono and Gran had emptied the bookshelf then struggled to pull it away from the wall.

Help had come from a surprising source, the landlord's brother, who'd arrived with the film crew and immediately spotted the PR opportunity of rolling up his sleeves and getting stuck in. To be fair to the man, he had seemed genuinely interested and had made a very public commitment to renew the lease for at least three years – not only to the small crowd who had gathered both in and outside the shop, but in front of the cameras as well.

Then, of course, they had had to put everything back as it should be for the book club, which they had managed to do just in time, although even now there were stacks of books on the floor next to the till. They could wait. Tomorrow morning would be quite soon enough to put them back in their places.

Claire had been concerned that all the fuss would overshadow the book club discussion of Luna's choice, but once everyone had settled down, the members had voiced their appreciation of the beautiful yet heart-breaking book. As usual Karmela had led the conversation and she'd seen Luna hug her afterwards, so she must have been pleased with the outcome. The comfort Luna was increasingly feeling in her new skin made Claire smile every time she witnessed it.

And this month's book … well, Claire had chosen it herself. Not only did the title reflect her mood but the message seemed appropriate as well. She looked from Karmela to Luna to Vedran as he topped up their glasses. Even at herself. No one travelled through life without collecting some baggage, that was for sure, and she hoped that every one of them could relate to this story.

Claire glanced across at Karmela as they settled around the table. She'd been more than a little nervous when Luna had told her she and Ezra were trying to track down Karmela's remaining childhood friend as a thank you. At first it had seemed almost impossible, but now they were creeping closer, with Luna beginning to message the most likely Nejlas through their social media accounts. So far they had drawn only blanks, but Luna refused to give up, and right at this moment, with so many other miracles already in the bag, Claire found herself believing as well.

The four of them sat for a moment in silence, watching the reflected pink hue of the sunset over the distant horizon clip the top of the courtyard wall, merging with the terracotta tiles in a surge of colours that to Claire were Dubrovnik and Dubrovnik alone. Then they clinked their glasses together, toasting The Welcoming Bookshop and its book club's future.

Vedran cleared his throat. "I have some news too. Something to celebrate, although to be honest it's more of a relief than anything."

"What's happened?" asked Luna.

"The police statement saying they've found Didi has appeared in *Dubrovački Vjesnik*. It's only a small piece, but at least it's out there now."

"It should be the main headline, after everything you went through," Luna huffed.

Vedran looked thoughtful. "No, no. The last thing I want is for all the fuss to kick off again. I just want to get on with my life, but at least I now have something official if anyone does say anything."

"But why did it take so long?" Karmela asked.

"Apparently it took time to track her passport through the Albanian authorities, then for the local police in Antigua to question her."

"I hope they made her bloody uncomfortable," said Claire.

Vedran grinned at her. "Do you know what? So do I. But tonight isn't about me, it's about all of us, about the book club, and it certainly won't be the same without you, Karmela."

Karmela smiled in response. "But that is the thing about book clubs, they are so much more than the sum of their parts. People come, and people go, but they continue to exist, because the point of it all is the shared love of books, of reading. In some ways who the actual members are is not that important."

"Well, I think you're wrong," said Vedran, leaning forwards and setting his glass on the rickety little table. "The four of us have achieved something very special, and if each of us had been different people with different skills, it might not have turned out this way."

"Go on," said Karmela.

"Well, it just so happened we had what it took to see this through. Your knowledge of Ragusan history was absolutely key. None of us would have known a thing about that coat of arms, or even thought to look for it. And if I'd been … say … a plumber, I wouldn't have known how to negotiate with the landlord."

"So what about Claire and me?" Luna asked him. "We just work here. We could have been anyone."

"Not at all. Have you any idea how many people would have just shrugged their shoulders and found a new job? You're both pretty damn special to have seen this through to the end. Special and brave."

"And Luna was so clever with all the social media stuff," said Claire.

"Not to mention having a techy friend to help me. I wouldn't have had a clue about the right hashtags and all that without Ezra and his analytics."

"His what?" Karmela asked.

"Exactly!" Luna giggled. "Just what I would have said a month or so ago."

"Where is Ezra anyway?" asked Vedran.

"Book club isn't his thing," said Claire. "He's not much of a reader, truth be told."

"Then it was doubly good of him to help," said Vedran.

"Except he had an ulterior motive," Luna added, punching Claire on the arm.

Vedran nodded. "He seems like a great guy, but he'd better not hurt my little cousin or he'll have me to answer to."

"No chance of that." Luna rolled her eyes. "He's besotted. It's Claire this, Claire that, all the time. It's just as well I love her too."

Claire didn't mind being teased, but this was going a little too far. "Cut it out, you two. I am here, you know."

"I think," said Vedran slowly, "before Karmela goes back to Zagreb we should have a party to celebrate what we've achieved. Not just us, but all the book club members and everyone who's helped, like Ezra."

"And Senada and the others from the jazz café," added Luna. "Maybe we could have it there?"

"Good call," said Vedran. "I'm meeting a new client in town tomorrow morning so I'll drop by and see the owner afterwards."

Claire sat back in her seat as the sky turned a velvety charcoal above them, and listened as they discussed it. Who would have thought, even a month before, that Vedran would be planning a party? Oh, she knew that inside he was still very fragile and confused, but maybe today's statement would be another small stepping stone on his path to recovery.

But what about her? Much as it would have seemed impossible back in January for Vedran to be planning a party, it would have been equally unlikely for her to be looking forward to one. How far they had both come!

She thought of her own fears, on her first morning at the bookshop, walking down the steps to Ulica od Puča, telling herself to fake it until she made it. Which to her great surprise, she had. The fact that Ezra and Vedran had been the only ones to catch Covid after a whole day together had put the final seal on her confidence. She was ready to reclaim her life. But she had a life here now, one she cherished more than anything, and not just because of her growing closeness to Ezra.

That was the biggest irony of all. That now she felt ready to leave and to see the world, all she wanted was to stay.

Luna

Luna knew the beat of the ferry by heart. Without even looking up from her book, she sensed they were almost at Suđurad from the way the rocking lessened, just before the boat slowed to enter the bay. Not that she'd been able to read. She'd been trying to find even some of the right words to tell her mother she was gay. But they were still eluding her, bastard things. She hoisted her bag onto her shoulder and stood. She'd just have to wing it like she always did.

Just two days ago she'd had no idea she'd be doing this. Well, she'd kind of known she'd have to, but kept putting it off. Then she'd been cornered by Senada and Claire and eventually they'd managed to persuade her to go on a weekday and tell Mama on her own. It hadn't entered Luna's head they'd meant now. As in really now. But before she knew it, Karmela had agreed to help in the shop and there'd been no going back.

The ferry bumped as it docked against the quay, lowering the great metal mouth that led to the car deck. Her fellow travellers were all tourists, clamouring to climb down the steps to explore the village and secure their place on the narrow beach. A small

334

group of backpackers looked as though they might spend a few nights on the island, and a German family with two white-blonde children had more than enough luggage for a month.

Luna followed the straggling group along the harbour, the air thick with the chirp of cicadas and diesel fumes from the small trucks lumbering from the ferry's dark hold. The tongue of water to her right was the clearest pale turquoise, the inland side of the short concrete mole crowded with trip boats and water taxis, close-packed in the swell. It was super-pretty here; she could see why people came, but it wasn't home. Not anymore.

Music from the beach bar on the corner filled the air. Modern music. Her sort of music. Not just for the tourists, she reminded herself. It was easy to forget there were still young people on Šipan, some of them anyway, and as if to underline the point two girls she knew from school walked towards her, one pushing a buggy.

They hugged, chatted and Luna of course exclaimed over the baby. She wasn't only being polite; bumping into them was a great way to put off seeing Mama, but even she knew she had to decline their suggestion of coffee. Now she was here, she needed to get this done.

Crossing the scrubby patch of ground that served as the village square, Luna headed inland. All was quiet as she threaded her way through the narrow streets, past the outdoor restaurant, which was just waking up for the day, the aroma of lamb *peka* drifting from its kitchen; past the wine shop, its window display thick with dust. Fuggin' hell; it felt as though she had stepped back in time. Perhaps she had.

Her parents' smallholding was at the edge of the village and she stopped at the end of the drive. The property opposite had signs advertising tastings for their wine and oil, but her father sent their olives to the co-operative in the way he had done since before Luna was born. Resting her hand on the worn stump of wood that had once been a gatepost, she hesitated. Nothing here would ever change. Was she wrong to even try to tell her mother? But Claire and Senada would probably frogmarch her over here on Sunday if she turned around now. And that didn't bear thinking about.

Mama was in the yard behind the house, her long black hair pulled away from her face, secured by a colourful scarf. Chickens scratched the dry earth around her feet as she pegged towels on the line, but they scattered the moment she rushed towards Luna, arms outstretched.

"My darling, darling girl. It has been so long and I have missed you so much."

"I've missed you too, Mama, but the shop has been so busy. Then Ezra got Covid—"

"The shop is closed on Sundays," her mother said.

"Yes, but if I come home on Sunday there is always a row about church with Tata."

"Would it really hurt you to come with us? Just sometimes?"

O bože, not this already. Luna smiled at her mother. "Let's not spoil today. We don't have very long, after all."

"No, you are right. And it will be just the two of us until lunchtime because your father is taking the aubergines to Šipanska Luka."

"Then shall I make the coffee?" Luna asked.

"No, darling girl. You must be working so hard. Let me spoil you a little at least. Go and sit on the terrace and I'll bring it in just a moment."

Luna chose her favourite spot on the old swing seat and looked out over the olive grove. Greenfinches flitted between the trees, the yellow flashes on their wings catching the pale morning sunlight as the silvery leaves rustled in the gentlest of breezes. She felt different here, as though she was caught between two worlds. The very slowness of the place was dragging her down. If it wasn't for her mother ... but she loved Mama dearly. And then she felt bad for not coming home more often. *Sranje* and *sranje* again. She didn't need this. Not right now.

Her mother set a tray on the table, laden with the cups and plates she kept for best, and her special *kiflice*, drenched in sugar and rich in vanilla, which Luna had loved since childhood. Her homecoming was clearly an important event in her mother's life and it broke her heart to know she was about to shatter her happiness. She'd give so much not to, but now she understood that it had to be done if they were to remain close, because the reality was that Mama barely knew her daughter at all.

She listened while Mama spoke of families they knew in the village, of the new hotel that might open on the island, of the success of a neighbour's wines in a national competition, her courage ebbing away with each new story. All she could think of to tell her mother was about the friend she had seen with her baby on the way from the ferry. It felt like safe ground. Common ground.

"Ah, Maria is lucky to be a grandmother, even if her daughter has not yet married the father. Of course Tata does not approve, but times do change and move on, although I would not like to be the one to tell him that."

Was this her opening? Luna's mouth felt dry, but before she could speak her mother carried on. "I don't suppose you have a boyfriend yet?" She laughed. "I expect you will tell me you are much too busy."

Luna swallowed hard. OK, this was it. Now or never, before her mother spoke again. "Mama. I will not ever find a boyfriend."

"Oh, don't be like that, darling girl, the right man will come along, just you see."

Sranje! Had she got the words wrong? Or was her mother deliberately not understanding? "No, Mama. I will never find a boyfriend because I am not looking for one. What I would like is a girlfriend."

"But surely you have plenty of friends…"

"Mama, please listen. This is hard enough as it is. What I'm trying to tell you is that I prefer women to men, that I'm a lesbian." There. She had used the word. The actual word. Now she was holding her breath.

The air hung thick between them. Her mother's eyes were downcast, could not meet hers. Finally she asked, "So have you spoken to anyone about this? Like a doctor, I mean."

It took some moments for her words to sink in. Mama actually believed that being gay was an illness, something that could and should be cured. Luna slowly set her coffee cup back in the saucer, her head spinning slightly.

"Why should I speak to a doctor? I am perfectly well. But I'm finding it hard to accept that you believe what I have told you means otherwise."

"Then a priest. Talk to a priest. Anyone, Luna, who might help you to live a normal life. I do not want this for you. No mother would."

"And if I want it for myself?"

Her mother folded her arms. "Then you are making a mistake."

So that was what Mama thought. Since the moment she'd mentioned the doctor, Luna had tried to stem her disbelief, tried to tell herself she was misunderstanding her intention, her words. But she wasn't. This was it. All of it. She gazed at the cracked plaster on the walls of the house, at the dark green shutters, the pots of geraniums lining the window ledge. It was entirely possible she would never see them again.

Luna wanted to weep. But not here, not now. That would only make her mother think she was right. Instead she stood, her legs shaking, and praying she could keep it together. "I had hoped you might understand, which is why I wanted to speak to you alone, because I know that Tata never will. And I still hope, when you have time to get over the shock, you will come around to accepting who I am. I still love you, Mama, I always will. But I can't listen to you talk like that."

Her mother stood, her fingers gripping the table between them. "And I love you too, which is why I want to help you to fight this."

There was nothing else Luna could say. It would be completely pointless. If she paused for a moment, even to look into her mother's eyes, the tears she was desperately holding back would flood her cheeks. All she could do was gather her strength and walk away, and hope against hope that one day her mother would change her mind.

Karmela

Karmela had been a little surprised when Claire suggested they meet for a Sunday morning coffee, with the old town so crowded with tourists, but all the same she was looking forward to it. She would be returning to Zagreb in just a few weeks, and she knew she was going to miss the friends she had made. Not just in the book club, but Rafael as well.

Of course she would miss the city too. Even sitting in a side street so filled with tables that people had barely the space to squeeze past, and with the café's burgundy-coloured awnings blocking not only the sun but the view of the buildings and higgledy-piggledy steps above her, she loved it. She could still reach out and touch the rough old stones that made up the outer walls of the café, and listen to the clock on the bell tower at the end of Stradun chime the hour, as generations of Ragusans had before her.

Karmela had learned so much since she had been here. Not simply in academic terms, but about human nature and about herself. That she did not always have to be an outsider, for one, but also that the most unlikely people could make the staunchest allies and closest friends. Part of opening up to others meant that it would hurt to leave them, but now she understood it was a small price to pay. What was it Shakespeare had written? That parting was such sweet sorrow? She had never understood that before, but now she needed to view it as another valuable lesson.

The thought occurred to her that maybe she could turn around her rather lonely existence in Zagreb as well. Make some friends. And although the idea was rather frightening, she did not want to close herself off from people and from her own emotions again. Maybe a good place to start would be to join another book club. Take her mother along, perhaps, because it was a shame that they were not closer too.

Alongside her research Karmela had begun to make notes about the novel she was hoping to write. It would be based on the Ragusan women, as Luna had suggested, but not a romance. It would be about their friendship; how their lives intertwined and their relationships with each other changed and grew. She was not quite sure she could do it, but she was certainly relishing the challenge. If nothing else it would be something to fill the long winter nights at home and bring her back to Dubrovnik in her heart.

The most daunting part was writing their emotional journeys, but at least now she knew where to start. With something that came from deep inside her, something precious and new. She had brought her notebook with her to work on ideas while she waited for Claire. She knew there had to be three women, and a loyal steward to help them. Not just for herself, Claire, Luna and Vedran, but more importantly for her childhood sisters in all but name, Emina and Nejla.

These days she was actively seeking her happy memories, and this novel would be her homage to all they had shared. Emina would definitely be the poetess, no doubt about that, and in her heart of hearts Karmela could see no further than casting herself as Filipa. Which meant Nejla would need to be Nikoleta. Perhaps she could make her a secret artist as well as a businesswoman. Where could fact and fiction blur?

Her coffee half drunk in front of her, Karmela closed her eyes, picturing the three Ragusan women in the comfortable, tapestry-lined living quarters above what was now the bookshop, talking, writing, sketching... But instead she found herself back in her parents' apartment in Sarajevo, stretched out on the bedspread with Emina, while Nejla sat at the desk and drew pictures. Such a happy memory, but tinged with the weight of loss all the same.

"Karmela?" The voice was tentative, but she knew it, or she thought she did. Was the memory so strong she could actually hear it? But no, the voice was an adult's, not a child's. Karmela's eyes shot open, and there in front of her was a tall, slim woman whose slightly upturned eyes and long straight nose meant she had to be Nejla.

Karmela opened her mouth to speak, but no words came. She felt hot. She felt cold. She felt sick. But most of all she wanted to burst into tears as a tidal wave of absolute joy coursed through her. How could this be? How could Nejla really be standing in front of her?

Nejla pulled out the chair opposite and sat down. "I've shocked you, haven't I?"

Finally Karmela found her voice, although it was shaking a little. "Especially as I was just thinking about you and Emina."

"I think about the three of us as well. I should have tried to find you, but..."

"I should have tried too, but I was scared ... scared to go back to Sarajevo, scared you would treat me as an outsider because we left."

"Never! But it was a bad war, Karmela. You were lucky your parents took you away. For the longest time we had no home and it was difficult to do anything but survive. And then, just as we were getting on our feet I became pregnant. So I married, but it was hard, with two children, and working, and finding somewhere permanent to live... Too hard to think about the past and the people in it."

Karmela's tears spilled over. "I am so, so sorry." Oh, it was almost impossible to bear how unimaginably hard her friend's life had been.

Nejla grasped her hand. "Don't be. Everything is fine now. Good, in fact. I am blessed. And even better I have found you again. Or rather, you were found for me."

Karmela shook her head slowly from side to side, trying to clear the fog. This was like some sort of surreal dream, but one she did not want to wake up from. "Found for me?" she echoed.

"Yes. A few weeks ago I had a message on Facebook from someone called Luna, asking if I'd had a childhood friend called Karmela Simic. So of course I said yes. And she told me you had been so kind and so wise for her, that you had saved her job, she wanted to do something special in return."

Luna. Dear, dear, Luna. She had gone to all the trouble ... thought of it even... Karmela was almost too overwhelmed to speak. "I cannot believe she would do this for me," she whispered. "Or that you came all this way."

"Why would I not? From what she told me I realised that wherever life had taken you, you were still the Karmela I knew; head always in a history book, looking for life's answers there, but the kindest, most loyal person I ever knew. Emina and I cried for weeks after you left."

"I cried too. It is strange, I had forgotten that. I think because afterwards for the longest time, I never cried again. Until I came here, and... But no. We should order more coffee and some cakes, and you can tell me all about your life."

Nejla took Karmela's hand across the table. "War damages us all in different ways."

"I know that now, but it took me a long time to learn it. I thought, because I had left, I had no right to feel hurt, no right to my grief. It was having to read a book, then meeting an old Dubrovnik Defender…" Karmela wiped her eyes with the back of her free hand. "But this is no time for tears, it is a time for joy. Tell me about your children."

Coffee and cakes became lunch with a small glass of wine, because Nejla had to drive back to Sarajevo that afternoon.

"I cannot believe you have come all this way to see me for just a few hours," Karmela said once they had finished eating.

Nejla laughed. "You have to believe you are worth it. Surely you know the value of friendship?"

"I do now. It was something else I had forgotten until these last few months."

"That book club has a lot to answer for. Do you think you will come back to Dubrovnik? To live, I mean. You seem so happy here and from what you have told me, that hasn't always been the case in Zagreb."

Karmela laughed. "I hope I have not been moaning too much. The thing is, Nejla, I think I can make my life there better too, now I know how to. But that does not mean if a suitable role came up in the university here, I would not apply for it."

"And Sarajevo?"

"That, if I am honest, I do not know."

"But will you visit?"

"Of course."

"Then in October, on my birthday. Please come for that. For the weekend if you can. We have so much to catch up on still, and Sumeja would love to see you too."

"Thank you. I will."

Karmela walked with Nejla back to where she had parked her

car. They hugged for the longest time, and a feeling of disbelief settled over her as she watched her friend drive away. Had she really seen Nejla again? How had it still been the same as it ever was, after all each of them had been through? How strong a bond true friendship was, how enduring. It was hard to think of anything more precious right now.

She took her phone from her handbag, but Luna's mobile was on voicemail so she left a message thanking her. But how would she ever be able to thank her enough? She was undoubtedly in the young woman's debt, so... But as Karmela walked along the street, the noise and the fumes of the traffic engulfing her, she realised. Or perhaps, remembered. It was what friends did; they were thoughtful, kind, put each other first. There were no debts in friendship. That was not how it worked. And it had taken two very special young women who ran a book club to teach her all that.

Claire

The soft fabric of her new maxi-dress swirling around her ankles, Ezra took Claire's hand and helped her out of the taxi. It was their first proper date since becoming lovers a few weeks before, and Ezra looked handsome as hell in his open-necked blue and white striped shirt and smart pair of jeans; so much so her fingers tingled as he led her up the steps to the restaurant terrace.

As the waiter showed them to their table looking out over Zaton Bay, Ezra smiled down at her.

"We hardly ever go out, just the two of us, so I thought it was time we did."

He was right. Even if they went out to the old town they almost always ended up at the jazz café, so perhaps that was why he had chosen this place. And from the comfortably upholstered seats and fanned white napkins standing to attention, Claire could tell it really was quite smart.

They ordered their drinks and gazed out over the water. Behind the wooded peninsula opposite, the sun was setting, flooding the sky with an orange glow and tingeing the sea that washed gently around the rocks below them with a bronze sheen. Ezra raised his beer glass to her gin and tonic, making the ice clink.

"I feel as though I'm on holiday," said Claire. "Thank you."

"This place reminds me of home," Ezra told her. "My father is manager of a restaurant like this one. Vedran tells me eating here is good."

"I thought he might know it."

Ezra laughed. "How do you think I found it? I'm a virtual hermit. I know nothing about these things."

"That's what Vedran and I called ourselves in January when I first arrived. Gran wanted us both to get out more, and neither of us wanted to go anywhere at all."

"But that's changed now."

"Yes. It's still early days for Vedran, certainly socially, but he did go for a drink with some colleagues this week, and of course he's organising the book club party. I'll never forget he has you to thank for that, Ezra, and neither will he."

"Me and Luna. She was the one who involved me, and I'm so glad she did."

"I wish we could do something for her. She was really down when she came back from seeing her mother."

He took Claire's hand. "My *mama* tried to talk to hers, but the result was the same. I think it helped Luna to understand the problem really wasn't her. And that the whole of Šipan isn't like her parents."

"They do seem to be throwbacks to another age. But having a rift like that with your mum ... it's hard to imagine."

Ezra stroked her thumb. "You must miss your family."

"I do. But they're finally coming over for a holiday in early September, before Belle goes back to uni. I can't wait for you to meet them."

"I would be honoured. Perhaps we could take them to Šipan for the day. And Fran and your *nono*. It would be fun."

"I'm sure we could all squeeze onto Nono's boat, and I'd love to see where you and Luna grew up."

"Then we'll do it."

The waiter was hovering nearby, so they turned their attention to the menu, ordering a cheese platter to share as a starter, then Claire opted for mussels while Ezra chose steak. On the opposite side of the bay, lights began to twinkle as dusk fell, and somewhere inside the restaurant an acoustic guitar started to play.

Ezra cleared his throat. "You said this reminded you of being on holiday. Would you like to travel again? Do you feel ready?"

Claire sensed this was more than a casual question and she weighed her answer carefully. "I do feel ready, yes. But I've just this week committed to the bookshop until Simeon can come back to work. Nadia's consultant is finally being a little more positive, but it's still likely to be a long old road."

"Luna didn't say."

"I asked her not to. I wanted to tell you myself. You see, when we got together we both thought it would only be for a few months, and now I could be here for another year. That could change everything."

Ezra's brow furrowed into an unfamiliar frown. "I don't see why."

"Well, I was thinking … a few months was sort of low risk. Maybe not too much heart-ache when I went home. But being together for longer—"

"Is what I want," said Ezra firmly. "There is no point in not putting my cards on the table. However, if you feel differently, then we will enjoy this evening then part as friends."

That sounded most unlike Ezra and rather like an ultimatum, but she got it, really she did. When she knew she'd be staying longer, she'd expected to be scared about the potential for hurt in getting more involved, but instead she had just been excited. Somehow, though, she had still felt the need to take responsibility for his feelings as well, to point out the risks to him. She guessed some things were too deeply ingrained in her to change, and she could live with that.

He was looking at her, waiting for her answer. "I don't want to be your friend," she said, "I want what we have at the moment. Maybe even more."

"Then why scare the hell out of me by suggesting…"

"I'm sorry, I'm sorry. It's just … if I'm going in eyes wide open, I need to be sure you are too."

"Right from the start. Practically from the first time I met you. I knew, if you felt remotely the same, and if I could make it work, I wanted to spend the rest… Anyway," he cleared his throat, "there's no reason for you to go home when Simeon comes back to work. I wondered, well, if perhaps we could go travelling. You know, see the world."

Together? His words were rushing and tumbling over Claire, reminding her of every fairground ride she'd ever been on as a child; a shock of delicious excitement running through her, tinged with fear. But a wonderful, thrilling fear at that.

She took a gulp of her gin. "Carry on."

"When we first met, before we were going out, I remember you talking about wanting to travel, to volunteer overseas, and that chimed with me because I'd always fancied being a digital nomad. But maybe … making plans for the future together … maybe it's a bit early to do that." He ground to a halt, picking up a piece of cheese and putting it back down again.

"Look, Ezra, we really like each other and we've both always wanted to travel. What's the harm in keeping it in mind as an option, once my job here finishes?"

"You make it sound so simple, while I'm overthinking everything. As per usual."

"Perhaps you're thinking like me, that maybe we're running before we can walk, that we have no business making plans when we've only been together a couple of months. But really, we're not actually planning anything, are we? We're just discussing the possibilities. Exciting possibilities at that."

He reached across the table and grabbed her hand. "I'm in new territory here, Claire, that's the problem. I wasn't looking for anyone and I wasn't intending to, but then you walked into my life and I knew I couldn't let you pass me by. I had to take that chance, but now I'm stumbling around all over the place in my head, worrying it's happening too fast, that you don't feel the same… *Sranje!* I never meant this evening to go this way either. I'd hoped it would be romantic, but perhaps I don't know how to do that either."

"It's strange," she told him. "Just a few moments ago I had the impression of being on some crazy fairground ride. But do you know what? I rather like it. I've spent so long being scared of life, being scared of being scared, really. I don't want to live like that anymore. I just want to dive straight in, but it will be easier if you're holding my hand." She stroked the back of his with the tips of her fingers.

His voice was thick with emotion when he replied. "With you, I think I can do anything. Shall we see if I'm right?"

"Yes, I think we should." They sat for a moment, gazing out over the bay, the lights from Zaton opposite twinkling on the water, the gentle guitar music drifting past them and over the boats rocking in the swell.

"Oh, and Ezra…"

"Yes?"

"This really is very romantic."

"Thank god for that!" He picked up his beer and downed it in one, belching loudly, making them giggle like a couple of children.

Luna

Luna ran up the stairs and stopped at the door. This was amazing. Two long tables almost filled the private room above the jazz café, fans whirring overhead and windows flung wide to let in the soft night air and music from the trio playing below. Almost everyone who had helped to save the bookshop was here and the buzz of conversation filled the room. Luna gulped back a tear. These people were her family now.

She had to believe it. After Ezra's mother's efforts with Mama had proved no more fruitful than her own, she'd accepted there was no going back. Not for the moment, anyway. She had always known her father would not approve, but her mother's reaction still cut deep. One more chance; she'd give them one more chance. Next Sunday, while her parents were at church, she and Ezra would collect her remaining belongings and leave a note to say she would be waiting at the Baca's house until the five o'clock ferry. She didn't hold out much hope.

But tonight was no time for negative thoughts. She'd never had Vedran down as a party-planner, but he'd excelled himself.

There he was, standing at the end of the table nearest her talking to Jadran and Karmela's friend Rafael, and she ran over to give him just the biggest hug. He picked her up and swung her around, making her dizzy, and everyone else laugh.

The waiters appeared, bringing huge oval sharing platters as starters, and Luna made a beeline for her nominated place, while guests scurried to sit where they could. She was at the head of one table, with Karmela at the foot, Claire and Vedran taking the same places on the other. It was a shame to be split up like this, but they had shared a bottle of champagne in the courtyard behind the shop before coming here. A bittersweet celebration because it was the last time the four of them would be together before Karmela returned to Zagreb. Luna was going to miss her something rotten, and who'd have thought that, the first time she walked into the book club?

From the look of the man sitting next to Karmela, Luna would not be the only one. Luna had been intrigued to finally meet the mysterious Rafael, the person who had perhaps played the biggest part in saving the shop by persuading the landlord of the political capital to be gained for his brother by thinking again. *Bože*, he was big, and there was something a little scary about him too. Scary but cuddly, like a freakily large teddy bear. Luna giggled.

The focus of his attention was completely on Karmela, but Luna had to admit they would make an unlikely couple. His unruly beard and exaggerated gestures were at complete odds with Karmela's precise neatness, and although she looked at him fondly there was no hint of flirtation between them. Of course, he was so much older than her, but on the other hand… No. She shouldn't imagine everyone in happy coupledom. But she was going to make sure Rafael was included in the book club circle once Karmela had left.

Maybe it was Claire and Ezra being together that was making

her try to pair people off. Now those two really did fit; the book geek and the tech geek, finally getting a life. But no. That was hardly fair to Claire. After all it was Claire who had overcome her fears to bring Luna here in the first place, and look at everything that had started. Everything, everything good.

Senada, sitting to Luna's right, interrupted her thoughts. "You seem miles away, Lepti, what is it?"

Whenever Senada used the pet name she had given her, Luna felt a little bit gooey inside. It came from the word for butterfly, and Senada had told her it was because she was rarely still. In return Luna called her Pčela, because Senada was such a honey. It didn't mean their relationship had progressed beyond friendship, although Luna believed that one day, when the time was right for them both, when she was secure enough to commit, it might well do so. Which made her super, super-happy. Sod what her parents thought. Here she was surrounded by love.

"I'm fine," she replied. "Just taking it all in. It's so great to have everyone here. Each and every person helped us in their own way to save the shop and that's so amazing. You and the students with the social media, Meri and Dusana putting up posters … and Fran and Paulette must have handed out literally thousands of leaflets to tourists, which Vanesa printed at work. I still have to pinch myself to believe it really happened."

"It wouldn't have done without you and Claire at the centre of it."

"Oh no. I was a wet weekend most of the time. I was ready to give up when Simeon dissed the virtual bookshop idea, but the others kept me going. I'm so glad Claire's staying. I don't know what I'd do without her."

"Believe me, Lepti, by the time she goes back to England you'll be ready to spread those beautiful wings of yours and fly. When I think how far you've come from the tearful little girl who rocked up here in the spring … it's only a few months and already you're right at the heart of gay life in the city. Such as it is."

Meri, sitting opposite, joined their conversation. "I've been thinking, you know, perhaps we could harness the momentum from the bookshop and organise a Pride event this autumn. It's a travesty the only ones in Croatia are in Zagreb and Split. We need to be heard here as well."

Luna could not stop herself bouncing up and down on her seat, making Senada laugh. "That's a great idea. We can take everything we've learned about publicity from saving the bookshop and use it. I don't suppose it will be as successful, but…"

"It might be. We can reach out to Pride organisers all over Europe for virtual support, so you never know."

They were still exploring the possibilities when Vedran tapped on his glass to quieten the room, and Claire stood to speak.

"Tonight is to thank you all for the parts you played in saving The Welcoming Bookshop. I've always loved the fact the shop's name underlines the fact that everyone is welcome and that certainly holds true when I look around the room. Not only members of the book club stood up to be counted, but so many others, from war veterans to the gay community; from family to friends to total strangers.

"There are, of course, a few people who have been at the very centre of things since we were told the shop would have to close. First I would like to thank my cousin Vedran, who led the negotiations with the landlord and is still working behind the scenes on our new lease, to make sure it's fair to everyone involved.

"Next is Karmela, or should I say Professor Karmela Simic, who never gave up and instilled the fight to carry on into all of us. It was also her idea to spend a Sunday pulling the shop apart to see if we would find any history worth saving, and as we all know, her hunch proved right. As if that wasn't enough, it was her friend and neighbour Rafael who persuaded an influential city councillor to listen and to take our side.

"Finally there is Luna, who thinks she has done so little, but has in fact done so much, at times running the bookshop single-handed while I've been up to my neck in business plans. But more than that, since I've been in Dubrovnik she's become my very best friend. From the moment I arrived in January she's slowly but surely pulled me out of my shell. And, of course, introduced me to her gorgeous flatmate Ezra, the man behind the analytics that made the social media campaign so successful.

"I know not everyone here is a book club member, but I'm hoping tonight will change that. At the very heart of what we have achieved is a love of reading, and more than anything that's what we've preserved by saving the shop. Along the way we've discovered our own stories together, and I do hope you'll all join us in discovering some fascinating books this autumn."

Claire raised her glass. "To The Welcoming Bookshop and the Dubrovnik Book Club. And its members past," she saluted Karmela, "present, and future." She downed her wine in a single gulp, then grinned. "Right. That's the serious bit over. Let's party!"

Some people applauded, others thumped the tables until the cutlery bounced up and down, while Luna jumped onto her chair to lead the whoops and cheers. She glanced in Karmela's direction, and although she was smiling, tears were cascading down her face. Rafael offered her his handkerchief but she shook her head, so he tousled her normally perfect hair with his giant paw of a hand, making Karmela laugh.

Vedran had his arms stretched around Fran and Jadran, who were seated on either side of him, and at the other end of the table Ezra was hugging Claire for all he was worth. There was so much love in this room, Luna thought, love for everyone and love to spare. And she vowed never to forget it, to cherish it inside her, ready for the times when perhaps life would not be so good. But for the moment she simply wanted to bask in its glow and have some fun.

Tonight was a night to party.

Vedran

I t was almost midnight when Vedran slipped onto *Safranka II*, his weight on the deck and the gentle swell of the waves making her rock on her mooring. He was tired, but far from ready to sleep, so he settled himself onto one of her moulded plastic benches and gazed into the velvet blackness of the sky above the old town.

Music pumped from the nightclub just outside the Ploče Gate, drifting over the low rumble of taxis waiting on the rank for their next fare. Behind the boat's cabin the lights from the smart hotels that lined the shore would be sparkling on the water, but he preferred to look towards the harbour and the city he loved.

Although later in the party he had ended up dancing with the best of them, before dinner he had been talking to Tetak and Rafael. Well, not so much talking as listening. Tetak seldom spoke about his war, but in the company of another veteran the stories had started to flow, leaving Vedran in awe of the bravery of ordinary men.

He had grown up in the shadow of the conflict, so of course he knew about it, knew that both his father and his uncle had been

Dubrovnik Defenders, but he had never considered exactly what that meant. They had risked their lives for this city on a daily basis, and Rafael had been one of the few who had pulled off the miracle to save it.

Vedran sat up and hugged his knees. The cost had been terrible, of course. Rafael still had a haunted look about him, and over the meal Tetak had told Vedran about his reputation for unpredictability and issues with alcohol. Tetak himself had taken years to recover from the loss of his wife and daughter. Twenty endless years, blaming himself for not shooting down the mortar that killed them. That was a hell of a lot of baggage to carry for such a long time.

That was what the latest book club choice had been about, wasn't it? The book they'd discussed at the meeting before the party. Something one of the characters had said, close to the end, about no one travelling through life lightly. It was true, wasn't it? Tetak, his father, Rafael and Karmela, all in their various ways damaged by war. And Claire by Long Covid, and Luna, battling her religious upbringing to come out.

And himself? God, he was the prime example. Didi had dumped so much baggage on him, sometimes it felt as though he couldn't even look over the wall of it she'd imprisoned him behind. Like the woman in the book, with the towers of boxes that filled her house. But in the end she had begun to unpack them. Could he do the same?

Saved to the bookmarks on his computer was the counselling service for abused men in London Claire had told him about. Did he dare to make contact? But thinking of Tetak, of Rafael, even of his own father's inability to settle in one place after the war, he knew he had to. No, he hadn't fought for his country; his battle was an intensely private one, but if he didn't face up to the consequences, the effect would be the same.

Almost without thinking his fingers ran over the sleeve of his shirt that hid the scar from Didi's hair straighteners. He would always carry it, and it was far from the only one. But *how* he carried it was up to him. In physical terms he could even get a tattoo to cover it, if he wanted to. And that would be his choice. His way of wresting control of his life back from his past. From Didi, come to that. He could never erase what he'd been through – no one could – but there were definitely steps he could take to lighten his load.

No way was it going to be easy. But perhaps where he'd been going wrong before was that he'd been desperate to erase what had happened, go back to the person he was before. The discussion about the book, even though once again he had failed to read it, had cast everything in an entirely new light.

Accept the baggage. Get the help he needed to learn to live alongside it. Just the thought made his stomach churn, but now he recognised it had to be done. He had one shot at life and he shouldn't waste it. He needed to move forwards, even if it was just one tiny step at a time.

As Vedran gazed across the harbour, the flame of hope that he'd barely known had been burning inside him seemed to splutter into life. Around *Safranka II* reflections rippled across the water and in front of him white light flooded the dome of the cathedral that rose above both buildings and walls. The quay itself was punctuated by the golden orbs of the streetlamps, echoing the colour of the stone, and even at this hour people strolled along the waterfront, no doubt enjoying the warm night air, entranced by the magic of this beautiful city he was privileged to call home.

His eyes fell on the arches of the Arsenal restaurant, where waiters were clearing the last of the tables after a busy night. He fingered his phone in his pocket. It was too late to call Malina now, and he was more than a little drunk, but he would do it, and soon.

He'd invite her for that drink he'd promised her to celebrate her promotion. He understood there was no going back for them after the way he'd hurt her, but the fact she'd never doubted his innocence counted for a lot. Perhaps they could even be friends. It would be a good long while before he felt ready for more, but tonight, under the glittering sky and hugged by the comforting arms of the harbour, he could almost believe that one day, one day in the distant future, he might well trust himself to love again.

Because he had to. Because his life was still ahead of him. Because a chain of events that had started with a reluctant visit to a book club had set him on this road. Because he owed it not only to his parents, to Tetak and Fran, but to Claire, and Karmela and Luna. But most of all, he owed it to himself.

The Book Club Books

JANUARY

The Thursday Murder Club by Richard Osman

Britain's top-selling book of 2021, it just had to be Luna's inspiration for wanting to solve the mystery of what happened to Didi Kelmendi. I loved the characters in Osman's book and they made me giggle quite a few times, which I think is what cosy crime should be about.

FEBRUARY

Coming Back to Me by Marcus Trescothick

In terms of a sporting autobiography this book was ground-breaking when it came out in 2008, dealing with the England cricketer's battle with his mental health. I worked in the rather macho world of cricket at the time and it was definitely a subject that was brushed under the carpet until Trescothick was brave enough to tell his story, which proved a catalyst for attitudes to change.

MARCH
Ordinary Thunderstorms by William Boyd

Probably the first read for my own book club I didn't want to pick up but ended up devouring. It features an unlikely cast of compelling characters woven into a faultless narrative that only a really skilled novelist could pull off. Oh, and it has a fabulously apt title too.

APRIL
Sense and Sensibility by Jane Austen

Honestly, was there any other book Karmela could pick? She loves the classics and in so many ways is Elinor Dashwood. Just as in so many ways she isn't.

MAY
Black Butterflies by Priscilla Morris

One of the best books I read in 2022 and it fitted perfectly into Karmela's narrative, set as it is in Sarajevo during the siege. Initially I was concerned it was a bit too obscure, but while I was writing this book it was shortlisted for The Women's Prize for Fiction.

JUNE
Swimming in the Dark by Tomasz Jedrowski

I knew if I waited long enough for Luna to make her choice she could make it LGBTQ+ fiction, and this book is so achingly beautiful it made me tingle right from the first few pages. Set in Poland in 1980 at a time when homosexuality had to be hidden, I was sure it would have resonated with Luna.

JULY
Everything Is Beautiful by Eleanor Ray

In many ways the last book was the hardest to choose, but I wanted it to be something ultimately uplifting with a wonderful title. As I read it I was far from sure I'd picked the right one, but when I reached almost the last page the theme of the book became crystal clear and had so much relevance to my characters too.

Acknowledgments

Even as I was writing *The Collaborator's Daughter*, an idea was spinning around in my head for what might happen to Vedran in the future. I felt so very mean to do this to him, but I just sort of knew what his story was, if that doesn't sound too weird. And then a title came to me – *The Dubrovnik Book Club*. I didn't know what it had to do with Vedran at first – after all, he's not much of a reader – but then it began to fit together.

It was fair to say that when I mentioned the book club idea to my editor, she was delighted. Charlotte Ledger has been such a champion of my work since she signed me to One More Chapter and I will be forever grateful. As I am to the rest of the OMC team, and to you, my reader, who has taken the time and trouble to reach this point in the book. My sincerest hope is that you have enjoyed it.

Dubrovnik is my favourite city on earth, and I do hope you have enjoyed your trip there with me. My parents went there on a cruise in 1986 and my mother felt the same, so it was high on my list of places to visit after she died. It was the first day of our Dalmatian cruise and our tour guide, Darko Barisic, being a registered city guide as well, showed us around. Little did I know what a great friend he would become. Thank you, Darko, for your continued patience with all my questions about Croatian life and language (you've taught my characters to swear beautifully). And for naming the bookshop.

I also have another Croatian to thank: Kresimir Pehar, owner of Dubrovnik 4 U Transfers and all-round good guy, who has become less of a driver and more of a friend during our visits to the city to research this book.

I would like to explain a little about gay life in Croatia. I had a hunch that a girl from a small island would not find it as easy to come out as her counterparts in London, for example, but I only realised the extent of the issue when I began to research the character who would become Luna. Normally Darko can open just about any door, but not this time. The silence from his contacts was deafening, and that spoke volumes. Naturally my own enquiries met with a similar response, so I needed to rely on websites, blogs, and the experiences of my own friends who came out in England thirty or so years ago.

I would like to point out that Luna's views about religion and churches are entirely her own, forged because she is so hurt by her parents' intolerance. I firmly believe it is as important to accept a person's religious beliefs as it is their sexuality, so I hope no one will be offended by her opinions.

The jazz café in the book is based on the Troubadour Jazz Café in the old town where the owner was proud to tell me his family had been welcoming everyone since 1986, and that things were a lot tougher during the communist era. If you're in Dubrovnik, do drop by for a drink, meal, or coffee and give them your support, if only to thank them for the way they have supported the gay community over the years.

Sadly the bookshop is not real, but is an amalgam of many of the shops I traipsed around one drizzly Saturday. Thank you to all the staff who welcomed and assisted a slightly eccentric British woman who wanted to take pictures of their ceilings and stonework! Their helpfulness summed up the city's friendliness perfectly.

On an historical note, the Ragusan women Karmela is researching are real historical figures, and there is still so much to be discovered about them in the untrammelled depths of

Dubrovnik's city archives in the Sponza Palace. As I do not speak Croatian (or rather medieval Serbo-Croat or Latin), there is no point in me going there, but I have spoken to a history student at Dubrovnik University who assured me it is the case. My main source was Robin Harris's *Dubrovnik*, a definitive history of the city in English.

The company and advice of other writers are so important to me, and while I was working on this book I attended (once again) Rosanna Ley's retreat in Spain with close writer friend Angela Petch. We laughed so much, and worked so hard, in the heart of a wonderfully supportive group. Thanks also go to Laura, Sandra, Sue, Alex, and the fabulous Cariads for all their support, not to mention the five-star beta reading and willingness to do so.

As ever the biggest thank you goes to Jim. At least this time we travelled to Croatia early in the season, so my wonderful husband didn't have to roast on my behalf. It takes a great deal of patience to live with a writer, and I thank him from the bottom of my heart.

YOUR NUMBER ONE STOP

ONE MORE CHAPTER

FOR PAGETURNING BOOKS

One More Chapter is an
award-winning global
division of HarperCollins.

Sign up to our newsletter to get our
latest eBook deals and stay up to date
with our weekly Book Club!
<u>Subscribe here.</u>

Meet the team at
<u>www.onemorechapter.com</u>

Follow us!

@OneMoreChapter_
@OneMoreChapter
@onemorechapterhc

Do you write unputdownable fiction?
We love to hear from new voices.
Find out how to submit your novel at
<u>www.onemorechapter.com/submissions</u>